The Poisoned Table

MERCER
UNIVERSITY PRESS

Endowed by
TOM WATSON BROWN
and
THE WATSON-BROWN FOUNDATION, INC.

The Poisoned Table

A Novel

Diane Michael Cantor

MERCER UNIVERSITY PRESS | MACON, GEORGIA

MUP/ P517

9 8 7 6 5 4 3 2 1

Books published by Mercer University Press are printed on acid-free paper that meets the requirements of the American National Standard for Information Sciences—Permanence of Paper for Printed Library Materials.

ISBN   978-0-88146-546-4
Cataloging-in-Publication Data is available from the Library of Congress

In loving memory

Betty Goldstein Cantor
Who believed kindness the greatest wisdom and lived her life that way

Leon Cantor
Who never ceased trying to recover despite insuperable blows

Frances Anne "Fanny" Kemble
"The last Renaissance woman"

For
TEIII, David and Sarah
LWIB

Preface

The Poisoned Table is a work of fiction that interweaves the author's invention, nineteenth-century actress Isabel Graves, supporting characters in her life, fictitious news accounts and correspondence, and an imaginary anti-slavery play performed on the British stage with the life of renowned British actress Frances Anne "Fanny" Kemble. For many years I studied Kemble's journals and researched her early life in Britain and her theatrical career in Britain and America. Her first-person account of slavery witnessed on her husband Pierce Butler's Georgia slave plantations formed the inspiration for the novel along with depictions of actual events and imagined situations, which although plausible, are conjecture. I read the original version of *Journal of a Residence on a Georgian Plantation in 1838–1839* by Frances Anne Kemble (New York: Harper & Bros., 1863) in the reference room of the New York Public Library and have benefited greatly from the scholarly research and annotations in the edition of *Journal of a Residence on a Georgian Plantation in 1838-1839*, edited with an introduction by John A. Scott (Athens: University of Georgia Press, 1984). *Fanny Kemble: A Passionate Victorian*, by Margaret Armstrong (New York: The MacMillan Company, 1938), provided additional detail of Kemble's life. I have quoted the works of William Shakespeare, the old English folk song "The Seeds of Love," and the spiritual "Go Down Moses."

In depicting the destruction of Kemble's marriage based on her abhorrence of slavery and her absolute opposition to Pierce Butler's conviction in his right to slave labor, I have quoted "News from Washington," in the *New York Times*, Washington Dispatches, 22 April 1862; "The Arrest of Pierce Butler," in the *New York Times*, 21 August 1861; Reviews and Literary Notices, *The Atlantic Monthly*, 12/70 (August 1863); *The American Annual Cyclopaedia and Register of Important Events*, 1863, Google Books Search; and the "Sale of Slaves," reported for the *New York Tribune*, New York; and the *Archives of the American Anti-Slavery Society* (2004–2008), Anti-Slavery Project, Arizona State University English Department, in collaboration with the e-server of Iowa State University.

The *Narrative of the Life of Frederick Douglass, An American Slave: Written by Himself*, authorative text edited by William L. Andrews and

William S. McFeely (New York: W.W. Norton, 1997) provided further perspective on the widespread conditions of slavery that Kemble decried.

I highly recommend these works to those who seek greater understanding of this horrific period in our nation's history.

Diane Michael Cantor
Savannah Georgia
February 2014

1

An Oath

I could have enjoyed squashing her like one of the tiny bugs which burrowed into my flesh in the poor lodging houses that became my home after she stole my part. No matter that I had been brought up to aspire to Christian virtue ever since I was a small child. I still harbored hatred that she took what I had earned by memorizing lines long into the night and practicing relentlessly my elocution lessons to eradicate all traces of my uncultured origins. The Christian charity was, after all, my mother's, not my own, and acquired by living with my father's debauches her entire married life.

I had every reason to believe I would be Juliet. Staring out over the heads of the audience listening to my audition, trying to focus only on Shakespeare's words and the phrasing I had chosen for my delivery, I heard through my concentration their appreciative gasps at my gossamer appearance on that great stage. She, on the other hand, no matter what they, or audiences after them, would say about her voice, could not match my appearance. My complexion then was as clear as it is still now despite so many passing years, and no one could have pointed out any flaws in my face that needed the assistance of stage makeup. Juliet, to everyone's taste, should display the unspoiled beauty of a young girl, and there was no doubt that I possessed this quality in my graceful figure and skin, much closer to porcelain than hers could ever be, despite the likenesses they sold of her in the street once she gained fame on the Covent Garden stage. My glossy, golden ringlets were all my own, though I have on the authority of those who attended *her* at the theatre, that her long tresses were not genuine.

My audition was merely a deception perpetrated so that her father, that failed manager who ran England's most glorious theatre into bankruptcy, should not appear to show favoritism toward his own daughter, who, though she might be many things, was by no one's judgment *Juliet*. They made their statements about her magnificent voice, comparing it to a rare instrument for which there was no match, and said I had not the presence to fill a large theatre. The real truth was much simpler; her father wanted his daughter to have the role and all the glory that would follow and save his family's fortunes by her rise.

I shall never forget my moment of triumph after I had read my part. Despite my fears and my father's drunken threats of what would happen to me and to our family if I were not selected, and my mother's tears at his drunkenness, which she considered an assault on God's will, I was confident. No one, I was certain, could witness my performance and not believe that I was everything Shakespeare dreamed that Juliet must be. And if my father were correct and Covent Garden's survival depended on this play's success in London and the tour to follow, then how could I not be chosen? *She* was so plump that, in all fairness, she was far too stout to portray Juliet, and though from the stage perhaps an audience could not detect the imperfections of her features, I had heard that when she was a young child she had contracted small pox, and even her fine, dark eyes could not save her face from its ravages.

Then I learned that I was not to have the part. *She* was to be Juliet, not for any talent that outshone my own and not for personal charm or advantage, but because it was her father's wish. There was nothing I could do besides go with all of London to see the performance lest someone say I was spiteful or jealous for not having been chosen. But I looked at her costume, the bodice straining across her great bosom, and thought how much more graceful I should have appeared if only I had been given my fair chance.

"She cannot hold a candle to you, dear Izzy," my father said later that night, as he drank his third port and lemon by the fire. "I might have known you hadn't a chance against management's choice no matter how beautiful you looked or how magnificently you recited. You could not win, my darling." He hiccupped drunkenly and left sloppy kisses on my cheek.

I made myself a promise that very night, after my younger sisters were asleep in our bedchamber. I crept out of bed to sit at my dressing table, pulling back the curtains to let in the moonlight, just as Juliet herself might well have done. I took out my Bible, not trying to read it in that faint light, but I put my hand upon it and made a solemn oath. I whispered, lest I wake the little ones in the bed behind me, yet still saying the words aloud so that they should be spoken in truth as lines in a play: "I lay my hand on this good book and swear by the grace of God and all who have held this book before me that I shall not be unfairly passed over again." I thought of *her*, who came from no better stock than I, her people having once been strolling minstrels, I had been told, but who somehow imagined herself better than I.

2

She was to be the heroine while I, as her understudy, might never even step upon the stage. I cried out, "Not I! I shall do better." And even though the little ones stirred at my words, I could not cease. "I shall have my revenge," I swore and then blew out my candle.

Honor Bound

(April 21, 1844: *The New York Ledger-Journal*)
"New Yorker Stands Bravely on Field of Honor"
by Martin Fitzweiler

On a sunny Monday morning just one week past, James Schott of Philadelphia, a prominent business leader and philanthropist, stood up in Bladensburg, Maryland, to defend his honor in a duel with Pierce Mease Butler, also of Philadelphia. The duel was fought at Mr. Butler's insistence despite Mr. Schott's incapacitation from an inflamed right foot that was so painful he could not place full weight upon his heel. Mr. Butler, as the challenged party, demanded that the combatants should not separate and walk the more customary ten paces before turning to shoot, but upon the count of three should turn immediately and fire. These rules further exacerbated the disadvantage to Mr. Schott, who was incapable of wheeling and turning quickly on his disabled foot in order to aim accurately. Remington pistols belonging to Mr. Butler's family were the weapons employed, and two rounds were fired by both parties, although no one was injured. The seconds, his brother John Butler for Mr. Butler and Dr. Colleton Bridgeport for Mr. Schott, could not determine whether it was the intention of the two gentlemen, who had formerly been great friends, to fire into the air or whether all shots missed due to a defect in the pistols themselves. Mr. Butler, upon hearing this line of inquiry, became incensed at dispersions cast on weapons in his possession, which he had used previously in several such engagements. Dr. Bridgeport, who was reached later in his medical practice, said, "I am only relieved that so fine a man as James Schott has escaped unharmed, particularly after the injury he has suffered from a man whom he considered to be his closest friend. As for Mr. Butler, it should not have been a tragedy if a true shot had ended his useless life there on that grassy knoll. And as to whether he should have gone then to his Maker or to some other destination, Christian principle shall not allow me to speculate."

Neither Mr. Butler nor his brother was available for comment.

The dispute erupted over a complaint by Mr. Schott that upon paying an unexpected visit to his New York residence in early March, he discovered an intoxicated Mr. Butler making unacceptable overtures to Mr.

Schott's wife, Ellen. Mr. Butler's wife, the formerly acclaimed British and American stage actress Fanny Kemble, was in Philadelphia at the time of the alleged incident. This is where Mr. and Mrs. Butler currently reside with their two daughters at Butler Place, just outside of town.

As previously noted, Mr. Butler is no stranger to the custom of dueling. It should also be noted that the late Major Pierce Butler, Revolutionary War hero and Mr. Butler's grandfather, married Polly Middleton, a South Carolina heiress, and that the Southern states have long upheld the practice of dueling to resolve matters of honor, often with tragic consequences for one or both parties. Hampton Point, a Georgia property in which Pierce Butler holds an interest, was the location where Aaron Burr found protection from authorities in New Jersey after he killed Alexander Hamilton in a duel in 1804.

(April 19, 1844: *The Philadelphia Star-Report*)
"Philadelphian Stands for Honor"
by Haverford Curtis Banks

On April 15th, a chilly Monday, Philadelphian Pierce Butler bravely strode onto the field of honor accompanied by his brother, John, to answer the allegations of his once close friend James Schott, also of our city. Schott charged Butler with improper behavior towards his wife, which Mr. Butler categorically denied. Bearing no enmity toward Mr. Schott, Mr. Butler commented to spectators that he was "proud to stand up with a man as admirable as James Schott." He stated further that though he denied the accusations, he felt it his obligation as a gentleman to grant Mr. Schott his satisfaction.

When questioned as to why he, as the challenged party, should select rules that placed undo pressure on Mr. Schott, who suffered from an injured right heel, Mr. Butler protested this erroneous conclusion. "It is outrageous that anyone should suggest anything so false. In stipulating that we immediately wheel and fire, rather than walking the customary ten paces, I sought to spare my friend, who should have been put to great disadvantage had I required him to walk ten paces on a badly swollen foot."

Witnesses report that both men fired two rounds but that no one was injured. Mr. Butler stated that though he had been bound by honor to defend his good name and accept Mr. Schott's challenge, he felt fortunate to have escaped unscathed. "Though I possess greater experience on the field of honor, descending as I do from my grandfather Major Pierce Butler, a

Southern gentleman and hero of the Revolutionary War, I am not Mr. Schott's equal with a pistol or a saber," he said modestly.

Mr. Schott could not be reached for comment as he and his wife, Ellen, are presently bound by ocean steamer to Europe. Mr. Butler was contacted at his Philadelphia home, Butler Place, where he resides with his two daughters and his wife, who until their marriage was the noted British and American actress Fanny Kemble.

My Most Terrible Role

I was a slave.

As a young woman, I did not, of course, conceive of myself in this way. Such an appellation would have seemed preposterous to describe Fanny Kemble, the recent favorite of the British *and* the American stage, an actress from the most celebrated theatrical family in London, and wife of one of the wealthiest Americans. Nor had my parents brought me up to be a reticent, cowering flower on some clinging vine. From earliest memory, my parents, brothers and sister, and my aunt, Sarah Siddons, certainly the most famous actress of her day, greeted warmly even my most childish pronouncements as evidence of an emerging genius and poet. And Pierce, my young husband, had wooed me so persistently and with such admiration I should never have imagined he could ever deny me anything or imprison me. If anyone had even suggested that his handsome face might become distorted with loathing for me, my younger self would have laughed in astonishment and told him not to insult me or Pierce by such an antiquated, demeaning view of marriage.

"The very idea!" I should have protested, and I could easily have decried the image in our modern age of a wife imprisoned in her husband's bower and permitted to communicate with respected friends only according to his whim. It would have seemed not unlike the plot of some tawdry play from an earlier era in which a woman who loved her husband and was a loving mother was cast aside like an old vestment in favor of the new design, even if it was of a vulgar fit and style. I could never have imagined such treatment in my own home.

Yet in reality it was not my home. Everything in it belonged to my husband, even the dresses that I wore and the shoes upon my feet. I had given up all my money, a considerable fortune, to my father before he returned to England from our American tour so he could reverse the dreadful condition of our family fortunes and save Covent Garden Theatre. Although I had published my play, *Francis I*, as well as my girlhood diary and another revealing my early impressions of America, where I had heard audiences shouting my praises, *I* could not speak freely. I had been invited to dine in the finest houses in the land and been taken on personal tours of every artistic or natural wonder in America, but I was my husband's prisoner. I had played Portia and Juliet to sold-out theatres in Europe and America, but without Shakespeare, I could make no speeches with power sufficient to save Pierce's love for me.

Our romantic courtship and marriage in 1834 when my husband's love seemed boundless, gave way to punishments and privations, not least of which was daily coldness instead of affection. The man who had adored me, whom I had chosen above all other suitors at the height of my celebrity, and for whom I had given up the stage, had tired of me. I could only watch in horror as I was supplanted by that *woman*, neither a fit teacher nor one I would have selected for any scholarly merits she could offer our children. As my husband imposed her into the daily midst of our family life, I was forced to sit across from her at the breakfast table, a fragile cup of tea trembling in my hand, since he had made it abundantly clear to me, and certainly to others by his innuendoes, what she really was to him. Still I endured these humiliations, swallowing my mortification for the sake of tiny Fan and Sal, my precious babies. Finally, I was banished from almost all contact with my husband, despite my silent acceptance of his cruel decrees against me, as evil in their own way as those of ancient Pharaoh toward the Israelites.

I had ample food and fashionable raiment. My husband was too mindful of society's good opinion to starve me or to exclude me from any public event where my absence should have drawn notice. And I realized early on that any supplications I might make to him were hopeless as cries before a deaf man. I would have foregone the choicest offerings of his table and should have gladly feasted on bread and water if I could have broken bread with our children. I should never have excluded him from family life as he barred me, until almost any food became distasteful and I could not eat and appeared sickly even to my own eyes. I, who had been presented at the White House and had dined with royalty, and in my father's house had called as friends distinguished poets, authors, and statesmen, began to dwell in dreary isolation.

Pierce Butler turned me away from my own children, limiting me to brief appointments with them during precious hours that passed too quickly and made us shy, so fearful were we of the next parting. Each time we were reunited, I felt the moments slipping away like sands in the hourglass. My two darling daughters would grasp my skirts with their tiny fingers, hoping if they should catch hold of me I could not be separated from them. When that woman pried them away from me to take them off to their lessons with *her*, I looked down and saw my skirts were wet from the tiny flood of their tears mingled with my own. Yet I was powerless as a slave isolated on an island rice plantation with no chance of escape save through the treacherous swamps, crawling with snakes and alligators, leading to the ocean and freedom. I was a free Englishwoman, brought up to abhor slavery and to cherish the rights of self-determination, yet I was cast as a slave before my own servants and my children and visitors to our Philadelphia home.

Now many years later, my face grown old as time, I am embarrassed to recall that hopeful fool I was, struggling to recapture Pierce's love, unwilling to believe his full deception. How strange that an actress who had played many roles fashioned around lost love and broken vows should have been unwilling to perceive what was happening in her own life, unless my obtuseness was the creation of my dreadful vanity, stoked since birth by the admiration of my family and then inflamed by adoring audiences. And in the early days of our romance, I had but to express a girlish whim for Mr. Butler to rush to satisfy it. Once he purchased a ridiculously expensive, intricately carved Italian piano without even hearing its sound, because I had casually admired it as we strolled by a shop window.

In whatever ways I was blinded in my youth, I now see clearly through the eyes of a woman nearing the end of days. Sitting up late now in the evenings, as I often do, recognizing that final sleep will come all too soon, and oddly now, even after long, refreshing walks, finding myself unable to sleep, I reflect on those days. I do not find myself at fault for failing to rebel sooner against the fullness of my imprisonment. After all, I had seen *true* slavery. It had breathed its foul breath in my face on Butler Island, where I came to know the "people," the term my husband and his family favored instead of slaves.

I had witnessed brutal violence as women were tied up for beatings with their naked bodies exposed to the lash. I had attended slaves dying on cold, dirt floors with blocks of wood as their only pillows, shivering, sick with fever, covering themselves with filthy rags. So it is no wonder that I should not recognize my own bondage, surrounded as I was by those who suffered in the field and retired in the evening to scant rations that could not staunch their hunger. I was never beaten, nor struck even once, despite my husband's terrible temper whenever his pride was enraged.

Yet the greatest heartbreak reserved for slaves was also possible for me. My children could be taken from me at his whim with no thought for their feelings or mine, just as any master was free to sell off the children of his slaves. But I am getting too far ahead in this tale, like a playwright impatient to reach the heart of his drama. I shall tell, in good time, how I came to go upon the stage, a life I would never have sought if family fortunes had not depended upon it, and how I became Mrs. Pierce Butler, living frivolously unaware of the human beings who slaved in Georgia to support our existence at Butler Place near Philadelphia. It was these eight hundred slaves who comprised the "property" he had never defined for me before we were married, saying only that he had land and investments in the South and upon his aunt's death would, with his brother, gain much more. This was the inheritance he never questioned, and which became my shame.

4

Stage Center

Late at night, I overheard my parents' angry voices. They spoke always so very gently to each other that I was surprised to hear them arguing. I stood at the top of the winding stair, not eavesdropping, but investigating the sounds of their disquietude. My father, Charles Kemble, handsomest man upon the English stage, who could have attracted the attentions of any woman he pleased, was blind to every woman's charms save my mother's, and he treated her with great consideration. I had never heard their voices raised to one another unless dictated by the stage directions of a play.

"I don't know what I shall do," my father said, his deep voice straining with worry, "with the theatre empty night after night. Unless I can *immediately* construct a scheme to bring patrons back, we are lost. And with Elizabeth now abandoning us to sing at Drury Lane, we will surely lose the following of England's favorite duchess. Her audience will abandon us no matter what plays we perform. There will be no future for this family or Covent Garden. We shall not survive this season."

Though I could not see my parents, I could feel his agitation and imagined my father pacing before my mother's wing chair by the fire, where she sat quietly sewing in the lamp light. It was a room of muted, tasteful colors, a Persian carpet of violet hues, pink damask draperies and a peach-colored, elegantly arched mahogany sofa flanked by family portraits of many other Kembles, who, like my mother and father, had proudly acted for their bread, never feeling shame for their profession, even in the days when the earliest Kembles were strolling players.

"Charles, if you don't sit down, you will drive me mad," Mother exclaimed. "This is not a stage. Though if it were, I am certain you would make some better occupation for your character than this incessant pacing. I understand you are very distressed," she said more kindly, "and you are right, we *must* devise a plan. But why speak of it at this hour? In the morning, I shall tell you a plan that might be accomplished if you wou—"

"And pray, Therese," I heard him answer sarcastically, in a tone he never adopted with her, "would *you* be so good as to enlighten me as to the details of such a plan? Perhaps the reason I, and my brother before me, have been so unsuccessful in saving Covent Garden and providing for the fortunes of this family is because without your intervention, it has never occurred to us to devise a plan."

"Oh, I *am* sorry, Charles." My mother's apologetic voice rose softly up to me. "I did not mean to seem a know-it-all when I understand nothing about the stage except how to act upon it. My dear, I humbly beg you—"

"No, my dear, the fault is all my own. I should not be so easily vexed. Yet what am I to do when I see new circulars plastered daily at the theatre threatening foreclosure and attendance is so wretched? I offer them Shakespeare, but they would rather frequent puppet shows and carnivals."

I heard the creaking sound of the sofa as he sat down and reached for her, and then his lips leaving their kiss on her hand and his penitent voice, "Please forgive my bad temper, my dear Therese. When I have no answers and you are so kind as to conceive a plan to save us."

"You must not allow yourself to feel so desperate, Charles. This family is far from requiring *saving*," she said encouragingly. "We always have our home and our craft. Surely you will always command the stage before a full house any night you elect to be there, playing any role you may choose. And *I* can return. I supported my family before I knew you. There is no reason I cannot do it again. Or if we must, we will sell everything. Really, I do not care about these *things*," she said disdainfully. "They are very beautiful, but sell them all!"

"How much do you think they would fetch us?" he asked sadly. "This house and all of your charming furnishings, if we even owned them outright. Which we do not," he said wearily, his despair ruining his rich voice. "It was all mortgaged for Covent Garden. And where shall we find the money for William's equipment or Adelaide's training? You know she must have several years in Italy. She has a brilliant voice. We owe it to her."

"That *damned* theatre," Mother said, almost inaudibly, no doubt embarrassed by her own outburst, disapproving as she did of coarse language. "John never should have taken responsibility for managing Covent Garden, nor should you have accepted his failure *and* debt as if they were your inheritance instead of a terrible burden. We are *actors*, not managers. How did you ever imagine you could succeed in such a venture? Could you not learn from John's disastrous example without losing our savings as well?"

Listening to the crescendo of her words, I expected my mother to say something more, but at first there was silence and then my father softly comforting her as she began to cry. She broke free of him and sobbed that we would all be turned out into the street. Kembles would soon be strolling troubadours once more, not because we sought this itinerant existence for romance or experience. She feared we should be forced to do it because we would have no home.

From my vantage atop the stairs, I began to feel guilty, first for listening to their conversation instead of making my presence known, and then for causing them so much expense. I was a young woman, but in many ways still a girl, just returned to London after sheltered, nurturing years in my French boarding school, where every possible lesson had been lavished upon me. I had read history and philosophy and studied Italian, French, Latin, and German until I was reasonably fluent. Piano and singing lessons had equipped me to amuse myself and others, and I sewed well, this having been a requirement of my school. I excelled most in writing, having since early childhood easily put my thoughts to paper, and still read late into the night, novels which would have been forbidden by the teachers back at school. I had begun to have small pieces published and had almost completed my play, *Francis I*. I loved to write, and, thinking I should never have to worry about earning my living, had imagined I would continue composing plays, poetry, and journals in my parents' home, since I was liberated from the constraints of school. I had anticipated afternoons engrossed by the many books I longed to read, delighting in the fresh pages I would cut with a small silver knife.

Yet it was suddenly apparent the existence of the very library table at which I hoped to sit was threatened, and that while I had been taking dancing lessons and appearing at school parties and balls in fancy frocks, my parents had been approaching ruin. This was not my fault, though I felt it painfully, as if their troubles were of my own making. I longed for some way to help them and to save Adelaide, who was peacefully sleeping in the chamber down the hall, blissfully unaware of the impending tragedy which would leave her rare singing voice untrained, her talent squandered.

"Oh my darling, please do not cry," my father said. "We are not lost *yet*." I imagined him drying her eyes with his fine handkerchief of Irish linen. "Could you possibly tell me now about *your* plan, my dear?" he asked delicately, seeking more to demonstrate his respect, I felt, than for any help he thought my mother could bring to a hopeless circumstance.

"It was only this," she said sheepishly, since what she had to offer at most was an artist's sketch of a dwelling rather than a finished house for a family without a home. "You must find a new actress. A rare beauty. A fresh talent seen *nowhere* before in England. And you must bring her out in a new production, so elegant in its staging, costumes, and music that *no one* will dare to miss it."

"That's all very well. And if I could once again bring forth Marie Therese de Camp, just as you were when I first saw you on the stage, I should regain our fortunes at once. We would take London and could tour all of Europe to full houses. Only, my dear, we *cannot* turn back time and there *is* no one today who could be another you," he said gallantly.

"Oh, but there is, Charles. *Fanny* is home now. She is twenty, and she is a Kemble. She would make an enchanting Juliet. It is in her blood."

I could be still no longer. I ran down the stairs to assure my parents I would gladly put aside my own pursuits to assist them. Although it frightened me, and I had no more than a schoolgirl's knowledge of acting, I said if it was their wish, I should appear on the stage of Covent Garden. I would do anything to save our family. I was a writer. I was sure of that. Yet if it were their will, I would become an actress. A *Kemble*. Overnight.

5

A Bit Player

There were no second chances for Isabel Graves on the London stage. I could not bring myself to stand once again rejected and humiliated in front of her or to accept the role they offered me as a lowly understudy. I would not shame myself. If I could not play Juliet in the finest company, then I determined I would not play her at all. My father had never raised me to stand in the shadows behind someone else. I had far too much pluck for that. Even if I had wanted to hide myself in that way, my manner and my beauty, if I may say so, would never have allowed it.

Instead, I went away, leaving London for the farthest provinces. My father knew a man, Mr. James, who had a traveling troupe that specialized in performances composed of recitations and song, with even a few jugglers and acrobats thrown in. Sometimes he included short plays that called for actors quick about their wits who could learn many different parts and disguise some of Shakespeare's famous roles with bits tossed in of our own and dances and songs made better with fancy costumes. I had at home always shown a talent for singing, not being one to turn shy in front of company. When my father had enjoyed a few cups of wine, I had often sung along while he played the piano in our parlor. I had a quick ear for tunes, and Mr. James had told my father more than once he ought to let me go on tour to give me the seasoning that any actress requires to become a success upon the stage. At the same time, he promised, I should likely gain a following, easy as it was for the eye to rest upon my blue eyes and golden ringlets.

At first Father would not allow it, insisting we were a respectable family, not one to let its daughters go traipsing off like gypsies, particularly one who turned men's eyes as quickly as my figure was wont to do. He maintained he must also think of my younger sisters, since what would be their future if it were widely known I had traveled unchaperoned round the countryside playing in places that would not meet muster in decent society. I despaired at his attitude, thinking I might faint away with boredom if he should keep me restrained yet miserable at home, waiting perhaps hopelessly for some man to claim my hand. I feared no man of substance would ever ask for me, since though I had been amply blessed with feminine charms, my pocketbook was empty. Our family connections were so dubious aspiring men of any standing would not call on me, and of those who did, I held their oafish manners in disdain.

When Mother had given up all hope of peace for our household, Mr. James came calling again to sample my father's port and listen to my singing. He mentioned that he had a new comic piece he thought perfectly suited to my voice if father would only permit me to travel. And this time, he offered an inducement to soothe Mother's qualms and which my father's greed for silver could not withstand. Mr. James's own sister, whose likeness he carried in a golden locket around his neck, a pretty likeness of a solemn woman in her thirties, was past hope of marrying and seemingly demure in all her ways. If Father should allow me to join the company, Mr. James would promise his sister, Violet, should watch over me. She would share my bedchamber and look out for me as if I were her own daughter. He reassured them that she was not herself an actress, but traveled with him as his wardrobe mistress, and since she also wrote a fine hand, helped him with such correspondence as was warranted by the tour.

Father continued to withhold his approval, perhaps out of concern for me or maybe just to exact a greater price. Yet when I begged him, literally clinging to his knees, protesting that I should surely die if I were to stay home with nothing to do save helping mother about the house, I could see him weaken. I convinced him there was no future left to me if I could not be Juliet. At least if I traveled perhaps I would be discovered on tour and offered a contract with the chance to travel to France and Italy or even to the United States. I told him if I did not leave home soon and make my fortune, I might remain on his hands always, an old maid, earning a pittance assisting mother with her sewing.

And so he acceded to my wishes. Mr. James promised his sister should never leave me unattended save when I was on the stage. He offered a generous advance if my father should sign the contract and that each month my father could expect to receive my salary. He said my talent and beauty would be such an asset to his staging that he should not even take his normal deductions for boarding and travel expenses. In truth, I think it was my bosom, as he imagined it in the revealing bodices of his costumes, which inspired his generosity.

Finally, my father, who suffered from a gentleman's tastes without his income, signed the contract and pocketed his gold coins. "Here, Izzy, my darling," he said with great fanfare, placing one coin in my hand. "Take this for yourself for some treat you may want along the way. And be a good girl now. I will not have you causing any trouble for Mr. James. We shall miss you, my dear," he said, kissing me noisily on the cheek. "Yet next time I see you, I would not be surprised if you have attained a following far surpassing Fanny Kemble's."

I cannot say that my father really believed his words. I fear he may have said them solely to justify his selfishness in selling my services, and then contemplated immediately how many of his vices he might satisfy with the advance, using only the smallest portion to appease his most insistent creditors. I do not believe he meant me harm, and resilient as I was, probably supposed Mr. James's sister should easily manage to take good care of me. She would see that I would come to no harm while I gained confidence on the stage and satisfied my longings for adventure by seeing a bit of the world.

And perhaps she would have seen properly to my welfare had she not been so fond of her toddy. At night when the rheumatism in her hands and feet badly troubled her, she dosed herself with generous portions of hot tea and lemon laced with rum. Some evenings she required three or four tumblers before the pain would ease enough that she could drift off to sleep. I will not say that it was right, and I'll surely own that it was wrong of me, to take advantage of her pain, yet I was hardly more than a girl at the time, so certain allowances must be made for my actions, and in the end no one suffered more for them than I.

I had spent too many evenings watching my father in his own stupor not to recognize someone who had taken a measure too much. I could not respect Miss James, whose auburn wig tilted to one side after her third toddy, and sensed that her pain grew most intense whenever she observed a bottle of rum on the table. Her deception was so obvious to me, I saw no reason I should not deceive her as well. I would remain very quiet sitting in my armchair by the fading fire in the various bedchambers we shared on our tour, watching moths circling in the lamplight, and when I cautiously turned back the coverlets, often observed the flight of tiny, greasy bugs. I waited patiently for her eyelids to flicker and then gradually shut as she drifted off.

One night when I could tell that she was lost in slumber, I rose gingerly, my shoes in my hand, and tread softly to be certain the floor would not creak and give me away. I hurried stealthily down the stairs like a thief and hardly dared to breathe until I had run several streets away from the house. Then I began looking all about me, hoping to find a glimmer of excitement to call my own, some place that I might hide myself away to enjoy the evening streets and the entertainments of people gathered in the shops and doorways.

I wondered how I should make it back into the house without detection. It was too late to cry over my foolishness in not having considered this necessity before I ran outside. I considered that I might as well enjoy myself since punishment would surely happen when I returned. I even imagined that Mr. James, concerned as he was about my virtue, might send me home in disgrace to my parents once he knew that I was wandering the streets unsupervised. I felt in my pocket the weight of the gold coin my father had given me and thought I might change it and spend a bit on an ice or perhaps a shawl or piece of finery from one of the shops.

I was standing in the shadows considering my plans when suddenly I heard a familiar voice behind me jovially calling my name. "My girl, how nice to see you. But how do you happen to be out all alone in this neighborhood of strangers? Where is my sister and what can she be thinking of, leaving you out here all alone?" Mr. James asked critically, taking my arm.

"Please promise you will not blame Miss James," I implored him. "She has no idea that I am out here. Her rheumatism troubled her so badly this evening that she had to take several toddies. When she finally drifted off to sleep, I came out on my own," I shamefully admitted. "Please do not be angry. I met no harm. I had to come out this evening for a walk. I think I would have died sitting in that room all night."

"You must promise not to misbehave in this way again," he answered sternly, still holding my arm as we walked along. "I made a promise to your father you would be entirely safe in my care. I cannot keep my word if you engage in such unsafe practices. Do you wish to harm yourself and make me a liar in your father's eyes?"

Then he smiled so kindly at me that I felt quite ashamed for the aggravation I had caused him and knew I was blushing with embarrassment even though there was no glass in which I could see my face. I remembered the shame from my childhood when my parents had caught me taking forbidden sweets from the sideboard. I could not bring myself to meet his eyes.

"Well, we shall say no more about it," he said soothingly, taking in my distress. "After all, there is no harm done. And it is both of our good fortune that you should have run into me as you have. Now come along and I shall get you a bit of refreshment and then escort you safe and sound back to our lodgings."

We soon approached an inn from which the sounds of musicians and celebratory voices escaped out into the street. Mr. James ushered me inside and then into a private room. I would rather have remained in the common room where I could observe the goings on and the excitement. Only Mr. James, after observing the admiring glances that came my way from gentlemen looking up from their table, spoke to the innkeeper, and we were soon seated in a small private dining room where the table was set with a white cloth and candles. After we were brought our bread and meat and tea, Mr. James called the waiter back to bring us some wine. They consulted over the board for a few moments, and then shortly afterward, I was served my first champagne. I had never before tasted anything so delightful, and Mr. James seemed to grow merrier by the moment. He refilled my glass frequently, yet needed to replenish his own glass much more frequently.

I felt quite dizzy from the bubbling wine though also very happy, no longer concerned about anything that might happen to me. Miss James could certainly not complain about my behavior if I returned under the protection of her brother. And the evening, which had seemed desolate and unpromising just a short time before, seemed suddenly full of promise.

"Although I cannot condone your running away this evening," he said, "I am pleased that your escape has given us this opportunity to become better acquainted." He refilled our goblets with the last of the champagne. "I have been admiring your work with our company. Your voice, your singing, your appearance. You are most talented, you know, my dear. I have been thinking of more ways to feature you on our next tour," he told me.

I felt my future blossoming before my eyes. I knew that his was only a poor company, nothing to approach or even to be mentioned in the same breath as appearing as Juliet on the Covent Garden stage. Still, Mr. James had praised my appearance and my work. This made me as giddy as the cold wine.

"There's only one thing that I believe will enhance your performance, dear Isabel," he told me. "This is not a criticism and please do not take it as such." He spoke slowly, carefully choosing his words, as if I were so delicate that his words might bruise me. "I believe your artistry, whether you are singing or acting, and you are certainly gifted in both respects, cannot be fully advanced, until you know more of life. I speak particularly of love," he continued, leaning closer to me and exhaling his winey breath, made even more pungent by the glass of some other liquor, which had just been brought to him. "You will see in time what I am referring to," he continued, wiping his mouth on his linen napkin. "No artist can portray great passion until he or *she*, as the case may be, has known the heights to which the human soul can soar."

I waited, expecting Mr. James to further enlighten me as to how I might attain the breadth of feeling essential to my craft, but he turned suddenly quiet as he drained the last amber spirits from his glass. Then he settled our bill, and we walked out into the night. I was pleasantly imagining what would happen next when Mr. James pointed out the poster plastered in the entry where we had sought shelter while he lit his cigar. It seemed so unfair that even in a small city so distant from London I should still be haunted by her face. For there, again, was Fanny Kemble, staring out at me with her haughty eyes and her long white dress. The artist had graced her with dark tresses much more abundant than her own, and a figure graceful and youthful as Shakespeare's own direction.

"Oh, pay her no mind, my dear," he said. "Your beauty will long outlast hers. Perhaps she occupies a finer stage now. This shall, however, change. I have confidence in you."

He motioned to one of the elegant carriages with their glowing lamps, and then the driver drew up in front of us and Mr. James ushered me into the carriage. He pulled the curtains closed across our compartment and announced that he would take me for a little drive before we returned to our lodging house.

"I imagine after this evening, my sister will maintain a very careful watch over you. There will not be opportunities for late-night rides," he advised, while calling to the driver to take us away from the town out onto the country road that followed the river.

I was by this time tired and ready for my bed and feeling slightly woozy from the unaccustomed wine. I had no desire to drive further than the lodging house as the movement of the carriage made me feel strongly all the wine I had consumed. Yet I feared I should seem ungrateful expressing my displeasure when the ride had been offered for my sake, since surely Mr.

James had long ago had his fill of horses and carriages. So I lay back against the cushions, closed my eyes, and tried to think of thoughts that would help dispel the dizziness rising inside me.

"You have the loveliest skin," Mr. James said, stroking my cheek ever so gently with his fingers. "I have never known any finer."

I wanted to tell him to take his hand away and demand that I be driven immediately back to the lodging house. Yet I was afraid to offend Mr. James or to make myself appear childish in his sight. I had already that night committed the most childish act of all, running away like a schoolgirl. I didn't wish to compound it by my ingratitude. I remained quiet, listening to Mr. James's idle chatter about the passing scenery, which it was far too dark to see, and struggling to keep open my tired eyes.

I do not remember falling asleep, yet that can be the only explanation for what happened. I woke suddenly in the most severe distress, gasping for breath. It was very dark. The carriage was moving much more slowly, and I realized I could not breathe because the weight of Mr. James's heavy body was upon me. His tongue plunged deep into my mouth, and struggle as I tried, I could not budge his weight or still his prying hands. For just a moment he leaned back, and releasing my mouth, he quickly stopped my cries with his handkerchief.

"Listen carefully, dear Isabel," he commanded, breathing hard. "There is no one to hear you, and now we must finish what we have begun. No man can stop when he has reached this point of desire," he insisted.

As I came fully awake, I shivered, finding that he had removed all my undergarments. And though I had never before seen a man aroused and could not truly see him then in that form, I felt him press against my leg and then grow harder as he forced his way deep inside of me. It seemed as if he were made of something much harder than flesh. Still choking on his handkerchief, I heard him sigh and groan and wondered how much longer this piercing pain would last.

Then it was over. He rested on top of me and reached beneath himself to straighten my garments. He whispered fiercely in my ear that he was about to remove the handkerchief unless I screamed, in which case he would throw me out of the carriage and leave me in the road. I would find myself alone in the streets far from any stage or the prospect of ever reaching one.

And though I was dazed with pain and badly frightened, I could still think clearly enough to realize if he pushed me from the carriage, I should be ruined. I could not go home. My parents would learn quickly enough what had happened to me, and my father should surely kill me. I doubted he would believe Mr. James had used me in this terrible way, for that would then reflect on my father's dreadful judgment and greed, which had placed me in Mr. James's care. And I knew I could not expect any assistance from the driver. I was certain he placed greater value on the generous fare he should shortly receive from Mr. James than on any damage to my person. I was not his daughter after all.

So I submitted until it was soon over, and Mr. James heaved himself up and quickly withdrew. He smoothed out his handkerchief, using it first to clean me and then himself, before he settled back on the seat beside me. He parted the curtains and told the driver to drive us back into the town.

"This needn't change anything," he told me calmly. "And as for love. There is not much more to it than that."

He seemed to be waiting calmly for me to answer him as if nothing had passed between us more than conversation on a late-night drive. I wished so much that I could reverse the few hours which had passed and find myself once again watching Miss James sleep and snore in our bedchamber instead of finding myself seared and shamed and confined in a carriage with the very man who had harmed me.

"Whatever will become of me?" I finally asked, my voice small and pinched, addressing my words as much to the black night all around us as to Mr. James, so deep was my despair.

He answered me right away, matter-of-factly, as if I had been waiting for his guidance, as I might on any ordinary matter regarding the stage. "Oh, you'll be right as rain by tomorrow," he replied. "I should recommend you get a good night's sleep, and in the morning you shall rehearse with the others and we shall be in Portsmouth by evening and have full houses there by my calculations. And well as you have been doing, my dear, I should think you'll make a very fine name for yourself. And this," he coughed slightly, alluding to our recent relations, "shall remain our little secret. I am certain you understand why that must be."

I could not escape him. I knew full well I would see him in the morning at the breakfast table and must act as if nothing had transpired. I could not express the terrible pain within me and perhaps was so young I did not understand every word he had ever said to me was uttered only to gain from me what he had wanted. Still, I asked him, accustomed as I was to looking to him as the theatrical agent who would launch my future.

"You said that an actress could not truly reach her powers without knowing the 'heights to which the human soul can soar,'" I reminded him. "Is this it? Is this what it means?" My voice was fierce and raw with the pain I suffered as the effects of the champagne subsided.

"With a bit of music and poetry time to time, if you are fortunate," he said. "Though perhaps that is only possible for actors on the stage with Shakespeare's lines at their disposal."

I wondered what Fanny Kemble knew of love. Had she experienced it, or had she known it only so long as she was Juliet and then watched it disappear once she had wiped away her stage makeup and taken off her costume.

6

Stage Fright

I was wooden. No post could have been less animated than I appeared reciting Shakespeare for my parents. I had studied furiously, first Juliet, every schoolgirl's romantic favorite, and then Portia, my own heroic ideal. After I had seen the handbills plastered on Covent Garden, advertising the auction of all contents prior to the sale, I knew how seriously my father's fortunes had fallen. I stayed up several nights, closing my eyes for only brief moments, memorizing every word until I could have been shaken from a leaden sleep to exclaim, "O Romeo, Romeo! Wherefore art thou Romeo? Deny thy father and refuse thy name; or, if thou wilt not, be but sworn my love, and I'll no longer be a Capulet." Or with all the precision taught in my school elocution classes, yet without an ounce of grace, I would have intoned drably Portia's timeless words, "The quality of mercy is not strain'd, it droppeth as the gentle rain from heaven upon the place beneath...," obliterating their poetry.

My mother tried to be encouraging, making her suggestions very gently, "You know it is actually quite all right to move, my dear Fanny, or even to take a breath. Actors *do*, you know, time to time."

When I had finished my recitation, for that was all it was, certainly it was not acting, staring straight ahead and pressing my nails into the palms of my hands, she thanked me for my hard work. My father silently left the drawing room, and I could not contain my tears, so ashamed as I felt for disappointing him. I knew I had shown myself to be the possessor of a prodigious memory without the Kemble voice or subtlety.

"I hope you do not think your father dissatisfied with *you*, Fanny," my mother quickly said, handing me her handkerchief.

"I have let him down, Mother, when he was counting on me. And I have shown myself to be an oafish actress who destroys Shakespeare when *no* Kemble has ever done that befo—"

"You misread him completely." She put her arm around me. "He is overcome with regret that his circumstances and, yes, even I must say, his mismanagement of the theatre has brought such a sad predicament upon our family that even you, a talented writer, should have to act."

"You speak as if acting is something horrid. When you have both given your lives to it."

"By necessity and by our own choices. And we had not some of yours. How many seventeen-year-old girls could write a play like *Francis I* and be asked to publish it? You are a *writer*, dear. That is all you have ever cared deeply about, and your father feels it quite wrong to pull you from it."

"At best I am only a *reader*, Mother. That is what I should most like to do. Read Shakespeare aloud for my living so everyone might find the sheer joy of his words. Yet I doubt I shall ever find anyone to pay me to do that. And I have far to go as a writer. I fear my efforts are still those of a fledgling. And now Father has seen that for all the talk of Kemble blood, it clearly does not run through my veins."

"Oh, but it does, dear Fanny," my father assured me, taking us by surprise, much as if our drawing room were the setting for a play in which he was once again the leading man. "I am *so* sorry if I gave the impression of displeasure, when that was not what I felt in the slightest. I was truly overwhelmed," he said, embracing us both, "at how you had labored through the night. No one but a *Kemble* could memorize both Juliet *and* Portia in two days. And now it will take but another Kemble to show you how to find the poetry of acting. Most study for years to find it, and you have but a few weeks." He offered his arm playfully. "Come, madam, your carriage awaits to take you to the theatre."

From the stage, Covent Garden did not convey the splendid seclusion of the boxes or the comfort of the red plush seats in the orchestra, from which the audience relaxed into the actors' and the playwright's magic. I had been attending performances by my parents and my Aunt Sarah for many years, yet I was completely unprepared to stand upon that formidable stage, the center of all attention, in a part of no lesser importance than Juliet.

I was still wooden, having in no way shaken my fear, and even worse my aversion to displaying myself in front of people, even in the privacy of my parents' drawing room, much less in the most august theatre in England. My Aunt Dall had assured me, as she stood with me in the wings, waiting for my entrance to be called, that once I stood upon that stage, I would be fine. Shakespeare's magnificent lines would take hold of me and inspire me to find my own voice. The costume mistress told me that I looked lovely, and that the simplicity of the white gown and my long flowing train accentuated my youthful grace and beauty. She promised me the audience would gasp with pleasure at the first sight of me.

And so they did. When I walked out upon that stage, crisscrossed by lights, I could hear the audience's sighs and whispers so that I forgot instantly and completely the words that were to come from my mouth. My father had earlier cautioned that I must forget the audience. "Pretend they are not even there," he had advised me. "Or if you must look at them, conceive of them as row upon row of cabbages. And who would ever let herself be upset by the opinions of cabbages?"

But I *was*. I could not think. I felt more lost than at any time in my life as the audience's murmurs reached me. I could hear their voices, as if they were speaking in my own ear, while at the same time the actors on stage could not have seemed more remote had they addressed me in a completely foreign tongue. I struggled against the tightness in my own throat, wishing the nurse were my own nursemaid so I might throw myself in her arms for comfort or that Lady Capulet were my very own mother.

Finally, coaxed by these two fine actors, who all but said my lines to me, I began to speak. At first, when finally I was sufficiently composed to speak, it was a very tiny voice that said haltingly, "And stint thou too, I pray thee, nurse, say I," while the cabbages still whispered and grumbled. Yet phrase by phrase, I began to gain my own strength, until the cabbages grew completely silent. And by the time of the balcony scene, I held all the cabbages in my hand.

Romeo, in this production, was not a romantic youth to enchant me or the audience, but an actor of my father's age, known best for his proficiency in drawing-room comedies. I heard the audience again whispering that it was a shame he was such a poor excuse for a Romeo. Then suddenly I understood that they meant this in contrast to *my* Juliet. Before them I had been transformed from a reluctant schoolgirl, trembling on stage, into an actress. I was Juliet. Or as the voices all around me pronounced, no longer in whispers, I was a *Kemble*.

Those who detest me, and there are certainly some besides Mr. Butler, as well as others who love me, and I have been most fortunate in that regard as well, may still upbraid me for my vanity and a self-important way of stating my opinions. I cannot deny such accusations, yet I tell anyone who makes them that it is hardly any wonder after all that was made of me. From the first night I played Juliet, I became the darling of the London theatre, and only if I had been a statue of stone instead of a young girl could this not have affected me.

Flowers were thrown up onto the stage with loving epistles or sent to my dressing room in such quantities as to fill a hothouse or to make it seem as if someone had surely died. Letters and callers came to our house at all hours. Gentlemen of whom no one in my family had previous acquaintance sent round their engraved cards. Most of these my parents would not admit, only making exception for those whose names were known to them, and only then if my parents or my Aunt Dall were present. Contrary to what many people, particularly Americans, seemed to believe of actors' mores, we Kembles followed the strictest propriety in our deportment. Still, crowds waited in the street for a glimpse of me as I left Covent Garden, where gentlemen literally stuffed their letters through the carriage windows.

Most of these were preposterous offers of money that no honorable woman could consider. *"If you will but grant me one hour of your time, any evening that you shall select, I will pay you 3000 pounds."* My sister and brothers and I began to laugh at them—I suppose unkindly—as we opened them sitting around the fire in the afternoon. *"If you will not speak with me soon, I will certainly perish. I have already lost two stone since I first saw you on stage as Juliet,"* one writer claimed. *"You must consent to see me."* My brother Henry became so uproarious reading that letter that he upset his tea, insisting that the writer was probably older than our father and weighed *four* stone too many before he had even heard of Fanny Kemble.

Yet, miraculously, it seemed that everyone *had* suddenly heard of me. Famous artists clamored for the chance to paint my portrait in every role in which I appeared. Shop windows at Christmas featured dainty porcelain miniatures of my face. I was painted more often than Princess Victoria when but months before I had been an unknown girl, acting only in Parisian schoolrooms. Sadly, I could no longer take my daily solitary walk through Russell Square's graveled paths, memorizing my lines or contemplating Byron's most solemn couplets as I went round and round, my eyes on the privet hedges, without attracting an admiring horde. Every performance at Covent Garden was sold out if Fanny Kemble was announced, and happily, even some nights when my name was *not* listed, since no one could imagine the staging of any production in which I would not take part. I had *become* Covent Garden. Hours before each performance, men stood outside the theatre waiting for the box office to open, in hopes of paying any price for but a single ticket.

My father's creditors and their demands could be held at bay. Covent Garden would not, at least temporarily, be sold or lost. There was once again unbridled gaiety and laughter in our home late at night after the theatre was put to bed. I had but a child's knowledge of finance and assumed we had surely earned so very much money—I envisioned endless golden heaps of coins—to release me from a profession whose glamour did not captivate me and which I found distasteful, since it forced public attention upon me. I longed to resume my writing energetically instead of scarce moments stolen for my journal. But then my father was invited to make an extremely lucrative American theatrical tour. By his own reputation, he could have achieved illustrious notice, yet his best offers, assuring the most extraordinary financial success, were promised only if we should tour together.

"It is only for two years," my father consoled me. "They shall pass quickly as exciting travel always does. You will return to London before you have had opportunity to miss it. Think of all the new material you shall gather, and while we travel, you will surely find many hours to write with absolutely nothing to disturb your concentration."

7

An Escape

I could not bear to look at Mr. James throughout the course of each day. No matter how I tried to escape his notice, I always felt his eyes upon me, watching fixedly as I studied my lines or ate my porridge or walked in the lane with the other young ladies in the company. Even before a full house, I could sense his presence in the midst of two hundred faces. At meals, I could not eat, knowing he observed even my everyday motions of chewing. He often stared at me so intently that all conversation at table would cease. I was certain, although I had never confessed to a soul what he had done to me, that everyone seated around us could tell as surely as if they had been in the carriage that dreadful night.

We toured the West Country, appearing at festivals where large crowds might turn out audiences sufficient to meet Mr. James's expectations. I was featured in song and dance and in the scenes from serious dramas he selected to please the most ordinary tastes. Every evening we performed the balcony scene from *Romeo and Juliet*, and the worst insult of all occurred when Mr. James, who denied his age, corpulence, and baldness in his supreme vanity, was my Romeo. It was injurious enough that Fanny Kemble had unjustly stolen the role of Juliet from me on the great stage I should have graced, but to add to that insult, the horror of nightly appearing with Mr. James and to be subjected to his disgusting embrace was a wretched cruelty. I tried to turn my face and give him only my cheek, yet he managed by his superior height and weight to turn my lips to meet his own. I felt I should certainly perish from this assault, and even thought a few times, perhaps inspired by Juliet's own sad example, to take my own life, so desperate his advances made me feel.

Yet through it all, I could not give up my dream to take the stage as a leading actress. I knew that I had earned it by my talent and determination, but if I resisted Mr. James before an audience or in the presence of the members of our company, he would punish me. Even though it was my beauty that drew audiences, particularly the gentlemen who purchased the tickets for their families, I knew Mr. James would not tolerate insolence from me. I had no doubt I could be replaced or, if it pleased him, sent home in disgrace to my family, who should never learn the true events behind my banishment. And after what he had done to me, I worried daily that there should soon be about my person evidence that should escape no one's eye of what had passed between us. Young as I was, still I had no doubt that if it came to determining the truth of my account or the false one which Mr. James should surely construe, I would, of course, appear to be a liar.

"We tried to do our best for her," Mr. James would ruefully exclaim. "I even placed your daughter in the care of my own *sister*," he would declare, to demonstrate the special efforts to which he had gone for my benefit. "Yet still she would run away, time after time, attaching herself to the very lowest of companions. It is no wonder she finds herself in this state," he would continue, sadly shaking his head and looking away from me in my misery. "I am afraid I can no longer control your daughter or vouch for her safety. I must return her to your care, sir," he would advise my father. "'Tis a great shame, sir, for such a fine family. Yet I think it is a hopeless case. She is simply a *bad* girl and will doubtless come to a bad end."

It seemed the only path left me was to run away. Only I knew I could not hope to manage without a sum of money I could rely upon. To flee without it would be to doom myself to a shameful reunion with my parents or the sad fate I knew befell girls in the streets.

So I waited. I knew that Miss James kept about her person a large pocketbook, which she wore on a belt around her waist, the keys of which were always in the pocket of her dress. Only before bedtime when she changed into her night garments, did she take the pocketbook from her waist and place it for safekeeping beneath her pillow. I knew it contained a great amount of money, since she kept in it her own funds as well as a portion of the company's earnings for each week, which Mr. James entrusted to her for safekeeping, concerned as he was of apprehension by thieves or by his many creditors.

One afternoon when she was badly afflicted with her rheumatism and had taken at least three large toddies, I promised to sit by her bed and watch with her until she had fallen off to sleep. She was very grateful since she had confided in me often before that until her "medicine," as she called it, had taken affect, the pain frightened her. I took up some needlework and sat down in the rocking chair beside her bed, smiling soothingly at her, in what I hoped was a convincing portrayal of the devoted companion, and waited while her eyes slowly closed and she drifted into a peaceful sleep. I watched carefully until she was breathing very deeply, and then I rose carefully, making not the slightest sound, and began to fuss about her pillow. I had decided that if by any chance she awakened, I would pretend to be retying her pillowcase. I would tell her that as her head shifted upon her pillow, I had observed that the laces had come undone and was concerned that the goose feathers being released should set her to sneezing and disturb her sleep.

Fortunately, although she started once or twice so that I feared she would wake, she did not open her eyes. When she finally rolled upon her side, I took the opportunity to slide my small, slender hand beneath the pillows to pull out her pocketbook. I knew far better than to take it with me, for to be caught with such a well-known item in my possession could not be explained. Once it was in my grasp, I quickly removed the key from her dress pocket and opened the pocketbook. I seized a handful of golden sovereigns and then replaced the pocketbook beneath her pillows. I secured the coins in my handkerchief and then pushed this small parcel deep into my bosom so if I should be detected leaving the inn, there would be no obvious sign of stolen goods upon my person. I left my needlework upon the chair. If she suddenly awakened, she would think I had merely left the bedchamber for a moment.

Then I returned to the adjoining dressing room that I shared with several other girls, wondering how I should explain my packing or make excuses if they asked where I was going. But it was my good fortune that they were taking exercise in the park so that I could put on a few extra garments beneath my dress and place a few necessities in a hatbox. I waited until I felt assured that the corridor was unoccupied, and then I ran from that inn, not once glancing behind me. I did not pause for a moment even to consider my course until I saw an approaching carriage, which was unoccupied. I showed the driver one of my sovereigns so he would know I was in earnest and possessed the means to set out upon my journey. I asked him what would be the fastest way for me to make my way to America, promising him handsome payment for his assistance. He agreed, for a considerable sum, to drive into the wee hours of the night to take me to a ship leaving early the next morning for America. Although it was costly, I much preferred this plan to stopping at an inn where by fate's unfortunate hand I might encounter someone who knew me or had seen me perform with Mr. James's company. I could not risk detection, so I gratefully pulled the shawl he offered around me to keep out the drafts, and closed my eyes. I drifted in and out of sleep throughout the long drive and did not breathe an easy breath of air until I was actually standing aboard *The Peacock*, a small vessel bound for Philadelphia. I knew no one in America, and not a soul aboard our ship, yet the captain seemed kindly. And when he asked how I came to be traveling alone, he was most sympathetic when I explained that my mother and sisters had been taken suddenly by a pernicious fever. Though my father feared having me go on alone to Philadelphia, he was more apprehensive of my remaining with him since so many others, almost all ladies, saddled with delicate constitutions, had already succumbed to this malady. I would be safer aboard an ocean-bound vessel where fresh air should be plentiful, and afterwards in New York, where my father's brother, my Uncle Silas, would care for me. I was to share a stateroom with an elderly lady, the only accommodation available, and I immediately expressed my great interest in retiring to my chamber to take my rest.

The captain pronounced me a very brave girl to take on such a lengthy, solitary journey after such tragedy had stricken my family. He said I was a credit to my parents and he would personally keep his eye out for me. "You will be perfectly safe and secure upon *The Peacock*," he told me. "You shall have such good health and spirits by the time we arrive in port," he promised, "you will be a changed young lady. Your own uncle may not recognize you as the worn, tired creature you are tonight. I hope he will allow me to show you both some of the attractions of New York before you continue on your journey to Philadelphia. You will certainly require rest after such a long journey, even on a ship as fine as *The Peacock*. There will be much to entertain you, and I shall be delighted to be your guide," he said smiling graciously, yet still awakening in me the fears which my encounter with Mr. James had left within me.

I smiled gratefully, assuring him that both my father and my Uncle Silas would be very thankful for his kindness to me and then begged that I be permitted to retire, so exhausted was I by the travel I had already undertaken. He tipped his cap gallantly and told me that if I would not think him presumptuous, he would tell me that in his fantasy, he always envisioned Juliet looking exactly like me. He had been fortunate to see the brilliant Fanny Kemble at Covent Garden when he was last in London, and all that was said about her acting was certainly true. Her voice was magnificent, yet even at the vantage actors appear from the stage, he could assure me that there was no comparison between us.

The elderly lady into whose stateroom I had been placed turned out to be a milliner. Mrs. Chestnut owned a small, elite shop in Philadelphia, from which the city's most famous and influential citizens waited for weeks to obtain her creations. She was on her return home after purchasing English ribbons, bows, and lace and studying the latest fashions. One night as we sat companionably by lamplight in our stateroom, she showed me sketches of her most recent designs. She had created hats for queens and countesses, the wives of presidents, famous opera singers and actresses, and the wives of the wealthiest men in Europe and America. She told me with pride that could not be concealed that in Jean Clemenceau's famous portrait of Fanny Kemble, often copied for miniatures and figurines, the lovely plumed hat she was wearing was one of Mrs. Chestnut's very own creations.

I listened silently as she described Fanny Kemble's exquisite taste and style. She seemed greatly surprised that I did not express admiration for my celebrated countrywoman or gratitude for opportunity to study details of her wardrobe. "You are so serious, my dear Isabel," she told me. "So unlike all the other young ladies who crave any tiny detail about Fanny. How is it you have not caught this fever which makes every girl wish to become a famous actress like Fanny?"

I could not tell her of my own fever and was relieved that she could not detect it. She seemed quickly to develop a motherly affection for me, sharing dainties that she brought on board and treating me to specialties from the ship's table which I should never have indulged in, so intent as I was to spare my small purse. Mrs. Chestnut had no children of her own, and since her husband did not enjoy excursions, she was traveling on her own. She had been hoping to find an assistant, someone to learn her craft and to assist her since her creations were in such demand. From my sewing skills, which she had observed when we did embroidery together in the evening in our cabin, and by her assessment of my tasteful arrangement of my own wardrobe, limited as it was, Mrs. Chestnut told me she had concluded that I was the perfect young lady to become her assistant.

"And it will not hurt at all, my dear Isabel," she whispered confidentially, "that you are so very lovely. In a millinery, the most important customers are men. Everyone supposes it is women," she said laughing. "I find, however, it is always men who commission the most expensive hats. And when they walk by a shop window and see someone like you at work over a lovely creation, they always come inside, sometimes bringing their wives and mothers or their sweethearts with them. Though most often they stop by all alone to place their commissions."

While working in Mrs. Chestnut's Philadelphia shop, I first encountered Pierce Butler. I was sitting in the large front room, trimming a lilac hat with white ribbons and lace, when I became aware of a gentleman watching me through the plate glass window. He did not stare fixedly, as would a child staring at display of sweets. He glanced at me furtively, turning away whenever I looked up and saw his eyes upon me. Each time he would quickly look away until finally he met my eyes with an unwavering stare and then came inside.

By this time I had spent several months in Mrs. Chestnut's shop, having decided if I did not accept her protection, I would surely never separate myself from *The Peacock*'s good captain, who searched among the crowd of people who came to meet his passengers for my Uncle Silas. I had forgotten this imaginary relative over the course of the trip and wondered how I should produce him until Mrs. Chestnut came to my rescue. When she heard me explaining to the captain that there had been a misunderstanding and that my uncle Silas, somehow miscalculating the date of my arrival, was actually in England and not present to welcome me, she urged me to stay with her until word could reach my uncle. She warmly hugged me and assured me I was more than welcome since she already thought of me as the daughter she and her husband had not been blessed to have.

I readily accepted her offer, recognizing it was certainly the best that should come my way. After noticing many gentlemen traveling aboard *The Peacock* staring unashamedly at me, I felt certain I should harm my reputation without someone like Mrs. Chestnut to protect me. I had heard that America, being a new country, was not so unforgiving as England of the transgressions in which a girl might innocently be entangled, yet I feared I could not achieve my dream to appear upon the New York stage if there were doubts about my reputation or my past. My escape from England would have been for naught.

"You are so very beautiful, my dear Isabel," Mrs. Chestnut assured me. "I would be content to simply have you sit in my front window modeling my hats. That alone should be sure to bring me business if you do not wish to pursue this craft. I am so very happy to have you with me."

But I preferred to work and learn the business, I told her. I had no other plan of how I would earn my living until I could be discovered by someone who would place me in the play that would assure my fame. The kind old lady was so taken with me that she became devoted to my welfare. She told me that as she had no living relations beside her old husband and two ungrateful nephews, that if I should work diligently and assist her in her old age, she should gladly will her shop to me.

I saw no reason to tell her of my ambition for the stage. I knew they must be postponed until I saved sufficient money to establish myself in New York or had made connections with a theatre, which seemed very far off at that time. Late at night in my despair when I could not sleep, I feared sometimes the nearest I would come to the stage might well be by trimming some actress's favorite hat. Then everything changed when Pierce Butler strode briskly into Mrs. Chestnut's shop, ringing the bell on the door and immediately calling attention to himself and to me when he asked if I might wait upon him.

The other girls were watching as he walked up to the counter. I had been concentrating on positioning four different flowers on a velvet bonnet. Mrs. Chestnut had insisted that the customer wanted all four flowers, yet every time I tried to arrange them, the result was overcrowded. I had tried to affix them three different ways and was so displeased I did not pay attention to the commotion Mr. Butler was causing until Mrs. Chestnut called me to the counter.

It seemed Mr. Butler insisted that *only* I could wait on him. There was no reason someone else could not have assisted him, Mrs. Chestnut whispered to me. She also explained that he was one of the wealthiest men in Philadelphia, actually in the whole United States. His grandfather had been a Revolutionary War hero, and he and his brother were leaders of Philadelphia society. He had never looked into her shop window before, much less come inside. I noticed immediately by the proud way he held himself that he was accustomed to being noticed by others and watching his wishes carried out. He was not at all a tall man; still there was no mistaking the elegant tailoring of his clothes and the commanding way in which he strode into the room. His mustache was waxed and his beard neatly trimmed about his face. His wavy, dark hair fell over the velvet edge of the collar of his suit. There was the fragrance of cologne about him, though he had just come inside from riding. He wore fine leather gloves and held a riding crop beneath his arm.

"Mr. Butler, I am so pleased to welcome you to the Chestnut Millinery," Mrs. Chestnut said differentially. "I should be glad to wait upon you myself, yet knowing you have requested to have Miss Graves assist you, I have asked her to stop her work so that she may show you any style of hat you desire."

Mrs. Chestnut spoke cordially in her most welcoming tones, yet having spent so much time in her company, I could see she was somewhat affronted by his attentions to me. It was her shop, and it did not please her to have a member of Philadelphia's high society walk past her to be assisted by a mere shopgirl. I was tempted to tell her she was truly mistaken if she believed Mr. Butler to be interested in her hats, no matter how imaginative their design. I was offended that after seeing me in the window, he vainly thought he could come in and ask for me as if I, and not the hats, were for sale.

"Thank you very much, Mrs. Chestnut," he said, tipping his hat and addressing her with formal courtesy. "I have often noticed your charming shop on this corner. I am glad I had the opportunity to come inside today. There is a lady for whom I must select a special gift, and I am certain I shall find it here."

Mrs. Chestnut looked as happy as if he had already purchased ten of her most costly hats, before she was called away to assist one of her regular customers.

"Is there a particular hat you would like to see?" I asked, trying to cultivate the helpful tone Mrs. Chestnut took with customers even though I had not waited on anyone before.

"I was watching you from the window. I'm not sure if you noticed," he said awkwardly. "Did you observe me watching you work?"

"Yes, and everyone else did as well. Now they are angry with me, since when you came in you asked for me," I confessed.

"You needn't worry," he reassured me. "I will purchase whatever amount will make the owner feel happy. She seems a rather simple little woman. It should not take much to please her," he said condescendingly.

"What did you wish to see, sir? Was it something we have in the window?"

"There was only one thing I saw in the window," he said softly, placing his hand on the counter very close to mine. "Alas, sadly it is no longer on display."

"I believe you are mistaken, sir. Nothing has been sold out of the window," I told him, unable to hide my perplexity. "Everything remains that was in the window when you arrived."

"No, that is not so," he said solemnly. "You are no longer in the window. And you are the only reason I came into this shop."

I felt so nervous that my hands began to tremble. He must have noticed my shaking since he placed his own on either side of mine to steady me. To anyone watching, it would have looked as if we were studying something together.

"What can I show you?"

"Nothing. Nothing at all. Simply box up for me two of your most expensive hats. It makes no difference what color or design. I want to please Mrs. Chestnut so she will be pleased when I call for you."

"For me?" I was startled by his audacity. "Why would you be calling for me, sir?" I tried with great effort to keep my voice calm, though I feared that everyone in the shop was staring at us and that the only voices that could be heard in that busy place were our own.

"You need not speculate. I shall be delighted to explain if after looking into my eyes you do not know the answer yourself," he said, leaning over the counter that separated us, feigning interest in a fawn-colored hat to which I had been affixing small grey feathers.

I was determined not to embarrass myself by returning his penetrating glance. Yet immediately I had it, I dismissed my resolve not to look at him. Though I could feel the flush of shyness coloring me pink from my cheeks to my temples, I looked into his eyes and returned his smile.

"When you wrap that up," he whispered, taking out his purse and to all appearances busying himself counting out his payment for two hats, "be certain to write on this card where I may expect to meet you for tea this Sunday at three o'clock. I shall anticipate finding it wrapped in tissue beneath a hat. Please do not disappoint me."

I did not eat the day I was to meet Mr. Butler, nor could I drink my tea that morning. I dressed slowly, selecting carefully those blue garments that would best accent my eyes and my pale, perfect skin. I tied back my golden hair with blue ribbon. I cannot say what I expected from this meeting with a wealthy Philadelphia gentleman, yet I did not see what harm could possibly befall me in a public tea shop. My life of long hours in the shop, chores at Mrs. Chestnut's house, and the required church services left little time for enjoyment or any hope of attending the theatre, much less appearing on one of its stages.

I had selected Couper & Roundtree as our meeting place since it was some distance from Mrs. Chestnut's house, so there would be little risk of encountering her or any of the other shopgirls. I knew she would disapprove of this meeting and suspect something inappropriate between Mr. Butler and me, and the girls themselves would likely tell tales out of their jealousy that I had attracted the attention of a distinguished gentleman. So when I entered the establishment, I looked carefully around to be certain I was not being observed before I approached Mr. Butler, who rose from the table where he had been seated, as if he were greeting a great lady.

He ordered an English tea for us, and when it came he asked if I would serve since I was both the lady at table and an actual Englishwoman at that. It unnerved me that the entire time I poured the tea and passed the cakes, he did not take his eyes from me.

"What is it?" I asked, concerned that I had in my nervousness committed some error in tea-table etiquette. I could imagine no other reason I should receive such intense scrutiny from his dark eyes.

"Oh, I do beg your pardon, my dear," he said taking my hand and pressing it in his own for a moment. "I did not mean to stare. It was quite rude of me. It's just that you are so very beautiful."

I felt the delicate teacup shaking in my hand, so I put it down for fear I should drop it. I could not think quickly of anything witty to say in response to this worldly man who seemed so genuinely drawn to me.

"I cannot understand what you are doing in a milliner's shop, Isabel. Surely there must be something else in the world you wish to pursue," he inquired kindly, seeming to suggest that I might easily do anything I wished.

"Not everyone can do exactly what she would like in life. We must make our living and have not all your advantages," I answered boldly, then worried that he might be offended I referred so frankly to his wealth and position.

"Nor do they have yours," he said gallantly, again looking deeply into my eyes. "Not one in a million is as lovely as you. I believe you could be anything you desire. So tell me, what is your desire? What would make you truly happy?"

"In England, in a very small way," I explained hesitantly, my voice barely reaching above a whisper, "I was in the theatre. I had the chance for a very large part. Actually to play Juliet with a prominent company until the part was *stolen* from me by someone who received partiality from the theatre manager," I told him, my heart still stinging from the insult. "So if I might choose anything, I should wish to be a success upon the American stage. Only I have no influential friends to assist me in making my way," I told him, feeling particularly alone in the strange country where I had fled to escape those who had harmed me, yet also leaving behind all that was comforting or familiar to me.

"Oh, I would disagree with you there, Isabel," he answered warmly, taking my hand for a moment. "I should never wish to be accused of exaggerating my own importance, yet I do not feel it would be doing so to assert that I have at least some influence in this country. And I do hope I am not being presumptuous in claiming to be your friend." His expression seemed very gentle as he looked tentatively at me, his face inclined to the side, as if so much depended on how I might assess him.

"I am very honored by your friendship, and so very far away from all my friends and family," I told him, speaking as if they were many and loving. "Do you think you could actually help me find a part with a theatre company?"

"I am certain I could help you if you would permit me," he answered graciously. "I know many people who are involved in music and theatricals and am, in my small way, a musician. I play the flute."

I could not believe my good fortune to have made such a helpful new acquaintance. Only recalling my recent experience with Mr. James, I was fearful. Kind as Mr. Butler was, and obviously wealthy and distinguished, I puzzled why he should wish to assist me.

"Forgive me, Mr. Butler, I do not mean to sound ungrateful for your kind offer. Yet I must ask. Why do you take such interest in me when you surely have so many accomplished acquaintances?"

In probably the only honest statement Mr. Butler ever made to me, he said, "Isabel, I am a patron of the arts and have always admired what is most beautiful. And in all my life I have never encountered anyone more lovely than you."

And so it began. Pierce Butler promised to help me find my place in the theatres of America from Philadelphia and New York to St. Louis and Chicago. He also professed to love me, and I believed him when he promised that we should have a great future together. He convinced me that I must immediately leave Mrs. Chestnut's employ. He said as long as I was occupied long hours each week trimming hats, I would have insufficient time to prepare myself for the stage, nor would any director hire a milliner's assistant as a leading lady. When I explained I had only the most modest savings and relied on my wages for my survival, Mr. Butler implored me to put my trust in him. He would purchase a small cottage for me and should provide me with the monies I needed for my regular maintenance and for the wardrobe appropriate for an aspiring actress who should soon be auditioning in Philadelphia and New York in theatres where he would introduce me. When I asked how I should ever repay him, he said he gave his assistance freely and it never need be repaid.

Less than a week later, I found myself living in a small white cottage covered in vines on a lovely cobblestone-paved street lined with trees. I had far more luxuries than I had ever known before, as well as Mr. Butler's daily company. I accompanied him to concerts and plays and for the elegant late dinners he arranged to be served to us at the cottage, with champagne in silver goblets sipped by candlelight. And true to his word, Mr. Butler introduced me to playwrights and theatrical agents and took me to their gatherings. I had finally the opportunity to appear, as no one's understudy and in no one's shadow, as Juliet and Portia. It was very far from Covent Garden in these small companies, yet I was on my way. I had outstanding reviews, praising both my acting and my beauty, and soon I had not just Mr. Butler's friendship, but his attentions.

He was devoted as the most loyal suitor, showering me with small gifts, escorting me home from my performances, and writing me tender letters. Still, he was not my husband. When I asked him when we should actually be married, something he had promised me, he told me that I must be patient a while longer.

"If it were up to me, dear Isabel," he assured me, "I should wed you this very day. I shall undoubtedly never find any lady who will please me more. Only the decision of who shall be my bride is not my own choice. I have very little income without my inheritance, and my good aunt, whose fortune I shall one day receive, a fortune so vast in property and money you cannot even imagine, insists that I shall marry someone of substance with family connections of whom she can approve. I mean no disrespect," he said, lowering his eyes deferentially, "yet I cannot be persuaded that the past and the patrimony you have described to me would be acceptable to dear aunt. Yet I am encouraged that if we are patient and wait only a little longer until you have truly won the heart of America as a leading lady of the American theatre, I believe she will be persuaded to sanction our marriage. Your celebrated achievement should then mitigate your low birth."

"How can you speak so cruelly of my family and even of the secrets I shared with you?" I could hardly hold back my tears. "How can anyone who claims to be a gentleman, descended from one of America's finest families, behave so ungentlemanly towards someone whom he professes to love?"

Mr. Butler fell on his knees before me, beseeching me to understand that his actions were motivated solely by his love for me. The only reason he could bear to postpone our union was so he would first inherit the where-withal to care for me as he felt I deserved. If his reference to the difference in our respective stations had been too strong, it was only to make clear to me why he struggled to win his aunt's approval. He regretted terribly that he had hurt my feelings. I could actually see tears in his eyes as he tenderly embraced me. I believed they represented the tenderness and authenticity of his feelings. Now, looking back, I believe Mr. Butler's acting abilities far surpassed my own.

That very night was the first time I slept in Mr. Butler's arms in the bed he had provided for me in the ivy-covered cottage.

"If you are sure, Isabel," he said gratefully, "that you truly want me, then let this be our wedding night. A temporary one until we shall receive my aunt's blessing. And I shall care for you just as a true husband should, now and when we are properly united."

I confided to him my horrible treatment by Mr. James, and still he gallantly insisted it made no difference to him. He should not blame me for my ill treatment by a disreputable man. It made no difference to him except if he should ever encounter Mr. James, he would not trust his temper and would flog him within an inch of his life. Then he carried me in his arms to my bed. He was very tender with me, running his hands over every inch of my body so that I should know pleasure, many subtle pleasures, where once I had only known pain. And during the night, waking in his arms and feeling the warmth of his body when before I had lain alone, was a delight to me. He soon spent more nights in my company, and I believed it would not be long before I should appear in a New York theatre as a leading lady and he would feel comfortable introducing me to his aunt as his fiancée.

About this time, Mr. Butler told me he would be away for a time on business in New York City. I asked if I might accompany him perhaps to attend New York plays. I hoped to advance my standing so Mr. Butler should feel he could introduce me to his family, and we might announce our engagement and should never again have to be separated. He assured me that if he were not to be so completely immersed in business, he would relish my company. As it was, he told me, smiling in his charming way, he feared my presence would distract him from the many matters requiring his attention.

He was routinely away from Philadelphia so that his answer did not concern me. I was accustomed to his absences, yet I became distressed when after a few days he had not responded to my letters. I longed for his company, yet reassured myself that he was only away from me to pursue business interests necessary to assure our future. I continued with my performances and patiently awaited his return.

One afternoon I returned home after a matinee performance at the Walnut Hill Theatre, pleased with how well I had acquitted myself. I was surprised to find a gentleman waiting in the doorway to see me. In truth, he did not behave like a gentleman in manner, as his tone was harsh and abrasive, despite his neat suit. He handed me a letter from the law firm which employed him, informing me that the cottage which I had come to think of as my own was to be sold. I must vacate in thirty days. This *gentleman* was actually prepared to take an inventory of all contents except for my personal effects, since the contents were scheduled to be sold as soon as the house stood empty.

"This is outrageous," I exclaimed, hardly able to catch my breath and stuttering as I tried to express myself. "I m-m-must get hold of my fiancé, Mr. Butler." In my alarm, I actually referred to him by that title, although we had never publicly declared our intentions. I had not appeared with him where he might be recognized, in order to protect his prospects with his aunt. "He is traveling in New York and I am uncertain of how to reach him. There is some dreadful mistake, I am certain. He would not sell this house."

"There is no mistake, madam," he said, looking at the gold numbers on my letterbox and comparing them to the address on the papers in his hand. "Mr. Butler gave these directions himself." He extended the paper so I could see the signature at the bottom of the order. "Before he left town, he directed our firm to make the arrangements."

"I can read what it says on your papers, sir, but that does not mean they are accurate," I told him, feeling so faint that I held tightly to the railing. "Mr. Butler is, as I am certain you know, a gentleman of considerable property. Perhaps in his hurry to attend to other business, my fiancé confused the address. He would, after all, never intend for his own fiancée to be turned out of her dwelling."

"I cannot speak to his intentions, madam," he said, looking away from me in a way that puzzled me until he cleared his throat and went on. "It is really not my place to do so. But he did ask that I officially notify you, since he will be away from the city for some time on a journey to celebrate his wedding to the famous actress Fanny Kemble. Now if we may go inside, I can make my list of contents and leave you to your packing."

8

Entrances and Exits

In 1832 I sailed for America with my father, leaving behind every association, save his company, that had been familiar or comforting to me. It felt very different from the many times I had left home in the past. In England and in France, my schooling had required parting from my parents, yet after the pangs of separation eased, I had always excelled at the one thing that was expected of me: scholarship. Suddenly I was forced to assume a new role as actress instead of scholar, along with the expectation that I would daily display myself before audiences, a practice which filled me with aversion. Traveling on the continent had always brought me great pleasure. I spoke French, German, and Italian and enjoyed travels with my parents and visits to the home of their friends. This time all I could think about was two years away from home in a strange new world, where they might speak English, but from what I had heard, did not understand it.

"My dear, 'All the world's a stage,'" my father quoted, trying to distract me with a jest, which was very unlike him, since he revered this favorite speech for its serious import. I looked at him with uncomprehending eyes, filled with tears, for those who could no longer be identified, but who still stood waving from the receding wharf.

"I only meant that you should not be so sad thinking of all you leave behind. You will find America and Americans not to be so different from people you have already known," he explained. "We are all certainly 'merely players...and one man in his time has many parts.' Wherever he may go."

"Oh father, could we please simply forget the theatre for one *moment*." I could not control my exasperation.

"Ah, that is something I have never been able to do." His tone was matter-of-fact, not melancholy as the words might suggest. "It is exceedingly odd for me to consider that for the majority of people it is only an *entertainment* and not a life."

I did not answer him. Yet as the ship moved further out into the open sea, I was certain that it could only be the former for me.

Pierce Butler's handwriting distinguished him from the others. Their letters were brought daily to my dressing room along with gifts of chocolates and flowers and impetuously scrawled notes on the backs of calling cards accompanying bottles of fine champagne. Some wrote to me of my "devastating beauty," something which a bout of smallpox, albeit a light case, had left me severely in doubt of, and others wildly declaimed their love of my "brilliant acting." Mr. Butler wrote to me of Shakespeare, quoting sonnets and commenting on my varying inflections as Juliet and Portia, my most frequent roles, and how they affected him as he followed us on tour.

That was the first knowledge I had that he watched me so carefully. Aunt Dall, my mother's sister, who had traveled with us to America to help watch over me, so concerned were my parents for preserving my good reputation, was impressed not only by his knowledge of Shakespeare, but also by his penmanship.

"He writes a very good hand," she observed one evening. "In such a bright blue ink, Fanny. He is evidently quite taken with you, my dear," she remarked, reading further. "And quite accomplished in his own right, dear. He has even obtained permission to play his flute in the company orchestra in order to be near you. Isn't that flattering, Charles?"

"A bit sappy, since you ask," my father answered. "But a nice enough chap whenever we have spoken. And very wealthy to be able to devote all his time to following a touring company. He must not have any business concerns which require his daily hand."

"I have heard that in Philadelphia he is a man of property," Aunt Dall replied. "Very well educated, descended from a leading family, and said to be one of the richest men in America."

"What sort of property does he have?" I asked curiously, truly revealing a girl's frivolous interest in houses, country estates, and carriages, all the things which the Kembles' daily struggle to support a theatre could not provide.

"Fanny, you *cannot* ask such impertinent questions. Though I'm glad you ask them now of me rather than risk offending Mr. Butler. In polite society you do not ask a man the composition of his property anymore than you would inquire as to the balance of his bank account," Aunt Dall answered in dismay. "Isn't that so, Charles?"

"I suppose you are right, Dall," my father answered. "Though I have had little enough of either property or money to answer very knowledgeably. Besides, so much discussion of Mr. Butler's property makes me uncomfortable. It is not as if Fanny is searching for a husband, are you, my dear girl?"

"Of course not, Father. Certainly not to an *American*. That would keep me far too far away from home."

"Oh, but gentlemen like Mr. Butler travel widely," Aunt Dall informed us. "He has told me enchanting stories about the time he has spent in London, Paris, and Florence. And Philadelphia, where Butler Place, his home, is situated, is the most delightful of cities. Much cleaner than New York *or* London. I have heard it said that his investments, which are attached to large farms in one of the Southern states, are managed by his aunt. He and his brother have really nothing more strenuous to do than count their money."

It certainly seemed that Mr. Butler had no pressing business confining him to Philadelphia. He appeared regularly at most of the cities on our tour, or if, on occasion, he did not follow us to New Orleans or Boston, since even he had *some* obligations, he would always be waiting in New York to greet us when we returned to that city. If we suffered from the oppressive heat, that beastly discomfort of cities, he sent round sherbets and iced drinks and was always in attendance to address our every need.

"You must be famished after such a performance," he would say flatteringly, waiting in my dressing room until I had escaped the last of Juliet's real-life admirers. "What would you like, and I shall gladly go anywhere to fetch it. Or I will take you to any establishment in this city. With, of course, your father and your aunt," he hurriedly added, nodding to Aunt Dall, who sat in the corner of the room, ever-watchful yet demure over her needlepoint.

After many such evenings when he had become a regular of our party and had created a stir in the newspapers by playing his flute in the traveling orchestra simply to be near me, I grew accustomed to his presence and *expected* his attendance. He was manly and strong-featured without the handsome, at times, even insipid good looks of many actors I had encountered. When it was determined that we should at last take a deserved holiday from performing, he helped design the itinerary for our travels up into New York state to see the remarkable countryside. My father was very grateful since he worried I had grown piqued from the long hours and poor air of cities, but knew so little about the country and the distances involved to have planned such a journey. Mr. Butler was glad to take complete charge of all the arrangements, even though he was not the only gentleman besides my father to be included in our party.

In retrospect, I fear it makes me appear shallow and flirtatious to acknowledge that before that journey, I had not necessarily valued him over the other young gentlemen who complimented me by their attentions. I found Mr. Trelawney more eloquent in the content and style of his writing, and though it seems very silly, had deemed him more worthy because of the handsome way his curls fell over his forehead and the excellent cut of his riding jacket.

Yet all of my impressions changed the day we embarked on that steep walk up to Crystal Falls. I was not certain I would make it, so marked was the incline, had Pierce not taken my arm and encouraged me onward until we saw together that magnificent sheer cascade of endless water. I have always been so drawn to water, it is surely my magnet, and Mr. Butler revealed that day it held the same power for him. He held my arm tightly and drew me so near to the edge that quickly we were both drenched, much to Aunt Dall's displeasure, but still we could not stop laughing. I have always responded more to nature than to any man, transformed by its unfathomable beauty, which no artist can ever recreate. And in that powerful, shimmering setting, with certain death from an almost bottomless plunge if one slipped barely inches away, I felt a rare feeling take over me. Standing at the edge of that towering falls, clasping tightly Mr. Butler's strongly muscled arm, dampened by the icy spray, feeling my own thick locks curling in the mist, while our laughter rang as one voice, I felt something new.

I understood for the first time that I returned the affection Mr. Butler had showered upon me for months. I realized I had deceived myself in the weeks before our travels, convincing myself he was of no more consequence to me than all the others who were attracted not by any charms and talents *truly* attributable to me off-stage, but simply because everything they had read and heard proclaimed *I* was the most desirable young woman in America. But suddenly I knew that if Mr. Butler should lose interest and begin to court the daughter of one of the old New York or Philadelphia families with lineage much closer to his own, I could not *bear* it. I believe the change was noticeable in both our faces as we came down from the falls, Mr. Butler gallantly offering me his handkerchief *and* his waistcoat when that small square of cloth was clearly insufficient to hastily dry myself before we took our places in the carriage. And from Mr. Trelawney's downcast expression, which he quickly tried to conceal, I knew that he could sense the change in our feelings.

Still, if not for the accident, I do not believe we would have married. I had made an immense fortune in America, by the standard of that day and even of today's. For two years, I had saved almost every penny of my earnings, planning to turn the entire sum over to my father so he could completely unencumber himself from Covent Garden's debts, for which he was responsible as its manager. Then, with our entire family, we would happily resume the English life that was so dear to us. I should act in a limited way if it were urgently needed for the family's financial purposes, but not of my desire. As soon as it could be managed, I would return to writing and study in a complimentary confluence.

This seemed quite possible until our terrible misfortune occurred. In America in those days, country roads between towns were rougher and much more poorly maintained than those travelers enjoy today. Even an experienced driver might come quickly over a hill and be unable to avoid a hole large enough to bury a hound in or might drive his coach into a ditch trying to make way for a speeding carriage coming from the other direction. I cannot say with certainty what occurred to the coach conveying our party, but after a terrible lurch, we were all thrown forward and then the coach turned over on its side.

My poor Aunt Dall took the very worst of it, suffering a terrible gash in her forehead and the crushing weight to her small frame from all the other passengers who fell against her. I tried to make her comfortable as best I could in the ruined coach while a rider was dispatched by horseback in search of a doctor. Days later, after we had managed to situate her comfortably in a tolerable inn, where a doctor treated her injuries and assured us that none were serious enough to endanger her life, she still did not improve.

I sat by her bed, futilely urging upon her sips of tea and spoonfuls of gruel and broth, which I could tell she attempted to swallow, not out of her own desire but only to please me. Pierce, as I had begun to call him in our new intimacy, instead of Mr. Butler, stood by my side, leaving me only when it would seem I wished it or to consult with the doctor about new medicines or treatments. Several weeks passed in this way almost as one unending, grey twilight.

As she always did, Aunt Dall tried to reassure me, patting my hand, urging me to rest myself lest I ruin my own health caring for her. A few times, at Pierce's insistence, I rested for a few hours in my chamber while he sat with her, holding her tiny hand in his large one, as if by doing so he would keep her connected to the life on earth that despite our efforts seemed to be drifting away from her. She was a second mother to me, always devoted to my safety and welfare. Without her guidance during our American sojourn I should surely have misstepped and impetuously brought disgrace on my family instead of the accolades I had accumulated like garlands.

Several weeks more we waited, taking hope when she opened her eyes for brief moments and faintly called our names or pressed her small hand into our own. The doctor, still coming by time to time to listen to her heart and take her pulse, urged us not to despair despite her weakness and to pray for her recovery. But she would not eat and could not regain her strength. She declined daily, and then, true to her quiet, gentle way, Aunt Dall passed away with hardly a flutter of her eyes or a gasp for breath. And I could no longer control myself. The pain of watching her languish for weeks, ill and suffering, and the thought that I no longer had her love or her protection made me inconsolable. I feared at her funeral that my tears, so constant and so profuse, would never cease.

Fortunately, our tour was over, since I could have convincingly acted no part during those awful days save one of a grief-torn mourner. Then, as my father made preparations for our passage home to London, it became painful for me to think of leaving Pierce, who had put aside all his own concerns to be with me throughout Aunt Dall's long illness. My father, intent as always on Covent Garden's fortunes, was already speaking of next year's season and the plays we should perform, as if he were unaware of my plans to leave the stage. He could not believe that anyone, given success such as I had known, with children and young woman decked out everywhere in "Fanny Kemble curls" and crowds still storming the theatres for a glimpse of me, could abandon her public for a writer's desk.

Only Pierce seemed to understand. "You must not return to England," he implored me. "There is no reason for you to do so. You *know* I adore you. I will provide all the things you have ever wanted. You say that appearing on the stage is your most painful duty." He took my hand firmly in both of his own, and I felt the rising emotion in his husky voice and in his eyes. "And so you shall *never* do it again. If you wish to write, you shall write plays and fill journals to your heart's content without anything in your daily life to disturb your efforts. Oh Fanny, *marry* me and be free of all that confines you."

My father was horrified at the prospect of leaving me in America to marry Pierce Butler. Father had come to like Pierce and felt indebted for his attentions during our travels, yet Father knew the full force of my mother's anger would fall on his own head once she learned of my plans. Father had promised we would be away only two years, which had already seemed an eternity to her. Now he would have to write that I would stay behind and be connected to our family only through letters and occasional visits. This would be a painful hardship since our family closely shared our pastimes and our occupation. We spent not only days in each other's company as other families might, but many nights of each week we acted together.

My father was deeply saddened by his own loss of my company. He had always been closest to me, defending me when others criticized my outspoken ways and devoting much time to playing with me. When I was but a tiny child, he had taught me to read poetry and to recite famous lines of Shakespeare. Though he was too much a gentleman to utter a word about it, I understood he feared the loss of my presence in the company. I was withdrawing just as my success was saving the theatre to which he had devoted all his talents. He recognized that he could not command such crowds and ticket sales without me.

I was so completely in love and confident of my own happiness that I proudly told him, "Father, before you go, I want to make over to you all my earnings from this tour. I shan't have any need of money as Mrs. Pierce Butler. I gladly give it all to you."

He would not hear of it. "It is nearly ten thousand pounds, Fanny. There is no way I could ever hope to repay it if I should borrow it from you. It is *your* money and though it should completely satisfy my debts, let no man say Charles Kemble ever took money from his own daughter."

"It is freely *given*, Father. That is the great difference," I said, passing the notes to him. "You *take* nothing from me. And you have given me *everything*. After all, without this tour I should never have met Pierce or embarked on this new happiness."

Pierce did not witness this conversation since if my father had requested assurances about the fortunes of my betrothed before accepting my gift, such scrutiny would have posed a great insult to my future husband. And Pierce, a man of sound judgment and business acumen, had proved himself completely devoid of avarice as well by heartily expressing his approval when I had told him of my plan to make over my entire fortune to my father. I loved and admired him even more, since surely no one but a man of great magnanimity could blithely accept the transfer of so large a sum away from his own control.

We were married very quietly since it was still a time of mourning for Aunt Dall. I was weary from two years of touring, acting a different role almost every night, and still grieving her loss. After my long separation from my mother and my brothers and sister, I had come to depend on Pierce's devotion. I felt very secure in his love and relieved to depart the stage and all that accompanied it for a new life at Butler Place. I imagined a serene world centered around the wide terraces, fountains, and manicured lawns of English country homes.

"You've only to let me know, Fanny," my father assured me when we parted, "if you become lonely in America. You will tell me," he earnestly implored, "if you should wish to return to the stage or if you should have second thoughts about your money?"

"Let us agree not to mention any of this again, Father," I beseeched him. "It is *your* money. As Mrs. Pierce Butler, I shall lack for nothing material I shall ever desire, and I have made my farewell to the stage. You have seen yourself Pierce's love for me, Father. My future is assured."

And so it seemed to be as Pierce and I began our wedded life, first savoring golden days of honeymoon, lying long abed and dozing dreamily away entire mornings. It felt sublime to close my eyes with my head nestled against his chest and his strong arms wrapped tightly round me. There were times when I should have preferred to kiss and relish a long embrace, feeling so tender and so alive whenever our bodies should touch, but Mr. Butler was determined always that we complete "the consummation of love," as he delicately referred to it. And so sensitive as he had always acted towards me, I was surprised when he would pull off my nightgown and lean over me, staring down at my complete nakedness, to offer comments about my bosom or my hips. Once, reaching beneath my buttocks and squeezing them between his hands, he commented, I felt very indelicately, "So I, among all men, am the only man to know what a fine and ample bottom the great Fanny Kemble possesses."

"My love, must you really speak of such things?" I entreated him, longing for his love, yet still shy of this new intimacy with a man and even self-conscious about his assessment of my feminine attributes. I tried even to silence his words with a kiss.

"Oh, I have embarrassed my dear bride," he observed, a little more gently. "This was never my intention, dear Fanny. I beg your pardon if I have discomfited the very one I had hoped most to please," he said, leaning over me to leave a trail of soft kisses down my neck. Then he paused and leaned back, looking quizzically into the candlelight as if he expected to find there the answer to a difficult riddle that puzzled him. "It is really quite strange, dear Isabel," he said softly, turning back to me, "that someone who has so often portrayed Juliet is made so uncomfortable by the language of love."

"*Isabel!*" I exclaimed, startled, searching his calm face for clues. "Why do you call me that? What does it mean that you should call me by another lady's name?"

"My dear Fanny, you are mistaken," he said with certainty, grasping me strongly. "I never called you Isabel. You misunderstood my words. I could not myself repeat precisely what endearment I just uttered. For who has a memory for words at a time when one feels everything so passionately?" he asked lovingly. "But I assure you there is no reason on earth I should call you Isabel."

His face grew almost stern in his determination to convince me that my ears had erred. I was equally certain that they had not. Much as I loved him and wished to believe some logical reason for his utterance, I could not help but wonder who Isabel might be and what she had meant to him.

9

Rescue

I engaged a driver to take me with my few possessions to an inexpensive rooming house since I could not spend the night sitting on my valises in the street. In one afternoon I had gone from believing myself engaged to one of the wealthiest men in America to being abandoned by him on the streets of Philadelphia. I had only a modest sum separating me from destitution and knew if I did not quickly find myself a safe place to stay, I risked the loss of my respectability, and once damaged, it could not be regained.

Yet when the carriage was in motion, I knew I could not stand to remain in Philadelphia. If I were to encounter Mr. Butler on the street, I could not abide seeing him with Fanny Kemble at his side, beaming proudly at his new bride and her celebrity, when in all rights I should have been his wife. Nor could I continue in the theatre. Although it had not been publicly declared, the manager of the company knew that I was soon to wed Mr. Butler, and since the news of Mr. Butler's marriage to the famous Fanny Kemble was likely to be widely known, a respectable company could no longer safely feature me. I would do best to leave Philadelphia to seek roles in a theatre in some less fashionable location where my beauty, which others had given much notice, and my talents, of which I felt confident, should secure me a part, and my unfortunate association with Mr. Butler would be unknown. I decided it would be wiser to depart immediately rather than waste my limited funds on lodging. I could purchase a train ticket instead of paying for a cheap room, where, in my agitation, I surely would not have been able to sleep, and at the same time would distance myself from my mortifying humiliation.

When the carriage arrived at the train depot, I asked assistance from the driver to convey my valises and one small trunk to the waiting room. I consulted the large board on which the arrivals and departures of trains were written out clearly in chalk letters of yellow and white. I considered that Baltimore, a city that Mr. Butler had often described to me as both attractively designed and rich in culture, could be easily reached without a lengthy journey. It seemed exceedingly fortunate that a train departed for that city in less than an hour's time. I purchased a ticket at the window and then returned to my luggage, trying to remain as inconspicuous as possible, which was difficult, attired as I was in the even least flamboyant of Mrs. Chestnut's hats.

I settled myself in the rear of a car, filling a row of seats with my belongings, and immediately busied myself with needlepoint. I bowed my head over my work so no one would be likely to engage me in conversation. As the conductor walked up and down the cars taking tickets, I hoped we would depart before anyone should sit opposite me. But in the last moments before our departure, more and more passengers came aboard and crowded into its compartments. Still, I looked away, hoping that a posture of indifference should make passengers wish to avoid me.

But then a tall man, even-featured, with graying reddish hair and a distinguished prow of a nose and deep-set grey eyes, asked courteously if he might occupy the seat across from me. I glanced up from my work, fully planning to ask that he not make such a request when there must certainly be other available seats, believing with certainty that his was but a guise to make my acquaintance. But when I looked around me, I saw that in the last few moments the train had been filled with men, women, and squalling children. I had no right to refuse him, and after taking in the rowdy comportment of several other passengers, I preferred he should sit near me rather than mothers with noisy, complaining children and lunchboxes smelling of overripe cheese and sausages.

At first we rode in silence, avoiding each other's eyes and turning from time to time to look out our windows without making any comment to each other. As often is the case in such situations, we kept looking up at the same time, our eyes resting upon each other until we each turned self-consciously away, he studying his newspaper and I returning to my needlework. It was terribly stuffy in our compartment, almost as if the original air taken in by the first passengers had been exhaled, and then mixed with stale tobacco smoke and perspiration and the remainders of food. I had tried when I entered the car to open the windows, but they seemed permanently shut, and the conductor was too occupied with taking tickets to respond to my entreaties. I was very gratified when my companion bestirred himself to attack the windows. I watched his powerful arms and shoulders flexing as he struggled with the intractable latches, finally managing to raise one window a few inches so that a small, delicious breeze passed through.

When he briefly absented himself, I assumed he had gone to freshen up since his exertions had made him quite red in the face. But when he returned smelling faintly of cigar smoke himself and bearing two glasses of lemonade, his mission became clear to me. I was surprised and also pleased when he presented me with a frosty tumbler of lemonade. Its alternating tart and sweet flavors tasted heavenly to me in that hot, unpleasant compartment.

"I hope you do not think me presumptuous in bringing you a bit of refreshment," he said gently, smiling shyly, as if exchanging pleasantries was very difficult for him. "I could not have enjoyed my own lemonade if I had not brought you some."

He wiped his forehead with a white handkerchief, and for the first time I noticed his hands, which were red and rough, as if they were regularly accustomed to hard labor. I determined that despite his frock coat and silk neckerchief and highly polished, unscuffed boots, he must be a tradesman and not a gentleman by birth.

"I take it as a kindness, not a presumption, sir," I answered at once, wishing to put him at ease. "It is stifling in here. If you had not so generously brought me this refreshment, I might have fainted. Please accept my thanks."

"It is nothing, miss. You make too much of it," he answered, his kindly face reddening from his apparent bashfulness in speaking to me. "I am sure you would do the same for a sister or brother in need." He smiled approvingly. "I see you wear a cross, and that is very nice to see. You probably have no idea of how many lost souls I encounter every day. It is reassuring to meet someone who wears Christ's symbol proudly around her neck."

I could not imagine what he would say if he knew how rarely my family attended church or that I had lived with Pierce Butler as husband and wife without benefit of a marriage ceremony. And that all that had stopped me from continuing this illicit relationship was Mr. Butler's own treachery, certainly not the teachings of Christianity. The very cross I wore at my throat had been given me by Mr. Butler, who had behaved to me in as unchristian a manner as I had ever heard anyone describe.

I felt again my companion's gaze upon me as I sipped my lemonade. As I looked into his quiet, grey eyes, his kind expression kindled a peacefulness in me, since I was friendless heading towards an unknown city. But then a sensation of melancholy enveloped me, much as the sound of carolers singing Christmas music often fills my eyes with tears. I started several times to speak, yet never managed to utter a word, so overcome as I felt. I noticed him watching me with concern and tried to quiet my racing heart, but found I had not the power to do so, and suddenly tears were cascading down my cheeks and I was sobbing.

"My dear young lady," he said, jumping to his feet with alarm. "What has come over you? Is there something I may get for you? Are you unwell?"

I could not compose myself sufficiently to answer him. I accepted the handkerchief he offered and buried my face in it.

"Has something happened on this train?" He looked at me with grave concern. "If someone has harmed you, you've only to tell me who he is and I'll attend to him at once," he said, clenching his fists.

"No, truly, I have spoken to no one save you and the conductor. And you have both been most polite to me."

Seeing that I was regaining my composure, he took his seat opposite me. Though he continued watching me with concern, his tone expressed much less alarm as it became evident I was not in imminent danger or recovering from a dreadful assault perpetrated by someone concealed on our train. He smiled encouragingly and urged me to take small sips of my lemonade that it might calm and revive me.

"My name is Thomas Meacham," he said soothingly in a deep, calm voice. "It troubles me deeply to see you so distressed," he assured me when I was sufficiently calm to introduce myself. "I am a farmer in corn and garden vegetables and dairy cows in a small way and the finest Maryland chickens in a larger way. I have been visiting my sister and her family in Abbotsville. I do not like to spend so many nights away from my own farm, but time to time in my business I must do so." He sighed and took a long drink from his own tumbler. "Just this past summer, my own dear wife passed away," he said softly, his voice breaking a bit over this revelation, "and my sister has been after me to visit for so long that I could not rightly delay it further. She worries about me, though I am well cared for in all ways," he said proudly. "I have a beautiful farm. As pretty a piece of land as you might ever want to see and very convenient to Baltimore if one is ever called upon to go there for business, or pleasure for that matter. But she worries that I am too much alone with only Mother, now dear Catherine is gone. It was my parents' farm, you see," he explained, "and now Mother is hardly able to go out anymore, so crippled as she is by her rheumatism."

Ordinarily I would have found his rambling tedious, but in my emotional state I was quite relieved to listen without having to share a word about myself or where I was bound. The longer he spoke, the more I was convinced Mr. Meacham's talkativeness was intended as a kindness. He had no particular desire to tell me about his farm and the new barn he had constructed with the help of several of his neighbors or the prizes his mother's sweet butter always took at the county fair. He had observed my tears, as well as the calming effect his words had upon me, and would have spoken gladly of the weather or the price of hay to soothe a fellow creature. He was determined to distract me from my sorrow, and despite my hesitance to speak with anyone as I departed Philadelphia, I felt myself becoming less agitated, and my breath rose and fell much easier as I leaned back against my seat.

"I am fortunate to have such fine neighbors to watch over Mother in my absence," Mr. Meacham continued. "Her wants are very simple and she never complains, good soul that she is, despite the terrible pain she daily endures from her affliction. And the slaves are very devoted to her, so I have had no worry that she has not been well cared for." He stopped suddenly and stared at me, gravely concerned. "Now what is it, my dear? Has some worry come over you again? Or did *I* say something to disturb you? I assure you that nothing could have been further from my intention."

I should have liked to remain silent and let him speak on in his reassuring cascade of ordinary conversation, yet felt I must speak up quickly lest he break the silence with questions for which I had no answers. But I did not dare tell him that I was stricken to learn that he owned *slaves*. I had, of course, known slavery was common in America, but had no occasion to observe it in Philadelphia. In the newspapers and in snippets of conversation I overheard in Mrs. Chestnut's millinery, I had heard such dreadful accounts of harsh treatment of slaves and wondered how someone who seemed as kindly and well meaning as Mr. Meacham could own and oppress other people.

Once I assured him he had said nothing to disturb me and that I felt greatly improved by the lemonade and his kindness, I inquired about slavery, both to satisfy my own curiosity and also to engage him further and postpone inquiry about myself. I struggled at the same time to conceive a personal history that would serve me when I reached Baltimore and should also give him a satisfactory account of myself.

"Have you many slaves, Mr. Meacham?" I delicately inquired. "So recently arrived from England and never having visited your farmlands, I have not seen them. But I hear much discussion in Philadelphia about their condition."

"Now, Miss Isabel, do not let yourself be taken in by the false statements of the abolitionists," he answered, his face reddening with the intensity of his feelings. "They would have you believe all Southerners mistreat their slaves when that would make no more sense than if we abused our own horses or our fine dairy cows. Such practices would be to our own ruin. And does not the good book make very clear our Christian responsibility to the beasts the good Lord has provided for our service and sustenance?"

I feared he expected an actual response from me when I could conceive of no answer which would not offend his convictions regarding the Lord's distinction between men and beasts, including men held in bondage. Young as I was, I could not believe men of any color should be considered, like horses or cows, the property of others. So I was overcome with relief when he cleared his throat and proceeded to answer his own question.

"You are yourself a Christian," he continued, his eyes fixed on the gold cross at my throat. "You know that Our Lord would find us severely lacking should we not treat all the creatures of his dominion with Christian charity, whether they be the beasts of the field, our own good neighbors, or the slaves He entrusts to our guidance. I do not possess a great plantation. I own a family farm and small dairy and have but four slaves. One is a man, Caleb, who helps me with all manner of farm work, and there are also old Moses and Rachel, who have been with my family since my father's time. She helps my mother with the cooking and cleaning, and he is an excellent carpenter and very good with livestock. And their daughter, Minda, is a clean and neat dairy maid and much in demand throughout the county as a midwife, there being few doctors nearby when a lady or a slave comes to her time and is in distress. I assure you that our *people*, as Mother and I do call them, are well fed and clothed and want for nothing we can provide them. They even receive a small ham, a fruitcake, and a bag of peppermint stick candy every Christmas," he proudly explained.

Then he seemed to have said all he wished about slavery and his property and turned his attention to me. "I am most heartened to see that you are feeling better," he said, smiling gratefully, as if my happiness meant much more to him than simple interest in the welfare of a stranger. "But I fear I have gone on far too long about myself. Much more, in fact, than good manners allow. So now please tell me about yourself, Miss Isabel, and what your plans may be, since you have not been long in our country."

I feared telling him I was an actress, since zealous as he had shown himself to be about religion, he would think me very evil and the rest of our journey would pass in remonstrations. In the fragile state into which I had fallen, still reeling from my abandonment by Mr. Butler, I needed Mr. Meacham's kindness. It was quite presumptuous of me, yet I already felt him to be my protector, and truly in the world there was no one to whom I could turn for comfort or advice. I knew that we would go our separate ways upon our train's arrival in the Baltimore depot, but still I could not bear with a few words to change his friendly aspect to animosity, as any account of my recent history would surely do.

"Please do not be shy, Miss Isabel," he encouraged me. "We still have a long way to travel, and you have told me nothing save your name." He smiled warmly as he stretched out his long legs, making himself comfortable as he turned his welcoming gaze upon me. "And I have been able to surmise that you enjoy cold lemonade."

The compartment seemed suddenly much warmer, despite the open window and our recent refreshment, as I felt Mr. Meacham waiting for me to speak. Everything that had transpired with Mr. James and my escape from him and then my heartbreaking disappointment with Mr. Butler was entwined in my head with my dreams of the theatre. I was certain Mr. Meacham should immediately disapprove of me if I acknowledged my hope of appearing on the Baltimore stage. I tried to speak, but when I opened my mouth no words came readily to my lips or even to my mind, and my palms and forehead were suddenly damp, while a drawstring was pulled tightly around my throat. I began to gasp for breath.

So ghastly had my appearance quickly become that Mr. Meacham rose from his seat and in his own arms supported me so that I might not fall from my seat. I felt his breath on my face and his strong arm behind me as well as the gentle feel of his hand blotting my face with his handkerchief. Even ashamed as I was by such a display of my emotions, I could no longer restrain my tears and began to weep from the depths of my being, sobbing as deeply as a child torn from her own mother.

Mr. Meacham was so startled by my condition that he threw propriety to the winds, taking off his waistcoat and fashioning it into a pillow, which he placed behind my head, thus helping me to recline upon the hard seat. Then he covered me with his coat and sat on the edge of my seat in his shirtsleeves, concerned that in my weakened state a sudden lurch by the train might send me crashing to the floor.

"You must answer me at once, Miss Isabel," he implored me. "I can see that you are terribly distressed, but if you cannot speak so that I may understand that you are not at risk of expiring, I shall have to direct a porter to rush through this train crying out for a doctor." He squeezed my hand firmly. "Please tell me what is troubling you."

I was sufficiently frightened by the prospect of becoming such a public object of display that I managed to speak, despite my apprehensions. "It is only that you are so kind, Mr. Meacham, which has made me feel so much at peace, but once this train reaches the depot I shall have no friend left in the world. I shall be all alone in a strange city, and I am certain that something dreadful will happen to me."

Immediately his voice grew calmer though his face looked stern as he examined me suspiciously. "If you have committed some wicked offense," he said, fixing his eyes upon me. "If you have stolen goods concealed about you or in that valise, or if you have harmed anyone or caused another's demise, than I shall have no recourse but to turn you over to the authorities and let you face your fate. I shall not harbor a criminal. You may be certain I shall not do that. So now speak up," he nearly shouted, startling me from my weeping. "Or I shall call the porter."

"Please wait," I implored him, clutching at his sleeve. "Do not call for anyone. I have done nothing that is a crime in this country or in my own. I am truly more sinned against than sinning, and find myself in such desperate circumstances. I have been encouraged and then abandoned and left to make my way alone in a strange country. I *promise* you, Mr. Meacham, I seek only honorable work to support myself. I am going to Baltimore to secure a place in a milliner's shop, as I have some skills and experience in that way." I felt myself blushing under his scrutiny. "When I set out this morning I felt brave enough in my resolve to find employment. Then when you were so kind to me, and I realized that soon we would bid each other farewell and I should be once again at the mercy of an unknown land without *anyone,* even a kind stranger such as yourself, to feel concern for me, I felt suddenly so frightened. And all the rest you have observed yourself. I could not breathe, try as I might."

I did not truly wish to find myself employed again as a milliner's assistant, nor did I perceive that I should have anything but a sad life living on poor wages in an attic room above such an establishment. But I was indeed afraid to share with Mr. Meacham my ambition to resume acting once I had found a company in Baltimore that would recognize in me the beauty and talent that even Mr. James had discerned. I feared his religious beliefs might cause him to consider the mere existence of my ambition constituted a severe blemish upon my character.

"If your distress is born of fear you shall be abandoned," he said softly, patting my hand, and then retreating to his own seat, "then you need worry no more. Clearly from your accent it is apparent that, as you have claimed, you have not been long in this country. I could not in good conscience allow any young lady to travel unprotected and to arrive without any friends or connections in Baltimore. I have not been blessed with daughters of my own, and my own dear wife is but recently departed. I should never square it with my own conscience if I permitted a friendless young lady to make her way alone in even so fine a city as Baltimore. So this is what I propose," he said, his countenance once again kindly and unperturbed. "My farm is situated some twenty-two miles into the countryside outside Baltimore. You are welcome to come to stay at our farmhouse. There is plenty of room, and I am often bound for the city on market days so it will be easy for you to accompany me and at that time to make the acquaintance of milliners who may be seeking someone with your abilities. And I shall be assured that no harm shall come to you. You may even help me, if you are willing, with some of the fine mending with which we have fallen behind due to my wife's long illness and then her sudden passing," he said, lowering his eyes with either true sentiment for her or out of feeling that it was proper to comport himself in this way when speaking of the departed. "Not that you must do so, but if you are concerned that you should be idle or unhappy, I wish to reassure you that there will be ways to occupy your time. And not, of course, with the sort of chores the slaves take daily care of."

"I should not want to be a burden to you, Mr. Meacham," I said tentatively, grateful for his offer, but also frightened since I had never seen him before that very day. After my recent experiences of Mr. Butler and Mr. James, and even my own *father*, I was worried lest I put my faith in someone whose protection might prove worse than what should simply befall me on my own. "You are so kind to be concerned for me. Thank you for all you have done on my behalf," I continued, sitting up very straight and returning to him his waistcoat and his outer jacket. I busied myself with the lacing of my boots, which he had loosened in the moments when he sought the source of my collapse.

"Then please, Miss Isabel," he said, again speaking to me with friendly regard, "do me the honor of stopping at Meacham Farm until you have established a reasonable plan. Then I shall not suffer the worry that some mishap has befallen you in a strange city. If you fear that there be anything improper or unseemly in my invitation, please recall that my mother resides with me. I am not suggesting that a young lady of your age should live unchaperoned with me. Every care shall be taken to preserve both our good names, and you should not undertake any labor about the household that is not to your liking. It will be a mutual kindness, as you say you are quite alone, and my dear mother has been poorly since my dear Catherine was taken from us, and will surely benefit from such pleasant female company. Hers is a gentle, sweet nature, given to tenderness even towards the slaves, and now without Catherine's companionship, she is very lonely. Mother's health makes it so difficult for her to call upon even our closest neighbors. So how delighted she shall be to have someone who sews well to assist her with her embroidery and her quilting. And you shall enjoy the finest of vegetables and poultry, all raised upon our own land, and from your window you shall have a view of fresh green fields and my cherry and apple orchards. Surely that shall please you and free you from the agitation in which you now find yourself?"

Though such an offer was unexpected and even overwhelming in the short span of our acquaintance, I considered that I had nothing to lose and, perhaps, had much to gain. A young woman who has already been ruined cannot again suffer the same misfortune. Mr. James first and then Mr. Butler had taken from me all claim I had to a good name. I was truly friendless, and at the very least, with Mr. Meacham's assistance, I might find myself a position through association with *his* name. There was no longer any good connection I might hope would come to me from my own, which had been unfairly tarnished. I reasoned that I should always be free to leave if the arrangement proved unpleasant, and I should be no worse for having tried the experiment. I was, after all, not a slave, confined to my master's property. If Meacham Farm proved disagreeable, then I would work even harder to find employment with a milliner in Baltimore until a theatre company engaged me in the occupation closest to my heart.

"Now come join me for a breath of air," Mr. Meacham said, calling me out of my musing and offering me his arm. "I am certain a stroll will do you good, and we shall discover if there is something more refreshing upon this train than lemonade and cookies. I believe you could do with a bit of nourishment, my dear Miss Isabel."

It was difficult for me to believe that I *had* regained my appetite, after recently feeling so feverish and queasy. I should not have been surprised to find my complexion a ghastly green. Yet instead I felt restored and ready to enjoy whatever nourishment Mr. Meacham could secure for us. The bad feelings were banished, and I felt again healthy and optimistic about what life might offer me.

I did not feel her great dislike for me upon being introduced, but I quickly learned that however friendly her son might be towards me, Mrs. Meacham begrudged every crumb of food I brought to my mouth and suspected me of robbing her larder. At table when I helped myself from the plentiful serving bowls of vegetables or platters of meat, she exclaimed indelicately that she would never have imagined a slip of a girl should require such great quantities of food. She claimed to *marvel* where I put it all. Once when I reached for a second helping of her buttered biscuits, she laughed aloud, exclaiming that she had only seen slaves snatch up food rapidly as I did, though perhaps it was just an English custom to grab up one's food. It was probably not considered impolite across the ocean, she surmised, just as European guests rarely followed the American custom of placing the fork in the right hand before transporting food to their mouths, instead of the European custom of omitting this step, which was faster but so much less graceful.

Despite these incidents, she rarely voiced other criticisms in Mr. Meacham's presence, as this would have disturbed her amiable son, who had made immediately evident his friendly intentions towards me. When we sat down to table or in the parlor in the evenings, she addressed me with cold politeness and seemed most concerned with her own maladies, real or imagined. Her son had mentioned her rheumatism when we first conversed. I observed that she regularly dosed herself with tonics, and when Mr. Meacham was present, she seemed barely able to lift so much as a fork or bend over to pick up a dropped knitting needle without whimpering from the pain. Yet when we were alone during the hours when Mr. Meacham attended the enterprises of the farm, she moved spryly without complaint, which was surprising for a large, heavy-boned woman who might have been expected to suffer from the weight of her years or simply of her ample person. And sometimes when I was seated by the fire in the kitchen mending all the items which that week had been placed in her sewing basket, still trying to do anything that might win her good will, I heard her irritable voice droning in the parlor. I rarely could discern all her words, yet I could tell, from his placating tone as he answered her and from the complaining voice in which she held forth about someone's "laziness and greedy appetite" and "distracting the slaves from their work with all her questions," that I was the source of her dissatisfaction.

I had only to compare the overflowing darning basket to the neatly folded, mended garments I returned every week to disprove her claims of my indolence. Yet I could not, in truth, deny I had delayed the daily work of old Rachel, as well as her daughter, Minda, who was younger and eager to discuss the larger world outside Meacham Farm, with my questions about their lives, as they were the first slaves I had ever encountered.

Rachel, a tall, motherly woman who seemed always to have a kind word and a shortcake and a seat by the fire for anyone who seemed lonely, still appeared wary when I wandered into her domain in the farmhouse kitchen. I sensed she feared saying any word to me, a stranger, that might be repeated to her master. She confined her comments to matters relating to daily activities about the farm, speaking with great care and signifying nothing in her tone that might convey her personal feelings or any criticism of those who had sold and purchased her and who continued to enslave her. When finally she responded to my questions about memories of her early days, she spoke softly and reflectively as if conversing with herself.

"I do not remember my mother and cannot say where I was born," she told me one morning as she prepared pastry dough for small meat pies, favorites about the farm for luncheon, along with her fruit pies and tarts, which were filled with berries and apples from Meacham Farm's own brambles and trees. Interested as I was in her history, I worried about the time she took to relate it, since as she became rapt in bits of memory, her hands grew slower in their kneading until they almost ceased, and I feared at any moment Mrs. Meacham might interrupt us and demand some terrible penalty for Rachel's tardy performance of her required tasks. Yet so enraptured was I by her story that I forgot to caution her to continue working while she related her sad history. My own troubled passage, at first friendless and with scant savings to sustain me, and terribly concerned as I was about what might befall me in an unknown world, seemed ridiculously easy when compared to the miseries of a slave's crossing, which Rachel described to me.

"I cannot say if I was born aboard a slaver," Rachel told me. "I do not think it so. The tales the older people share about the heat down in the hold where they were stacked like sticks of firewood, everyone chained together and no one able to move or breathe unless the captain gave the crew leave to move them on deck, makes me think it could not have been possible for me to survive if I had been born on one of those evil ships.

"But I cannot remember being held or hugged or even given a crust of bread by my mother or rocked in her arms. My early life passed away long before I came to have memories. I have been told that the slavers preferred not to sell females with babies or small children since they knew well how wretched the conditions were in which they would transport the slaves to their markets and did not want the added burden of grieving mothers who might wail and moan for days if their children sickened and died on the journey across the ocean. I have heard tales of mothers clutching the slavers' legs until their arms were pried away, begging that their babies not be taken from them. But, I am told, babies were grabbed up and little children dragged away and thrown into the ocean to drown while their mothers looked on. And some of the old people remember mothers who managed for a short while to conceal tiny newborns about their bodies beneath their ragged robes, only to have this found out at sea, and then the captain would toss these babies into the ocean. They say old Satan followed every slave ship and that the cries to be heard came from those he had already committed to the fires of hell, but I believe the cries must have come from those poor mothers sobbing and moaning, as they watched their babies writhing in the waves before they drowned or were eaten by the hungry sharks. Because on those journeys over, with men and women dying from disease and hunger and sadness, the old people say bodies were cast overboard every day. And so the sharks followed those ships, circling round them patiently waiting. They hardly ever had cause to be disappointed."

I could not speak a word nor meet her eyes, so heartbreaking was the story she told. I knew that I was not personally responsible, yet glancing down at the pale color of my own skin, I felt to blame for the gross suffering she described brought about by people of my own complexion. My sadness must have shown plainly in my face, so hurriedly did she attempt to comfort me.

"Now Miss Isabel, don't you fret so or Massa Thomas will be angry with old Rachel for upsetting a guest of this house. I did not mean to make you so sad. You need not weep for me. I am all right here, and there is no way to change what the Lord has made to be. We have no power for that, and in church they say that we must wait for our reward at the Judgment Day."

"You do not fear that there may still be slavery in heaven?"

"No, I do not see how that can be, Miss Isabel," she said contentedly. "In heaven there is always rest for the weary and angels need not lift a finger except to strum their harps. Everything is peace and calm and there is not a single task to be done. There will be no need for slaves."

"And do you imagine that the black and white angels will then sit side by side in choirs?" I asked, surprised she could believe in this benevolent view of heaven for slaves told her by white masters and ministers.

"Perhaps not in the same pews," she conceded after reflecting for a moment. "It may still be as it is on earth, where the white folks sit downstairs in church and the slaves sit in the balcony. But in heaven they will all be angels."

Minda, Rachel's daughter, did not describe for me her visions of heaven. She stared at me with large, dark eyes, which appeared to look right through me, so steadily were they fixed upon me, shining in her perfect oval face. I tried not to flinch under her scrutiny, but so carefully did she study me, I felt uncomfortable and had to turn away.

"Why do you look away, Missy?" she asked, her voice gentle and concerned, but her eyes still set upon me.

"I was...you see...just looking at something else," I said, stuttering awkwardly in my discomfort under Minda's continued, unwavering stare. My stomach threatened once again, as it had been doing for several days. I barely managed to rush outside before my breakfast rose in my throat so that my face grew ashen and I had no choice but to lean into the bushes to relinquish my sour meal.

"I know what is bothering Missy," Minda said sympathetically, following me into the farmyard garden and wiping my clammy forehead with a damp cloth. "But do not worry, Missy. I do not think old Mistress or Massa Thomas can tell. You still have time."

I pulled away from her kind ministrations, horrified by her words, which though intended as a kindness, seemed a dreadful accusation to me. I wanted with all my heart to run from her, but at that moment felt far too weak to even rise. My feet, even in my light slippers, were so heavy I could not escape her, and as I tried to force myself to flee, I was again overcome by my rising bile.

"I do not know what you think *you* can tell about me," I said harshly, defending myself from her knowing looks. "There is nothing about myself I should not wish anyone to know," I said, less sharply, regaining my composure and not wishing to address her with the condescension expected of masters and mistresses, which I had been cautious to avoid. "How mistaken you are to suppose you can detect some secret malady in me when this, I am certain, is only the consequence of yesterday eating too many of those fine oysters in cream sauce. Nothing more," I told her, regaining my calm, until moments later I was forced to fly through the kitchen door, soiling my soft tan, leather slippers when I could no longer contain myself. I could feel her eyes on my back even without turning.

A few days later, Mr. Meacham asked me to accompany him on a ride down to the far pasture to inspect his new calves. Although I was not so uncharitable as to wish his mother discomfort, I was pleased she could not join us on this excursion due to the pain she felt in her joints from the jostling of the farm wagon. I was at first concerned, based on my recent queasiness, that I should myself suffer from the rough ride across meadows or on the rutted roads of the farm. But I had no return of my symptoms, and the fresh morning air and the gentle feel of the sunlight on my face refreshed me and chased away my apprehensions. My well-being must have shown in my face, as Mr. Meacham commented upon it when it was not usually his custom to remark about my personal appearance.

"You look quite radiant this morning, Miss Isabel," he observed shyly, the color rising in his cheeks. "I had been concerned that you might well have contracted spring fever or some other affliction." He smiled warmly, turning to look at me, the reins held firmly in one hand, his eyes scarcely noticing the road, so familiar as it was to him. "Mother, too, has been asking after you," he assured me. "She did not want to embarrass you, sensitive as she is to a young lady's temperament," he explained, "and also sharing my concern and regard for you as a stranger in our midst. I am so pleased you are feeling better since Mother was planning this morning to inquire of Minda if she might know what has been ailing you. She is only a slave, but as you know, Minda is relied on throughout the county for her doctoring, particularly her care of ladies at their time of confinement and for other female complaints. Now I shall be able to tell Mother that you are restored and that she need not consult Minda." He smiled and sighed deeply, which I had observed was his way of showing he was at peace. "She shall be so relieved, concerned for you as she was."

I could not refrain from snorting in disbelief, an unladylike trait my mother had often sought to cure me of, so incredulous as I was to believe that this disagreeable lady had any concern for me other than her son's friendly demeanor towards me. The only matter that bothered her more than the quantity of food I consumed was the amount of time her son desired to spend in my company. I wondered what trouble should greet me when we returned to the farmhouse. Perhaps Minda had conveyed her opinion, which I still prayed was incorrect, of what was troubling me. Perhaps Mrs. Meacham had devilishly coaxed it out of her by tempting her with a large slice of ham or a plate of buttered biscuits or with the most serious inducement of all: speak up or suffer the penalty of the lash.

We had arrived at the paddock behind the barn where the four new calves were walking haltingly on their stilt-like legs with their mothers nuzzling them gently to encourage them. While Mr. Meacham inspected them under their mothers' watchful eyes, great dark ones that I marveled at in their sweet and gentle faces, I could not contain the tender feelings they evoked in me. I stepped down from the wagon to rub the velvety blaze between the calves' eyes and soon found my own filled with tears. With a sudden shudder I could not hide, I remembered with horror what my mother always said when she saw a young woman or girl carrying on over babies. "There's more there than meets the eye," she would whisper knowingly. "It would not surprise me if somebody has a little *bundle* of her own before long."

When we returned to the farmhouse, Rachel and Moses waited anxiously on the front porch, pacing as if looking out for our approach, not daring to allow themselves to sit down. This was not usual behavior, as Rachel would normally have been inside making her preparations for the evening meal while Moses headed out to the fields to check on the work Caleb had accomplished that day. Although their complexions were of the darkest black, still they appeared grey with worry. They seemed so stricken that even Mr. Meacham, so pleased by the fine condition of his new calves that he hardly noticed anything around him, recognized their uneasiness.

"What is the matter, Rachel?" he asked, standing at the foot of the porch steps looking up at her. "Has something happened?"

For a moment she did not answer him, looking to Moses as if she had lost the power to speak.

"I am very sorry, Massa Thomas," Moses said softly in his deep, quiet voice. "But it is Old Mistress. She said she felt right tired after her breakfast and so she went to lie down. She told Rachel to call her when she was ready to pour the new preserves into the jars. You know she likes to be certain those jars are sparkling clean with nary a speck on any one of them. She would rather pour the preserves herself to make sure each jar has its share of—"

"Get to the point, Moses," Mr. Meacham interrupted harshly, sounding very unlike himself in his agitation. "I don't give a damn about the preserves. Where is my mother?"

"That's just it, Massa Thomas," Rachel cried out, regaining her voice. "I knocked on her door, just like she told me to when the preserves were ready for her to pour. When she did not answer, I knocked again, and then I went in to see why she was so quiet." She reached out to pat her master's arm and lowered her voice as kindly as if he were her friend and not her master. "I am so sorry, Massa Thomas. There was nothing I could do. She was already gone. I 'spect she must have passed away in her sleep."

Mr. Meacham ran past her so intent as he was to see his mother. He moved very quickly for someone usually so deliberate in all his actions, and I could see that his face was white with shock as he stood by her bed.

"She feels no more pain, Massa Thomas," Minda soothingly assured him. "You can look at her face and see how calm she was. I believe she drifted off in her sleep and never even knew it was her time."

Mr. Meacham knelt beside her bed and took his mother's cold hands in his own. "You devoted your life to me," he cried. "I was going to repay you and now this can never be." He struggled to say more, but his words broke off in deep sobs.

Rachel and I stood awkwardly watching his pain, uncertain of what to do, she imprisoned by her slavery, which called for following directions but certainly never issuing them to her master, and I, confused by my irregular position in his household, feared even to touch his shoulder. In that farmhouse, where only night stilled its ceaseless industry, we were suddenly silent, frozen beside this sobbing man.

The funeral was held in the small family cemetery surrounded by maple trees and small apple trees started from shoots from the adjoining orchard planted by Mr. Meacham's grandfather. The neighbors from the surrounding farms and friends from Mr. Meacham's church all gathered at the graveside. Mr. Meacham, who had regained his normal composure, was still terribly despondent without any family close by to support him in his loss. Although it had been his wish to delay his mother's funeral until his sister could be present, his minister, Rev. Woodley, convinced him that the distance involved and the inevitable delays, as well as the increasing warm weather, made it essential to proceed with the ceremony. He should send word to his sister of their mother's passing, though she might only learn of this sad news after their mother had been laid to rest.

The words of Rev. Woodley's eulogy and the songs selected by members of the church choir made little impression on me. I stood silently and listened, swallowed up by one of Mrs. Meacham's own black dresses, as I had none of my own. The morning had begun very clear without a cloud in the blue sky, but then as Rev. Woodley concluded his words and the gravediggers began to cover the casket with shovelfuls of dark black dirt, the skies opened with heavy rain. The mourners then all hurried to the farmhouse, where Rachel and Minda had already set out a tray of small sandwiches, platters of turkey and ham, and several salads. Tea and coffee had been brewed and set out in a silver service beside cake stands displaying Rachel's finest yellow cake with lemon icing and a spice cake topped with nuts and chocolate frosting. I busied myself acting as hostess, although certain Mrs. Meacham should have detested seeing me in this role. Mr. Meacham smiled gratefully across the room to me as I passed sandwiches and made certain that Minda and Rachel steadily replaced all the refreshments to accommodate so many guests. I was pleased to have this occupation, as otherwise I should have felt uncomfortable amid so many strangers when my status in the household was so unclearly defined. Mr. Meacham, who usually responded to any curiosity seekers about how I had come to live among them, was far too distracted to speak to anyone.

I perceived something serious was being discussed, observing Mr. Meacham in hushed yet intense conversation with Rev. Woodley, while both of their eyes kept turning time to time in my direction. Then Mr. Meacham, seeing that I was for a moment standing on my own, came quickly to my side and asked if we might step outside for a breath of fresh air, the rain having passed, so that he might ask me something of importance. I followed him outside to the porch of the farmhouse where several gentlemen stood smoking their pipes and cigars. He took my arm and led me down the steps. Though I could feel the curious glances and murmuring voices of others following us, no one was more curious than I about what he wished to discuss with me.

"I do not know how to thank you, Miss Isabel, for all you have done to assist me on this sad day," he said quite formally. "I am not certain we could have managed to properly honor my dear mother without your hand in the arrangements."

"No thanks are necessary for what little I have done, Mr. Meacham," I assured him, "after all you have done for me. I am glad if I have helped you in any small way. Now would it not be better if we rejoined your guests?" I asked, eager to interrupt a conversation that I could sense, from his own agitation, was turning in a direction that made me most uncomfortable.

"We may certainly return to the others, Miss Isabel. Yet first, there is something that I must ask you. In fact, Rev. Woodley has insisted that I discuss with you your plans, and my own ideas concerning them, since now that my dear mother no longer lives among us," he stated with some difficulty, his voice still catching with emotion, "he has advised it is inappropriate for a young woman of marriageable age and a widower like myself to live together with no one else save the slaves."

My mind filled with troubled thoughts as I tried to keep my expression calm. I had never planned to stay long at Meacham Farm. It had all along been my hope to resume acting once I had recovered sufficiently from Mr. Butler's treachery to manage my expenses, and from Meacham Farm I had hoped to soon make my first forays into Baltimore to inquire of milliners. But my situation was suddenly gravely changed by my certainty that I was with child. The signs could no longer be disputed, and no lesser authority than Minda had even whispered to me early that morning, when she had come upon me trying to conceal with powder the mottled aspect that had taken hold of my countenance, that "no hand on earth can hide the mask of motherhood." She referred to a blotchy change of coloring around the nose and eyes, which she had noticed particularly affected ladies like myself of very pale skin. "You have no need to worry on my account, Miss Isabel," she reassured me. "You have been very good to the people. But before long, it will not matter how carefully we keep your secret. It will show, and I believe it already tells in your face."

I wondered if my greatest fears were about to occur. Would Mr. Meacham accuse me of defiling his household by coming among them as a fallen woman? I could not believe he would seem so subdued if this were to be his accusation or if he had just been exhorted to denounce me by Rev. Woodley. But I said nothing, trying hard to calm my trembling heart, and waited for him to speak.

"My dear Isabel," he said, addressing me much more familiarly than had ever been his custom. "I am certain you know the deep regard in which I hold you. It would be inappropriate on a day such as today for me to regale you with accounts of your beauty and your kind ways, yet I do believe you are aware of my feeling for you." He looked down in sympathy and humility, lest I feel he was forcing me to make an affirmative answer. "Please do not go away to Baltimore as you had planned. Stay here with me and be my wife."

I was surprised by Mr. Meacham's proposal, though, in truth, from our first meeting he had always been receptive to me. But until that moment, his feelings had remained unspoken. I had always supposed I would escape one day and never imagined I should marry a man so many years my elder, no matter how much he esteemed me. I wished immediately to run away where I should never be enveloped in his embrace, until I considered how deep was the trap into which I had fallen. If I were to leave and go to Baltimore, after but a short time I would be so obviously with child that no theatre would ever offer me a place in its company, nor would I even be kept on in a millinery shop. I would be disgraced and should soon have no way to earn my bread or even pay for the most meager lodging.

It had never been my wish to remain at Meacham Farm or to find myself nightly enfolded in Mr. Meacham's strong embrace, yet I saw his arms would provide my only solace. My misgivings about allowing Mr. Meacham, who had been so generous to me, to believe this baby was his own were abated in my frightened heart by the memory of Mr. Butler's dreadful deception. Knowing that Mr. Meacham's long marriage had been childless, I felt assured he should be delighted to finally become a father and should never have cause to know the coming child was not his own. The joy of fatherhood that he would enjoy, I convinced myself, far outweighed the necessary deception. Perhaps we would have other children, and when I felt more sure of him and his secure affection for *all* his children, I might tell him that our first child was not his own. Kind man that he was, I felt certain he would not turn upon me, but would, from his great religious conviction, forgive me. It grieved me that I should no longer fulfill my dreams, but considering my serious predicament, I accepted my hope of becoming a great actress should never come to be. And if I married Mr. Meacham, I should at least be safe from harm's way, and by my acceptance of his offer, I would make this stalwart man very happy. If anyone dared to trifle with me, he would heartily defend and protect me, which, though less than the most romantic reason to marry, certainly offered reassurance for someone having endured my recent abandonment.

"This matter has long been on my mind, Isabel. I had wanted, even before I took you to see the new calves, to ask if you might consent to share permanently this life with me, but then poor Mother passed away. I would wait now to grant you all the time you might need for consideration, since you are so much younger than I, but Rev. Woodley has helped me see today that I must not delay lest I harm either of our reputations." He smiled warmly at me, concluding very tenderly, "And as for that, I should not give a fig for what anyone might say about me, dear Isabel, but I could not stand by silently while anyone utters a word against such a pure and exemplary young person as yourself."

His kind regard made me cringe with regret, knowing how I should deceive him if I accepted his offer of marriage. But even my hesitation he misread, interpreting it as maidenly modesty and reserve, which had made me overcome by such a substantial offer as his own to someone so new to his acquaintance with unknown family connections across the ocean. As he waited patiently, I resolved there could be no great wrong in a solution that would provide my baby and me his name and save Mr. Meacham from the great loneliness that afflicted him. I knew him to be much attached to me, and if I could not return his feelings, I accepted that I could at least remain true to him. My greater unhappiness would be to give up all hope of the stage, and since I would have no choice but to do so as his wife, I felt he would have no reason to complain of me. My own sacrifice in marrying an older man for whom I could feel nothing save friendship, and in saying good-bye forever to the stage and all its adventure, seemed to diminish my deception.

And so on the following Sunday, we were married at his church with Rev. Woodley officiating. As we were still in mourning, it was a very modest occasion without a large dinner or luncheon to follow. My husband promised me that we should undertake a wedding trip when the mourning period was over, and in the interim he should ask his sister and her family to come from Pennsylvania to welcome me to the family. Since I had already been accustomed to assisting his mother with the sewing and mending and other household chores, and much of the running of the household was well attended by Rachel, I saw there should be little change in my daily life, save in one respect.

I knew I must tell Mr. Meacham that I was with child, *his* child, as soon after our marriage as possible before he might notice changes in my appearance. I supposed if my condition were quickly known, then my husband and others should not remark about it and might not calculate too carefully how soon after our marriage our child was born. Even if they did whisper to each other that the date of my lying in came too soon, at the worst they would then imagine that Mr. Meacham, widowed and lonely as he had been, had become intimate with me before our marriage. Though they should certainly disapprove, safely married as we were, it could be forgiven and forgotten as our Christian life together proceeded quietly and productively at Meacham Farm.

On our wedding night, I prepared myself to receive his attentions with every consideration for what would make myself most appealing. My husband had always expressed great admiration for my blonde hair, so though I had of late taken to wearing it up, I washed and perfumed it and left my hair flowing loosely over my shoulders. My nightgown was decorated with embroidered flowers featuring periwinkles, which set off the blue of my eyes. I had taken care to be certain that my hands and feet were silky smooth, using a lotion which Minda made from crushed berries mixed with hog fat, honey, and dried flowers. I settled myself comfortably beneath the sweet-smelling sheets and blew out all but one candle, thinking that a darkened room should make my husband more receptive to romance. I felt none myself, yet would play the role I had determined for myself as his enthusiastic partner so that I might quickly have right to proclaim myself with child.

When my husband entered the bedchamber, he was completely covered by a long brown robe, which he did not remove until he had climbed into the bed beside me and concealed himself beneath the covers. I could see his smiling face in the candlelight as he turned to me, and as his robe opened, his strong shoulders, powerful chest, and heavy belly were all revealed. I turned my head slightly aside so that he could not reach my mouth and might content himself with· moving quickly to the act of procreation. I hoped his religious principles required this and at the same time precluded our engaging in actions to prolong our relations for my pleasure or his own. I willed myself silent, closed my eyes, and waited for him to proceed.

I heard his heavy breathing as he lowered himself upon me, but I felt no sign that his ardor was increasing. I reached up to clasp my arms around his neck, hoping that this close embrace should encourage him. Yet my attentions seemed not to have such an effect, and he soon reached up to remove my arms and fell back beside me like some great bear, making a resounding thump as his body hit the mattress. I feared that somehow I had offended him by my silence, although there had been so little contact between us I had not known in what manner he had expected me to respond. We both lay very still as the silence grew deeper between us in the darkened room.

"Is something wrong, my dear husband?" I finally ventured, holding my voice to a conciliatory whisper. "I hope I have not disappointed you in some way."

"Of course not," he answered huskily, and I sensed that he was embarrassed. "You are quite lovely. Let there be no doubt of that. I believe I am only overtired and have indulged too much today in rich food. Let us rest now and speak no more of it. We shall try again on the morrow. There is, after all, no hurry. Surely when Providence decrees it time for the fruit of your womb to ripen, then this shall occur. Do not be concerned, my Isabel," he said soothingly, turning to kiss chastely the spot where my hair met my forehead. "All in God's good time."

Yet after a week passed, this situation did not improve between us. Mr. Meacham, as I often still considered him in my thoughts, felt no particular hurry to conceive a child. I knew time would pass quickly by and should our relationship not soon be consummated so that I could happily announce I was with child, my own changing appearance would make him aware of it. Each day I struggled to find clothing which would fasten around my growing waistline and noticed also the swelling of my breasts and the greater definition upon my face of that mask that Minda had observed. I knew that the continued queasiness, which overcame me without warning at all times of the day, could not much longer go undetected by my husband. He would become suspicious of this peculiar malady that afflicted me, or if he did not, then surely someone else would observe my distress and ask him about it.

I waited, hoping with all my being that one of his good-night caresses would lead to more than a good-night kiss. When this did not occur in our waking embraces at night, I decided to see if while he was deep in slumber I might bring him to readiness. I listened for some time to my husband's breathing, making certain that it was deep and regular. Then I reached into his long night shirt, moving gently as I could so as not to wake him before there was some sign that he was responding. I placed my hand upon him and began to tighten my warm fingers around him, but after a few moments there was no outward change in his breathing nor any visible sign of his arousal. I prayed he would soon waken and turn to me in a passionate embrace. And indeed, he stirred, and softly he called out my name. I turned to him, keeping my hand in place and putting my arm around his neck, hoping he would soon be ready to take me so that the pretense of romance between us should no longer be necessary. I could declare myself with child, and then each in our own way, this child, my husband, and I, should all be safe.

But when my husband fully wakened and turned to me, he showed no love or passion or even tender affection. He roughly pushed me away, sitting up in bed, adjusting his nightshirt so that it fell well below his knees. He lit the candle on the table beside our bed, and turning his angry face towards me, he condemned me. "You jezebel!" he cried out in disgust. "All this time I have believed you to be a lady, capable of showing proper womanly regard, but you have deceived me. You could not even wait for me to come to you as any honorable wife should. Against all of God's teachings, you have tried to force yourself upon me. Have you no shame?" he asked angrily, and before I could attempt to answer him, he had angrily left our chamber.

After that evening, my husband never again touched me. In front of friends and neighbors, and whenever the slaves were present, he behaved with all appropriate courtesy. But when we were alone, he barely spoke to me. He continued to share my bed, fearing, as he disclosed to me, that if he moved to another chamber it would soon be known and discussed in the village. He refused to allow our personal relations to become the subject of gossip. I begged his pardon and pleaded with him to grant me another chance to prove I would not offend his standards of decorum. I promised in all our relations to wait patiently for him to lead the way, but he would no longer touch me except when his hand might touch mine as he passed me my plate at table or handed me down from a carriage. If it had not been so necessary that I declare myself with child before it became generally known, I should have been relieved to avoid my husband's embrace. But as it was, I feared terribly that if normal relations did not commence between us, I should be ruined. Distasteful as it was to make further efforts to ingratiate myself into my husband's affections, I tried determinedly to do so. But he would not come near me and slept as far from me in our bed as was possible without risk of falling out upon the cold, wood floor.

I began to wonder if my husband had a serious impediment that prevented our successful relations, and if he were secretly pleased to use my transgression in attempting to arouse him as an excuse for failing to perform his husbandly responsibilities. I considered that the first Mrs. Meacham had borne him no children. In speaking of their childlessness, he had always referred only to the Lord's will, which it was our duty to accept, although it was sometimes hard for mortals to understand. I wished I could know whether his present difficulty had affected his relationship with this lady of whom he always spoke with tender devotion or if it only occurred when he came close to me. There was no one, save my husband, to whom I might ask such a question, and I knew such a personal inquiry would mortify him. So I continued my efforts to charm him, applying creams and lotions to my face and hands, perfuming myself every night, and washing and brushing my golden hair to its finest luster, hoping that I should attract him. Yet still every night he turned away from me the second he had extinguished the candle.

I finally approached the time when I could no longer conceal my condition. I had been forced to sew several new dresses since I could not contain my increasing body within my old garments. One day at church, I had even heard the Rev. Woodley comment to my husband that he was so pleased to see what a fine figure of a woman I had become. "Nothing of the spare, young girl about her any longer, my good man," he smiled approvingly. "It would appear that she has taken on well the duties of your household. I am wondering if you shall soon be telling me that the Lord has blessed you with a child?"

My husband politely demurred, yet I worried he should soon himself ponder how full-figured I had become. This should seem all the more strange considering the peckishness of my appetite and the queasiness to which I had been subject. I knew that if his mother had still been alive, she would have already discerned my secret, and I wondered if anyone else would share their doubts with him in her stead. I decided I must summon the courage to confide in him and hope that still within him were the instincts of that caring man, who had so benevolently befriended me on the train.

The only other choice was so unspeakable I could not say it aloud to myself even when I was quite alone, walking in the pastures early in the morning when no one could possibly hear me. I could not bring myself to try to kill the baby growing within me. When I had been at Mrs. Chestnut's I had heard the other girls speak of remedies to end pregnancies and of a few poor girls who had taken dangerous potions which unintentionally ended their own lives as well. And there were tales of others who injured themselves falling from horses or attempting to do so, and who gained nothing save a broken leg for their efforts. I knew no doctor to whom I could make an inquiry, and as Minda performed most of the day-to-day doctoring on the farm and the attendance to ladies when they approached their time of lying in, I was again without anyone to whom I could confide. Although she liked me, I knew I would be putting her in terrible peril if my husband should become aware that she had tried to assist me to achieve such an end. I could not imagine what punishment should befall her and wondered if she might, despite her value as a skilled slave, be sold down the river away from everything familiar to her, or even be put to death. As much as I loathed bearing Pierce Butler's child, it seemed I had no means to avoid this fate, nor, despairing as I was, could I consider any action that might endanger my own life, so precious as it still was to me.

I waited to approach my husband when I was certain he had enjoyed a very pleasant day and was well satisfied after a hearty evening meal. I found him ensconced in his armchair beside the sitting-room fire, dozing contentedly, his hands folded across his chest. He looked quite peaceful and amiable, and I convinced myself that I might make my revelation and the kind man sitting there should find it in his heart to forgive me. I knew what I must share of my past would appall him, yet had heard him speak so often and movingly of Christian charity and forgiveness that I believed he would forgive me and in his heart might still find his way to love a child not his own.

Finding that I sought a serious conversation with him, my husband bestirred himself to come sit beside me on the settee, where we could speak intimately and I should not be required to call across the room to him. He turned to me with the most sympathetic of expressions, and said soothingly, patting my small hand with his large one, much as a parent would console a child, "Now then, dear Isabel. What is it that you wish to tell me?" Seeing that I still hesitated, the apprehension turning me paler than ever, he gently encouraged, "Please take your time, my dear, but do tell me what is troubling you. I am most concerned that you look so unwell. Shall I call Minda?" he asked, feeling my quickening pulse.

"No, you must not do that," I cried out anxiously, so great my concern that Minda might fear so for my health that she would feel obliged to inform my husband of my condition. I realized that any revelation she made would not be a matter of disloyalty to me, but would stem from her own vulnerability as a slave. Though Mr. Meacham seemed a tolerant master, who fed and clothed his slaves far better than customary and was loathe to use the lash, he would never countenance secrets kept from him by his new wife and one of his slaves. I was, indeed, her mistress, but he was her *master*, a far superior position, and also a relationship of far longer duration than my own. She would, if she were wise, tell him right away, and if she remained silent, then her fate would rest upon my own head if some dreadful punishment befell her when Mr. Meacham learned, as he inevitably would, of her prior knowledge. So, haltingly, I forced myself to answer him.

"When I first came to America," I explained, thinking it wiser to gradually make my confession, rather than to blurt it out at once, "I was left friendless when I had believed I should be well protected. When you met me on the train, I was completely alone in the world, having been shunned by those who had promised to care for me."

"Do not worry us both with this recital of old history best forgotten," he said kindly. "It would appear your companions treated you ill and were not worthy associates for one who would become my wife, but let us put this to rest. Since you have been living here at Meacham Farm, you have admirably comported yourself and have known those of only the finest character, so pray put your former associations behind you. Unpleasant as they may have been, at least they have not left you with any lasting harm, my dear."

"I wish that were entirely so. But I am afraid that I was harmed in a way that was not apparent to me at the time we met, sir, but now does me considerable harm," I answered vaguely, trying to summon the courage to make a full confession.

"Are you ill?" he asked with alarm, and then looked slightly away, as if to shade me from his scrutiny lest his questioning shame me. "Or has someone beaten or harmed you in such a way that you fear to tell me you may not bear children?"

"I have been badly treated," I answered, feeling myself trembling anew as we reached the point in the conversation where I must reveal to him the true source of my unhappiness.

"I shall not pry into your past, my dear," he responded with greater sensitivity than I should have expected him to summon under the circumstances. "What is past is gone forever. And if you were harmed by someone, unless you are in pain and should require treatment, in which case I shall take you to the most learned specialists, I say these former hurts must reside in the past. Let us not bring them up." He kissed me tenderly on the cheek. "And if it should come to pass when we are intimate that still you cannot conceive a child, then we shall accept that it was not meant to be. God has another plan for us, which shall be revealed in His good time. Although I would be sorry that I should not see you become a mother, nor myself realize this second chance to father a son, I should accept it as God's will." He patted my hand once more. "And so should you. There is still much more to life, even if a woman should be barren."

It might have been easier had he not been so understanding. Then I might have told him more gradually. But as it was, I was unable to contain myself a moment longer. "I am not barren. I am with child."

"But this is impossible," he cried. "We have not yet even consummated—" He stopped abruptly, and stared at me with a look that can only be described as horror. "What are you saying, Isabel? That you came to me knowing that you carried another man's child?"

"No, I did not know it. I had not yet felt the signs. They were late in appearing. I was bound for Baltimore, just as I told you when we met. Certainly you cannot imagine that had I known I should have been setting out for a city where I had not a friend nor any promise of employment once my condition should become apparent?"

"How can I say what is imaginable at this point?" he immediately protested. "It should never have occurred to me when I met you on the train, an upright young woman busy with her needlework, that you were not virtuous. You even seemed hesitant to converse as if you were concerned it might not be seemly to do so," he further reflected, as if he were reciting aloud his thoughts. "Or was this simply your ruse to obtain the protection of a farmer who took pity on you, poor and friendless as you appeared, and in so much distress?"

"But I *was* all of those things. There was no pretense. I had been abandoned by a gentleman who had promised to make me his wife. I was foolish to have put my faith in him, but that I did, and he left me for a prominent lady with whom he became smitten after he had already pledged himself to me."

"And then before you parted, this scoundrel forced himself upon you?" he asked hopefully, I believe desiring for a reason which should permit him to forgive me. "Who is this *gentleman?*" he asked, fairly spitting out the word in his contempt. "Tell me his name so that a plain-speaking farmer, clearly his inferior in birth and advantage, may take him to task for violating a young woman who did no wrong save to love him. Who is this cad who forced you against your will to this dishonor?" he asked, pleading in the same breath for me to name the perpetrator of my assault, so deeply did he wish to believe me innocent of any wrongdoing.

"I cannot say, in truth, that he *forced* himself upon me. That would be untrue," I admitted. Much as I then detested Pierce Butler, I was unwilling to portray him as an attacker whom my husband might challenge to a duel to avenge my honor and in this way lose his own life. "Yet he did lie to me about his intentions, leading me to believe that it was his fondest wish to marry me, when I see now this was never his plan. He cast me off as if I were no more than a house cat for whom he had suddenly lost interest. Yet if I had actually been his pet I believe he would have left me a saucer of milk or a bowl of scraps from his table, while, in truth, he left me nothing when he departed Philadelphia."

"And so you married me solely to protect yourself and your bastard child," my husband said resolutely, his voice still even, but his efforts to keep it so apparent in the strained manner in which he spoke, his fists clenched so hard upon the table that they turned white.

"It was not that way at first. Surely you must believe me. When you offered me the opportunity to stay at Meacham Farm until I should regain my strength, I had no knowledge then of my condition. I was only relieved to have a safe place to rest and replenish myself. I asked nothing more of you. And, in truth, I did not even have to ask. It was you who suggested— who truly *insisted*—that I should stay."

"But when you did know, you chose not to advise me," my husband said icily, his grey eyes taking on a coldness I had never before observed in them. "You had no reason to think I should not behave fairly towards you. Had anything in my demeanor towards you, an unknown young woman whom I had befriended out of Christian duty to a stranger, given you reason to fear me?"

He seemed to be waiting for my answer, and though I was generally voluble to a fault, I struggled for words. Anything I thought to say seemed on quick reflection likely to give him cause for complaint.

"Just as I thought. You had every reason to confide the truth to me, but instead you chose to deceive me so that I should marry you and conceal your sin. This is the reason you have tried night after night to press yourself upon me," he cried out, "when you had no true affection for me. You sicken me, Isabel," he said, rising so precipitously that he nearly toppled the rose-colored lamp, a family heirloom, from the nearby end table.

I dared not meet his gaze. He had always spoken so kindly to me, only then I felt his quiet fury brewing to a dangerous rage as he reflected on my deceit and perhaps his own inability to consummate our relations. "How dare you desecrate my home!" he shouted, moving angrily towards me as if he might strike or shake me, but then stopping abruptly to stare at his own hands, as if shamed by how nearly he had laid them upon me.

After some minutes when I scarcely breathed, he calmed himself. "You need not be afraid, Isabel. I shall not cast out a woman with child," he said evenly. "I would not show so much cruelty to an unborn child," he continued, his voice wrought with pain, "even though you shall be its mother. But once you have given birth then I shall divorce you," he said matter-of-factly. "I shall settle a small amount of money upon you so that you shall not be destitute, on condition that immediately after the birth you shall leave this state and never contact me again. But I shall not call another man's child my own, though that was your intention," he said hotly, unable to stave the accusation which tormented him. "And on the morrow, in the presence of Rachel and Minda, you shall appeal to me to permit you to sleep in a separate chamber since you are with child and are so often now taken suddenly with illness. You shall ask them to make up my mother's chamber and to move your clothing there so that you shall not disturb me so often during the night. I shall see you at meals, and you will accompany me to church, but you shall be my wife in name only. And I shall pray for the day when you will leave this farm and we shall never meet again."

Then he quickly left the farmhouse, striding purposefully across the meadow towards the barns, to all appearances like a farmer with many matters occupying his mind concerning his livestock. Rachel, who had been waiting to bring in fresh tea, but had dutifully delayed her entrance on hearing our raised voices, set the tea service upon the table and quickly filled my cup.

"Missus should not worry," she said comfortingly. "Massa Thomas, steady as he is, time to time is taken by dark moods. He frets for every lamb and calf upon this farm. But he will get over it. So you drink up, missus. It will do you good, poor as you have been feeling."

"I believe I have terribly upset him, Rachel," I confided, thinking it best to tell her, although I was not strictly following my husband's instructions. "I just told him I am with child and that he shall be a father before five more months shall pass. I do not believe he was prepared for this to have occurred so quickly."

"Now don't you pay him no mind," Rachel answered, solicitously arranging a footstool before me. "He will be used to it by the time he comes back from the barn, after all these years he has waited and waited for a child on this place, and Missus Catherine could never give him one." She smiled happily and wrapped my shawl around me. "I expect, missus, you have believed massa vexed with you when he is merely overcome that what he has always wanted has finally received God's blessing." She looked out the windows facing the field where my husband could be seen, a purposeful figure striding away from us. "I will make a special dinner tomorrow, missus. You have given massa a joy to celebrate he never expected to know."

To all observers, my husband's behavior towards me was unchanged, unless it might have been judged to be even more solicitous of my comfort. He instructed Moses to see that a fire was burning in the sitting room all day long and into the evening to assure there would be no chance for me to take chill. Every morning before I rose, the fire was lit in my bedchamber and Rachel brought me my breakfast in bed. About the household, everyone assumed that this hot breakfast, brought to me on a tray while a fresh stone was placed in its muslin wrapper beneath my covers to warm my feet, was due to my husband's deep concern for my health. But I knew they were all mistaken, and that my husband wished me to breakfast in my chamber so that he might be spared the sight of me before he went out to spend his day upon the farm. He rarely returned any longer for luncheon, but instead sent Caleb up to the house to retrieve the basket Rachel had prepared for him. In this way we were relieved of the pain of each other's company as the days and weeks and months passed heavily.

I busied myself making clothes for the baby, since there having been no children at the farm, there were no garments to be passed down or refitted for the baby. I knew my husband was not an impetuous man, and so assumed he intended to keep his resolve and would put me out along with my child as soon after the birth as I could safely travel. I had no idea where I might go or what occupation I might find with a small baby to mind. So with all the energy that I possessed, I set myself the task of devising tiny clothes, replete with lace and bows and tiny booties to match, to keep my mind from my unknown future. Rachel and Minda both marveled at my skill in creating these tiny garments and waited on me most graciously, bringing me strengthening eggnogs and cool drinks in the afternoons and urging me to refrain from performing even the slightest task which might tire me.

"Missus must be *our* baby until she has her baby," Rachel told me, smiling warmly. Minda said nothing, but always watched me carefully, ever cautious for my welfare. I could not know if she had genuine concern for me or if she merely assessed wisely, as a slave who was the area's only midwife, how severely she might be chastised if her master's own wife should befall a calamity while under her care.

My husband insisted that I should be attended in my lying in by Dr. Baldwin, the physician most highly regarded by the ladies of Baltimore. I begged him to reconsider, feeling that I should be so much more comfortable with Minda, who would never be so disrespectful to her mistress as to inquire why her baby was arriving far sooner than my marriage to Mr. Meacham should reasonably allow. I soon understood that in this matter my husband's conviction was unyielding. Just as he was determined to have no more to do with me than civility and propriety should demand, he had also resolved I should have the very finest available care and treatment so that no man should be able to say, if ever my true tale should be known, that my husband had not done everything in his power to provide for me, despite my shameful behavior.

The worst of my queasiness ebbed as the months passed and I grew heavier with child. Despite my worries and the uncertainty of what lay ahead for me, my appetite improved and the rose of health returned to my countenance. I cannot say that I welcomed their return with joy, so difficult was my predicament, but when the tiny motions of the child moving in me could be felt, much like a darting butterfly, I, breathing deeply, knew that my time drew near.

And then a very strange thing occurred. Nearly two months before the date that seemed likely for my baby to arrive, I awakened in the middle of the night wrenching with pain and shortly afterward found my nightgown sopping wet around me. I cried out for someone to help me, and though he had grown as cold to me as ice, my husband came quickly to my door and assured me that he would send immediately for Minda to attend me and should ride immediately to Baltimore with Moses to find Dr. Baldwin. He set Caleb to work bringing more wood to the kitchen so that water should be boiled in large quantities, and soon the entire house was alive as if it had been midday instead of the middle of the night.

Minda tried very hard to calm me, assuring me that babies often arrived earlier than the date their mothers had calculated. She bathed my face with warm cloths and helped me change to a fresh nightgown during one of the times when the pains abated for a few moments. She tied back my hair and helped me back to my bed, which she had warmed with hot bricks. Then she sat beside the bed and let me squeeze her hand as tight as I could when the pains became too strong for me.

"Do not try so hard not to cry out, missus," she told me when I bit the sheet trying to stifle my cries in the folds of cloth. "Massa is still off fetching the doctor. And you have no cause to hold back around me. I have heard lots of crying, fine ladies and the *people* of all the farms and plantations. I am used to it."

I was so thirsty I begged her for a tumbler of cold water, but she told me if I gulped down water, even a small amount, I would likely vomit and further weaken myself. I had no strength to rise to find my own water and so had to content myself with the small sips she allowed me when she gently washed my face with a damp cloth. I tried to close my eyes so that I might rest completely between my pains, but soon they came closer and closer together, and still my husband had not returned with the doctor.

"It is best you let me look now, missus," Minda said, drawing back the covers. "I believe fast as your pains keep coming and hard as they are, the baby cannot be long in coming."

"Where is Dr. Baldwin? Surely he should be here by now," I cried, thrashing side to side with the pain. I both wanted Minda near me, frightened as I was, and also feared having her close by, much as she knew about my circumstances. My husband knew the worst, but I worried that I might cry out something in the midst of the birth that might be heard by Minda, and then the secret my husband had so determinedly sought to hide would be revealed. I feared a sudden revelation would inflame his anger against me.

"We could not find him," my husband said, rushing into the room, as if he had heard my question and thought it directed to him. "He has gone to attend a planter's wife the other side of Baltimore and no one knows when he shall return. I am afraid, my dear," he said, wiping my brow, almost *tenderly*, "you must rely on our Minda to do her best. And she has safely brought many babies into this world."

There was so much kindness in his tone that I believed at that moment he had made up his mind to forgive me, and if I could safely bring forth this baby, particularly if it were a boy, my husband might be content to accept him as his own. I should not be suddenly left all alone with a baby, and hoped once the terrible pain receded—I think I was not completely clear in my thinking because of it—our life could continue. My husband should be pleased finally to be a father, and though I had never planned for nor wanted the role, I would come to enjoy motherhood.

Then the pain was so intense that I lost awareness a few times of what went on around me, or perhaps this was caused by the herbs Minda mashed into a paste and pressed to my nostrils when the pains grew most intense. Until suddenly I was vividly awake with all of my senses about me, and I smelled the scent of blood, which immediately I knew must be my own. My husband was no longer standing beside my bed. The room seemed at once very dark. I thought at first that many hours had passed, but then I observed that all the candles had been extinguished save one, which burned smokily on the table beside my bed.

"It is done then, Minda?" I cried in relief. "It is over?"

At the sound of my voice, she quickly came to stand at my side. She had been washing something in a basin and hastily she dried her hands on her apron, leaving bloody marks upon it. But it was very curious to me, that despite my questions and her usual deference to my every request, she did not answer me.

"Let me see my baby, Minda. Is he sleeping?" I asked, looking across the room at the basket we had so carefully prepared.

"Do not talk so much, missus," she said. "You are very weak, and it is best you rest now."

"Then bring him closer so that I may see him, Minda," I insisted. "After all the pain and trouble his arrival has caused, let me make his acquaintance at once," I continued, trying with all my heart to bring some levity into that dark, somber room.

"I am so sorry, missus," she said finally when it became apparent to her that lest she satisfy me, I should try to rise from the bed to see for myself. "You are right, he *was* a fine boy. Handsome as a little prince, with golden hair fine as your own upon his head. But he never took even his first breath. When he slipped out into my hands, that cord was twisted tight around his tiny neck, and though straight away I pulled it loose, it was too late. Nothing I could do would start him to breathing, and his little body was already turning cold."

"But where is he?" I asked, again trying to rise. "Certainly still I must see him. Bring him to me at once," I cried, my voice, high and strained, sounding strange to my own ears.

"I cannot, missus," she told me. "Massa wrapped him up in swaddling cloth straight away and carried him off in his own arms. He went down to the barn with Moses and Caleb, and they are fashioning the tiny coffin that shall hold him."

"But they cannot do this," I cried in a voice I could still not recognize as my own. "Not until I see him," I insisted, trying to raise myself from the bed even though my body felt as if it were weighted down with stones.

"I am so sorry, missus, you are too weak to get up from this bed," she said softly, grasping my hands as she eased me back into the bed and covered me. "And Massa Thomas said you must not see the baby. He shall be buried straight away." She wiped tears from both our faces. "I have brought many babies safe into this world, missus. I have seen it happen before, missus, to slaves and ladies alike. No one can say why."

She then held up my head and fed me spoonfuls of broth from a pink-flowered china bowl. I tried hard as I could to swallow it, and determined as I was to rise from that bed, I could not even find the strength to take more swallows of soup, and closed my eyes.

"It will be easier when you have rested, missus," Minda reassured me. "Massa already said he is taking you away as soon as you are able to travel to the Virginia mountains. The air is very fresh there and you shall have no one to disturb you while you build up your strength. In a while, you and massa will have another baby," she said soothingly, as if she did not suspect that my baby, albeit conceived early, was not her master's.

"No, that cannot be, Minda," I told her, still too unsettled to hold my tongue, and frightened that my husband wished to spirit me away before any stories associated with this sad birth might arise. "There cannot be another baby."

"Of course there can be, missus. There is nothing the matter with missus that time will not soothe," she said encouragingly. "And those that used to say massa was to blame that Missus Catherine could not have a child must now hold their tongues."

"No, Minda. I shall be frightened to try again. No one shall make me," I insisted, again speaking out despite my intention to remain silent.

"I am sure that is true, missus. Massa knows how poorly you feel right now. And he would never, as some gentlemen do, force himself upon his lady." She shuddered as if a cold wind had come into the room. "You do know some gentlemen do that. *Particularly* with their slaves, who have no say. The gentlemen say it keeps the blood fresh among the slaves, adding their massa's blood. But you have no need to worry," she said, moving the candle across the room so that the chamber should be darker near my bed and I might sleep. "Our massa has never held with that, missus. Though we are not free," she said sorrowfully, "our blood has always been our own."

Then she placed my hands inside the quilts to warm them and moved her chair away into the shadows so that I should still be comforted by her presence, but encouraged by her silence to fall asleep. I heard the sound of birds in the yard and the even creaking of her rocker as I began drifting towards sleep, and I thought of freedom. I could not conjure clearly what I was free to do, but I knew I was not a slave and no longer forced to be wife to a man I did not love or a mother when my own childhood had forever soured me to the role of mother or child. My eyes were heavy as if weights had been placed upon them so that I could no longer keep them open. But even as I fell into slumber, I knew that soon I would be free.

When I woke, no one spoke of my having given birth. I was no longer treated as the mistress of the house, but was now considered an invalid recovering from a serious malady, who had to be kept in a darkened room free of distractions. If Rachel and Minda passed in the hallway outside my chamber, they spoke in whispers, suggesting that even the sound of everyday voices might prove too disturbing for me. Minda continued to nurse me with broths, custards, and hot cups of a soothing tea she brewed from herbs she collected in the nearby woods, but she did not pause to converse with me. She seemed, in fact, eager to leave my chamber as soon as she had attended me, as if she had been bidden to speak to me as little as was possible. And in that silent chamber, kept darkened by drawn draperies and the light of only one candle, I dozed in and out of slumber, hardly noticing the coming and going of day for night.

In this way I passed several days, sometimes waking briefly and finding myself in a fresh nightgown without remembering even raising my arms so that the old gown could be lifted over my head. I could not remember anyone shifting me to a chair or even asking that I turn to one side so that fresh linens might be placed upon my bed, and yet I found my face pressed against a pillowcase whose pattern I could not recall. And finally at one point when I opened my eyes, expecting to find myself alone, I found my husband rocking in the chair beside my bed.

"I trust you are feeling somewhat improved, Isabel?" he inquired, his tone neither warm nor cold, but somewhere in between. "You look rested, and it has now been three days since you were stricken. Is it all right if I speak now to you about the future?" he considerately inquired.

I nodded, supposing that he would doubtless proceed no matter what I responded and actually feeling far too tired to object. It seemed as good as any time to discuss what should next come to pass.

"I wish to offer my condolences upon the death of your child," he pronounced formally, always careful to proceed in the manner he felt Christian duty prescribed. "I am sorry that Dr. Baldwin could not attend you. I promise you, Isabel, I did all that was in my power to convey him to you. And I believe Minda could not have done anything more to save the baby. She never left your side."

"I am certain in both matters that what you say is true. It could not be helped," I said wearily, actually so fatigued that I felt I was speaking of circumstances affecting someone other than myself.

"I believe you should now be examined by Dr. Baldwin," he said solemnly, looking away from me, as if he had to avert his eyes after making such an indelicate suggestion. "I have arranged for him to come tomorrow afternoon to assess your recovery. And if he says that you are well enough to leave this house, then I shall arrange for you to travel to the city of your choosing so long as it is outside this state. Here, take this," he said almost brusquely, thrusting a brown leather purse into my hands. "As I promised, you shall want for nothing. I have seen to it that you shall leave here with the means to comfortably establish yourself. There are only a few matters to which you must agree so that we may divorce and be free of each other."

"Thank you for this," I said, taking the full purse and placing it beneath my pillow, having no time to think of any other place to secure it. "I am very weary, but if you wish to tell me now what you require of me, I will try my very best to listen. It is generous of you to act as you have, and I cannot believe there is anything you should ask to which I would not agree."

As my husband listened to my words of gratitude, I was surprised by the look of remorse that passed across his face. I could not imagine what he had to regret, except for the fact that he had married *me*.

"I should not want you later to feel surprised by the complaint that shall be filed with the court." My husband paced before me in his agitation until I wanted to cry out for him to be still. "You do know that in a divorce there must be a guilty party and a complaint?"

I had not actually considered how such matters were managed. It had not concerned me directly, not having sought marriage as a lasting state so much as a temporary refuge when I felt most friendless. In my time of desperation, I had thought only of the present and had not contemplated the means by which marriages might be dissolved nor could I imagine what possible complaint I could lodge against Thomas Meacham. It seemed unlikely, though, that a man as chivalrous as he should make accusations against a lady prostrate before him in her sickbed.

"Since you do not answer, I will explain," he said methodically, as if he were making a speech. "I have but two choices, Isabel, adultery and desertion. And as the child is now...," he paused, nervously clearing his throat, "no longer a present concern, and since you do not disclose his father's name and he was born while you were wed to me living under my roof, there would be no grounds for a charge of adultery. However, once you leave, and you shall leave in the night without mentioning to anyone in this town, free or *slave*, where you are bound, it shall not be difficult to successfully establish a charge of desertion. And though I have no wish to damage your reputation, I shall not impugn my own. I must obtain a divorce so that my life shall resume its regular course. I believe I am owed that much, Isabel," he said mildly, "having been so badly misled by you."

"Where are you sending me to begin my desertion?" I asked, finally summoning sufficient energy to sit up and consider where I might be bound.

"I have asked if there is anywhere outside this state where you wish to go, but you have given me no answer. Do you now have one? Some place where you have a friend or familiar association?"

"I have no one to whom I may turn, sir. If I had, no doubt we should never have met on that train."

"That being the case, it seems best for you to go to Virginia," he said coolly, as if he were making plans for someone with whom he was hardly acquainted and not someone whose bed he had recently shared. "I have located a very suitable small hotel, the Virginia Manor, in Richmond. The owner is a widow of good reputation, who serves wholesome meals and keeps a respectable establishment. Several members of our church resided there when they attended a wedding so large that all guests could not be accommodated by the host or in the homes of neighbors. If after a few months you should wish to go elsewhere, you have, as you know, ample means to do so. By that time your disappearance and desertion shall have been published. You may resume your millinery work or may travel wherever you wish to go." He studied me critically, and in his countenance I could perceive his struggle between his desire to humanely treat me according to Christian doctrine and his contempt for me and the sin I had brought into his household.

Several days later, Dr. Baldwin pronounced my recovery to be quite satisfactory. A hired carriage came for me after nightfall when my departure should not be easily observed. The wind was blowing mightily as a cold rain fell. I feared this might be emblematic of a dismal course for the next period of my life. But though friendless, I had the protection of a sufficient purse. I could afford to reside at the Virginia Manor, a well-appointed establishment as far removed from the dirty rooming houses of my past as are elegantly attired actresses and actors on a theatre stage from strolling minstrels performing in the dirty streets.

I could not easily overcome my recent suffering, nor regain all I had lost of love and the modest place I had assumed in the theatre before Pierce Butler betrayed me. Yet as I regained my strength, I also reclaimed my hope. A fellow lodger offered me the way to rekindle my dream. I was no longer an innocent young girl, the perfect Juliet. But I *was* still Isabel Graves.

10

A Leading Lady

There were no gardens at Butler Place. Its name had made me envision the lovely English homes I had visited in my youth. I was not so naïve as to think America old enough to have produced the great country seats of Europe, nor was I accustomed to living in daily grandeur, yet I had expected more than a charmless farmhouse without distinction or beauty of any kind. Pierce had been staying at the home of his brother in Philadelphia, and I joined him there temporarily until Butler Place, which my husband was redecorating in my honor, could be made ready for our arrival. The painters and carpenters could not apply their paint and wield their hammers fast enough for me, as I was eager to leave the bosom of a family I sensed disapproved of my husband's choice of wife, convinced as they were that my family's profession was of questionable taste. Yet I would not have been so desirous of establishing our family at Butler Place had I anticipated what awaited me.

I cannot claim that my husband had misrepresented his home. He did not ascribe to it bucolic flourishes, which existed only in my mind's eye when he told me Butler Place was situated six miles outside of Philadelphia on three hundred acres of land. He had mentioned an avenue of maple trees leading up to the main entrance, and so I had imagined manicured lawns with shrubs and hedges and lovely gardens for all seasons, when in reality there were none. The road approaching the main door was very rough and so close to the house that clouds of dust were stirred up in the dry weather and muddy ruts greeted any visitors once the rainy weather commenced.

By all that I could see, the Butler family considered any kind of vegetation that did not immediately serve the kitchen table as wasteful frivolity. Pierce had casually mentioned to me farms and a dairy, which I had reflected pleasantly upon, remembering months of my childhood spent in the English countryside when the air was fragrant from mowing and we would assist with making butter and gathering eggs and other pastimes children enjoy when they are not required to attend them every day.

Finding it to be a working farm with cornfields to the left of my front door, an apple orchard to the right, and barns and a dairy to the rear, I thought at Butler Place I should at least be surfeited with fresh butter and cream. But even that was not to be the case. When I walked out to the dairy to introduce myself to the dairymaid, I made what seemed to be a very simple request that I be provided with fresh butter each morning. This young woman, whose white cap and person looked none too clean, spoke to me as if our roles were reversed and I was *her* servant.

"Now, I've much too much to do a'ready. And if you think I'm to find time to be churnin' for you every mornin', you're much mistaken."

Pierce laughed when I told him of this exchange and urged me to have patience with the staff. "They are not accustomed to English ways and habits," he said, putting his arm around me and bearing me close to him as we went inside to our tea. "Nor does it impress them to receive instructions from the leading lady of the British stage."

I wondered by this remark if he were making fun of me or insinuating that I thought too much of myself. Yet when I looked deep into his brown eyes, I felt that he had but answered directly without any hidden implication. And because at that time he was still everything to me, I asked him, flirtatiously as I imagined Jezebel must have spoken, if at least I might take comfort that *he* was still impressed by the charms of an actress acclaimed in both the Old World and the New.

His response was shattering to me. We were seated in the small drawing room. Butler ancestors looked down sternly from the pale blue walls, quiet but omnipotent. Still, the room was warmly lit by candlelight and Pierce's Newfoundland Caesar, stretched out black and massive on the Oriental rug, sighed companionably at our feet. I thought Pierce would surely take my hand, profess his love anew, and draw me to him, perhaps suggesting that we read together again the poems of Tennyson and Byron, as we had done so many afternoons of our courtship. He had seemed then to love literature as much as I did, particularly when I read to him. He had said *no* other voice brought poetry so fully alive to him.

"Fanny, I have married you. Surely that should be enough for you," he said with an impatience his voice had never conveyed to me before. "I am too old to keep up indefinitely this youthful flirtation, and as you know, you are two years my senior," he continued, pressing this matter of our ages, which had formerly never seemed of importance to him. "Let us simply get on with the business of marriage and family, Fanny. We have responsibilities you know. We are not living upon a stage."

I was speechless, a condition that those who know me well say is rare as rain in the desert. I thought perhaps he was merely out of sorts, a condition which possesses all of us time-to-time. So we were quiet for a while, and I assumed his cross mood had departed, like a headache, and I asked if I should read to him. Anticipating his pleasure at a suggestion he had favored so often during our courtship, I picked up the red leather-bound copy of Keats my father had given me at parting. I thought we should sit close together by the fire while I recited his favorite odes. It had seemed indelicate, his reference to the "business" of marriage, but as I was still so very much in love with him, I sought to please him before we went up to bed. It seemed a fitting prelude to what he might have in mind.

But he answered coldly that he had no patience for poetry. He actually took his gold watch from the pocket of his vest to consult the hour, as if to demonstrate to me how pressed he was for time. I commented mildly that in the past he had always found time to read with me. He had attended every performance in which I appeared, sometimes driving through the night to reach me. And now he had no time to spare me when we sat together in his own drawing room after night had fallen and surely no business could be transacted.

"Oh, Fanny," he said sorrowfully, as if it pained him to be forced to respond to a difficult child. "I thought you had seen enough of the world to understand that courtship *ends* with marriage. It is supplanted by love, true enough, but you cannot have supposed a man would continue with all the practices of attendance towards a young lady after he has married her?" He stroked my hair, resting his hand in the dark waves of it, but no longer so tenderly as he had but weeks before. "I have made you my wife. What greater honor could I bestow upon you?"

I told him honestly that I suffered from the loss of his company. I could sense his withdrawal from me when just weeks before he had lingered over my every answer to his questions, and only months earlier he had proven his love for music and for *me* by learning the difficult flute accompaniments to several of our plays, simply to be near me. Now that we were alone and married, I told him, he showed *no* interest in music other than to have purchased for me a rare rosewood piano and an ornate harp to adorn our music room. I had imagined we would play duets in the long evenings at home, yet unless we had company, he never wished to join me. I sincerely did not regret the loss of my audiences, since as he well knew, public performances were a misery to me, but I beseeched him to tell me how I was to manage without *his* society.

"I am so sorry, dear Fanny." His tone was calm yet patronizing. "I am a man of business, not a musician. I thought you understood that." Then kissing me chastely on my brow, he bade me good evening, excusing himself to attend to pressing business interests which required his immediate attention. I said nothing, although I heard a carriage approach in our drive and the servant's voice greeting a man who had entered. I heard his companion's laughter from the foyer and knew no business had called my husband away. I was convinced he merely wished to pursue his own amusements.

Then I could not contain myself. "What business takes you out so late, my dear husband?" I asked, trying to take all vexation and irony from my voice. "Could it not wait until tomorrow?"

"That cannot be your concern, Fanny," he answered, fastening his cloak around him. "It is men's business and nothing which involves you nor about which you need be informed. It is unseemly in a wife to question so closely her husband's whereabouts. Surely you are not saying you *distrust* me?"

I assured him I did not. And at *that* time I had no suspicions about his conduct. I only wanted to feel again the reassurance of his love and companionship.

I began to write feverishly. It was my only relief to fill page after page with all my thoughts, especially those too barbed to speak. I had written continuously since childhood and had imagined this time as a married lady, without a financial worry to disturb my concentration, should be the period of my greatest productivity. I would also be able to engage in the most active correspondence of my life, freed from endless lines to memorize and long nights of performances followed by endless trains, steamboats, and stagecoach rides in order to reach my next engagement.

I wrote often to my father and mother and to Elizabeth Sedgwick, my dearest American friend, who lived in Lenox, Massachusetts, which seemed at that time worlds away from me with its intellectual discourses by the fire and debates on philosophy, politics, and history, men and women speaking together in harmony. Yet I could take little joy in my writing, so lonely had I become, seeing hardly anyone besides the Butler family members, who disliked every choice I made in home decorations or even in my personal attire. They were not themselves Quakers, the family having long attended Christ Episcopal Church in Philadelphia. Still, they were heavily influenced by the Quaker tastes surrounding them and felt all homes, and those dwelling in them, should be dressed in somber black and grey. When I made a few minor changes in furnishings and selected an amber, patterned wallpaper for the drawing room at Butler Place, I thought my sister-in-law might need to be revived with smelling salts. They believed I dressed always in gowns of bright colors, in a style that should not have drawn any but favorable attention in England and which had always been my taste, simply to annoy their sensibilities. I denied it at the time, but with the passage of years, I can perceive in my actions the mark of youthful rebellion. For one who had just retired from the stage, where my every movement was adored, it is not surprising that I should have been quite lonely standing outside the footlights or that I should have wished to defy the narrow, muted tastes of my husband's family. Yet I am convinced I did not regret the loss of attention from the multitudes nor feel deprived of a profession I had never sought as my own and could have in time adapted to their more somber world if I had not lost the affection of the *one* man who mattered to me, whose eyes no longer attended me.

I would be committing an injustice if I portrayed Mr. Butler as neglectful of my wants. Sensing my melancholy, he purchased a magnificently spirited black horse, Forrester, for my sole use. It had always been my greatest pleasure to ride, and Americans bred mounts as fine as any to be had in London. I was delighted to no longer face the isolation of Butler Place by having a horse completely at my disposal. But even riding, I brought Pierce's displeasure down upon me. It was my joy to ride long distances in all weather, and one of my favorite rides was down to the river near the wharves. On one of these rides, I encountered a gentleman, an acquaintance of my husband's, who hardly spoke to me beyond the raising of his walking stick to touch the brim of his hat. However, he noticed me sufficiently to take it upon himself to tell Mr. Butler how surprised he had been to encounter me in such a questionable location, one he would not have sought out himself if not for a business call which required it, and a place he certainly would not wish his *own* wife to frequent.

I would not give up riding, my husband's suggestion in his first anger, since it was my favorite exercise. I *tried* to be more circumspect, which meant going out earlier than was my wont, to avoid the scrutiny of other good Philadelphians. However, I still inflamed Pierce by even my choice of guests at Butler Place. My family had been received by kings and queens and on any evening might sit in our drawing room with the most celebrated philosophers, poets, and musicians of our time. I had *never* been taught to feel myself above or beneath anyone's company or to feel that as actors my family was socially inferior to anyone. Yet when I wished to invite my mother's friends Mr. and Mrs. Charles Matthews, English actors of our long acquaintance, to dine with us at Butler Place, Pierce would not hear of it. I reminded him that he had been only too delighted to be introduced to all the actors and artists who traveled in my family's circle when he was courting me.

He responded with his usual infuriating calm, saying in a most condescending manner that he would never have wished to insult my family or our company, and that such companions might have been fine and appropriate for me as long as I was on the stage, but I was there no longer. Fanny Kemble, the *actress*, could understandably be freer in her associations than could Mrs. Pierce Butler of Philadelphia. Good society would simply not permit the eccentricities in associations that I deemed appropriate. He offered, and I am certain he thought he was being very charitable, to invite them to a banquet he was giving in town to honor Sheridan Knowles, since it would not involve receiving them in our home.

"What of Thomas Sully, then," I shouted, admittedly raising my voice to him. "You have no qualms about admitting *him* to our home or having me sit hour after hour as he paints my portrait. Or Mr. Trelawney, for that matter. He is much more outspoken than both of the Matthews together and yet you seek out his company."

It was due to family connections, he explained, that such artists should be welcome at Butler Place. He knew he had appalled much of Philadelphia society by his own choice of me, coming as I did from a family of actors and with a mother who descended from mere *farmers*. But he had been smitten with me, as had all of America, and had been willing to flout public opinion because of how very extraordinary I was in every way. He made no apologies for that to *anyone*. Yet surely I must understand that in Philadelphia, Thomas Sully might be a painter, but he was first a *Middleton*, one of America's oldest families and Pierce's own cousin besides. And Trelawney could also boast impressive lineage dating back to the original colonial governors. Certainly I must be able to understand what family meant to him.

Had he not changed his own surname according to his grandfather's request so that the Butler name would live on?

I was aware that he and his brother John had changed from Mease to Butler, solely to meet the terms of their grandfather's will in order to receive their inheritances. But I managed to hold my tongue and not contradict him, hoping that the conciliatory tone he was then taking towards me might indicate his desire to restore warm relations between us. This was all I longed for at that point, praying that he was not so hardened against me as it appeared. Nor did I tell him that to be a *Kemble*, a member of Britain's most famous acting family, gave me ties to history and talent far greater than his claim to Major Butler, who, though a signer of America's Constitution, should never have been asked to sign this illustrious document if he had not been married to Polly Middleton, daughter of a South Carolina governor. He had been an Irish soldier without noble connections to laud over the Kembles.

Still, I took the hand that Pierce extended to me and tried hard to smother my rage. It has been my misfortune when I am angry to shed tears at the slightest provocation, often giving antagonists the impression that they have injured me severely, when in reality I am *infuriated* by their unfair remarks. It has always been to my advantage as an actress to feel a range of emotions quickly and powerfully, but as a woman I have found it painful to be exposed so often to others' proud victory when they perceive that they have brought me swiftly to submission.

My tears, at this instance, must have triggered Mr. Butler's chivalry since he offered me his arm as he tenderly wiped them away with his own handkerchief. "I am so sorry you are unhappy, my dear Fanny, and for any part I have taken in making you so." His words were spoken so quietly and directly that I am certain he meant them and also that he was not, despite marrying into the Kemble family, of sufficient skill to imitate our acting prowess.

Later, as we lay together, our love again secure, our trust—at least my own—complete, and the bedclothes wrapped completely around us so that outwardly we could have received anyone, though underneath we were as sweetly entwined as I have often imagined Romeo and Juliet to be, he began to trace my profile with his finger.

"It is a splendid face," he said admiringly, tracing my profile, "but I have often wondered why it is so changeable."

"Are we not all changeable," I asked, "our moods coming and going like the seasons?"

"No, I meant your complexion." He looked down at me, studying my face, even drawing the candle closer on the night table to aid his examination. "Sometimes it is a face of such clarity I cannot describe it. And then other times I see the marks. They seem much darker, as if they had just been drawn by a heavy hand."

"You needn't point out my imperfections," I said angrily, turning away from him. "I told you before we married that I had contracted smallpox as a child. How cruel of you to throw it up to me."

"I meant nothing by it," he said sleepily, blowing out the candle. "It should not be surprising to you that a husband should notice it or wonder about it. But I did not mean to hurt you, my dear. Particularly at a quiet moment like this. Yet it occurs to me that I know the explanation for your variability."

"It is no *mystery* that requires special understanding. I have told you the marks vary according to my emotions or perhaps some aspect of the temperature or the humidity."

I could feel his gaze fixed upon me though we lay in near darkness of a chamber lit only by the dying embers of the fire and one small candle. "It occurs to me that it might have been the stage makeup that you wore. Perhaps that was why it was not so apparent in those earlier days."

"Or perhaps then you were in love." My voice could not conceal its irony. "'Love bears all things.'"

"Oh, Fanny," he said, taking my head in his hands and lowering himself again upon me. "I am still in love. There is nothing you could do or say which would diminish my desire for you."

Our daughter, Sarah, my darling Sal, was born nine months later, and born of love or not, she has always brought such joy to me.

11

Upstaged

No matter how perfectly I tried to play the role of Mrs. Pierce Butler, conforming to my husband's image of a socially accomplished American lady, I was constantly upstaged by my past, as the written word is inescapable. I certainly did not aspire to be accepted into Philadelphia society, yet knowing this was so important to my husband, I tried desperately to please him, inviting ladies to tea and keeping my conversation to safe subjects such as the weather and the health of the queen. I had quickly learned that in Philadelphia society, proper ladies were discouraged from discussing subjects of any seriousness, as this was considered unseemly. Unfortunately for me, no matter how much I might elaborate on the glories of my window boxes or the recent summer's preparations for jam-making, my past writings condemned me.

I could not expect Mr. Butler, nor truly anyone of his acquaintance, to understand the pressures of economic necessity I had felt seeing loved ones suffering for lack of funds. He and his brother and the set in which they traveled were accustomed to satisfying their every wish no matter how quixotic, unlike my own family, where money was often in short supply for the daily needs of life. Because I had gained a high degree of celebrity soon after arriving in America, and had shown myself not incapable of expressing myself freely and with a certain flair, my thoughts became a commodity I could sell.

I had kept journals since earliest childhood when I first learned to write, and had always been asked by members of my family to share selections from them. So it was very easy for me to agree to publish my perceptions of America. In our early days in New York, I was approached by Mr. Carey of Carey, Lee & Blanchard, a well-established Philadelphia publisher, to tell all I would of my impressions of Americans. He offered such an extremely handsome sum that it had seemed silly to refuse him, particularly when he said I could disguise names to protect the feelings of those who had so kindly opened their homes to me. Mr. Carey flattered me, and naïve young woman that I still was despite my celebrity, and highly susceptible to being made much of, I was bewitched by his invitation to share with the world what Fanny Kemble thought of Americans. I was an actress, after all, and he offered me an unprecedented audience and a much larger stage than I had ever before commanded. I also felt the strain of providing for Aunt Dall, who had nothing to sustain her in her old age, having never married and having devoted herself entirely to the welfare of my family. There were also pressing financial concerns for my sister, Adelaide, whose magnificent voice required training so she could pursue the operatic career for which she was destined. I knew that my father could not possibly provide for them, strapped as he was by continuing obligations to Covent Garden and the costs of my brothers' schooling. If I did not help them, it seemed that my beloved Aunt Dall and brilliantly talented Adelaide should have the bleakest of futures.

Mr. Carey had read a portion of my journal and found it highly entertaining. There seemed no foreseeable harm to his proposal of publication. On the basis of my fame, he offered me far more money than I had ever received for *Francis I*, a five-act play. I signed a contract with provisions for only minor revisions to the text, and considered myself to have made a very fine bargain. I could not predict how long my acting career would endure, knowing well the fickle loyalties of audiences, as well as my own discomfort on stage, and I had been drawn always to literary pursuits.

In the midst of Aunt Dall's illness and death and my own marriage, I quite forgot about my American journal's upcoming publication. But Mr. Carey did not, and Pierce was furious. When the manuscript arrived at Butler Place for my review, Pierce became so enraged he knocked over a small table, smashing a chocolate pot and set of four robin's-egg-blue demitasse cups that had been most prized by his Aunt Frances.

I was holding Sal, a mere babe in my arms, when he began madly thumbing through the pages, becoming steadily more incensed. "How *dare* you say such things!" he shouted, his pale skin growing flushed. "Generous people who welcomed *you*, an actress," he said with unconcealed distaste, "to their tables and into polite society. And this is how you repay them!" He threw the manuscript down on the tea table, sending cups and spoons clattering and causing poor Sal to cry as if she had been struck.

I attempted to calm him, reminding him that he had read my earlier journal, "Records of a Girlhood," and had even commended it for being well phrased and amusing. I asked him, in my complete ignorance, why this publication should be so different.

"Because, madam, you are now Mrs. Pierce Butler. You may no longer do and say anything you like as if you were still a mere actress. Your father may not have been bothered by your reckless impertinence, but I *will* not have it."

"How very odd that what you formerly admired in me, dear Pierce, you now find so abhorrent," I responded, truthfully not comprehending his displeasure. "You told me it was refreshing how I thought for myself and put to paper what others left unsai—"

"That was *then*. Now you are Mrs. Pierce Butler making rude comments about the leaders of New York and Philadelphia society. Fanny, what could you be thinking?" He gathered up the pages of the fallen manuscript and crammed them roughly into their brown leather portfolio. "This shall not be published. Of that you can be certain."

"There is a contract, you know," I said mildly, hoping this logic should satisfy a man of business. I was still trying to soothe little Sal and hardly dared look at him. "Mr. Carey is not likely to change his mind. I asked once if I might withdraw the manuscript, not being fully satisfied with the writing. It is quite *juvenile* if you must know," I admitted. "But he was quite adamant that it is the style and form he desired and that I had signed a contract to write it."

"Well we shall see what Mr. Carey has to say when he hears from me," my husband said menacingly. "I am going into my study. I do not wish to be disturbed until I have finished reading this entire manuscript. Then I shall make whatever changes *I* deem necessary. If you were unaware, madam, then let me enlighten you. No wife may publish anything without her husband's approval. Your property is *my* property. Surely you must have known that. But oh, I forget," he said derisively, "that I am speaking to a *leading lady* of the theatre. Who can possibly ascend to the mighty sphere of *her* thoughts?" He shook his head ruefully side to side. "Yet no one is to blame for this circumstance save myself. I would have done well to listen to my family and the fears they had about this marriage. I *should* have known better."

I sat outside his study door like a naughty child relegated to the darkened schoolroom to wait for the master to return with his cane. Finally, after what seemed the length of several afternoons, he summoned me. The manuscript was spread across his secretary, much marked up in blue ink in the fine penmanship Aunt Dall had once admired.

"I have done the best I could with this, Fanny," he said more calmly. "I believe that Mr. Carey might have been dissuaded not to publish, but it seems not the proper expedient after reading your contract. I find it wiser to simply amend the most offensive sections and to improve the constructions."

"And have I nothing to say in this matter?" I heard my voice turning shrill despite my best endeavors to control it.

"If truth be told, you have not. But before you allow yourself to become so distressed, examine my revisions." His anger spent, Pierce's tone towards me turned conciliatory. "I think you shall find it much improved."

I carried the manuscript to my room. I knew I could not stand to read it with his eyes fixed upon me. I would have felt so vexed to see my work defaced by his corrections, that even if they represented genuine improvements, I could not readily have accepted them. As I read, I saw that in places his skill had turned the rambling reflections of an impetuous girl into much clearer usage. Setting aside my anger at his husband's powers over me, I had no real complaint with much of what he had changed. Even his modifications of persons and places to more adequately conceal identities of my subjects seemed reasonable. I had composed this journal never imagining that I or my future husband should live among these families. Yet I was infuriated that he had deleted every reference I had made to my first contemplation of slavery.

"Why have you done this?" I asked when we were reunited in his study. "You have stricken every word about slavery from my journal. Certainly, you, and naturally, Mr. Carey, know that I am an Englishwoman with an Englishwoman's aversion to slavery in any form. Why do you find it improper for me to express how it makes me feel to see rich Americans performing no work themselves and living off the sweat of others?"

"I hardly think you have seen anyone, black or white, *sweating* in your presence, Mrs. Butler." He had regained his composure and spoke pleasantly to me, if not due to his change of mood, then perhaps because of the half-empty decanter of brandy sitting before him. "I cannot deny you your right to think whatever your conscience directs you about the institution of slavery. But I *must* absolutely object to your writing about it."

"And why is that?" I insisted. "Have I not the right to freedom of speech?" I tried to lighten the tone of our discourse with humor. "Or are you saying your freedoms do not apply because I am an Englishwoman?"

"I suspect you are acting as usual. Or do you *honestly* not understand, Fanny?" Pierce searched my face carefully, looking for a sign that I was ridiculing his sensibilities.

"I understand your objections to my references to actual persons. You need not explain that further. But what possible objection can you have to my expression of revulsion for one people's ownership of another?"

"Only that everything we have, the food you eat, that lovely gown you are wearing, your magnificent Italian piano, even the chair you sit upon, all exist because of it. My property is not just in lands, madam, but in the slaves who tend it on two plantations, one in rice and one in cotton. Eight hundred and eighty-six slaves at last counting, and I am graced by God to have every one of them." He paused to stare coldly at me, allowing his words to find their mark. "And so my wife shall refrain from condemning a system which she knows nothing about and which supports her and her child and our baby-to-be in luxury."

He pounded the arm of his leather easy chair, recognizing that I was poised to make protest further. "You should *thank* me for this intervention, Fanny. If your diatribe had been published, some of our good neighbors, who own slaves themselves, might have burned down our home and everything we own. What hypocrites we should have seemed if you denounced the very enterprise that supports us."

It was in this way I first learned the nature of the property my husband and his brother had inherited from their Aunt Frances, and that by marriage I was also implicated as the mistress of two plantations, one on Butler Island and the other on St. Simon's Island, both off the coast of Georgia.

12

Learning My Lines

As actors, we are early taught to maintain the rhythm of the play even when someone forgets his lines. Pierce's revelations shocked me to silence, but I had to move forward with my life. I could not retire to my bedchamber to read novels and eat bonbons. I had a young daughter to rear and a baby in my arms. Despite our fundamental disagreement on this issue, I still had hopes of rekindling the love that had been so powerful between us. He had, after all, suspended his entire life for months to follow me, and I had separated myself from all who were dear to me in order to make my life with him. It had not been a pretense of love on my part, and if his infatuation for me had faded once I no longer portrayed great heroines on the stage and was instead an actual woman expressing her *own* feelings, I was determined to show him I still possessed sufficient charms to endear myself to him.

I also resolved, such faith had I in my husband's decency and my own good judgment, that I should learn all there was to know about slavery. I would read every article or book I could find concerning it and should speak to anyone who could bring me firsthand knowledge, so that I might discover if, as Pierce claimed, it was an institution which if humanely practiced brought ample benefits to master and slave. It seemed a preposterous claim that men could be improved by either being enslaved or enslaving others, yet I was forced to admit that unlike my husband, I had never observed slavery in practice.

I learned that the death of Pierce's Aunt Frances, who had for some time taken upon herself the complete administration of the family plantations, meant that he and his brother, John, must travel to Georgia annually to meet with the overseers and authorize the expenditures to be made on these two vast plantations. I begged to accompany them so that I might see with my own eyes and be reassured that conditions were far more favorable than my abolitionist friends, the Sedgwicks, and their associates had described to me. But Pierce would not hear of it, saying that there would not be room for us all on Butler Island, where he and John would spend the majority of their time. He laughed at my surprise that we should not be accommodated comfortably in a handsome, capacious plantation home with columns and a veranda. He explained they would be staying in the overseer's house, the only edifice besides the slave cabins on the island. The house was very primitive with only two chambers of any size besides the overseer's own, and a tiny office and kitchen. With the new baby, Fan, and the children's nursemaid, we should be impossibly overcrowded. He also insisted that the travel conditions were far too rude for an infant or young child and a mother recovering from childbirth. He described the lengthy journey, literally nine to ten days of stagecoach travel on roads rougher than what I had already experienced, trains on rickety tracks through swamps, cramped river boats, hotel rooms shared with strangers, and food not fit for man or beast.

His family was unified in the opinion that I should not accompany him. Pierce acknowledged that several of his cousins had been disturbed when they had heard me publicly condemn slavery at family gatherings, while at the same time defending the statements and articles written by Elizabeth Sedgwick and her family in support of abolition. They reasoned, I thought unjustly, that if I did not find slavery acceptable as it was practiced on the Butler plantations, I would foment dissent among the "people," as they called their slaves. Pierce's sister also appealed to me to think of how miserable my babies and I would be amid the primitive hygiene, the malaria-carrying mosquitoes, and the absence of fresh meat or milk. There were hardly any vegetables on the island, nor white flour, nor even the most basic entertainments to which I was accustomed. When she described such harsh living arrangements for white people, this only heightened my speculation and my curiosity about what conditions must exist for their slaves.

Inevitably, Mr. Butler and his brother set off alone. I was, as many new mothers, totally enamored of my own darling babies, and so not totally miserable to be left behind. It was, and still is, my opinion that many American mothers have such limited expectations of their children that their little ones are far less accomplished than British children of a similar age in their ability to read, figure, draw, and to speak other languages, not to mention English itself. I did not wish such a fate to befall Sal and Fan and took this difficult separation from my husband as another opportunity to lavish my attentions on my babies. I placed Fan's cradle near the piano and set Sal beside me so that she might be fully engaged in the music. I cannot believe that these early sounds do not help shape a child's way of hearing all the music around him. I also read aloud to them, cover to cover, many books from Mr. Butler's library, assuming that even the sound of words, if they could not grasp the sense of them, would still move them to share the passion for literature I have always felt and which for even a short time I shared with their father.

Elizabeth Sedgwick came to visit at Butler Place. She was, even in her youth, one of the wisest women I have known, and from almost the moment we were introduced she became my dearest and most respected American friend. I admired her entire family for their stand against slavery. While I was touring with my father, the time I spent with the Sedgwicks in Lenox, Massachusetts, provided me the most enlightened conversation I experienced in America. They came from a lineage rich in teachers and ministers, so it was no wonder that Elizabeth was possessed of great learning, as well as a calm, inspiring voice. I had not realized until her acceptance of my invitation to stay at Butler Place during my husband's absence why Elizabeth had always preferred to invite me to Lenox and declined to come to Philadelphia. She confessed, somewhat shamefaced, her brilliant blue eyes looking downward, that she had longed to share with me her distaste for Mr. Butler's outspoken support of slavery, which she and all her family were committed to abolish, but had felt it wrong to speak against a husband to his wife. Learning of his vast holdings in the South, she thought it proper to refrain from any discussion of slavery in Lenox when he and I had visited her together, since considering her own deep feelings, and those of all around her, a heated disagreement might have erupted. Mr. Butler's own hot temper, of which she had heard much discussion, made her fear he might react violently if his views, truly his very way of life, were to come under attack.

But once I became aware of my husband's property in human beings and had begged for her counsel, she no longer felt any scruple violated if she offered her advice. Sitting over tea, her lovely dark hair pulled back modestly, revealing a profile so noble it would have become Joan of Arc, she urged me to seize the opportunity that was before me. We spoke late into the night concerning the most honorable course I could take, understanding as I did that my daily bread was earned by slaves, and that my husband's conviction that slavery was an inevitable institution was sanctioned in many parts of the world. We determined I must implore Pierce to take me with him the next time he traveled to Georgia, when my children would be older and better able to withstand the long journey and life on the island. We could not deny we both believed the dreadful reports of slavery that we had heard and read, yet they were certainly contradictory to what Mr. Butler and many Southerners maintained. I must therefore beseech him to let me witness slavery for myself.

I would have to judge with my own eyes, and if I should find, as we feared, that the evils of slavery were accurately reported, then I should dedicate myself to alleviating the suffering of the slaves and speaking among the whites to convert them so that they would see the rightness of the abolitionist cause. Then at least I would not be idly watching, enriching myself by the labor of slaves, while their suffering continued. By my firsthand knowledge, I would also educate Elizabeth and others committed to the abolitionist cause in the North so that their lectures and papers might better speak the truth, whatever I should determine it to be.

In addition to such a companion to my soul as Elizabeth, I received calls at Butler Place from Pierce's family and friends. I was lonely during this first separation, and the irregular schedule of conveyances and the great distance that separated us made it possible for me to receive only infrequent letters describing Pierce's health and his occupations on the plantations. I longed to know more of what he was experiencing, and so sought out Amelia Pinckney, a cousin of Mr. Butler's whose family had plantations in South Carolina. She frequently came to see me and, like most other ladies, wanted only to talk of the stage and the famous actors I had known. I coveted what she knew of plantation life and the circumstances of the slaves. She was the only woman I knew who had *lived* on a plantation and witnessed actual slavery, not just the accounts others might render of slave life.

She possessed the sort of fair, delicate beauty, much revered by American gentlemen, so that without saying a word of criticism Amelia's very presence made me doubt myself. I knew that others questioned, and increasingly I wondered myself, why Pierce had been so taken with me, choosing me above all others, forsaking the standard which had been held up to him when surely I did not emulate it and had not concealed my nature. I recognized that since I had left the stage, I seemed destined only to anger or embarrass him. Amelia Pinckney would have felt no qualm about his censorship of her writing and would have respectfully accepted his exercise of a husband's prerogative to refuse publication. I naturally kept our conver-

sa[...] [...]t she might innocently, with an insider's
ex[...] [...]al character of life among slaves.
[...] [...] to share with me much more than
pl[...] [...]s until I suspected that she had actually
be[...] [...]iries. Then one day as we were drinking
tea [...] Sally were taking a stroll with their
nursemaid, I finally managed to loose her tongue, without even offering her
a glass of sherry.

"Do you believe the slaves are cruelly chastised?" I asked her, hoping a
direct question would yield more than the delicate ones I had tried to pose
with a subtlety Pierce claimed I exhibited only when acting. "Did you ever
witness the lashings I have heard of?"

"Now, Fanny, you must not permit yourself to be affected by the
writings of the abolitionists. You read far too much, my dear," she said,
glancing over at the secretary in the corner, covered by the books and
magazines I had been reading. "Those people have never even *seen* a slave.
And why would any master in his right mind allow such valuable property to
be abused? I can promise you," she said with pride, "that no Southerner
would even let a horse be abused, much less a darky."

I poured her another cup of tea and placed closer to her the English
scones of which I had found she was particularly fond.

"You need not concern yourself about the welfare of Mr. Butler's slaves.
A fine gentleman like Pierce would not suffer cruelty on his plantations, and
his overseer has served over twenty years on Butler Island. He would long
ago have been detected if he allowed cruel practices. Although, Fanny dear,"
she said, drawing closer to me on the blue damask sofa, "perhaps I should
not say this. I do not mean to give you any cause for alarm, nor have I any
personal knowledge that it is this way with the slave women on Butler
Island." She added more sugar to her tea and stirred it with a tiny silver
spoon, delicately crooking her little finger as she waited, attuned to her
timing as much as an accomplished actress. "But you see, dear Fanny, the
greatest concern for the wife of a planter is *not* ill treatment of the slaves. It
is the loose way of the slave women around our men. There is practically no
way for gentlemen to avert the way these women throw themselves upon
them, possessed as they are of such animal needs and urges. There may be
some masters who revel in this opportunity for adultery and the chance to
breed more slaves," she whispered, shuddering slightly at the thought. "Or
perhaps some who believe that from their own line the slave children they

beget shall inherit Christian virtues. But I believe it far more likely that men of weak character cannot withstand the wiles of these lewd, slave women. It is not for me to say, Fanny, and *our* plantation is not on a remote island like Mr. Butler's. Even knowing my own husband's devotion to me, I would not wish him to remain alone among those temptresses."

I then resolved to devise a way Mr. Butler should not spend another winter and spring without me on Butler Island.

13

Revenge

December 15, 1835

Dearest Izzy,

I feel disloyal writing to you, knowing full well how angry your father would be to hear of it. Yet as the song goes, "Christmas is a coming and the goose is getting fat. Time to put a penny in the old man's hat." And if a body can think of charity for anybody, then how can a mother forget her own daughter all the way on the other side of the world?

I understand well your father's anger with you, and we will never understand why you ran away from Mr. James and his dear sister after the great kindness they had shown you. How could you do that after all the time they spent teaching you to act so you might have the chance in the world that you always wanted?

You can hardly hold your father to blame, Izzy, I should think, for wanting no more to do with you after you ran off with money belonging to Mr. James just like a common thief instead of the young lady with breeding and education that we sacrificed for. I cannot mention all the shame you brought upon our family. But never mind now. Your father has managed to repay it, even if it has meant we have all gone without those things that are necessities and have some days had only potatoes to eat, morning, noon, and night.

And Christmas is coming and not to hear from you last year broke my heart, and though your father will not, as I have said, even mention your name, you must know that we think of you. And not to even know for sure if you are well or all alone with nobody to cook you a Christmas goose or set you down beside a warm hearth does break a mother's heart.

I was proud to know how well you were getting on when you wrote about your acting and that you had received a proposal of marriage from that wealthy gentleman, Mr. Pierce Butler of Philadelphia. And so at least at night I did not worry so much about you and only kept you always in my prayers. I had hoped that he might bring you back sometime to England and perhaps you could then make things right with your father. Particularly if Mr. Butler was to make him a present of the money your father has lost on account of your disreputable behavior.

So then I was more disappointed than you can know to hear nothing more from you about your wedding plans. And though I tried to reach you, I received no answer from Mrs. Chestnut. It is most humiliating to a mother to depend on strangers to tell her how to write to her own daughter, who she cared for tenderly.

Though I am thinking perhaps you are entitled to a bit of Christian charity, since hearing about Mr. Butler and his marriage to that Fanny Kemble. I can see why you felt far too low to write home. The newspapers were full of it last year with some of them crying out it was a crime for the leading lady of the British and the American stage to abandon her public to marry. And others were writing about the beauty of a love story featuring the magnificent English actress and the handsome, wealthy American. My dear Izzy, how betrayed you must have felt that this man, I cannot bring myself to call him a gentleman, should make you such promises, and then cast you aside like a broken doll, to marry another. And not just any other I should say. It had to be that Fanny Kemble, who had no call to think so well of herself. Were you not far more beautiful in figure and face? Could not everyone with eyes see that clear as the nose upon my face? And if she was not a Kemble nobody shall ever convince me that you should not have appeared in her place as Juliet at Covent Garden and then your entire history should have been different, not to mention your father's and my own, what with the struggles we have had since you left us in such unfortunate circumstances.

After she had already stolen from you the role you should have rightly played upon the finest stage in England before an English audience, now she has stolen from you the man you loved and who you had placed your hopes in. There is no fairness in the world that I can see that permits some people to prosper when an honorable man like your father struggles so. And how humiliated you must now feel with all the world hearing only tales of Fanny Kemble and her brilliant marriage. I know that it is probably for this reason that you do not take time to write to your own dear mother. Surely it must weigh heavy on your heart that you have been so misled when if you had only stayed with Mr. James your future would have been assured and you would not have caused your family to suffer.

Yet I do not write you now to berate you. What would be the Christian forgiveness in that? I imagine you must in your disappointment be suffering and it is my fond wish that I could comfort you. I have not wanted ever to belittle you, Izzy, and never thought you might come to such a sad state so many miles from your native land. I only pray that in your misguided love and trust for this Mr. Butler you did not permit him liberties that have resulted in your ruin and which should never have come about if you had remained in the safe haven to which your father had entrusted you. I am certain you now know, Mr. Butler could not have had honorable intentions towards you if he had set his sights on Fanny Kemble.

I hope this letter finds you and finds you well. I know you understand I had to follow your father's directions since it is his name and his honor you have disgraced. Yet in your sadness I do still feel a mother's love for you. Life has not been fair to you, dear Izzy, and I wanted you to know that I think of you. If you are not in debt or worse and are keeping well, I wish that you may find it in your heart to send a little something home to help repay your father for the debt you have brought down upon him and for the great trouble he took to help you make your way in the world.

I do not know when next we shall see each other, my dear girl, and for that matter, we may not be so blessed to see each other again, separated as we are by such vast distance and with my days coming towards their end. But be brave, Izzy, and know that your mother thinks of you, and though he should be angry that I say it, so does your father, though you have wronged him.

Blessings of the season,
Mother

I did not receive my mother's letter until late summer of the following year when I passed briefly through Philadelphia on tour and, in stopping by the postal authority, found her much-handled, rain-dampened letter. I was relieved I had not read it closer to the time she had composed it when I was still so devastated by Pierce Butler's treachery and my banishment from Meacham Farm. Had it come to me then, while I was convalescing at the Virginia Manor, with absolutely no hope of love or friendship, nor any way to resume my acting career, reading her letter would have convinced me I should end it all by drowning myself in a nearby river or running blindly into the path of horses pulling a heavily laden wagon. I had been so despondent that I should not have seen her words for what they were, the heedless thoughts of a foolish woman, who was so hopelessly enslaved to my father that she did not even acknowledge his treachery in entrusting me to Mr. James.

It was truly fortunate for me that by the time I read her words, I had returned to the world of the successful, those who need not beg their bread from any man and who wake each day with hope. This happened very much by chance, as I might just as easily have fallen among low companions or given in to my sorrow. But not long after my arrival at the Virginia Manor, I was sitting one evening in the parlor, observing the conversation of the changing guests and long-term boarders rather than facing the solitude of my room. I sipped from a cup of tea and, glancing through my Shakespeare, had not settled yet on which play I should read when a young man sat down in the chair beside me, intent on engaging me in conversation. He wore a suit so shiny that I wondered if he had been wearing it uninterrupted for several years. His blond hair almost completely covered his collar, making me suppose his finances were so constrained he could not even regularly afford the cost of a barber. Yet despite his worn clothes, and the rundown heels on his boots, and his straggling locks, he was a handsome man and spoke to me in a well-modulated baritone, to my ears, an actor's voice.

"I hope you do not mind if I join you?" he asked decorously, though nonetheless taking the vacant seat to my right without waiting for my answer. "It is not often I have observed anyone here reading Shakespeare." He smiled, showing strong, white teeth and blue eyes full of light.

"It is not my parlor. All seats are free to those that want them," I answered without much friendliness, recent events still weighing heavily upon me.

"Then let me introduce myself," he said formally. "Matthew Andrew Harrison." He enfolded my small hand in his very large one. "And dear lady, you are?" he asked as he adjusted the cushions of the small mahogany rocking chair, which creaked beneath his weight. He was not heavily fleshed, yet he was a tall man.

There seemed no reason to conceal my name. If I did not answer him directly, it would require little effort for him to otherwise obtain it. In the process, he might come to consider me odd, something I did not desire, friendless and alone as I was at that time.

"I am Isabel Graves." I smiled, and found it easy to meet his welcoming eyes, even as I retrieved the hand, which he held longer than I felt appropriate.

"Are you an actress?" he asked, surprising me by his question.

"Yes...well, no, that is, once in a small way I was...," I faltered, discomforted by his intense stare which made me reveal more than I had intended.

"Well, which is the correct answer?" he asked, laughing, yet not unkindly. "I suspect your first response to be the true one since the ladies of my acquaintance love to be *seen* at the theatre when Shakespeare is performed, but I do not come upon them reading him when no one is watching. In private, they choose much simpler entertainment." Again his eyes fastened on my own. "I wondered if you were perhaps reading him professionally, preparing for a part? In fact, I envision you as the perfect Juliet."

Little could he know how he moved me by this remark, while at the same time he added salt to the unhealed wound of my longing. Before I could decide how much I should share of the truth about my days upon the stage, and my stunted dreams, he had reached out and picked up the red leather volume from the small table on which I had rested it.

Opening it to the page marked by the ribbon, he observed with pleasure, "So you see, I am correct after all. You *were* reading *Romeo and Juliet,* and I dare say it was not your beauty alone that moved me to observe that you could surely play Juliet. I believe now I have come much closer to the truth. You have played the role professionally, have you not?"

Feeling the trembling of my heart, I did not trust myself to speak. I nodded, conceding his point, yet fearing that if I began to tell any part of my tale, I should burst into tears and be unable to continue.

"Then this is truly good fortune," he said, his face made radiant by his smile. "I am actually a playwright by trade, but as I imagine you know there is not likely a less profitable profession for one whose best plays are unpublished and unknown. And so I manage a small company and act myself when we are short of actors. Each night we offer a different play, and for the next few months we shall be playing mainly in Virginia and Maryland. And guess, if you can, what difficulty has befallen us?"

I inclined my head with interest, yet said nothing more, still unable to trust my voice.

"Our Juliet is with child and though she has struggled with ingenious staging and costumes, she is so close now to her time she can no longer play the role. If she did," he said smiling, pleased with his joke, "Shakespeare's tragedy should turn at once into broad comedy."

The horror must have shown quickly in my face, his story touching too closely to my own life and predicament. He hurriedly assured me, "Forgive me. I have given you the wrong impression, Miss Isabel. We are a completely respectable company. Our Juliet is a married lady. There is no shame or surprise here. She simply now cannot continue to play her part. But she is quite happily married, and to *Romeo* no less. In fact, he shall remain on stage while she watches from the audience.

"Forgive me if I have misread your interest, or if you should be unwilling to join an unknown company, albeit comprised of the most delightful players," he continued haltingly, as if he feared what he was about to propose might offend me. Then he playfully removed a pink rose from the bud vase on the table beside me and extended it to me as if it were a pearl. "But if you should, in fact, be willing to save us from the tragedy which faces us if we are forced to go before our audience in two days time with *me* portraying Juliet, then please speak up, dear Miss Isabel." His kind voice and eyes pleaded for my sympathy.

And so in that very parlor, with guests across the room gathered round a piano singing popular ballads, and two gentlemen talking loudly by the fire over their cigars, I looked up from my reverie and read for him from the balcony scene, my voice no longer trembling, my memory faithful, my diction true. When I finished, he was so completely silent that at first I supposed my rendering so dreadful he had not the heart to tell me how wretched it was. He even looked down at the floor, as if postponing the harsh comments he must make.

But when he again met my eyes, I could see he was quite overcome and his eyes were filled with tears.

"Please join our company, Miss Isabel," he implored me. "The pay is poor and sometimes quite irregular. I must not deceive you. Yet the actors are talented, you shall play to the most appreciative audiences, and you will never tire of your roles. For almost every night you shall play a different one. And perhaps, in time, if all goes well, I will have the joy of seeing you appear in one of my own plays."

"Are you truly serious with this offer?" I asked, hardly daring to hear the answer, so unexpected was this opportunity, so rare this chance to resume the dream I thought had perished.

"As serious as life and death," he said, never taking his eyes from mine. "I hardly know you, yet I can tell someone has hurt you terribly. And though I cannot promise you riches or glory, I *can* promise you that I will protect you. No one shall dare harm you or wrong you so long as I live. I shall love you sweetly, perhaps, if I am fortunate, even one day as your husband, and if not, I shall love you as your brother and your honor shall be as my own," he said passionately, as if he were reciting the hero's promise in a play.

"Recited so gallantly, sir, yet since this is our first conversation, would it not be wiser to put off your proposal of marriage until we have at least been acquainted for an entire evening?" I asked playfully. "Or else you may find that though your opinion of me worsens with longer association, you have obligated yourself to marriage."

"I should not regret any obligation made to you, dear Miss Isabel, no matter if it were a pledge solemn and binding as the marriage vow," he replied earnestly, fixing his eyes on my own with such determination that before I could prevent it, I laughed, embarrassed by his elaborate declarations.

When I observed Matthew was blushing crimson to the tips of his ears, I surmised the ridiculousness of our conversation had embarrassed him as well. Perhaps he felt it foolish to have made such effusive remarks to a single lady, whose acquaintance he had scarcely made. But when he spoke again, I saw I was wrong.

"I should have realized it is my lot never to be taken seriously. A writer of comedies cannot expect more. You would have taken my marriage proposal seriously if I were a tragedian."

"I cannot believe you intended I should seriously consider it. No one proposes marriage to a complete stranger." Seeing his crestfallen expression, I hurried to add, "Besides, you are wrong to say the authors of great comedies are not respected. Look at Shakespeare. His comedies are among my most favorite plays."

"Then why did I come upon *you* reading *Romeo and Juliet*? Now there's a cheery tale."

"Tell me about your comedies," I insisted. "I beg your pardon, but I am not familiar with your work."

"You deeply shame me, Miss Isabel," he replied playfully, not appearing to be. "How can I profess to be a well-established playwright if my plays are unknown to you?"

"Truly it is no reflection on your popularity that I do not know your plays. I have not been long in this country and do not often have the means to attend the theatre."

"You might easily have forgotten my plays even if you *had* seen a number of them," he said regretfully. "Mine is not a name known in society. My plays are drawing room comedies and amusements, well received and enjoyed *when* they are offered. The audiences go home smiling, content with their evenings, and likely forget all about me until the next time." He continued to address me, yet his voice drifted inward, as if he were speaking to himself. "But I am convinced there is an important play I should be writing. I do not know what its subject will be. But regardless of what may happen to *me*," he continued rather melodramatically, "this play will make a statement that shall not be forgotten."

He then looked at me, his eyes glittering with such intensity I could not be sure if he was intoxicated by the sound of his own voice, like so many people in the theatre, or if he suffered from a debilitating fever. I thanked him for his invitation to join his company, which I gratefully accepted, since I had no better plan to help me return so quickly to the stage. I bid him good-night and hurried away before he could engage me in further conversation, or in something else, as he was so handsome and looked at me quite longingly with his long-lashed, deep blue eyes until I feared I might succumb to temptation.

The next days passed quickly in preparation for traveling. Every morning in the parlor, we rehearsed the abbreviated versions Matthew had crafted of Shakespeare's most popular plays. I concentrated mainly on Juliet since *Romeo & Juliet* would be performed at every destination of our tour. And though Matthew heralded my appearance in this play as the salvation of the company, I soon learned that my sewing skills were almost of equal value. Poor as the company's costumes would have seemed in good condition, many of them had been made useless by a terrible storm which had drenched the trunks in which the costumes had been stored after the last engagement. No one had discovered this terrible accident until the chests were removed from the leaking attic, where they had been stored, and opened to reveal the ruined finery. It was customary in those days for each leading actor to travel with his own trunk containing the costumes for all his major robes. This chest was as much his tool chest as that of a carpenter, cobbler, or seaman. But for our company, which stored its costumes all together, the damage was far more ruinous than the loss of one actor's costumes. This disaster meant the destruction of an entire company's prospects. Hard-pressed as Matthew was for funds to provide food and lodging for the company, I knew he had no means to pay for the repair and replacement of all the company's properties. Without them, we could not perform.

When I saw the garments with their stains and tears and rotting plumes and lace, and witnessed the distress of the actors discovering their ruined finery, I went immediately in search of my sewing box. Soon I was instructing a small team of actresses, who became my assistants, while Matthew took the last of his savings to a dry goods store where cloth, thread, ribbon, and even bedclothes might be obtained. We worked late into the night, sewing and salvaging where we could to create costumes for gentlemen and ladies which might be passed on from play to play until we should raise sufficient funds to replace our costumes. I thought with dismay how paltry Mrs. Chestnut should deem my hurried designs, particularly my hats fashioned out of remnants. I was myself concerned that I had erred in offering to lead the reclamation of the costumes. I worried viewing the imperfect results, my companions might chastise me for worsening our situation and depleting all their savings in the bargain. I feared having to apologize to the entire company, and was instead delighted to have pleased comments issuing forth all around me, as everyone examined our new costumes and a few that had been reclaimed from the rubbish heap.

"Well done, Isabel," Matthew congratulated me, unfurling a purple lined cape in one hand and examining a pale blue ball gown draped over the chair in front of me. I sat on a low stool from which I was sewing a panel to cover the damage to a water-stained green silk frock, worn by a young woman who stood patiently before me, nearly sleeping on her feet.

Then he took my hand, gallantly lifting me to my feet, and urged the rest of the company to applaud me for transforming their ruined wardrobe chests. "It would have sufficed if you had only agreed to be our Juliet," Matthew announced. "Yet you have done so much more. You have saved us with your nimble hands," he said, and then before I could stop him, he fell to his knees, and kissed the hem of my garment, as if I were a queen.

"I am taking you out for a stroll now and will take no argument," Matthew told me as I prepared to protest, so much work still needing to be completed. "You have worked through the night bent over those horrible, nasty costumes. You need fresh air, rest, and a cup of tea."

I turned down the tea, having already consumed far too much during that day of toil and the long night that had preceded it. But I relished walking out with him for fresh air and a peaceful stroll through the early evening streets of Richmond. I admired the red brick fronts of the houses with their neat front gardens and boxwood hedges.

Until then I was startled by a horrible jangling of chains and the harsh voices of men on horseback, who cracked their whips as they called out to the slaves they were driving before them up the dusty street. There were men, women, and children chained together, and some of the women bore tiny babies in their arms, which they attempted to nurse whenever the pace of their progress up the street slowed enough to allow it. Their clothes were ragged, many of the men were shirtless, and all were barefoot. They stared straight ahead, looking neither to the left nor right, cowed either by the whips that cracked regularly around them or by what they had been told would befall them if they disobeyed in any way.

"It is disgusting, Isabel," Matthew said, shuddering as this pathetic parade of human beings passed by us. "I am so sorry that you have witnessed the most shameful part of life in this country. I imagine, working in a milliner's shop, you have not seen close by the horrors of slavery. Had I known they would be passing this way, I should never have brought you out for a walk."

I felt I must respond, yet did not wish to share any part of my past at Meacham Farm, nor reveal I had observed slaves as they worked, eaten food prepared by them, and been ministered to in my own time of need by a slave's kind and competent hands. Thomas Meacham's "people" had been plainly dressed, were neat and well maintained, and had wanted for none of life's necessities save freedom. I recognized that the cruel scene I had just watched in the street portrayed the more usual face of slavery. I closed my eyes so tightly that it pained me, yet still I could see their faces.

"Why do they not rebel?" Matthew asked me. "On many plantations, they far outnumber their masters. They are rarely kept in chains, especially in remote locations. I do not understand why they will not fight back against such cruelty."

"And where would you have them go?" I asked sharply, more angrily than I had intended. "They have no weapons, horses, or boats to carry them away. And no money to purchase food for their escape. If they were to head north and be captured, they would be sent back to the most unspeakable punishments." I, who knew something about escape from cruel treatment, could not fathom how difficult running away would be if one's skin were black, attesting to one's bondage, leaving no way for one to disappear in a crowd.

"All you say is true, Isabel." Matthew slowed his pace markedly, allowing the sad troupe of slaves to pass out of sight. "Yet every time I see them driven to market like so many cows or pigs, I cannot understand why they do not go mad and turn on their oppressors, even with only their bare hands to defend themselves. It would be futile, but I am surprised they do not pound their chains against the heads of their tormentors."

"And then be beaten or killed or have their children sold away from them like dogs?" I asked, incensed by his foolish notions. "That is what would happen. What you propose is the romantic stuff of plays. You have read or *written* too many of them. In real life, such dangerous risks cannot be taken."

"Perhaps you are correct," he admitted sorrowfully. "Though I cannot believe house slaves have not tried to poison their masters. Preparing all the food, it would be possible for them to poison an entire family as it sat down to table."

"And likely be blamed for it straight away. Who else could be held responsible? Any cook who should try it would be tightening the noose around her own throat or those of her entire family. There would be immediate retribution, and no one could benefit from such short-lived revenge."

"You're wrong, Isabel," he insisted. "If someone starved and beat you or forced you to endure his advances even when you loathed him, or grabbed your baby away to sell it the moment it was born, certainly you are not saying you should react logically and rationally? Might you not strike out at such evil?"

My heart was suddenly too full for me to speak. Matthew scribbled rapidly in the small notebook he carried always in his pocket.

"It is not improbable one day slaves shall turn on their masters," he told me as he wrote. "They clearly have more than sufficient cause to do so. It would not surprise me to learn a master somewhere has been served a poisoned soup. I shall think more about that. It would make a very daring and exciting play," he considered. "It could stir audiences, one person at a time, to condemn slavery."

"If you write and perform this play in America," I warned him, "do not be surprised if you are poisoned yourself. I beg you not to follow such a foolish course."

"Do not worry, dear Isabel. It is only an idea in my notebook for now. You've no cause to worry. At home in New England, it once seemed sufficient to listen to the abolitionists' speeches in church halls and to agree with them. But now, every time I see slaves in the flesh, I feel I must *do* something. I must write about it!"

This last he uttered with such feeling he was stricken, as he often was, with a fit of coughing. I asked if we should step inside somewhere to find water to soothe him. But he pushed aside this notion, saying it was nothing but a bit of dust caught in his throat.

Two days later when the company departed, I traveled with them, feeling myself to be in every way a full member. By carriages and trains, as we made our way, Matthew remained always at my side, looking out for me. He hardly let anyone come near me, determined as he was to protect my honor.

At first there were frequent nights when our poor company could scarcely pay our expenses and have money left to purchase our supper. Until gradually, our success became more assured, and I was recognized for my accomplishment as Juliet and other heroines. I even received notice and offers from more established companies. It was difficult to believe that but a short time after being turned into the street by Pierce Butler, I had established my own theatrical reputation and could easily make my own way, depending on no man.

But happy as I felt and comfortable as I became, I could not forget Fanny Kemble and the golden life which she enjoyed. She ate from a silver spoon and a bone-china plate while I struggled each day to earn my bread. She, my obvious inferior in face and figure, had *been* Juliet, while I was offered only the chance to be her understudy. And then when men of all nations were clamoring to be her suitors and she could select any of them for the color of his eyes or the cut of his coat, she had chosen Pierce Butler. He meant nothing to her while he meant *everything* to me, but she had always been served anything she wanted as if she were the only diner at a magnificent banquet.

I knew I should not succumb to envy and past resentments, yet I promised myself I should have my revenge upon her. I did not say a word to Matthew, who lived in a peaceful, golden light working on his play, unaware of who moved around him. He forgot to eat more than once and looked as thin and pale as the milk left at the bottom of the pail after the cream is skimmed off the top. I had never spoken a word to him about Fanny Kemble and how she had tortured my past. If I had, he would have advised me to reflect upon my own attainments rather than my slights, particularly those so long ago. He would have implored me to savor my joy that hardly a ticket could be found to our performances any night I appeared, and that audiences applauded soon as I took the stage.

Yet I remained true to my oath. I should have my revenge. No matter how many years I might wait to attain it.

14

"Alabaster Baby"

I could not believe, despite the deceitful characters I had read about and portrayed, that my husband would dishonor me. Nor did I imagine slave maidens should tempt him more than I, finding myself unchanged, after bearing two children, from my appearance when he first professed his love. I was prepared to plead my case to be allowed to accompany him on the long journey to his Georgia plantations, yet it became unnecessary.

John Butler, my husband's brother, had fallen into poor health, and his physicians advised him to avoid the exhausting travel and hardships on the rice plantation, even for the masters. Since Pierce himself was severely troubled by rheumatism, his family, not often my supporters, agreed it best for him to spend the winter in the mild Georgia climate. They expressed approval that I had *finally* put aside my troublesome writing and stage career to minister to my husband. I endured silently acerbic comments, which would usually have drawn retorts from me, so determined as I was to see slavery for myself.

Though Pierce wavered, seemingly from genuine concern for my safety, sad news arrived from England, which decided the matter. Without any warning, my mother had taken ill while visiting in the countryside near Surrey and had died suddenly before she could even be brought home to London. I was forlorn not to have seen her for over two years, and I felt so helpless to be separated from my family in England. Try as I would to compose myself—almost anything—seeing a painting, the playing of a piece of music which had been one of her favorites, or hearing someone quote a bit of poetry or singing a song that she had admired brought on a stream of tears. I told Pierce he must let me come with him to Georgia, if not for his own health, then for mine, since I could not stand to be alone at such a miserable time. Whatever differences we held about slavery, we were husband and wife, and I could not face this fresh grief as well as lonely months without him.

Since he was often bothered by my independence, I believe my husband was pleased that I beseeched him to let us accompany him. I assured him that our babies were old enough and so very healthy that with the help of our wonderful nursemaid, Margery, this journey should not be harmful to them. Despite Pierce's warnings of the rough conditions, I could not fathom any life so harsh that we could not manage it with the inducements of the river breezes and beautiful salt marshes and miles and miles of land where young children might romp freely. And though it disgusted me to consider it, we would have over eight hundred slaves to attend us. Mr. Butler had spoken very little about the slaves, but he assured me that despite the small overseer's house in no way resembling the plantation homes Amelia had described to me, there would be house "servants" to attend to our every need. After accepting my determination to join him, my husband's only remaining concern was taking Margery on our journey. He worried seeing a white woman in service would have a terrible effect on the slaves. But I prevailed. There was no way I could undertake such a journey without her assistance.

We departed Philadelphia on December 21, 1838, traveling by railroad to Baltimore. Despite the long days before us on stagecoach, riverboat, and barge, I felt great eagerness to begin this journey. We all were bundled up against the cold, including tiny Fan, just barely one year old, with only her pink, dear little nose showing amid her wrappings. And Sal, not my namesake but certainly my soul's companion, turned every moment to ask me yet another of her questions, beginning with "why," about all that she could see unfolding around her.

I love to travel, yet I have always been bored by other people's lengthy descriptions of ocean crossings, the menus of meals they consumed, concerts they attended, and plays they have seen, unless, of course, they allude to performances in which I have appeared. Therefore, my account of our journey shall be mercifully brief. There is, indeed, little new to convey about the nature of traveling with two small children and Mr. Butler's ancient aunt, who was accompanying us as far as Charleston. The deprivations we suffered, from the poisonous fumes of the coal locomotives and the showers of cinders they deposited upon us, the stale food, drafty rooms and carriages, no accommodation to even wash one's face or dry one's hands with a clean towel, and sleeping chambers shared with total strangers, were all so unpleasant, but it would seem an unnecessary indulgence in self pity to further recreate them.

For me, far more revelatory than any experience of food or culture was our first contact with the slaves themselves. The further south we traveled, we observed them more and more, attending to their mistresses and masters and carrying out all manner of work. Mr. Butler was displeased when I pointed out to him that those we saw who were not personal servants or coachmen were ragged and ill-clad. It seemed to me, contrary to Mr. Butler's assurances, Southerners clearly thought more of their horses, which appeared well fed, with their manes elaborately braided with ribbons, than they did of their slaves.

"You have not yet seen actual plantation life, Fanny," Pierce said reassuringly. "These are ramshackle farms with hardly a handful of slaves among them and farmers scrabbling to make a poor living. The laborers you see working on the roads are most certainly hired out and obviously not cared for as they would be by their own masters. You should not judge by these poor examples. Wait until you are among our people and see how you are received and how contented they are."

I made no reply, though I harbored doubts. Why, I supposed, should a farmer of modest means treat more poorly a slave whom he knows well, having no others with whom to confuse him, than a plantation owner with hundreds of dependents? My husband's argument was unconvincing to me, since the value of a master's human property, I reasoned, should logically increase according to its scarcity. But I made no comment, intent on rocking Fan, who had grown fretful in the intermittently hot and freezing railway car, dependent on the whims of the furnace-like stove, which was at times left oddly idle and then alternately stoked as if to represent the very fires of Hades. Then we were beset by the freezing draughts from windows that had been forced open by other passengers sitting closest to the oppressive heat.

In North Carolina I had my first taste of true "Southern hospitality." The horse-drawn coaches on which we were traveling, through the sandy, wasted land of barren pines, arrived at the desolate spot where we could make connection with the next train. Yet the people who were waiting about the platform, fierce-looking white men and women of the coarsest, roughest nature, told the gentlemen of our party that the train had been delayed and would not arrive before daylight. We had then the grim prospect of sitting through the long, dark night in these cold boxes on wheels, which did not deserve even the name of *carriages*, unless a temporary provision could be found for us.

Mr. Butler made acquaintance with one of the men, who had come forward to ask if he had about him some chewing tobacco. Mr. Butler removed his case from his waistcoat and offered the man a cigar. He accepted it quizzically, sniffing the aroma of the tobacco, yet clearly puzzled that anyone would roll tobacco in that way or smoke it as Mr. Butler proceeded to show him was the way in which a cigar was handled. It was then I noticed that several of the women standing to our rear, wearing silk gowns, which looked as if they had been worn several days without interruption, along with bonnets decked with bows and artificial roses, were taking tobacco in their gloved hands and were joining the men in chewing it, and, most disagreeably, spitting into the path before us.

After such pleasantries, as the darkness descended around us, Mr. Butler and several of the other gentlemen who were traveling with us gained word from our tobacco-sated companions that if we should walk only a short distance through the woods, we would come to the farm of old Colonel Mackey, a man of considerable standing in that neighborhood. By walking only one mile we should come closer to the connection with the railroad, and he would certainly offer us hospitality as he had graciously done for many travelers before us.

As the last traces of light were dying out around us, we made our decision to hurry as fast as we might travel to the colonel's home, burdened by sleeping babes and tired women and weary gentlemen as well. Mr. Butler paid some of these men to direct us while others went ahead to tell the worthy colonel of our arrival so that he might assemble dinner for our party as quickly as possible. As dark descended, we found ourselves worn out and famished, and the babies in our arms, no longer crying in their own exhausted slumber, seemed to have taken on the weight of heavy logs.

After a hard walk, we left the woods and came upon a few rough houses at the edge of fields where last year's remnant stalks loomed skeletally in the lantern light. The men leading us pointed out the colonel's dwelling, a true surprise to me, since I had supposed a colonel to hold a position of sufficient wealth to possess a dwelling of more distinction than the poor farmhouse we approached. I began to despair of what sort of dinner the scion of such a home might offer us.

I made my way to the front door, leading with me Margery, who, like me, was clutching one of my babies, and entered the house. We came immediately into one huge room where a large wood fire was blazing on the hearth. There, sitting by the fire, was a ruddy-complexioned man with long silver hair and beard. He welcomed us in a friendly way to draw near the fire.

Colonel Mackey, as he turned out to be, was in no way dismayed by the sudden appearance of our party. He encouraged us to make ourselves at home, and set to motion a host of staring Negroes, who brought us quickly some of the colonel's homemade blackberry wine. Since he urged us so strongly to make ourselves comfortable, we managed to drape an assortment of our cloaks across his gaping windows, which would neither open nor close, allowing in great gusts of wind. In one corner of the apartment stood a clean-looking four-poster bed, at which I must admit I looked with great want, but we situated ourselves as best we could in this rough-walled room on an assortment of rush-bottom chairs, most sagging or torn by the weight of years. But my babies were furnished with bowls of milk, and we all were comforted by the welcomed heat and light of the bright fire and the prospect of the fine dinner that had been promised.

Under the warming influence of the colonel's wine, we learned that he had fought with Washington and was indeed a local hero. Looking at the crude rafters overhead, hung principally with bunches of dried herbs and turkey-feather fans, I began to feel sadness that this old war hero, whose wife had died long ago, was reduced to living so rudely. The Negro women, who moved around us preparing our dinner, finally interrupted my ruminations by calling us to table to refresh ourselves. We were all quite hungry, as we had eaten very little the entire day.

I cannot describe our shock at the food that was put before us. Dirty water, I cannot deign to call it *tea*, followed by stale cheese, bad butter, and dry, hard biscuits. This was the dinner whose preparation we had eagerly awaited. And then to our surprise, the hospitable colonel, who had urged us to eat our fill, asked to be paid the extraordinary price of a half dollar apiece for each member of our party.

Remembering Amelia's warning to me, my spirits were further dampened upon learning that three of the dusky women who waited upon us at table were his own daughters. I wondered if even more of his "servants" were his own progeny, since, as we were leaving, a young Negro girl, whose very free way of speaking with us made us aware of this circumstance, said, with commendable pride towards her *benefactor*, "Indeed, Colonel Mackey is a father to us all!"

When we heard gratefully that the train was approaching, I was pleased to leave the colonel's shelter, no matter how venerated a war hero he was. I noticed that when I tried to catch Mr. Butler's eye to engage him in discussing my first direct experience with slavery, he averted his gaze and seemed very preoccupied by the passing scenery.

Announcing arrivals by the sounding of a great conch shell must be the most glorious herald of them all. If someone wishes to compose a truly American rendering of Shakespeare, I should absolutely recommend that herald trumpets be replaced by the low and then thundering magic from a crescendo of conchs. This is precisely how our arrival on Butler Island was proclaimed on December 30th, nine days after we had left Philadelphia, but seemingly after we had traveled to the end of all we had ever known. Our landing startled me, as I had fallen into a reverie when we pulled away from the steamer on two small boats that carried us across one of the branches of the Altamaha River near the little town of Darien.

We had entered into a narrow, artificial canal, which I was told had been dug by General Oglethorpe's men to aid his escape from the pursuing Spanish and Indians. The banks were dikes, guarding rice swamps. But once we had progressed a short way into the inlet to take us to the island, I was charmed by the beauty of all manner of evergreens growing thick and luxuriously beneath giant straggling cypress trees draped in that gray moss I have never seen except in these Southern woods. Although called *Spanish* moss, there was nothing about it to recall gay, Spanish dance or music. It cast the most singularly eerie and dismal aspect over those woods. The trees were draped as well in all manner of vines, thick as a man's arm, and some resplendent with berries. The calls of all manner of waterfowl and great hawks sounded all around us.

Thinking of my own dear family and of England so far away, I fell deep in thought while we passed a sisterhood of small islands dividing the noble river into several streams, each of them wider than the Thames. Then we approached the low reed and grass-covered banks of Butler Island, passing the rice mills and other buildings, which since it was Sunday, were all still. This silence, save the movement of the oars cutting the water and the birds overhead, made the sounding of the conch more sudden and more startling.

Then, as if on cue, Negroes came running from every direction, jumping, laughing, clapping their hands, and shouting in the most excited and extravagant ways to express their delight at our arrival. As we stepped from the boat, the crowd of Mr. Butler's slaves rushed around us, seizing our clothes, kissing them, clinging to us as if we were divines who had blessedly fallen from heaven into their midst. I thought these raptures would surely subside once we neared the overseer's house where we would be staying. But still the slaves crowded round the windows to catch a glimpse of us, even begging entrance and sitting outside the room where I sat rocking Fan, watching every motion we made as if we walked in a superior manner or moved our hands in a fashion that their own hands could not grasp.

Mr. Butler walked out time to time to greet slaves with whom he was particularly acquainted. They seemed to receive his words gratefully, smiling as they walked way, again as if they had been granted a private audience with their king. Then the door opened, and he brought in to see me an aged woman, whose frail, wizened body did not match her raucous, unbridled exclamation of delight at making my acquaintance.

"This is old Siba," Mr. Butler said differentially, leading the old woman, who seemed hesitant of taking too much liberty by meeting my eye, to stand beside my chair, where Fan had fallen asleep. "She has been with the family since she was born here on the island many years ago. She wishes to bring you an arrangement she has prepared especially for your arrival."

I quickly pressed the small nosegay of holly and berries to my face, wanting to please her. In this season of winter, even in that southern climate, she had obviously struggled to find these adornments, and who could say what sacrifice she had undergone to afford the cost of the red ribbon wound around it.

"Oh, massa," she exclaimed to Pierce, as soon as she drew near. "Now where you find this *perfect* alabaster baby?"

Thinking that she referred to Fan, whose complexion was truly delicate as alabaster, I turned the sleeping babe so she might better admire her. I knew also that my own countenance would never be described by anyone as pale and translucent, nor would anyone likely refer to a grown woman, the wife of the owner of this extensive property, in such terms. I was not surprised by her feelings. I thought, and I am *not* ashamed of my youth and pride in new motherhood that produced my belief, that everyone, be she slave or free, must hold tender feelings towards sleeping babes. And Fan's delicate cheeks, with just a dainty hint of rose, *were* particularly lovely.

"Oh, no, missus," she said, reaching out to touch the hem of my velvet gown. "Do not wake l'il missy. But look at her, massa," she continued admiringly, smiling at *me*. "You have chose a lily alabaster doll and brought her among the people."

When she had gone out, and we were temporarily alone with our children, Mr. Butler spoke with much satisfaction. "Now surely, Fanny, you *cannot* dispute the high regard in which we are received. If slavery were really so cruel, why then would these people be so overjoyed to see their master and their new mistress? They would instead hide in fear of us. With your generous heart, Fanny" he said, warmly kissing my hand, "you have troubled yourself unnecessarily."

15

New Mistress

I had worked all my life, not hard physical labor, as the slaves endured each day, but I had earned my own bread. And I had lived with servants and seen no shame in honest service or an employer's reliance on this arrangement, so long as servants were fairly paid and respectfully treated. But I was stunned to suddenly become the mistress of hundreds of slaves.

I worried that tiny Sal, serious three-year-old that she was, might readily become accustomed to the accepted division of free people and slaves and what horrible effect this might have upon her. As we began our daily rounds of the island, I watched with horror as all the people, male and female, old and young, fawned over her. They carved her crude necklaces from Cypress wood and made her dolls from corncobs and bits of fabric they could ill spare from their own scant allotments. She was carried so often that her little feet should never have touched the ground if I had permitted it, and her already determined personality turned bossier under the constant dotage of her adoring hordes.

"Why does it bother you, Fanny?" Pierce asked with obvious perplexity. "Let them enjoy her. A white child is a novelty to them, and they cannot harm her. Children of the South are brought up completely by black mammies and are just as fine as any childre—"

"They are spoiling her terribly, Pierce. She will grow up quite tyrannical. Already she expects to be at the center of everything, always talking and *never* listening to what they or anyone else says. She stands before even the youngest children as if she is their mistress, and I shall not have it!" I regretted immediately that my temper had escaped me, but we were soon embroiled again in one of our struggles.

"Well, whether you desire it or not, Mrs. Butler," his tone verged on insult, "it is a simple fact that you *are* the mistress of this plantation and your daughters are the little mistresses. There is no point in disputing it. You would do far better to direct your energies elsewhere."

Before I could tell him of my plan to do whatever I could during my sojourn of a few months among the slaves to help them better their condition, he informed me that our conversation would have to be postponed. He was required to meet with Mr. Ogden, the overseer, to consider pressing matters relating to the rice harvest.

And then, as he always prized the last word on any matter, my husband looked back through the doorway, his tone agreeable, though I felt his barely veiled derision. "This matter of Sal always having to be the center of attention. You may wish to reflect from whence that emanates, Fanny. I, of course, have not had benefit of your fine *English* education. I must venture that her disposition cannot in so short a time be affected by her time here. You might do well when you are holding up your mirror, to consider what daily example she has observed."

Though I was not granted opportunity to respond to this unkind accusation, I felt vindicated when just two days later I overheard Sal's conversation with Mary, a young woman who performed the services of a chambermaid and was, of course, one of Mr. Butler's—I cannot now and could not then bear to refer to them as my own—*slaves.*

Sal was watching Mary straighten the bedclothes in the room allotted to Margery and the two children, and said, with her blossoming importance, "Mary, some persons are free and some are slaves. I say, *I* am a free person, Mary. Did you know that?"

"Yes, missus," Mary said wearily, continuing her task.

"Some persons are free and some are not. Do you know that, Mary?"

"I know it is so *here*, in this world, missis."

Since I was nearby in the next room sewing, I could not refrain from joining the conversation. "Oh, then, Mary, you think it will not always be so?" I asked.

"Me hope not, missus," she said, her eyes turned away, looking inward as if she were praying.

I am afraid that this poor woman actually believed there could not be slaves in heaven, since in that place righteousness would be imposed. Since her concept of heaven was shaped completely by the white man's religion filtered down to her, I was amazed she could fathom a heaven any white man would believe in that did not include slaves to wait upon him, unless in paradise such service should be taken on by angels. Then I had to laugh bitterly to myself remembering that to most planters and to my own husband, slavery itself must be *heaven* or something preposterously akin to it.

With so many slaves at my disposal, I waited on myself more than I had ever done in my life. Besides my own aversion to the idea, much less the reality of persons in bondage, I cringed at the personal offensiveness of Mr. Butler's *people*. I met many Southerners who insisted the filthy habits of slaves were inherent to the race or that the slaves were too ignorant to avail themselves of plentiful water and soap. Yet in those days, such sentiments did not keep Southern women from hanging their infants at the breasts of Negro slave women and having one or more little "pet" blacks sleeping in theirs or their daughters' bedchambers like puppy dogs, nor planters choosing one or more favored female slaves to admit to their own beds.

My husband asked me directly why with so many slaves I would not suffer anyone to attend me. I told him I could not believe that he, after living in his brother's fine home in Philadelphia or even in the immaculate realm of the Butler Place farm, could tolerate such offensive personal habits among those who waited upon us on the plantation. It seemed preposterous to put the care of one's children, the cooking and serving of one's food, and the keeping of one's home, small and crude as our dwelling was on that island, in the hands of those who came in daily encrusted with dirt and wearing clothes which had been worn to rags and washed with no greater frequency than they had washed themselves. I imagined some of their clothes should fall to dust if submerged for the first time in water! And if this were the condition of house servants, by all accounts the best fed and easiest worked of the slaves, I told him I could not imagine the condition of the field hands or of those who were ill.

"You must stay away from the fields," he directed me sternly. "They are no place for you or our children. There are rattlesnakes concealed in the high grasses and mosquitoes which carry malaria. I will *not* have you endangering yourself or our children. But if you sincerely wish to better the condition of the slaves, then take your soap and water and go teach them all you like at the infirmary or in the slaves' cabins or at our own table about an Englishwoman's hygiene. But you must remember this is a working plantation, Fanny, not a country home."

I advised him I was not then, nor had I ever been, sufficiently accomplished as an actress to convince myself or an audience that Butler Island was a country estate. But I should be delighted to roll up my sleeves and turn buckets of hot water and soap upon the filth of our plantation.

I wondered what he feared so strongly, sensing it was more than snakes and insects, which in any case crossed my path daily, that he did not want me to visit his fields. But I contented myself with what I should teach the very next day to the girls and boys who tended the babies and small children who were left behind while their mothers worked the fields.

16

Love at Last

I was at last a leading lady. I had become, without dispute, *the* leading lady of our company when we took up residence in Baltimore. Through Matthew's excellent management, we returned from touring in the spring of 1839 with modest savings and found an opportunity in Baltimore when another company closed down due to its manager's fondness for spirits. We inherited their costumes, more varied if not more finely sewn than my own creations, and a theatre audience that longed for good acting after desultory performances during the last days of our predecessors. I confided to no one how strange it felt to finally arrive in Baltimore, where I had hoped to establish myself after Pierce Butler's betrayal, or that when taken from Meacham Farm condemned for desertion, I had not dreamed I should so soon regain the stage. A position in the rudest traveling company had seemed a greater hope than I dared to have, yet suddenly I was acclaimed in Baltimore for my acting and my beauty.

Everyone came to see Isabel Graves as Juliet, Portia, and Ophelia or any other role I chose to play. They rushed to my dressing room after performances beseeching me to sign their programs. Gentlemen sent me bountiful bouquets of spring flowers and long-stemmed roses bound with satin ribbon to protect my tender fingers from the thorns. There were always poems attesting that my beauty was "...much lovelier than the fairest rose" and cards and letters imploring me to accept dinner invitations or entreating me for even the briefest audience. Heart-shaped boxes filled with chocolates covered my dressing table, and amid them appeared the cards of more admirers. Yet plead as they did, I turned away all invitations, having good reason to be fearful of gentlemen, their promises and their passions, and the wrongs they might bring down upon me. I had been thwarted too severely in my quest to appear at a prominent theatre to permit love or romance to deter my success.

Yet gentlemen would not accept my refusals, and the most determined of them all was Matthew Andrew Harrison. At first, I misconstrued his attentions, thinking he was merely grateful for my acting and sewing skills, which had helped to change the prospects for his small company. Yet his distressed expression if any gentleman called on me and was not dismissed after a few moments, and by the way he waited each evening to escort me from the theatre, Matthew's devotion was always evident.

I had felt entirely comfortable in his company since our first conversation at the Virginia Manor. Although only a marginal actor, at *best*, Matthew possessed a personal grace, which was very reassuring, and the first day I observed him talking with the other players, it was obvious he was the favorite of all the ladies in the company. I deliberately held myself apart from him, fearing his tone of easy intimacy and not wanting to allow anything to discourage my path to the stage. But one evening when Matthew escorted me to the carriage that would take me home from the theatre, he settled himself beside me in the soft seat and made no move to bid me good-night. I would have spoken up in surprise, but before I collected my thoughts, we had taken off down the street. For the slightest second, I was frightened this carriage ride that evoked terrible memories of Mr. Jones's assault, was Matthew's attempt to abduct me.

My apprehension must have shown clearly in my face, since we had scarcely turned the corner when Matthew quickly assured me his intentions were completely honorable, though he felt compelled to ask me something he could not postpone another moment. Then pressing my hand, he beseeched me not to look so concerned and promised that once I reached my lodging house, if it should be my wish, he would leave me.

"If there is nothing to fear and your intentions are truly honorable," I told him, much annoyed by his actions, "then why are you behaving so strangely?" I felt very weary, and I was in no mood for anything to delay getting myself quickly to bed.

"I feared you would not see me, Isabel," he replied miserably. "Every night there are gentlemen fighting for the chance to exchange a few words with you. They are far more handsome and fashionable than I and offer you all manner of presents and compliments."

"What a ridiculous thing to say, Matthew. If you could only hear yourself!" I exclaimed. "You are as good a friend as I have had in my entire life. Why would you imagine you must steal into my carriage to speak with me? I would have met you anywhere you wished, though not now when I am exhausted and suffering the most dreadful headache." I disengaged my hand and turned away from him.

"Please hear me out, Isabel," he implored, taking back my hand. "I had to detain you in this way, or I should not have found a private moment to speak."

By this point I was greatly perplexed by his urgency and whatever caused him such terrible agitation. His face was quite flushed, as it appeared after one of his dreadful bouts of coughing, but, in truth, he seemed without any physical discomfort.

"What *is* it, Matthew?" I asked gently. "I would try to guess, but am a poor hand at games and intrigues. I have come to rely on minds far greater than my own to think up clever words for me to say," I went on, acknowledging him as a playwright.

"Then truly, you do not know what I wish to say? I must go ahead and say it?" he asked softly, his face inclined very close to my own.

"We shall be there any moment, Matthew. I do not know what troubles you, and we are too old to play guessing games like children."

He grasped both my hands in his own, seeming to fear that if he did not hold on I might flee the carriage. Then, in his most tender voice, a voice more filled with love than I had ever heard outside a stage directed at me, he said, "Dearest Isabel, I ask only this, and it is everything to me. Will you make me the happiest man in the world and take my hand in marriage?"

At that moment, marriage was the last thing I imagined he should suggest, though he had made no secret of his fondness for me. We saw each other every day of the week, yet still he pressed for my answer.

"I see you do not hurry to answer," he replied sadly, leaning back against the cushions. "Perhaps it was too much to hope that someone as beautiful and talented as you should consider marrying a poor wretch—"

"You must not say such things," I begged him. "I am honored you should feel so much for me, accomplished as you are yourself. And surely you know you are the sweetheart of every lady in the company, and that they all seek your good opinion over any other?"

"That means nothing to me. The only good opinion I seek is your own. It is all that matters."

"Well, that, of course, you have, had since the first day I met you," I assured him.

"Then you will agree to be my wife?" he asked expectantly, his voice rising with his hopes.

"If I *could* marry, I would gladly choose you, Matthew. If only I had met you years ago, before my life took certain painful turns..." I stopped then, feeling my own throat growing tight and tears filling my eyes. "But I am certain I shall never marry. I have suffered far too painful injuries from gentlemen I should have been able to rely upon. Marriage is not for me." I affectionately took his hand. "But since you are so kind and good, you shall, of course, find a worthy lady to marry. But it cannot be me."

"Why, Isabel? Please do not be afraid of being hurt. I should rather cut off my right arm than cause you pain. There is no one in the world for me save you. I am as sure of this as I am that I live and breathe."

I could not bring myself then to tell him of Mr. James and Pierce Butler, my false marriage, or the baby unwanted by me, who lay in a lonely grave. I would not speak of the ambition, which motivated my every breath, to claim my place upon a greater stage than I had ever known. I felt I should injure him severely if I told him I loved him, as I was sure I did, yet that I loved more deeply the theatre and my dreams of it.

"If you cannot love me, Isabel, then I do not care to live," he said, relinquishing my hand. He buried his face in my lap. "I have never felt this way before. I have adored you since the first moment I came upon you reading Shakespeare in the lamplight."

"Then there is nothing for it but for you to come in," I said, lifting his head and taking the handkerchief from his coat and wiping his eyes. "I cannot send you away after what you have said."

In truth, I feared he might do away with himself, dejected as he seemed. Believing marriage should bring me only unhappiness and bad fortune and that I should never again agree to it, I still could not let him leave me. My pain had lifted, and I was profoundly moved to see a face so filled with love for me.

Due to the lateness of the hour, we were fortunate no one was seated in the common parlor I passed through to reach my own chamber. I should not have known how to explain his presence. As it was, we were alone, and quickly as actors following directions to exit the stage, we escaped to my small sitting room. At first, I busied myself pouring out the tea that the maid had left in readiness and serving Matthew meat pies and sandwiches, which had been prepared for my late supper. I poured cream into my tea and added sugar.

"There is only one, so we will have to share," I said, offering him my cup. "I don't mind if it is all right with you."

"I cannot take a single bite or even one sip of that tea," he said, trembling as he set the cup down on the table. "I should not wish to waste a precious moment of the time I have with you in mere eating and drinking. I am certain I *should* go now, dear Isabel," he said, turning away. "Or else I shall not be able to take responsibility for what may happen. I do not think I may be trusted to remain alone with you."

"Do not hurry off, Matthew. How can you claim to love me and yet wish to hurry away?"

"You say you will not marry me, Isabel. You have given your answer quite plainly," he said, his face solemn and pale with disappointment.

"That is true. Thank you for not pressing me to change my mind and respecting that I do, indeed, know it. But though I have rejected your proposal of marriage, did you not hope I might feel differently about *love*?"

"You mean...you would consider—" he asked, too surprised to complete his sentence, "You would permit me to..."

"You talk too much, Matthew." I approached him quickly, and when he started again to speak, I silenced him with a kiss.

We left the sitting room and moved into the tiny bedchamber, which was almost completely occupied by the bed itself. I drew back the coverlet, and even in that drafty chamber, which had no fireplace, I soon felt warm in Matthew's arms. I had been undressed by other men, cruelly stripped of my clothing by Mr. James as he sought his purpose and disrobed by Pierce Butler with what I had perceived as love, yet this was my first experience of tenderness. Matthew touched me slowly and gently, the marvel of being together in this way making it hard for him to proceed.

Then gradually his confidence came to him, just as an actor finds his feet upon the stage. Matthew kissed me very deliberately. After he removed my stockings, he graced each of my toes with a long and lingering kiss, first one foot and then the other. His soft hands tenderly removed my clothing, until he himself trembled with the feel of nothing but silk underclothes between us. When not even this separated our warm bodies, I felt Matthew's sweet kisses at my throat as his hands caressed me. For the first time in my life, I responded easily from my own heart, wishing Matthew might remain with me forever in that warm place where I felt no awkwardness or pain or a man's pressing needs.

I had played many love scenes, and even in real life with Pierce Butler had felt love and excitement that a great gentleman should so desire and cherish *me*, as I had believed he did. There had been pleasure of a sort, but suddenly I felt a joy that I had never known. It came over me first in shivers and then in waves of pleasure so encompassing I was aware of no sound other than Matthew's and my breathing and the wondrous embrace of our loving arms, grasped around each other. Breathless, I could not speak nor even try to complete a thought. Even time was still. I no longer heard the loud, regular ticking of the clock upon the dresser or sensed the passing of the hours.

Matthew remained with me that entire night, warm and close. Waking once during the night when cats yowling in the street disturbed me, I did not mind at all my interrupted sleep, so pleasant as it was to rest beside him. He slept very soundly, and as I pulled the bedclothes up more completely around us, I recognized happily that this was love. And I told myself that if it did not disappear at first light like a passing fog or a vapor in the night, then I should surely know how to speak of it without requiring anyone to compose lines for me to recite. I should do well enough on my own.

17

"Water Not to Drink"

Elizabeth and I had determined before I set out for Georgia that I should maintain a careful journal so that all I observed of the actual nature of slavery might be preserved for the perusal of others. I would be as objective as I could, documenting the evil *and* the good, if I should be able to discern any evidence of goodness in it, so that no one could say my account was biased. We agreed that my primary purpose should be to improve with any means at my disposal the condition and the prospect of the slaves, and to this end I began to develop a scheme to teach cleanliness, even to the most minor degree, among the older children.

It is fortunate Elizabeth had convinced me to maintain such a careful record of my observations, since even painful and powerful images may be partially eroded from one's memory by time. Just as the great speeches of plays and the most sublime lines of poetry are often eclipsed by the years for even the most seasoned actress, less important recollections of daily life can easily be forgotten. Not wishing to disappoint Elizabeth, I did steadily record what I saw on Butler Island, weary as I was many nights and terribly discouraged by the pitiful conditions I witnessed all around me.

First, I noticed the absence of soap and clean water. Women are often accused by men of being *fussy* about the cleanliness of children, always worrying whether their little hands are clean and whether they are immaculately turned out in neat dresses, suits, and snow-white stockings whenever visitors are expected. And this *fussiness*, since it must be called such, is an abomination to me. I should never hesitate to drink from a fresh stream if I were thirsty or to pluck an apple from a tree, nor would I have desired my own children to be so awed by dirt that they would have hesitated to play vigorously or to exercise. Yet the opposite swing of the pendulum was in place on Butler Island when I came to dwell there. No thought was given to dirt or pestilence or even the most rudimentary ways of discouraging them.

In almost the same words used by my husband, the overseer Mr. Ogden told me that I might encourage cleanliness among the slaves. He had no objections to that sort of teaching so long as it did not involve reading and writing, which could surely corrupt them, but he warned me that I should find them intractable. "It is just the way of their race," he told me. "They cannot help it. They have a turn for dancing and cooking and brute labor. But a well-bred mare will look more to the care of herself and her young than a slave. It is a fact, ma'am, and you may not like it, but you will soon learn that you cannot apply a white man's principles to slaves."

Like a good journalist, I determined not to take his opinions for fact but to go out among the people so that I might see for myself. I had only been around the house servants, who were filthy enough, so I set out for the cabins where the field hands and their families resided. Our own dwelling, by far the most primitive place I had ever lived, with its bare floors and three main rooms attached to pitiful "closets" for Mr. Butler's and Mr. Ogden's offices, and a dirt-floored kitchen, was a veritable palace compared to the slave cabins.

These *houses* were organized in rows or settlements with a drainage ditch running behind them leading to the creeks and down to the river. All the waste from the houses, human or otherwise, was thrown there to spoil and smell until washed away daily by the tides. Each cabin was tiny, all of twelve by fifteen feet with a few smaller closets, closer than the staterooms of a ship, divided off from the main room by rough partitions. Two families, often eight to ten members each, resided in one of these mere huts, which had bare wood frames and windows open to all weather and a miserable fireplace that let in more draft than heat, but which was the only source for light, cooking, or heat.

The discomfort and the filth of the cabins was worsened by the practice of letting the fowl, ducks and chickens the slaves were permitted to raise and which were their only hope of improving their diet, run in and out as they might choose. These birds were drawn to the waste ditch behind the houses and fluttered in an out all day through open doors and windows, leaving their own filth and depositing more they had picked up from the ditch. The fowl also carried mites and parasites, and I soon learned, as my own clothes became infested after my visits, that the very sand on which these poor houses were constructed abounded in fleas more troublesome than bedbugs. Any time I stood among the people, I noticed that the fleas were crawling over their arms and legs and even their faces. So accustomed were they to this everyday pestilence that they made no effort to remove them. Since their ragged clothes and no doubt their crude pallets were crawling with vermin, perhaps they simply accepted them as part of their daily condition.

I discovered in almost every cabin, squatting around a hearth that had grown cold since the early departure of their mothers for the rice fields, small groups of children from four to ten years of age. The oldest held babies in their arms, whose sole care was their responsibility, since their mothers returned to the field three weeks to the day after they had given birth. These little nurses, as they were called, watched over the infants and carried them to the field to their mothers whenever they required nourishment.

"Why do you sit here," I asked them sharply, "letting these filthy birds into your house and watching your fire go out?" I pointed to the dirt and filth on the floor and admonished them to sweep it out and to chase the poultry from the room.

At first I thought these stunted little beings, hardly like any children I had ever encountered, could not understand me since they watched me so stupidly and remained huddled before the dead fires. So I began to pantomime and was encouraged when they startled to giggle as they watched me go through motions of sweeping and pouring water from a bucket to the floor, adding soap, and scrubbing. I took an imaginary cloth to my own face to wash it clean.

I was encouraged to see at least signs of playfulness and laughter in them, there being vitality and intelligence in laughter of even the roughest, most boisterous variety. So pleased was I at their animation that I asked the oldest girl, who seemed the leader of them all, to bring me a pail of water and I would show them more clearly what I meant.

"No need to fetch water, missus," she told me. "Plenty water for all us need right here." She graciously walked over to the hearth, balancing her small charge on her hip to better manage the weight of the large wooden bucket she brought to the table and placed before me. Reaching in, she pulled out a rusted dipper, bent by many hands and inclined it towards me. "Missus very welcome. But we have no glass," she said, cordially as any hostess presenting the best of her table to a guest.

I could see dirt suspended in the dipper itself and insects floating on the surface of the water. I felt all eyes in the room upon me as I emptied the dipper back into the bucket.

"Missus not thirsty?" she asked, puzzled.

I explained, almost gagging at the thought, that I did not plan to drink that dirty water. I exhorted her to empty that bucket into the ditch and to send one of the larger boys to fetch some fresh water.

She quickly chose a boy and sent him to dump the water in the drainage ditch, stirring up much squawking among the fowl that were pecking in the refuse there. And as he walked away, lugging the bucket, which seemed enormous on his small arm, she asked curiously, unable to contain her amazement, "If missus not thirsty, why she want water not to drink?"

Since all the cabins I visited showed a similar filth and their small inhabitants demonstrated total ignorance of the purpose or practice of cleaning their dwellings or themselves, I proceeded to show them. I asked my small charges to each fetch me a bucket of water using the stout wooden bucket, often better constructed than the cabin itself, found in each cabin. Seeing the scum in most of the buckets, I set the smaller children to finding small branches we might use as scrapers and brushes, since such items were evidently considered unnecessary housekeeping tools for slaves. All the while their eyes were wide with astonishment since they had never before seen anyone "make so much stir with water."

We began with their hands and faces. Since I had found no manner of towels or facecloths in any of the cabins, I had brought with me a supply of rags I had fashioned for the purpose. How pathetic it was that as these poor children had so little, even my rags seemed a gift to them. They were at first frightened by the idea of rubbing water on their faces "for no purpose," as one solemn boy told me, and much troubled by uncovering the heads of the tiny ones they watched so that they might, I feared for the first time in their lives, receive the attentions white children are given daily. It was a custom on the island to cover the heads of newborn babes, despite the fact that they were born often with a full head of thick hair, and seldom to remove these coverings. This increased even more the nesting place for dirt and vermin.

I had not thought to bring soap with me, imagining this to be a staple of daily life provided to these poor people, but learned quickly from the amazed children that they had never seen nor known soap. I therefore contented myself with "washing" their small hands and faces with water until I should endeavor to learn how to make soap with ash and lye and fat, as I had heard it was produced. I had not enough of my own hand soap to distribute to them all. I met with immediate approval from my charges when

I told them that every day each of them showed me his own clean face and hands, and the clean face and hands of the child he watched, he should receive from me a penny. There was no doubt to me that a penny earned meant more to these slave children, for whom all labor was unpaid and expected, than to any child I had ever known.

When all my water and branch carriers had returned, I showed them how to sweep, where there were brooms, and to use branches where there were not, to rid the houses of the dust and dirt of the ages and the droppings of so many fowl. We swept again with sand using our scrapers to scour the floors and then followed with fresh water, a commodity that had probably never touched those floors before. Then I taught the boys how to measure and fashion sticks to fit across the doorsills high enough to impede the fowl but not themselves and how to divide their bare windows with more sticks so that the fowl could no longer fly freely through their houses. I showed them the abundance of kindling wood all around them and encouraged them to gather piles of it. When we had built up the fires in all the cabins so that warmth emanated from each small hearth, and the babies were wrapped again in their poor coverings in rooms that if not wholly clean were much improved in appearance and fragrance, I felt very satisfied. Even these mere *children* had disproved the myth of their own brutishness. If only shown the way, they were quite willing to better their surroundings, and they seemed very pleased by the change in their own countenances. Since they had taken so easily to these modest improvements, I was certain there was much more they could accomplish. I looked forward to sharing their success with my husband, who might have been a "doubting Thomas," but who could certainly not deny the success of my experiment nor the improvement to his *property*.

Then one of the younger girls, Sikey, not a babe but hardly more than five, a serious and quiet child, tugged at the hem of my apron with her newly cleaned hand and implored me, "Now we clean, you give us meal, missus? We not eat since morning."

Their very languor, which I had mistaken for indolence, was then explained to me, learning that they had eaten only a few crusts of corn bread and remnants of porridge from the roughest corn grits left from the night before, very early before their parents were sent to the fields. They could expect nothing more until after nightfall when their parents returned. No wonder they had seemed listless lying around the cold fire. And I had bestirred these hungry children to work! I left them to return to our house to see what scraps and remnants I might find in our larder to share among them. I knew there would be very little since it seemed the practice to prepare only sufficient food for each meal, and what few scraps there were fell to the province of the house servants, for whom this was a great benefit of their *lofty* position among the plantation's slaves.

Mr. Butler came upon me scavenging for more grits and beans and any staples I could find to take back to my hungry charges. He was greatly displeased that I should have "been so taken in" by Sikey's entreaty for food, which had soon been echoed by all the others. "You must not permit them to beg from you," he instructed me. "Their mothers receive their rations, and if they are so improvident as to use them unwisely, then, madam, their children must suffer. You say they are to be respected as human beings, then let them show that they can manage their own affairs."

Although I made no complaint, I could not believe that those starving children ever had enough to eat or that their mothers had been supplied with plenty of food and had rashly squandered their weekly rations. When I returned to the cabins with my small cache of food, I was quickly surrounded by children clamoring for life's sustenance. I had not nearly sufficient means to assuage their hunger.

When their mothers returned from the field, I waited eagerly to see how they should find the improvement we had achieved in their quarters. Several weary women, stumbling to their doors, looked very surprised to see me and wide-eyed at the changes that just a few hours of work had wrought. I had hoped they would be proud of all their children had accomplished and what they could themselves maintain with just a brief period of work in the evenings. I promised to help make soap and together we would fashion towels and facecloths as soon as I could acquire cloth. But they were silent until Callie, a strong, tall woman, standing easily a head taller than I, who seemed to be a leader among the women, tactfully took me aside.

"It is all very good what you do, missus. But when we come back from the field so tired our backs most broke, we can do no more, missus. We leave when the sun barely up and we come back when the sun be to bed. Then we must fix our little food and then we sleep like stone."

That night when I told my husband about their willingness to be cleaner if they had the time to clean, he became upset with me. "*They* know their places far better than do you, Fanny. They know they are here to work, and work they must. What good are these English standards of cleanliness if they interfere with work? We are running a rice plantation, not posing for a portrait," he said disdainfully. Then in a softer tone he cautioned, "You must not consider their situation as if you were experiencing it *yourself*. They are accustomed to the way they live. It is all they have ever known."

I could not take consolation in his words, and wondered, not for the first time, how my husband could sleep peacefully while hundreds of poor beings suffered around him, longing for small comforts which he could well afford at little sufferance to his own fortunes. He denied them because they were slaves, who he did not perceive had even basic human needs, and who certainly could not protest the conditions in which they lived.

I sat at my dressing table, brushing my dark, thick hair, clean and sweetly perfumed, and could not help thinking of those who toiled but never felt the refreshment of a daily bath, nor the pleasure of vigorously brushing their hair before the mirror in slippered feet and a warm dressing gown with a soft bed covered with comforters awaiting them.

I heard Pierce calling me softly, more gently than was his wont. He had invitingly drawn the covers back that I might slip in and join him. His face looked tender in the candlelight, rested and unquarrelsome, reminiscent of days when the strongest differences we felt were over poetry or music. I was soon beside him, wrapped in his arms, warm and safe in the desire that still united us when we were alone and not arguing about my concerns for his slaves. As he caressed me and I felt myself responding to his touch and returning his kisses, I wondered if the slaves had any time for tenderness or if it was all animal-like mating for them, living in those tiny cabins crowded with many people. *Slaving* as they did from dawn to dusk, had they any chance to love, as we might know it, since even their husbands, wives, and children could be cruelly sold away at a master's whim? Surely this uncertainty constantly preyed upon them as a beaten dog always awaits his master's next blows.

I had not realized it, but my sad thoughts made me gasp as if I were in pain.

"My dear, what is it?" Pierce asked, his voice tender with concern. "Did I hurt you?" He brushed the hair back from my face and kissed my neck tenderly as if I were easily breakable. "What is it, my love?" he whispered.

I could not tell him I had brought his unfortunate slaves into our bed, and assured him that all was well. I clasped my hands behind his neck and drew myself close against his chest, attempting to shut out my visions. Soon he was asleep, and I composed myself anticipating I should find better conditions the next day when I visited the infirmary. Unlike some plantations, where seriously ill slaves remained in their cabins, further spreading their disease, or were isolated to barns like ailing beasts, on Butler Island there was a special building erected solely for their benefit.

From its exterior view, the infirmary was an impressive building, particularly when considered in contrast to the tiny, rundown slave cabins. It was separated from the entire settlement by a pleasant space planted in aged orange and apple trees. The two-story building was constructed of white-washed wood and appeared to have received more care in its design than the cabins, which seemed to have sprung up from a crude assemblage of old boards. Only the very ill, of whom I had been told there were few, along with pregnant women, who were taken there to give birth and be attended during their nursing in, resided there. From outside, so ample did the building appear, decoratively graced by fruit trees, I reflected it might be an inducement to bear more children, simply to peacefully reside there for three weeks away from the crowded cabins and the intense labor of the fields. Until I went inside.

I cannot adequately describe the spectacle of depravity I witnessed in that place designated to assist the weak, the infirm, the very old, and new mothers with their babes. It would be no exaggeration to say I feared I would become ill myself once I had begun to breathe the foul air. If I had not been so afraid of offending its pathetic inmates, I should have covered my mouth with my handkerchief and gasped its perfumed protection from such dreadful odors. Although nothing could have protected me from the sights before my eyes.

Upon entering, I was struck by the darkness and could barely see two feet in front of my own face. The ample windows I had seen from the outside were all shuttered, not due to blinding winter sunlight, but because there were no panes remaining in the windows. Sacrificing light, they had fastened the poor shutters, as many as would actually close, against the gusty winds. Even the panes of glass that did remain were so obscured by dirt that they revealed no more light than the shuttered ones. In the great fireplace, all that burned were the dying embers of what could certainly not have been more than a few sticks. Yet still, with some inexplicable hope, these poor wretches, these cast-off souls, lay as close as they could to the fire, as if by their very presence they willed it to warm them, though it barely smoked. The strongest among them, it was only women I could make out at first in the weak light, reached out their maimed, arthritic hands towards this poor fire. Of the others, a few were at least elevated on rude wooden settles, but the majority lay silent without aid of beds, mattresses, or pillows, wrapped only in filthy, tattered blankets, too weak to even cry out in their pain, on the cold dirt floor.

Some were obviously very old women, who perhaps but the day before had collapsed under their burdens in the fields. Then into this damp, drafty atmosphere, which must have increased their suffering and filled their last hours or days with the stench of other sweating, diseased bodies, they were left to die. Having labored since early childhood and given birth to nine or ten or even fifteen "good little slaves for massa," as I had heard them proudly exclaim to Mr. Butler, they were left to die miserably, aching with rheumatism, burning up with fever, without even a sip of cool water to moisten their parched lips, treated with less kindness than an old cart horse turned out to pasture to end his days.

In what seemed grotesque juxtaposition, the new mothers lay suckling their young, beside those in great pain, waiting for their children to be born. They, too, were shivering from the cold, which appalled me as I thought back to the tender, peaceful time I had shared with my babes when they were new. I shuddered, realizing I should have wished them to die in their cradles if I had known a slave's life or wretched death awaited them. I realized my husband would have discouraged my visit if he had considered the operation of the infirmary to be cruel or unjust, leaving me crushed by his heartlessness. That such conditions existed among new mothers and the very ill on a *wealthy* estate, where the masters were thought to be humane and the overseer decent and efficient, made it unfathomable what must transpire for slaves on poorer estates where greater economies were practiced and conditions were not so *humane.*

Elizabeth Sedgwick, always wise and forward-thinking, had advised me to make careful entries in my journal about observations such as these since they were likely to be renounced by the proponents of slavery. It is due to her influence that I am able to quote so precisely what I witnessed as well as the severity of my reactions. I was so overcome initially that I was silent, but when I regained my sensibilities sufficiently to prize away the desperate hands that grasped at my clothing, I was propelled to action.

I instructed old Rose, the midwife under whose superintendence the entire enterprise seemed to operate, to open the shutters covering the few windows that were glazed, so that we might receive even a small measure of light. I seized a large log that I had noticed in one corner of the room and began to drag it towards the fire.

Rose, indeed a motherly woman, which seemed fitting for her profession, exclaimed in horror at my efforts, "Let alone, missus. Let be. What for you lift wood! You have nigger enough, missus, to do it."

Soon an outcry arose from all the assembled bodies, strewn round the room like cordwood, so mortified were they that a white woman, albeit the only able-bodied woman in the room besides old Rose, who had twenty to thirty patients to attend, should lift a hand to help them. I exhorted Rose to send for water and rags so that we might begin tidying up that horrid space. I instructed her to collect the rubbish from the floor of this miserable apartment so that we might properly sweep away the filth in which these women lay.

"You must clean each day, Rose. This room has not been swept out in months, I should judge. And you are the one in charge of this place," I said, unable to keep my displeasure from my voice.

"Missus right. But old Rose care for the people by my lone self. Who to bring water or sweep the floor with all the weight upon me?" she asked, going over to attend the cries of a young girl, scarcely more than a child, who writhed on the floor, her massive belly incongruous, considering her stick-like arms and legs.

I could not deny the justice of Rose's words, as well as the foolishness of my own remonstrances. Even a skilled nurse could not have created decency in that filthy chaos, and should have rightly demanded several chambermaids and assistants to aid her in administering that "hospital." I sent off a girl, perhaps a daughter who had abandoned her own young charges to attend her suffering mother, to go off and fetch water, while Rose bestirred others to help her gather up soiled rags in preparation for sweeping. Rose's helpers seemed so weak I feared their health might be further compromised to satisfy my indignation and felt regretful of the activity my outburst had fomented. I was preparing to depart in search of Mr. Butler to beseech him in the name of all that was Christian to give some relief to these poor people when I was arrested by a dreadful moaning, far more animal than human.

The harsh circumstances of the women lying around me had so disconcerted me, I had given no thought to what suffering might be taking place above my head. But I could ignore it no longer after that moan and the ones that followed it. I passed through the other room of the ground floor, skirting the bodies, barely animate, of two old men whose glazed eyes did not even shift as I walked by them. I climbed narrow, steep steps, much more like a ladder than stairs, with Rose, standing below me, begging me not to ascend. Considering these rickety stairs and taking into account Rose's girth and advanced age, I doubted she ever attended the person who was moaning above my head.

When I came through the opening and bent beneath the low rafters of the roof, I found a solitary girl, somewhere between childhood and young womanhood, attending an apparition. I know no other way to describe it. Before me was the gaunt face of the creature who was making those ghastly cries. Its gender was not discernable to me by way of dress, since its body was covered by filthy blankets bound fast to a pallet. Spittle formed at the corners of its mouth, and all its hair stood out in wild ropes like so many of Medusa's snakes. The room was bare except for a bucket of water and a pan in which lay a few crusts of cornbread.

My terror, and it is no exaggeration to use that word, must have been evident in my face, since the girl I recognized as Patty, the daughter of House Mary, urged me calmly, "Missus not worry. Molly just having one of her fits. She will not hurt nobody."

As if to demonstrate the truth of her words, she approached this seemingly crazed creature and offered her a sip of water from a rusted cup she had dipped into the bucket of water. Molly, as I now knew her to be, docilely accepted the proffered drink.

"She not so bad between her fits. Nobody knows what bring them on today. But she be back in the field day after morrow. I watch to see she not hurt herself when the fits come on. Molly very good worker for massa when she well."

"Does anyone know what this illness is?" I asked, still shuddering as the poor creature began to moan anew.

"It begin when she in her twenties and just come on time to time." Patty studied her charge carefully and then turned to me with the full seriousness of any nurse discussing a patient. "She fine until her babies keep dying."

"How many children does she have?" I asked, fearful from the answers I had received to similar questions.

"Molly have fourteen children. But only four living," Patty recited matter-of-factly. "None of the boys living after Caleb. He run off into the swamp."

The writhing of this poor creature, mother of fourteen, who would soon be back in Mr. Butler's fields, and even the obliviousness of Patty, her poor attendant, to the cruelty that afflicted them both, was sufficient to make *me* have fits. But I climbed down, promising Rose to send soap and bandages and food. I left that place, my clothes soiled with dirt and crawling with vermin so that I wished I might plunge into the water rather than walk home in such a filthy state, which was merely the condition in which they lived all their days.

When I returned to our house, I learned an invitation had come for Mr. Butler and me to visit the McIntyre's in Darien. On several occasions, Col. McIntyre had pleased me greatly with gifts of produce from his ample garden, after I had shared my regret that almost no vegetables were cultivated on Butler Island, save rice itself. Once I had rid myself of the filth I had brought home, not just dirt but the fleas I could clearly feel and see on my own arms and legs, I was gratified by this invitation, not just for its offer of good food and pleasant company and the diversion from our isolated life, but because late that afternoon or the next morning on the ride home, I would have occasion to speak uninterrupted with my husband. Since Margery would stay behind with the children, I might have several occasions when Pierce would be in good humor after a fine dinner and wine, and we would be quite alone. I was certain God's hand had sent me to witness the terrible plight of the slaves in ways Mr. Butler would never know, as he rarely visited the cabins or the remote infirmary. I must make him understand that the improvements I advocated were a matter of life and death for his poor people. I prayed he would be appalled as I to their daily suffering if I could but get him away from Mr. Ogden, who saw the slaves as but so many replaceable spokes in the wheels of the plantation.

18

"The Cold, Dark Ground"

Mr. Butler was pleased by my ready acceptance of the invitation from Colonel and Mrs. McIntyre, since I had often shunned the company of planters, finding they sang unashamedly praises of slavery. I felt slightly guilty at my concealed purpose for our excursion, but said nothing to disturb his good spirits. The McIntyres were acknowledged many counties around for their fine superintendence of their slaves, the bounty of their harvests, and the exceptional quality of Mr. McIntyre's formal gardens, which, unlike those of most planters, boasted ornamental and exotic shrubs. The gardens certainly did not approach the scale of anything European, yet were so tasteful and appealing I had remarked upon them to my husband on a previous visit.

"Any of us could boast such lovely gardens if we had even one half of Col. McIntyre's fortune," Pierce had said disdainfully. "There would be nothing to it. But most of us have more pressing concerns than flowers and ferns. We have rice and cotton to grow. And lest you forget, madam, when you are at the opera or the theatre or cantering around Philadelphia, these simple, less aesthetic products of *my* garden provide the wherewithal for all you enjoy."

I longed to tell him had I known before I parted from my father what I had learned about the Butler *property*, I should never have permitted it to support me for a single day and would have gladly remained an actress. I thought of the hard decisions I had made, first going on the stage out of love for my parents, and then leaving it for the prospect of future happiness with a dear husband. I nearly confessed the terrible error I feared I had committed in becoming his wife, but thinking of our children and the love I could still feel for Pierce when the grip of slavery was not around us, I remained silent.

Soon we had arrived at that pretty estate so attractively cultivated, where the slaves, for like everywhere else in the South that was precisely what they were, seemed more like servants than people of bondage. They were neatly attired, and I could not help notice they were very clean in their persons, unlike the *people* of Butler Island.

"It is far easier to keep servants clean in town than on the island," Mr. Butler said when I commented upon it. "You will find the same when we visit our cotton plantation on St. Simon's Island. It is no magic fashioned by *McIntyre*." I thought I detected a bitterness in his voice as if I had diminished him by making my observation.

No magic, indeed, I thought. Other than soap and water and decent clothing and good food and treatment. But before I could actually respond, Col. McIntyre, his wife, and several of their other guests joined us. We were offered crystal glasses of his prized Dandelion wine and tea sandwiches, the first white bread I had seen in weeks.

"So what do you think of our darkies, Mrs. Butler?" one older gentleman asked me. "I understand that you had not been around them before," he said laughing in a way that suggested he had already consumed much more than the small glass of wine we had just been offered.

"My wife is, of course, an Englishwoman," Mr. Butler quickly interjected. I sensed his concern I might express a troubling declaration against slavery. "She has not had long to establish an opinion. Except for a brief time in New Orleans, she has not been South before."

"Ah, but Southern hospitality is readily apparent, Mr. Butler," this gentleman continued. "Even if your dear wife has only been among us such a short time, she can still tell us how she finds our customs. Although no household is likely to be so accommodating or as charming as this one, Mrs. McIntyre," he said, bowing gallantly to our hostess.

"Certainly not, though many may try," I concurred. Then before I realized fully the insult to my husband my impulsive words implied, I had already added, "Surely not on Butler Island," and then watched as Pierce's face reddened with anger.

"Oh, you are too modest, Mrs. Butler," Mrs. McIntyre graciously interceded, leading us to the table, elegantly set with fine silver and a lace tablecloth. "Life is so much easier here in town. We've many more advantages for entertaining and so can take very little credit if we occasionally succeed. And I will gladly tell anyone that Butler Island lamb is the finest I have ever eaten in America *or* in any of the countries of Europe. I believe this can be credited to the grasses of the salt marsh. Isn't that so, Mr. Butler?" she asked, attentively inclining her regal blonde head towards my husband, while slaves dressed very neatly, even elaborately by Butler Island standards, served a wonderful fricassee of chicken with fresh peas and golden, perfectly shaped biscuits.

"Likewise we can take little credit for that pleasant result," my husband responded, pleased at the compliment our hostess had paid him, "since all our grass is watered by the salt marshes. Hence, the excellent flavor you recall. But that is an area in which Mrs. Butler is really far more expert than I, growing up as she did in the land where the cultivation of lamb has been perfected."

My husband smiled encouragingly at me, I believe convinced he had safely steered me away from a possible digression about conditions on Butler Island to one on lamb and mutton, where surely I could do no harm. I regretted the earlier remark that had tactlessly escaped me and did not intend to create further discord, between us or among the party, yet an amusing story occurred to me.

"I would agree, Mrs. McIntyre, that the mutton fed on the short sweet grass of Butler Island and St. Simon's is raised under precisely the same conditions as the famous *pre sale* lamb that French gourmands especially prize. But I must tell you about the challenge we have had recently in the carving of it."

Perhaps I had myself consumed too much of the colonel's good wine or maybe it was only that the devilish side of my nature, too long confined, escaped at that moment, so that I perceived no harm in relaying a simple event which spoke no ill of Mr. Butler or his *people*. Yet as I began to speak, I saw my husband's countenance stiffen, despite encouraging glances from our host and hostess and the other guests, who, like all Southerners, relished a good story.

"We are served lamb or mutton frequently," I told them, "but it has been invariably brought to table in lumps or chunks of indeterminate shape or size, literally like blocks of wood. I asked our cook why a decent, usual Christian joint of mutton leg, shoulder, or saddle was never served. And I was told that the *carpenter* always cut up the meat, and all he knew was to cut it up much as he would blocks of wood, but that if I should be willing to instruct him, he would be glad to carve it up in any way that pleased me.

"Imagine my mortification when shortly afterward, they called me to the kitchen to meet with the carpenter and a freshly slaughtered sheep. I must confess a lifelong aversion to raw meat, the odor and even the touch of it, nor had I ever served as a butcher or even a butcher's assistant. But having seen their sincere desire to serve me well, which I do believe to be true of all the slaves I have encountered," I informed the gentleman who had originally inquired how I "found" them, "I tried to breathe seldom as I could and proceeded to carve closely as I could approximate, reasonable joints of meat. And now they are quite proficient at it, Mrs. McIntyre, and we should be ever so pleased to send over all that you might desire."

"What an entertaining account, Mrs. Butler. Your reputation is *obviously* well earned. You are clearly accomplished in more ways than I had ever imagined. I should surely be pleased to receive a few legs of your excellent lamb and a shoulder roast," Mrs. McIntyre answered graciously, "if not cut by your own hand then by your own direction."

I dared not look at Mr. Butler, but sensed from others' expressions that he was seething. I felt rescued, thankful as any actress for the prompter's cue from the wings when the older gentleman happily replied, "Well, I am pleased you have found your darkies wish to serve you well, Mrs. Butler. This is invariably the case where kindness and good treatment rule. But I am still curious to know how you find them. Some of the abolitionists tell such outrageous tales of mistreatment and cruelty."

I suppose as a loyal wife I should have deferred to Mr. Butler, much in the manner I had accepted his editing all reference or reaction to slavery from my earlier diary. I struggled to hold my tongue, thinking of the poor wretches I had visited just the day before, languishing in "kindness and good treatment" on that infirmary floor or hidden in its dark attic. I felt the pressure of Mr. Butler's shoe against my foot and suddenly there seemed no other conversation at the table. All the motions of eating and serving had halted as if a command had been given for their cessation.

"This is, as my husband said, my first experience living among slaves, sir," I answered, trying to keep my voice diplomatic as a pastor asked to comment on the beauty of the homeliest child in his parish. "So I have insufficient experience to comment on their overall condition."

"Oh, come now, Mrs. Butler. That is truly spoken like a diplomat," he replied. "You are among friends here. Surely you may simply share your impressions."

"Well, then, I will share them if I must," I ventured, seeing all eyes turned to me and feeling the slaves who served us were listening, ever still behind the masks they assumed as respectful servants. "I should have to say I find it as unnatural a state in practice as I had ever supposed it to be in theory. And although far crueler to the enslaved, harmful and disastrous for both slave *and* master."

"Yet you were just saying that you found our darkies—we do not call them *slaves*, you know—desirous of serving us well. Now why should that be the case, Mrs. Butler, if they are poorly treated?" the old gentleman asked, intent on pursuing the fault he believed he had discovered in my logic.

"For the same reason that a beaten dog still curries his master's favor. What recourse have they, sir, when every scrap of clothing and crust of bread and even the choice of whether their husbands or wives or their own precious *children* may be sold away resides in the hands of their masters?"

"But they are ill-suited to any but the most unskilled labor," he stated emphatically to the approbation of several of the company. "We must watch out for them and *someone* must be their masters, or they could not survive. Who would care for them in their illnesses and provide for them when they are old and can no longer work?"

And before I, or anyone else could comment, he continued, his tone again quite affable. "And have you not heard them singing in the fields, Mrs. Butler? They could not raise their voices so well if their hearts were heavy. There is a song some of the older darkies sing," he reflected happily, "that starts, 'Let the herald trumpets sound. For massa in the cold, dark ground'. Surely you must know it?"

I waited, hoping someone else would respond so that I should not be obliged to answer or suggest to this gentleman the ambiguity of the lyrics, which might as easily be said to celebrate a master's passing as to mourn it. Yet no one spoke, and I felt all eyes turned obligingly to me.

"I am more familiar with the song based on the Scripture of the ancient Hebrews, sir, I am afraid," I answered carefully, knowing that Mr. Butler should be displeased by my response. "'Go down, Moses,'" I quoted. "'Way down in Egypt's land. Tell old Pharaoh to let my people go.'"

"Perhaps, since we have finished dining, we should adjourn to the drawing room for coffee," Mrs. McIntyre suggested quickly, leading the way. "Thank you, Susie, for a fine meal," she said to the solemn, dignified young woman of beige complexion who directed the other slaves in attending us at table. I wondered, perhaps unfairly, if such graciousness to her *servants* was her rule or if it were done on this occasion to demonstrate for my benefit how kindly they were treated.

"I also love to hear the singing of our people about the plantation," she confided as we walked together from the dining room ahead of the gentlemen. "But tonight I hope you will avail us of a different kind of music, Mrs. Butler. I am told you sing beautifully, and your husband has confided to me that you miss your piano. I hope you will grace us with some music this evening."

I had not considered it until the moment of her invitation, but so absorbed as I had become in the hardships of our people, I had forgotten the pursuits that had formerly occupied hours of my days. I hardly read or played a single note on the piano, not having even the crudest instrument available on Butler Island, and only wrote daily the dreadful record of what passed before me, a transcription of human cruelty and misery devoid of any pleasure which true literary creation afforded me.

Once we were alone, Mr. Butler was livid, although there had been no evidence of this in his public countenance the remainder of the evening. He was quite charming and even consented to play the flute accompaniment to a lovely Scarlatti cantata while I played the piano and sang the soprano part. But once we had parted from the others, he upbraided me.

"I cannot imagine how you found it appropriate to discuss such things at table," he snapped at me. "I realize, of course, that *I* have not had all your advantages, but to bring up the carving of *raw* meat at table. What were you thinking?" he snapped at me, attempting to keep his voice down for fear our voices might be heard by the McIntyres or their guests. "And growing argumentative over the songs slaves sing in the field. I have listened willingly to all your complaints and the faults you find with everything that isn't conducted according to your own tastes and—"

"That is unfair, Pierce, and you know it."

"I know nothing except that I expressly asked you *not* to discuss your feelings about slavery with our neighbors. But you cannot desist, not even for *one* evening."

"I did not intend it. You know that is the truth," I pleaded with him, appealing to the better part of his nature, which I still believed would not be unfair, even in his embarrassment at the mention of anything reflecting ill on his plantation or rekindling arguments with his family about his bringing me to the South. "I had to answer, Pierce. He asked me directly, and you saw yourself, he would not desist until I answered him. If you wish to know what I truly believe, I think it much more likely the slaves are *dancing* when their masters are underground than lamenting their absence. Not after the conditions I have witnessed."

"Just what have you seen?" he asked suspiciously, pulling me around roughly to face him. I had been sitting at the dressing table brushing my hair in preparation for bed.

"You surprise me, sir," I said, pulling away from him. "You have hurt me." I pressed my advantage, rubbing my forearm where he had grabbed it.

"I am sorry, Fanny," he said sorrowfully. "I was agitated, but I *never* meant to cause you pain." His face seemed kind again, touched as it was by regret. "What was it you wanted to tell me?" Then he listened without interrupting as I described conditions in the infirmary and the daily hunger among the people. I watched him grimace as I described the filth, the cold, and poor, aged Molly moaning, tied to her pallet in the attic of the infirmary. "That damned Ogden," he muttered. "He should see to these matters. They should not descend to such a state that you need involve yourself."

"But I don't mind. If you would grant me the little means to do it, I should be very glad to make such small improvements as I can. It will not cost very much in cloth, food, soap, and firewood. I am already teaching them to clean, and if you should see your way to let Rose have a true assistant, it would make such a change in the care of the sick." Observing that his face had not hardened against me, I implored, "If I might have a carpenter's services for but two days to fix the windows and make more bedsteads, this is all that would be required. It is not much to ask for these people who have worked their entire lives for you. I *beg* you, Pierce."

"This time then, I shall provide what you ask, Fanny, since it concerns you so deeply. But such matters cannot become a regular subject of our conversation. I pay an overseer good money to assure the care of these slaves."

"Then you had best find another one if he deems it proper to send young women into the field only three weeks after they have given birth," I replied hotly, regretting at once, at the sight of his face, my interference in his business and my criticism of this man whom he considered such a credit to the estate.

"That may be *your* opinion, Fanny," he answered angrily, "but we are fortunate to have William Ogden. Not many would do as fine a job and produce such an excellent return on our investment or be willing to live in such an isolated place. Please do not forget that the plantation operates to make money, not to promote the comfort of its slaves."

"Have no fear that I shall ever forget that, Pierce," I responded with a bitterness that I can still feel even though many years have passed. "I am reminded of it every time I see their faces and their suffering."

I cannot say what reaction I expected from my husband, but to my surprise I saw that he was preparing to leave me. He had drawn his long cloak around him and pulled on his kid gloves.

"Where are you going, Pierce? It is very late. Surely everyone has gone to bed on this plantation and in town."

"As I have told you previously, it is very unbecoming of a wife to question her husband's comings and goings. I *shall* not account to you for my every movement."

"But *please* stay," I urged him, trying with all my might to detain him, dreading to see the state to which our relations had deteriorated and fearing what pastimes he sought at that late hour. "Let us talk as we used to, dear Pierce. Surely we can do that. Do not go out so late on this cold night."

"I shall be warm enough in this," he said, indicating his cloak and smiling coldly, chilling me to my heart. "Besides, it is not talk I seek."

"At this hour I cannot imagine what establishments you would find open to welcome you."

"There are places where a gentleman is always received, madam, regardless of the hour."

"Pierce, *please* do not leave me," I implored him, clinging to his arm. "If you are not yet ready to join me in bed, I will sit up awhile and read to you if that will please you. Or I am certain if you wish it, I could find someone to bring you some tea or a glass of whiskey. But please do not go away from me," I beseeched him, fearing what might come to pass if he did so.

"Your solicitude for my welfare is truly very laudable, Fanny," he said stiffly, almost as if he felt bound to thank a servant he held in poor regard for a service nonetheless properly performed. "It is, however, too little, offered far too late, since this very evening you saw fit to belittle me and Butler Island Plantation to our hosts."

I begged his pardon for my unfortunate words earlier at table, but also implored him to see how preposterous it was to expect me to witness the monstrous things I had seen and not be able to speak of them so that they might be remedied. No person of feeling, with a true heart beating in her breast, could be silent before such suffering.

"So there we are once again," my husband said triumphantly, startling me as he pulled my arm from his sleeve and firmly pushed me aside. "It is always about you, is it not? No one else has any feelings and the only point of view to be considered is your own," he continued, glowering at me.

"But, that is changing, Mrs. Butler," he said coldly, looking at me with such intense dislike that at first I believed I was having a terrible nightmare. "I should have listened to others *genuinely* concerned for my welfare, who warned me against marrying a spoiled, self-important creature like you. But I would not listen." He laughed cruelly. "I was too infatuated, like all of America, by the *great* actress," he said sarcastically. "Though right before me there was one lady, truly a *beautiful* young girl," he declared, staring unkindly again, as if drawing a comparison to every physical defect of my person, "who loved me and wanted nothing save to be married to *me* and to please me. She was so lovely," he said wistfully.

"Then you should have married her," I cried angrily, feeling my heart breaking with humiliation and wondering desperately who this young lady might be who still haunted him.

"In *that* observation, you are absolutely correct, madam." He drew his cloak around him and gathered tightly the cravat at his throat. "I should have married her and I *would* now be a far happier man. As she would not have constantly berated me to my face and to others about the management of my affairs," he wistfully reflected. "But alas, I did not marry her while I had opportunity, and now I have lost her. It is my own fault that instead of her devotion, I preferred the grand spectacle attending you, and so I am left, madam, with no choice but to play my part opposite you. But for now, I have my cue to leave this stage," he said, looking with gratitude to the partially open door. "I believe all my lines have been spoken." Then he smiled, seemingly pleased with his own wit. "I bid you good-night."

"Pierce, please, do not go off this way," I begged him. "I know you do not truly mean these unkind words," I insisted, trying to convince both him and myself. "It is simply your anger speaking. Indeed I have given you some cause for displeasure with me, I am afraid," I demurred, lowering my head to him. "But this is not so serious. It is only a quarrel that happens time to time in all marriages."

"You do not comprehend anything I am feeling, madam, nor what I have felt since we were wed. I believe you do not even understand your own feelings and actions, accustomed as you are to reciting fine utterances conceived by playwrights while audiences listen spellbound by the mere sound of your voice. But I am afraid that now, at least tonight, I cannot bear anymore of your speeches."

Then despite my tears, which should have softened the heart of any man who had so often professed to love and cherish me, Mr. Butler closed the door between us. I did not know then the truly serious import of this exchange, only that he was determined to leave me. He had spoken more coldly towards me than ever before, even when I had violated his wishes. I feared where he was bound that night and was desolate I had not the words or wiles to stop him. I hoped it was but a single night's disgrace and that he would regret the cruelty of regaling me with his memories of a previous love. I prayed it was an argument to be rectified on the morrow and longed for sleep to soothe my hurt, but it would not come to me, and I lay awake throughout the night, wondering the identity of this "beautiful girl" who still possessed my husband's heart, even as the skies began to lighten.

19

Tying Up

The next morning I had little time to brood over Mr. Butler's late-night behavior, since at breakfast he was very solicitous to my wants and encouraged me to share stories and anecdotes with our hosts that he found particularly amusing. When I expressed my desire to take a morning ride, since the colonel had graciously offered me the use of any of his fine mounts which might please me, Mr. Butler quickly offered to accompany me, something he had declined to do for some time. I was very relieved and also much gratified when later he was friendly and talkative as we began our journey home. I felt from his sociability that my husband regretted his unkindness, which made me hopeful of restored happiness between us, even though I should never know what pursuits or companions he had sought the night before after forsaking me.

As soon as we returned to Butler Island there were many matters requiring my husband's immediate direction, as well as two gentlemen who had traveled over to see him on business. He was so constantly occupied that for a few days, save at meals, I rarely saw him. But he was very cordial even in our brief encounters, and as one who is always happiest herself when actively occupied, I turned my attention again to bettering the condition of the poor people around me, still mindful of doing nothing to provoke my husband's displeasure.

When next I visited the infirmary, I found it remarkably improved. An aromatic soup or stew bubbled in a large caldron over a warm fire. The residents who could comfortably sit up had been pulled closer to the hearth to enjoy its light and heat. The floor was swept, and even those who were not in beds lay at least on clean straw pallets with blankets. There was a fresher odor in the room, and though some of the broken panes had only been covered with oiled paper instead of glass, the shutters were opened to fill the room with light.

There was even a lively hum of conversation. Before, the only sound had been poor Molly's moans and the pathetic cries of those imploring Rose to bring them food or water. It was still the most primitive setting imaginable for the beginning or the end of life or in which to restore the afflicted to health, but it was not the same place I had seen a week before. Instead of dirty rags on the floor, awaiting their next use, there was a neat stack of fresh bandages.

I did not seek nor desire praise or thanks from the slaves. It was sufficient for me to see that their suffering had been lessened. Yet as I moved through the rooms, I did notice a strange reserve among the patients. Women who had before joyfully greeted me with, "Welcome, missus. We be too glad to see you," averted their faces and appeared to feign sleep or deafness, literally anything that would permit them to avoid speaking to me. They would not even meet my eyes. When I asked how various ones among them were feeling, they answered uniformly, as if they had been coached, "How do, Missus. We much better today," and then turned wearily away as if they were all overcome by weariness.

"What is it, Rose?" I asked the busy midwife, whom I noticed was wearing a clean apron. "Why will no one speak to me?"

She who was usually so garrulous was silent, as if she also feared to exchange words with me. Then at my insistence, she confided quietly, "They be scared, missus. After what happened to Ruby, Sabine, and young Patty."

I was immediately chilled by her words, as I am when ominous tidings are first revealed through well-crafted foreshadowing in a tragic play. Observing the frightened faces all around me, I knew some terrible act had been perpetrated to make them fear *me* when on my first visit, I had merely dispensed the few comforts at my disposal.

"This morning, Mr. Ogden had them flogged for complaining to the missus."

"But they did *not* complain to me, Rose. They simply answered my questions."

"That may be, missus. But when Mr. Butler ordered this place be cleaned, Mr. Ogden come in here yelling. He say the women have no business complaining to you or massa about going to the fields when their baby be three weeks since that is how it has always been on this plantation and nobody is harmed by it. And that Patty wrong to tell you old Molly is like she is because she birth too many babies."

I thought of Patty, yet almost a child, beaten with that leather scourge I had seen hanging in the barn and carried by the drivers to the fields. And Sabine and Ruby, still weak from childbearing, torn from their infants and beaten because, lying weak in the damp cold of that bare room when I had stopped to admire their babies, they had bemoaned having to part from them and return so soon to labor in the rice field, after which, as Ruby had told me, "our backs feel most broke in two."

"But we got good soup now, missus, for the sick ones," Rose said, obviously concerned for *my* spirits, as she stirred the caldron which sent up such an appealing aroma. "It not much, but missus welcome to taste it." Then she patted my arm sympathetically. "Don't you take on so, missus. Only Ruby and Sabine was tied up. Patty only flogged," she reported reassuringly.

"Tied up? What *can* you mean, Rose?" I quickly looked around the room, expecting to see these two women bound and tied up in a corner. Having always, even in times of studious pursuits, been myself inclined to frequently move about a pleasant room, I contemplated the unpleasantness of being confined in a miserable one. I was relieved not to find them so encumbered. In fact, they were nowhere to be seen.

"Oh, they not here, missus," Rose explained, quickly gathering that I was searching for them. "Molly well enough to go back to the field so Patty gone, too. Sabine and Ruby had four days to come of their three weeks, but after what they say, Mr. Ogden send them back to work."

This seemed incredibly harsh for poor Molly. Despite her fits, which in a just society would be sufficient to excuse her from any kind of labor, she looked so aged that she seemed more ready for the cemetery than the rice field. For Sabine and Ruby, able-bodied though they were, their precious three weeks rest with their babies had been foreshortened when even the original interval was far too brief a time to recover from childbirth under ideal circumstances.

"Missus really not know about tying up?" Rose asked in surprise, interrupting my bitter thoughts.

I shook my head and turned to her for an explanation.

"On most plantations when they very angry, they tie up a slave," she said, speaking calmly, as if she perceived herself, because of her important stature as midwife, safe from such treatment or because she had witnessed this cruelty so many times she was inured to it. "They strips off your clothes in front of all the people gathered around and then they takes your thumbs and tie them together and then strings you up to a tree so your feet barely touching the ground on your tip-toes. This way you got no way to back away from the lash and it bite into the poor flesh harder. But that not the worst part."

I had heard accounts of slaves doused with turpentine or rubbed with salt after beatings to inflame their afflicted backs. Since Mr. Butler had assured me of the kind treatment of his *people*, I could not believe such practices were ever carried out on Butler Island. But already reeling from the knowledge of cruel floggings my indignation had spawned, I waited, steeling myself for what Rose would describe.

"The overseer calls on one of the men to do the flogging," she told me. "But not just any one of them. If she has a husband, he choose that one. If she do not, then he choose her father or the boy she courting. And if they tries, because some of them do, to go easy on her, then the overseer will give him even worse."

"Rose, how do they not run away from such a horrible thing?" I knew as *mistress*, my hated position, that I must never express to any slave my sorrow and horror at their treatment, or my feelings that they would be justified to flee, but my words poured forth before I could control them.

"Some do, missus," she said, shaking her head in dismay. "But it do no good. They got no food and no money. They just wanders round and round in the swamp not knowing where they going. If the alligators not get them first then the snakes surely do. Or finally they come back not looking like a person no more, all swole up from the mosquitoes and the fever and the snakes. If they *make* it back. But most end up like Molly son, Caleb. The men was rowing when they find his body—what was left of it—down by the river where the alligator drug it. And ever since she heard, Molly not been right in the head. First they try to beat the fits out of her but that not work. Now the driver send her to the infirmary when they come on her."

She surveyed the room, now fresher and more comfortable for those who remained by the fire or on the pallets about the room. I wondered if all those who lay with closed eyes were truly sleeping or listening to our conversation and hating me afresh for my part in bringing about these terrible punishments.

"Now, missus, you not fret so," Rose beseeched me. "This place much better," she said cheerfully, "and nobody expect to escape the lash forever. It come for us all."

Mr. Butler had no sympathy for my outrage about this unfair punishment of his slaves for merely speaking to me. So unperturbed was he by Mr. Ogden's actions that I could not help but fear he had ordered them.

"Do not make yourself ridiculous, Fanny, with such accusations," he said, drinking his morning tea and offering me a plate of biscuits, much as if we had been casually discussing the weather rather than the beating of young mothers and the turning of an insane old woman out to hard labor.

"How could you allow it, Pierce?" I had not intended to have this conversation in front of the girls, but there seemed no way to avoid it. Fan, always sensitive, began crying at the sound of our raised voices, and Sal, who had been so intent on her sausages that we had forgotten her, asked a thousand of her questions. "Why was someone beaten? Why was it Mother's fault? Why was someone insane—whatever that might mean—which rhymes with pain and Jane?"

"There, you see what you have done?" my husband said triumphantly. "You have upset our own children and made matters worse for the very slaves you wish to help. I hope this shows you why you should not interfere in the business of the plantation. How could you imagine I could not bring your concerns to Odgen, *egregious* as you described them? The operations of the plantation are his business, and I will not be able to retain the services of a skilled overseer like him if you or even *I* constantly meddle in his affairs. Besides, you saw for yourself that improvements *have* been made in the infirmary. This was expressly what you wanted." He put down the newspaper he had been reading and stood up. "Come, Sal, you shall go with me on my rounds this morning," he said cheerfully, scooping up the still sobbing Fan up and handing her to me.

"But I cannot exist, Pierce, where no one is even safe speaking to me," I insisted, following him outside. "I do not know what I shall do if the smallest improvements I suggest or any comment I relate to you shall result in punishment of these poor people."

"Please refrain from being so *dramatic*, Fanny," he said disdainfully, using the word he often chose when seeking to disparage me, "and leave the care of the slaves to those who best understand their needs. This plantation has run successfully according to a system established long before you or I came here. Besides," he said in parting, taking Sal's tiny hand in his own, "we shall be leaving shortly for St. Simon's. I believe you shall find yourself much happier with life at Hampton Point, both in its setting and by the condition of the people in a place much less remote than these rice swamps. They are making you far too gloomy a companion."

20

"My Brother's Keeper"

Besides despairing that my husband's love was fading, I feared the consequences of his gambling. Perhaps it is every wife's hope that this is the vice that separates her husband from her company, since the more common cause is far too disturbing to consider. In my case, having surrendered all my income to my father when he had returned to England, I worried that I, and my children, should be destitute if the *gentlemen* who frequently came to see my husband at odd hours for heated conversations, as well as his intense concern for one so wealthy about the most paltry expenditures of daily life, foretold financial disaster. His assurances that I should be happier on St. Simon's Island made me eager to go to that larger, less isolated place where we might spend more time in society, visiting with other families and sharing pursuits such as riding, music, and reading poetry, which had brought us such pleasure in the past. In a more cultured setting, I hoped that my charms, such as had once enraptured him, might dissuade him from cards and gaming and other vices I dreaded to contemplate.

I was also disturbed by his increasingly quarrelsome nature. It was humiliating that he insulted me during his fits of temper, but I worried if he should unleash his contemptuous temper on someone else, this person might do him violence and leave our children fatherless. After reading an account of a duel in the Brunswick *Dispatch*, I could easily picture Mr. Butler involved in such a ruinous, barbaric event. The article reported that two planters, Mr. John Wylly and Dr. Thomas Hazzard, both of our county, had been feuding for some time over a piece of land, disputing the boundary between their two plantations. So angry and heated had their argument become that they challenged each other to a duel, in the spirit and conventions of an earlier, uncivilized century. They stipulated that each should wear over the region of the heart a piece of white paper to encourage a lethal shot. The most horrifying aspect of their quarrel was their decision that whoever should emerge victor should have the privilege of cutting off the other's head and impaling it on a stick on the very piece of land that had been the root of their quarrel. It amazed me that such a ghastly plan was constituted by two *gentlemen*. It would have seemed more worthy of savages, as the planters considered the slaves to be, but no slaves I had encountered would have considered such a brutal undertaking.

More horrifying than their threats was their actual meeting, not in a field near their disputed property, but in the piazza of the Oglethorpe House, a refined hotel in Savannah. The newspaper account indicated that when they came upon each other by surprise and exchanged words of disagreement, Mr. Wylly struck at Dr. Hazzard with his walking stick. At that moment, they were separated by another gentleman of their acquaintance. But later the same day when their paths again converged in the doorway of the hotel, Mr. Wylly spat directly into Dr. Hazzard's face. The doctor drew his pistol, the ready equipment of any Southern gentleman, and fired from close range so that the ball passed directly through Mr. Wylly's heart, killing him almost instantly.

It was this same degree of blinding rage and anger in which I could imagine Mr. Butler embroiled. Although not born in the South, he appeared to have inherited, along with these slave plantations, all the intense pride and belief in honor, be it actual or false, that constituted the code of Southern gentlemen. His dignity was easily offended, and he was moved so quickly to anger, I could readily imagine his demanding satisfaction for even a minor insult.

A few weeks before, I had watched in shame and consternation when he passed angry words with a planter from Darien. It had begun as a simple exchange of pleasantries when our two parties chanced to meet in one of the establishments on the square. Mr. Butler was bargaining with the owner of the general store over a very large order that would see the plantation through the coming year. I had separated from him to examine several bolts of brightly patterned cloth that I knew would please the women on the plantation. Once they had discovered that I could cut the patterns for dresses and sew them up tolerably well, one of the benefits of attending a good French boarding school, they begged me to sew dresses for them and to teach them how they might do so as well. I had rolled out several bolts around me and was ruing the high price and inferior quality of these wares as compared to Northern goods when I was startled by angry voices behind me, the loudest of which was Mr. Butler's.

"Take back those words immediately," I heard him say. "Or with certainty, you shall answer for them!"

"Mr. Butler," the shocked man interposed, "I do beg your pardon. I made only a passing comment about the decreased value we are offered for our cotton. It bears upon us all. Certainly *not* just upon you," he explained. He was a tall man, far more imposing than Pierce, yet I sensed from his worried expression and his very deferential tone how deeply he feared my husband.

"Mr. Bryan," my husband replied, his face reddening with anger, "when you make remarks about the decline of Sea Island cotton, a matter about which I am certain you are also misinformed, you denigrate the enterprise to which my family's fortunes have long been committed. It has been noted at all the markets of Europe that ours is the finest quality cotton ever produced. *Nothing* and no one shall impugn its reputation. No competitors shall ever endanger it. How dare you insinuate that it is less valued in the world market!"

"Again, sir, I beg your pardon," Mr. Bryan said hurriedly, his voice shaking, and others gathered round, including his wife, who tightened her hold on his arm. "I meant no disrespect, sir," he continued cautiously. "It was my mistake entirely to assume that you, as most of us, might be planting more in rice to accommodate the declining market for cotton. I regret my error and meant no disregard for you or for Hampton Point's fine cotton," he said placatingly, the words perfectly correct, yet something in his obsequiousness suggested he spoke only to avoid my husband's irrational anger.

"I gladly accept your apology, Mr. Bryan." My husband extended his hand and shook Bryan's warmly, clearly of the mind he had well acquitted himself and preserved his honor, even though Mr. Bryan was absolutely correct about the ascendancy of rice in our fortunes.

I could hear others muttering in disbelief as we walked away. Leaning on my husband's arm, I spoke with animation about the cloth I had selected and my plans to organize a sewing class, hoping in this way to distract him from the comments that followed us, and which I knew would infuriate him. Pierce was gaining reputation as a volatile, imprudent man in spite of his wealth and position as the planter with the largest standing in the region.

The next morning, hoping to reassure myself that my husband shared the horror most people would find in the murderous quarrel between Mr. Wylly and Dr. Hazzard, I sought his opinion. After I had poured his tea and added cream and sugar to his liking, I asked how he viewed solving a property dispute in this way. I longed to hear him say he shared my revulsion over Mr. Wylly's violent, needless death. But that was not his answer.

"For a gentleman, there is only one choice, my dear. It is always an honor and an *obligation*," he said appreciatively, genuinely pleased I should consult him, "to stand up with another gentleman on the field of honor. A pity, though, about poor Wylly. I recognize that to a lady, his fate seems very hard. But there was nothing else Hazzard could do after receiving such insults."

I understood without further illumination why any person should deplore being struck with a cane or being spat upon. Still, I was shocked that Mr. Butler, a man of sophistication and education, should think being shot in the doorway of a hotel to be a death befitting a gentleman or a reasonable way to resolve a boundary dispute.

"I was not referring, my dear, to the physical provocations in this matter," my husband responded, "but to the insults Dr. Hazzard withstood. I have heard more of the particulars than this writer knew," he said, looking disdainfully at the newspaper I had resurrected to discuss with him. "There are words which once spoken to a gentleman *cannot* go unanswered. And I fear in such circumstances, there is only one answer which will suffice."

I pressed him to elaborate and must admit ashamedly I was hoping his answer related to words spoken against a man's wife. I *longed*, there is no other word for it, to have him say with his old gallantry that he would never allow words to be said and not retracted that spoke ill of his own dear wife. I should not, of course, have condoned dueling to amend such insults, but would have been pleased to know he still held me so dear.

I wondered if he knew of such circumstances in the sad matter we had just been debating. If so, it then seemed logical that Mr. Butler would believe emphatically that an insult to a gentleman's wife should affect him as powerfully as an insult to his own character or the quality of his cotton or the mettle of his horses. But this was not what he expressed to *me*.

"If another gentleman accuses one of dishonest dealings or cowardly actions, his accusations must be answered or one could no longer remain a gentleman. Many things one could suffer," he explained, meeting my eyes very solemnly, "but loss of the high regard of other gentlemen would be intolerable. If anyone should dare impugn my good name, I should gladly accommodate him with whatever weapon he might choose."

Other planters, as well as slaves, had informed me that as the weather warmed, it was not safe for whites to remain near the swamps surrounding the rice island plantations. The risks of yellow fever and malaria outweighed any benefit a master might make by superintending his own property.

"The mosquitoes too many and the fever too mighty," House Mary proudly told me, "for missus and master. Only the *people* can be here the whole year round."

It was a further revelation to me that during the hottest seasons of the year, even the *overseers*, white men still but not gods like the masters, could not remain safely on the rice plantations, so severe was the threat of sickness. Slaves themselves would occasionally succumb to the fever despite daubing themselves thickly with mud to escape the insects' bites, but whites were so endangered that for several months of the year, the head man of the plantation, himself a slave, maintained the sole authority on the plantation. He had no gun or other weapons besides his whips and scourges with which to subdue a potential uprising. Yet so absolute was this slavery, that no one spoke of any time when an attempt had been made to overthrow even the head man's authority. It would be very safe for us to depart Butler Island for the drier, safer climate of Hampton Point.

"Massa come and go like the seasons," head man Frank resignedly told me. "But we always here when he come back."

I was gratified by the fifteen-mile row, the labor not mine, of course, to reach St. Simon's Island. The fresh air was always delicious to me after the oppressive heat and stillness on the island. Near the end of our journey, we traveled through a veritable labyrinth of tributaries and branches into which the broad river raveled like a fringe as it stretched to the sea. As we approached, the conch was sounded just as our arrival had been announced on the rice island. After traversing a narrow *cut* or channel of water separate from the main stream, we came upon the famous long-staple cotton fields of St. Simon's, white and abundant as fresh snow.

As the slaves came rushing out to greet us, truly descending from all directions, I felt the excitement of their first sighting of us, just as we had been so regally greeted on Butler Island. In the spirit of exuberance that enveloped us, my recent parting with the *people* that morning was a painful contrast. On the rice plantation, the slaves had been so sad, even despairing, at my departure that I feared what might transpire for them after we were gone. I knew that the improvements I had wrought were small enough, but sensed their dread that without *my* small voice, all advancement of their condition should cease. I promised that we should return, and Mr. Butler assured them that I was correct and that they would hardly have time to miss us before we were back among them, but I still saw their tears and again had to pry their imploring fingers from my clothing.

In my desire to be once again on solid ground, I was longing to escape Butler Island, the place itself, since surely I could not escape slavery. With every possible inch of land given over to rice cultivation and the need by a system of dykes to flood the entire vicinity for irrigation, hardly any solid, dry land remained. There were no horses on the island, but even if I could have found a mount, there would have been scarcely space on Butler Island for me to enjoy my most favorite pastime. I walked the few paths that were dry enough and not so thick with snakes, but was mostly confined to rowing in the small boat made especially for me by Mr. Butler's slaves. Yet this was no substitute for a brisk gallop on a spirited horse. I looked forward to the *freedom*, a word whose context had become intensified for me, to pursue the pleasures that should be open to me once again on firmer ground.

I noticed immediately as we made our introductions among the *people* on St. Simon's Island how many were of light complexion. This was a startling contrast to Butler Island, where almost every slave's countenance was so dark as to indicate that the blood running through his veins was unadulterated from the beginning of time. I asked Mr. Butler why he thought this might be, curious to know if a darker complexion was considered better protection against the mosquitoes and so more desirable for slaves cultivating rice.

He laughed at such a foolish conclusion, advising me that it was merely a matter of proximity. "On Butler Island, there is almost no access to white people, other than the overseer and the owners. On St. Simon's more whites visit the plantations, socially and in the course of business. And though it is discouraged, there is more contact among the slaves of the neighboring plantations. More mixing is, of course, to be expected," he said matter-of-factly.

The contradiction of such logic struck me like lightening. The slaves were considered savages, yet when whites had opportunity to *mix* with them, they chose to take advantage of it. Why would proximity make relations with these *barbarians* suddenly more desirable? I did not think this *mixing* occurred only to produce more slaves for the plantation, or, in the case of their masters, solely to satisfy their sensual desires. I believed there was a lure on both sides, although on one, all acts were of free will, while on the other they were coerced or done for privileges as pathetic as a handful of sugar or a small morsel of meat or as urgent as a mother's hope that by winning her master's favor she might prevent her babies from being sold away. I even questioned the wisdom, as well as the morality, of creating a greater supply of slaves through this mingling of the races, since it appeared the mulattos on the plantation seemed quite the most dissatisfied and restless members of the slave population.

Renty, the obvious offspring of the former overseer Roswell King, who had come back to visit the plantation during my time on Butler Island, seemed more cursed than blessed by his lighter complexion. He complained whenever he was assigned heavy work and brazenly declared to Mr. Butler that he should be given special considerations, such as the right to own a small gun for shooting game, an unheard of privilege for a slave, "on account of my color." He was always looking for gifts that Mr. King might have left behind for him, although when he visited us, Mr. King took no special notice of Renty and certainly never acknowledged the young man's patrimony. But he had no need to do so. It was written on both their faces.

This same *writing* was much more apparent at Hampton Point. As we were making our rounds, I asked Mr. Butler, "Did you notice that child which was just presented to you? The little boy born since last you were here to that absolutely *filthy* woman wearing the soiled petticoat over her dress as if it were an apron?"

"Yes," he said, not truly looking at me, so intent he was on lighting his cigar amid the breeze blowing off the point. "What about him? A well-formed little fellow to my way of thinking."

"And of very light complexion."

"Yes. This happens time to time, Fanny. You *know* that," he said, impatience creeping into his tone. "Certainly this comes as no surprise to you."

"But do you not think that he bears a striking resemblance to Mr. King?"

"Very likely his child," he said in an off-hand manner, as if the matter were far too trifling to warrant further discussion.

"And what about Driver Bran? Would you not say that he also favors Mr. King exceedingly?" I asked, referring to the young man of quiet mien and grave countenance who exercised great authority on the plantation when the overseer was absent.

"Quite likely his brother, born when his father, the older Mr. King, superintended the plantation."

Later that noon, we were served dinner by a young man whose extremely light color and regular features also bore striking resemblance to Mr. King, although his sole acknowledged parent was a very black woman named Sinda. In visiting the cabins, I also made acquaintance with Betty, a dark and serious-faced woman who proudly showed me her cleanly kept room. I noticed that she, too, had a ten-year-old son of very light complexion, even though her husband, Driver Ned, was dark-hued as she. I could not curb my inquisitiveness and asked her how such a thing could come to pass, even though I felt certain I knew the reason. Still, I wanted to see how she would answer me.

"Jem is my son by Mr. King," she told me sorrowfully. "I tried to keep from his way but he would follow me. I could not say no or he would order Ned to be flogged, stripped of his job, and sent to the hardest field work. Ned is too old to stand up to that, missus. And it is the same for the women without husbands. If they complain to massa about the overseer, then when the babies come, soon as they eat from table, they are sold away. It will happen, if this be the overseer's will."

I could say nothing in return, other than to comment on how well formed were *all* her children. I had not power to assure her that such wrongs should never be allowed again. Though Mr. Butler still regaled me at our supper of the wonderful improvements made to Butler Island and Hampton Point during the tenure of the Roswell Kings, both father and son, I could not convey to him my absolute disgust at the conduct of his paragon overseers. Dreadful enough that slaves forfeited the right to their own labor, but even worse that they were bred according to their masters' or overseers' plans, as if they were beasts of the field, rather than men and women, husbands and wives.

I learned day-to-day of even further cruelties perpetrated by the former overseers. It appeared that old Mr. King "would not stand for quarrelin'" among the married couples. If he heard of husbands and wives who fought or even raised their voices in the Quarter, he would simply shift them to other cabins as indiscriminately as if they were curtains or bedsteads. It was the same for women who refused his advances or later those of his son. If they "kicked up a fuss," they would be bred with any man around the plantation of his choosing. They might bemoan their fates to the heavens, but who would hear them? Certainly not Mr. Butler. Even if he were present he would not *hear* them, since he cautioned me not to accept as God's truth all that was shared with me by the slaves. I believe it was from true conviction that he told me, no doubt aided by the thinking of his overseers, that "the *people* cannot help telling falsehoods. A lie comes much more easily to their lips than a simple truth."

Still, my husband did hear the lamentations one evening from a *gang*, as they were called, of the pregnant women of the plantation who had requested to speak to him about the severity of their work when they were heavy with child. Our domain there, a rambling farmhouse in need of repair, was more capacious than our dwelling on the rice island, but still afforded me, sitting with my sewing in another chamber with my windows open to the breeze, full account of what was said. Since so often my entreaties for these poor people caused much disagreement with Mr. Butler, I had purposely absented myself from this audience.

"Missus tell massa why we call?" I heard their leader ask tentatively. I recognized the voice of Nelly, a tall Diana-like woman, fine bodied and muscular.

"No, she did not." His tone was curt and unwelcoming. He was determined, he had told me previously, not to encourage them in their complaining as he said was *my* wont.

I could not see, but I could imagine the others standing so close to Nelly that their shoulders were pressed against hers, their swollen bellies tight under the rude clothing they were given. They were silent, but if she faltered, they would support her under the great scrutiny of their master.

"How massa feeling this nice evening?" Her tone was polite and very friendly, counting on whatever cordiality she might engender in that proud young man, who wielded all the power in her world. I knew *he* was not smiling, but sensed from the murmured greetings that they were all smiling. They were after all, his *people*.

"I am quite well," he said. "I believe the good air here is truly soothing to my rheumatism."

Then there were several outcries of pleasure. "Praise be." "That be a blessing." "Praise the Lord for helping massa." Their voices were so grateful for the health of their master, one might have imagined that he had already granted their wishes or that their own wretched health had been improved.

"Fact is, massa, many of the women suffer from the damp most dreadful. And now that we are carrying as we are, the weight 'most kill us. By end of day, our poor legs and ankles so swollen we have too much pain to sleep."

He said nothing, but I could imagine his countenance, handsome in repose, but so stern, even with me, when perturbed.

"We ask Mr. Odgen, but he say nothing to be done but to do our portion as soon as we can and then there be more time to rest. There nothing he can do to alter our task. The work must be done."

I had learned that both plantations worked on the task system, by which each slave, child to man, was assigned a task of work to be completed each day. If it were completed early, then the slave might occupy himself however he pleased for the remainder of the day. If the work were not completed, as the pregnant women complained was often the case for them in their later months, there would be grave consequences paid in floggings, increased tasks, and reduction in their poor rations.

"Mr. Ogden is correct, Nelly," he affirmed. "The work must be done, and it is the same on both plantations. You *know* this. It has always been the way."

"But many of us now older, massa. We 'bout wore out between working the fields and raising all the children. If you could lighten our load the last two months when we so large, massa, our dresses 'bout split and the mosquitoes so heavy in the field and the fever comes upon us."

Another brave voice called out, "If please, massa, could we rest from the field in the heat of day? When it pass, then we go back to tend massa's fields even stronger. If we could but rest when we so weary," she implored.

For a moment there was silence, solemn as if a prisoner in the dock of a great court were waiting for the judge to pass sentence. I could hear Mr. Butler's steps as he walked back and forth, considering his decision.

"Very well. I will have a word with Mr. Ogden about *whether* your tasks may be lightened slightly in your late months and if the *older* pregnant women might have a brief rest period during the middle of the day. But see that you make good use of it and that you finish the tasks assigned to you. We will *not* have slackers on this plantation. Now that is all. Good-night."

But then as they began to walk away he called them back, hardly needing to raise his voice, so attentive and fearful were they of his every word. "Do not try to plant any foolish ideas among the *people*," he admonished them. "You must still return to the fields three weeks after your babies are born. I do not want to hear from Mr. Odgen that any of you has kicked up a fuss about that. Three weeks gives you plenty of time to rest, since no work is required of you save the care of your new babies. You are allowed to rest all day, not even troubled by your other children."

I listened as he further recounted the beneficence of the plantation to them, and I felt sickened, especially knowing that Mr. Odgen referred to some among them as "good breeders" and that their children were not considered their own children, but instead so many colts or shoats or calves for sale at his or Mr. Butler's will.

Then I heard the sound of the women's happy voices as they walked away bidding him good-night. They had won a small victory.

"I hope you were listening, Fanny," he said proudly when he came in to join me shortly after that for tea. "Did you hear how easily their requests may be settled when both sides are reasonable?"

A most peculiar request came to me from Cooper London. He was one of the most highly valued slaves on the Butler Island plantation for his great skill in the manufacture of all the wooden tubs, barrels, and casks in which everything was stored, as well as for the great moral influence he exerted over the slaves as their spiritual leader. Cooper London was always very clean and neat about his person, and his clothes, although the poor raiment of all slaves, had been very carefully used. I imagined him to be a man of close to forty years with a wiry strength about him. He presented his request for prayer books with some urgency, knowing with summer descending on the islands, it would soon be time for us to leave.

He was the minister to the slaves, self-taught, dignified, and very accurate in his depiction of Scripture, although he had no advantages of education or training. The slaves were permitted only once per month to go into town to attend church, the moral instruction both valued but also *feared* since it might elucidate their poor treatment to these poor wretches or bring them too much into contact with slaves from neighboring plantations and foment rebellion. Therefore, Cooper London was allowed to conduct his own weekly service for the slaves and such weddings and funerals that received the approval of the master or the overseer. It was in attending one of these services that I first became aware Cooper London could read, a remarkable feat for a slave since they were denied all education, and anyone who taught them to read or write risked punishment by imprisonment or *death*, depending upon the severity of the offense.

"I very much enjoyed your leading of the service," I told him the very first time I attended. "The order reminds me of the service to which I was accustomed as a child. How did you learn to read so well?" I meant to congratulate him on his accomplishment, which I knew had obviously been garnered on his own time after arduous days of work.

Immediately, I saw the fright in his eyes, so similar to that seen in the eyes of a trapped animal. I had not meant to cause him pain, but clearly I had disturbed him.

"I can make out a few *words*, it is true, missus," he admitted. "But I cannot *read*," he insisted, his eyes downcast.

"But *certainly* you can. I have heard you reading the prayers to the people every Sunday. And you read them very, very *well*," I said, wanting so much to praise this good, somber man.

"It is only memory, missus," he told me. "I have always been that way. Once they have been read to me, verses stay in my mind. It has always been so."

"That may well be, and it is a blessing," I agreed, thinking sadly that this man's fine mind had been so misused by slavery. "But truly, who taught you to read? I have seen you do it. You have no need to be afraid to admit it. I should just like to know how you acquired the skill. One day I hope that all who wish to may learn to read."

"Well, missus, I just try." He struggled uncomfortably to respond, as if answering me would set him upon a bed of coals.

"Now, Cooper London, someone had to teach you," I insisted, in my own youth and indignation completely misinterpreting his reticence. "Who was it?"

"Missus, I just learn," he answered evasively, speaking softly and avoiding looking into my eyes.

"But how did you manage it? I remember myself how I was taught by my father when I was but a tiny girl," I told him, recalling with pleasure those sessions at my father's knee.

"I cannot say, missus. I suppose heaven helped me."

I was about to inform him that heaven might work many miracles but had not been credited with teaching people to read when I finally understood. He *dared* not tell me who had taught him and tried not to admit that he had such accomplishment for fear his teacher might be revealed and imprisoned or put to death for defying the laws regarding the education of slaves.

For this reason I was mightily surprised at his request for as many prayer books and Bibles as I could possibly purchase for him from the North so they might be distributed "among the people." I felt certain that for some, these books were perceived as powerful charms and amulets and not desired for any purpose of education, so inscrutable would the written pages have seemed to them. Yet so much did these people crave the bright and the gaudy that I hardly felt so many would desire the plain, black books I might provide if not to *read* them. I deduced that the art of reading was more widely spread among Mr. Butler's slaves than he had any idea.

"It is good of you to be so concerned about the welfare of all the people, Cooper London," I said. "I will do my best to obtain them for you," I promised. "What gave you the idea to ask me?"

"Missus has been very kind to the people, and so she would surely help if she could. And I must ask as minister to the people. For is it not written, 'Am I not my brother's keeper?' Just as massa is the keeper of all the plantation."

There was no irony in his face or tone. He had respectfully asked a question and stood humbly awaiting my answer. I could not quickly decide if it would be fitting to tell him that Cain was asked about Abel's welfare that he might show himself to his Maker to be a faithful brother, but his answer to God revealed his own duplicity in Abel's death. This passage from the Bible did not correspond with Mr. Butler's "keeping" of the slaves for his own benefit. I considered whether I should simply disregard his second statement and thank him again for working so diligently to instruct his people. Or perhaps implore him to enlighten me how he could maintain belief in a religion that afforded him such a horrid life and might put to death anyone who sought to open his mind to words.

In the end, I did not reply, but assured him I would find him some prayer books and Bibles, and in parting pressed into his hands a small Bible I had been using to teach Sally her verses. It was not a fine edition but had gold lettering upon its cover and a brightly colored frontispiece showing Jesus with his disciples.

"Oh, no," he protested. "This is *your* book, missus. It is much too fine for *slaves*. I cannot take it."

I pressed it on him and drew away quickly before he could return it. I did not wish him to see my tears, which I could neither contain nor dare explain to him.

21

The Poisoned Table

Matthew wrote late into the night, trying to compose the play that would convince Americans to abolish slavery. As he concentrated on matters to assure our company's future, he confided that he could no longer bear to write about love or laughter and drawing-room scenes involving the antics of ladies and gentlemen. These were our bread and butter, but he felt haunted by the suffering of slaves. Ever since encountering a coffle of ragged slaves being driven through the streets of Richmond, he believed it his mission to awaken Americans to the beastly cruelties of slavery.

We had begun spending all our leisure hours together, but there were many nights when I left him still writing when my eyes would no longer remain open, as well as mornings when I rose to find him laboring still. Before leaving for my morning walk, I would shake him gently to rouse him since he had collapsed into sleep over his worktable, surrounded by the crumpled, false starts of an entire night.

On a few occasions, in the morning I smoothed out the crumpled pages to see if a plot might be successfully emerging so that I might offer him encouragement. But a structure to support his ideas seemed uncertain, and his constitution clearly weakened from the late nights, lack of sleep, and poor diet. He rarely consumed more than a few bites at mealtimes, fortifying himself mainly with cup after cup of strong tea, and while he sought to conceal them from me, I heard him attempting to smother fits of coughing with his handkerchief.

"If I could only envision a compelling setting, I can convince them of the evil, my dear Isabel," he told me. "But I cannot simply recite a litany of evils. Audiences should not wish to see such a play and would just think me a didactic reformer. If only I knew someone who has witnessed slavery firsthand, watched masters working their slaves, eaten food prepared by them, and seen the sad course of their lives. Then I could create a protagonist through whose eyes the story could be easily told. But where am I to find such a witness?"

I said not a word, hoping he would answer his own questions as he so often did. I busied myself clearing away our tea so that my face should not betray my memories of Meacham Farm and the slaves I had known closely. Their condition was unlike the harsh stories I had heard during my American travels, yet they were enslaved and lived daily with the terrible knowledge that at any moment they could be sold away to fall under the cruel treatment of a new master. They carried with them the history of how they and their families, if they could remember them, had arrived in bondage in America. Rachel's stories would likely never fade from my memory, though I had not known Moses or Caleb well enough to know if upon their backs they bore scars from beatings suffered before they came to Meacham Farm. Perhaps when sufficiently riled, even Thomas Meacham, who had always comported himself so civilly, had exercised his right as a master to physically chastise his slaves because there would be no one to oppose him. I cringed thinking also of Minda, who had brought so many slave and white babies into the world and had surely saved me through her ministrations. In a different world she could have been a respected nurse. Instead, she was only a valuable piece of property.

"What is it, Isabel?" Matthew asked solicitously, rising and putting his arm around me. "You shivered just then as if you had seen a ghost, and your face is suddenly so very pale."

"It is nothing," I said smiling, returning his embrace and shaking off his concern. "Just an odd, passing thought. But tell me, Matthew. Why do you believe Americans do not comprehend the full cruelties of slavery? You are naïve to think them ignorant of its customs. Surely you do not imagine you will be thanked for informing Northerners who enjoy the fruits of slavery how its harvest is prepared, nor for showing Southerners what they already know is true yet prefer to forget?"

"My word, Isabel," he exclaimed, his eyes opening wider in surprise. "I believe outside of a play that is the longest speech I have ever heard you make. It is odd it should be about slavery when in your life as a milliner's assistant, you hardly encountered it."

"That does not mean I have no feelings about it," I answered defensively, still careful to offer no further explanation. I had never shared how I came to find myself "between engagements" at the Virginia Manor. I had revealed little to Matthew about my past besides my place of birth. London was such a large city, I had no fear he might make an inquiry or meet an acquaintance that would somehow lead him to my mother and father or Mr. James.

"I have never met such a secretive lady, Isabel, particularly an actress. In my experience they comport themselves as if they are on stage even when they are not and wish always to be the center of attention. One would think by your own reticence you are a fugitive who has committed an atrocious crime and is afraid she will accidentally incriminate herself."

"Let me reassure you, Matthew. Imperfect as I am, I am more sinned against than sinning. At least in the most serious matters. And if other actresses are so arrogant, can you not simply be happy I am not conceited?"

"I can be very happy with you, my dear Isabel," he whispered softly, his lips at my throat as he led me back to bed. "In all possible ways."

"Matthew really, I cannot," I protested, though I was fairly helpless against his tenderness. "I must get to the theatre. I have a rehearsal and a meeting with the costume mistress."

"They can all wait a short while. Remember you are *the* leading lady. They cannot do without you," he said as he cushioned the pillows beneath my head. "You should enjoy it."

"And I do. But it is not a good idea for me to be late and so convince everyone of my conceit."

"No one who knows you could possibly think such a thing. And if they do, I shall personally correct their impressions and tell them you were detained taking pity on a poor playwright suffering through the twentieth draft of a play that could not be written without your encouragement."

I speculated what kind of encouragement he referred to since he had begun kissing me—my eyes, my throat, and my hair—and was caressing me from head to toe, at first intensely and then reverentially, as if he were overcome with love for me and had put slavery aside. I cannot say how we became undressed, but quickly I found myself so tightly embraced by Matthew that I could not have extricated myself even if that had been my wish.

"We must be careful," I whispered, my pleasure slightly interrupted by my fear that I might again become with child and ruin my present success and all my prospects.

"If only you would marry me. Then we should not have to worry about that prospect," he whispered, clearly understanding my meaning. "We should not steal about like criminals instead of lovers and could instead be happy about whatever our love brings. But never fear, my darling," he reassured me, taking something out from beneath the covers. "The French are far ahead of the rest of the world in matters of love."

And shortly afterward, as we lay together in each others arms, I asked him teasingly, "Are you now encouraged?"

"I know you are having your fun with me," he said smiling down on me. "But actually, in all ways I am. In fact, I have just decided how I shall construct my play. It has occurred to me just this moment. I shall call it *The Poisoned Table*."

"Sounds awfully cheery, Matthew. I hesitate to inquire how it unfolds."

"I thought you would never ask," he said happily, propping himself up on one elbow as he proceeded enthusiastically with his description. "It is set, of course, on a plantation. I believe a fairly remote one. The master and the mistress of Golden Isle Plantation will be brutal people without a shred of kindness between them. They think nothing of meting out the cruelest punishments and are so mean that they begrudge their slaves an extra biscuit or crust of bread, and are much more concerned about the health of their horses than of their slaves.

"I have not sketched it out fully, of course, but I think the entire action shall take place at the dinner table in a handsomely appointed room where the entire family, waited upon by slaves, is seated at dinner. Picture a table covered with platters of food and goblets filled with wine. The slaves stand silent against the walls, serving their masters, but never speaking unless addressed. Suddenly one of the youngest children cries out in pain and falls out of her chair. And then everyone is writhing in pain or running from the room in agony."

"It sounds frightening, Matthew. But what can this possibly have to do with slavery?"

"Everything, I should think," he continued, slightly bothered I had interrupted him. "The cook, a trusted slave who has served long on the plantation, has poisoned them all. I have not figured it out yet, but I believe there will be another slave, an old woman who brings the cook some poisonous herbs, which are then cooked into the family's dinner. For their evil acts, as the agents of slavery, they are poisoned at their own table."

"It sounds dramatic, but how could such a terrible thing actually happen?" I asked incredulously.

"Why should it not? How could any retaliation be surprising from those who live daily in fear of floggings, starvation, and the fear that their family and loved ones may be sold away? Why should they not hate their masters and want to take revenge?" he implored me, his voice rising with passion.

"Because they are beaten down and hungry and without any friends to help them who are not slaves themselves. And they have witnessed so much cruelty they would be terrified of what might be done if they were apprehended."

"Perhaps it has occurred even if we have not heard of it. If it has not, it is only a matter of time, Isabel, before a courageous slave decides to right the countless wrongs. Wouldn't you strike out against anyone who harmed you or threatened to sell away your children or your husband?"

"How can I know, Matthew? You would do better to write something more believable. What if you wrote about one slave rising up against the overseer when he beats a woman in the field for not completing her task? He makes that stand, even though he knows it will bring down the wrath of his master. But still he does it."

"That would not be sufficiently important or symbolic," he insisted. "I want to attack the very foundation of slavery, the assumption that no matter how badly abused, slaves will continue to serve their masters. I want to show the defeat of slavery at the very table where the slaves are forced to serve. The perpetrators of evil will be served up portions of their own poison."

"Where could you perform such a play?" I asked incredulously. "It would never be shown in the South. I am uncertain it could even be performed without outcry in the North, where the abolitionists speak out. You intend to show slaves *murdering* their master and even their *mistress*!"

"But what a master and mistress they shall be," he said excitedly, warming to his story. "I shall cast you as Louisa Tarleton, the mistress, who chooses to be present when slaves are beaten and punishes the house slaves by starving them or selling their children away. You will be brilliant. It shall be your greatest performance," he exclaimed with true pleasure.

"She sounds *terrible*, Matthew. Thoroughly evil."

"You need not *like* her, Isabel, you have only to portray her so the audience fully comprehends what unbridled power does to those who possess it." He smiled, greatly satisfied with his own vision. "Besides, villains are the greatest characters of all, every actress's dream. One cannot always play Juliet."

I agreed, recognizing I needed to seek roles to demonstrate my full ability. I could not rest upon my beauty, which would fade, or upon standard repertory.

"Well, I must set to work," he said, rising and quickly pulling on his clothing. "Now that I know my direction, I must waste no time in accomplishing it." He leaned over to kiss my forehead, and then impulsively hugged me close to his chest so that he was speaking into my ear. "Just wait and see. You will be wonderful as the mistress of this tragic plantation. This role shall define you on the American stage. You will surpass even Fanny Kemble," he proudly predicted, little knowing the special meaning his words would have for me.

22

"Kicking Up a Fuss"

We had returned to Butler Island, weary and hungry from the slow boat journey on a breezeless day when I learned that a terrible event was about to occur. No one told me directly, but I detected an unusual quiet as the house servants went about their work amid a tension thick as fog. I saw nothing amiss among our possessions, poor as they were on that island. I looked them over immediately since I had heard of slaves flogged viciously over the breakage of a prized soup tureen. I did not wish them to suffer untold agonies awaiting my discovery that some object had been destroyed when I should never have complained of it, even if the object broken or mislaid had been of actual consequence to me. I had already witnessed Mr. Butler's displeasure at the theft of a ham, which resulted in a flogging and the cook's demotion from the relative ease and good rations of a house servant to the harsh labor of the field. I had tried to hold my tongue about so many daily cruelties, but knew I could not remain silent if someone were to be harshly chastised over a broken teapot or missing cup of sugar.

Happily, I found nothing missing and everything in its place down to the napkins for our table. I determined the best plan was to occupy myself with Sal's lessons, which she had been only too glad to neglect during the many rounds of visits on St. Simon's Island, to wait for whatever was amiss to be revealed to me. Several times that afternoon I heard my husband conversing heatedly with one of the men, but unlike some days when he reported to me on the decisions of his day, this time he stayed away. It intensely distressed me not to know what was transpiring, but I busied myself with the dress I was cutting out while Sal, at my feet, practiced letters on her small slate.

After a time, House Mary asked if she might speak with me. When I assured her we could discuss anything she wished, she remained silent, looking uneasily at Sal. Sensing she deemed what she had to say far too serious to state before a child, I called for Margery, who was tending Fan, an increasingly inquisitive baby, to take Sal away with her. Margery, who was bathing Fan, sent in her stead, Psyche, called "Sack" by all, her assistant nursemaid. Psyche was a pretty and tidy young woman, always neat about her appearance, as were her two children, both under age six. Like many of the *people*, she and her husband, Joe, were born on Butler Island, where their old mothers and fathers still worked. It was the entire world to them.

I had always observed Psyche's sad demeanor, which was not surprising to me, since I believed the daily experience of slavery so dreadful as to take away anyone's inclination to smile. But on this day, Psyche, as mythology tells us the personification of the soul, looked to me as if she had lost her own. I thought to speak to her, but with Mary standing patiently by and Sal carrying on with one of her child's tales, it was not the right time to inquire.

Yet soon as Sal had gone off with Psyche, Mary implored me, "Please missus, it not my place to interfere in massa's business. Nary before I ever say a word. But poor Sack, her heart about to break." Then she waited, watching my face for the sign that she had my leave to tell me what terrible fate was to befall Psyche at Mr. Butler's hand.

"What is it, Mary? You may speak freely to me."

"Missus not heard when Joe come from the fields to see massa. He find out just this morning before you return when Mr. King come by the cabins, that massa made a present of Joe to Mr. King. And he will take him to Alabama when he leaves end of the week. But he has no wish to buy Sack and her babies. They shall never see each other again."

I was so shaken to discover a family was to be separated in this way in a world that I inhabited, that I turned over my full sewing basket. Thinking of my own small children near the same ages as Psyche's own, I could at first not speak, torn as I was by the vision of having my own children sold *with* me or away from me or having my husband, an outrageous thought under the circumstances, given to someone as a *present*.

"Does missus understand?" Mary asked, watching my silent face, concerned that she had not made her meaning clear. "That why Joe was sobbing this morning. He say he never will leave his family or the island where he was born. Massa told him there is nothing to be done about it since massa owns Joe and Mr. Ogden owns Sack and her children. Will missus help?"

Mary's face was hopeful at the thought of my intervention, yet I knew how weak my powers were to help *anyone*. She was a woman of kind, gentle mien, inured to her burdens and never took advantage of her proximity to me to ask for favors. She had finally asked for my support, with obvious fear of angering me or Mr. Butler, and I felt helpless to assist her. If I expressed my horror at what Mr. Butler proposed to do with Joe, then I would be acting disloyally to my husband, but I felt I must intercede before this terrible tragedy befell poor Psyche and her family. I had heard of slaves hanging or drowning themselves to avoid being sold away and had never thought I should witness such sadness on the Butler plantations, where I had been assured kindness reigned.

Running out in search of my husband, I encountered first Mr. Ogden, who was coming into our house, which for most of the year was his office and *his* dwelling, to work on his books. I came upon him so suddenly I accidentally knocked the papers from his hands, and while we were gathering them up, he commented on my obvious distress.

"You seem in such an awful hurry, ma'am," he said, squinting, as was his way. "Any way that I might help you?" Even so many years later, I still recall his slow, deliberate speech. He moved clumsily like the great bear of a man that he was.

I asked if Joe would be sent to Alabama with Mr. King, leaving behind his wife, children, mother, and father.

"That is the case, ma'am. It is a rough journey where Mr. King is bound. He says he will not be bothered with a woman and young children. They would be much in the way. So Joe must leave them behind," he simply informed me. "It happens time to time."

My worst fears confirmed, I went to search for my husband, knowing there was nothing Mr. Ogden could do to change this dire situation. I felt him squinting after me as I hurried down the sandy path to the water where Mr. Butler was directing carpenters on the alterations to a light craft used for our afternoon excursions.

"Pierce, my *dear* husband," I said when I had gotten him off to the side for a moment. "I appeal to you, not just for Joe and Psyche, but for the sake of your *own* soul, please do not commit this cruelty."

He looked at me in annoyance. His expression showed the impatience one might feel towards a troublesome child.

"Still you persist in meddling in matters which you cannot help and do not understand," he said, sadly shaking his head. "This circumstance is nothing out of the ordinary. I am well within my rights to reward Mr. King with a gift commensurate with his meritorious service. It is my decision to make, Fanny."

"How can you make it and remain a moral man?" I endeavored to hold my voice down since Joe's fellows stood nearby, but so dreadful was this decision to me, to speak calmly was very difficult. "You have said yourself what a fine worker Joe is, a truly excellent model for all the slaves, and that he and Psyche maintain their children and their home so well. And *this* is how you reward them? You break up their family to make a *present* of this husband and father to Mr. King?"

"I shall not tolerate your interference in my affairs," he said, quietly seething with anger, glancing at the slaves who were watching us. "And your accusations towards my integrity incline me even less to listen to your arguments," he said calmly, as he turned away. "If you are so interested in the future of souls, concern yourself with your *own*."

Then he left me, I will admit, crying by the side of the road. I waited a few moments, hoping that when his temper cooled he might change his mind, as was sometimes his way. But he did not look back at me, much less utter a kind word to which I might make entreaty. I returned to the house feeling miserably about what I could not prevent, and at my husband's indifference.

Toward evening, after the children had been put to bed, I sat alone reading, or I should say trying to read, this sad subject still so much on my mind. I had not been able to eat a bit of my supper for the sadness of it. Mr. Ogden came into the room, our sitting room being the only place with sufficient light in the evening to permit him to examine his accounts. I asked if he had seen Joe that afternoon. I dared not bring up the matter again to Mr. Butler, and thought Mr. Ogden might pass on to me some word of how Joe was withstanding this ordeal. I still feared he might harm himself in his grief.

"Yes, ma'am, I saw him. He is a great deal happier than he was this morning."

"Why is that?" I could not imagine a mere day's time should make the separation from his family less troubling to him.

"Well, ma'am, he is not going to go to Alabama now. Mr. Butler told Mr. King that Joe had continued to kick up such a fuss about it. So Mr. King said if the fellow wasn't willing to go with him, he did not wish to be bothered with any niggers down there who were bound to be troublesome. He said he might as well stay behind."

"Does Psyche know this, Mr. Ogden?"

"Yes, ma'am, I reckon she does. I passed her just now and she was smiling like a child at Christmas."

I took a deep breath before I asked what I most wanted to know, all the while calculating in my head what might be the total value of all the ornaments, jewels, and trinkets I possessed. I doubted if they should fetch nearly enough to purchase a woman and two children, but I had no other money to speak of since making over my fortune to my father. It reviled me to think of actually *purchasing* slaves, but I realized that only if I became their owner could I really be certain Psyche and her children might not be sold away. Joe belonged to Mr. Butler, who surely would not now propose to sell him, if even Mr. King did not want him as a present since he so strenuously protested his separation. But Psyche and her babes could be sold at any time, singly or together, at Mr. Odgen's whim.

"Mr. Ogden, I have a particular favor to ask of you," I forced myself to say, ignoring the loathsomeness of becoming a slave owner in my own right.

"Yes, ma'am," he said agreeably, though his squinting still made him an inscrutable man with whom to converse.

"Please promise me you will never sell Psyche or her children," I implored him, "without first letting me know of your intention and permitting me the option of buying them."

Mr. Ogden rubbed his eyes and then turned to me as if trying hard to see me clearly. "Dear me, ma'am, I am very sorry, but I have sold them this very day."

I gasped aloud in horror at the hopelessness of these poor people's lives. Joe had been saved, but now this brutish man before me had just obliterated Joe's future and happiness by selling his family. How could he and Mr. Butler be so insensible to the brutality of their actions?

"I am so sorry, ma'am," he said again, obviously upset by my distress. "I didn't know, ma'am, that you entertained any idea of making an investment of that nature. I assure you if I had, I would willingly have sold the woman and her children to you. But I sold them this morning to Mr. Butler."

So it ended well for poor Psyche and Joe. Mr. Butler had resented my unmeasured criticism of the morning, but my words had not been without some good effect. He had brought these poor creatures under his protection, where I trusted he would secure them from any future misery of this sort. Still, I wondered at his silence, after witnessing my terrible anguish at our supper table when it would have been so easy for him to tell me my fears had been allayed.

Perhaps, I speculated, he did not want to give me the satisfaction of seeing he had taken my entreaties to heart or that I *could* influence him to make such decisions. Later that night as we sat together, he with his wine and I with my cup of tea, I thanked my husband for his kindness.

"I am glad they are happier now. And that *you* are happy," he answered, though he spoke without smiling and his expression showed no gladness.

We drifted into silence over our books. My husband's relaxed, untroubled expression, as he perused a popular novel, evinced no sign that he had so closely escaped a decision that no act of repentance could have vanquished. I worried that my respect for him might disappear entirely, just as the morning tide washed clean the shores and creeks of Butler Island, leaving nothing behind in its wake.

23

"Going Home"

I could escape slavery on the water. After instruction in rowing by Jack, a young man assigned by Mr. Butler to accompany me on my long walks and to serve as general man servant, I developed a fine proficiency in rowing my small craft, *The Dolphin*, named for those magnificent creatures who sometimes leave the ocean to swim up the Altamaha, where they cavort wildly, creating much consternation among the other creatures of the river. I had outfitted my craft with green-flowered chintz cushions of my own design stuffed with Spanish moss so that it was quite comfortable, even for Mr. Butler, who still suffered greatly in his joints.

Out on the water, where I could not observe the slaves working, I temporarily left behind their daily torments. I was exhilarated to be laboring with oars in my own hands, all the while enjoying the magnificent live oaks with wind-swept branches festooned with thick, trailing moss. I never tired at the sight of waterfowl, with their iridescent feathers and varied markings, and even the great, prowling birds of prey gliding overhead, ever watchful for their opportunities.

Whenever we were in company and I described my explorations to the other ladies, they were invariably amazed I should venture alone on the river or *wish* to exert myself when I had hundreds of slaves I could direct to row me the length of the river, if this were my pleasure. Since they themselves, in their ridiculous shoes, most unfit for walking, would never have considered walking even a half a block, they found my desire for exercise as disturbing as had I conversed with them in my camisole.

One lady I visited in Darien teased me good-naturedly as several of us sat in her drawing room intent over our needlework, an art in which, fortunately, I could well acquit myself, so they did not find me totally lacking in *normal* feminine pursuits.

"Perhaps this yearning for exercise is an English taste," my hostess mused, regarding me thoughtfully. "Like lamb and mint jelly or your numerous puddings. Since I have never before met a lady, Mrs. Butler," she noted with wonder, "who longs so much for work when all around her are so many hands ready to assist her."

She spoke, ever oblivious of the slaves who silently attended us, yet could surely have enlightened her about their "readiness" to perform their daily-enforced *exercise.*

"But I do not consider walking and rowing my small craft to be *work* at all. It is a pleasure to me. I think I should become quite ill if I did not daily take some vigorous activity to enliven my blood."

"Since you mention the matter of your *blood,*" another lady rather indelicately conjectured, "perhaps this fascination with exercise is a consequence of your former profession. Your *family's* profession."

She paused, perhaps to assess my reaction or to permit her comments to have full effect upon her rapt audience of neighbors. I felt my face flush and dared not glance at the other ladies, who waited for conversation to resume in a drawing room that had grown very quiet.

"Since until recently Mrs. Butler was a celebrated actress," she explained, obviously pleased by her own logic, "this explains her *need* for exercise. She is *accustomed* to far greater excitement than we are. Indeed, coming from an acting family, Mrs. Butler has lived always among ladies who *work,*" she continued, her tone seeming, at least to my ears, incredulous and disdainful. "For us, the regulation of our households and the care of our husbands and children provide sufficient occupation. But you are accustomed to the praise of admirers in London, Paris, and throughout our northern cities. It is no wonder you must now rely on your exertions to make up for the lack of such attentions in our very quiet world."

By this time I was certain jealousy colored her tone and explained as well the deprecating laughter of several of our companions. They envied the perceived glamour of my former life on the stage and yet still derided me, and my mother and aunt before me, for *working* to earn our family's daily bread.

I struggled with how to respond, feeling my temper rising but not wishing to anger my husband by sharp responses that might estrange me from those ladies and the place in their society he deemed so important. He had, in moments of recent annoyance, expressed his regret that he had fallen in love with a woman who found all the conventions of his world so unacceptable and who was intractable in polite company. I wished to give him no further confirmation that I was unfit to be his wife or to hold my place in such circles. Yet I wished to fling in their faces, along with their insipid tea so poorly served, albeit in fine Limoge, that I was proud to take on work of any honorable kind, nor was I ashamed that my dear mother had saved her own family from starvation by acting before she met my father. And that I felt only pride that my Aunt Sarah was uniformly acknowledged as the finest actress to ever grace a stage.

I sensed these ladies valued me only slightly above slaves and poor whites, who were *forced* to work for their sustenance, although several were sufficiently hypocritical to have implored their husbands to take them to see the "magnificent Fanny Kemble" in the capitals of the North or in New Orleans, where tickets for my every performance had been in great demand. How greatly several of them disliked me, I surmised, from their haughty stares. I felt a powerful longing to be *home*, not meaning Butler Island or even Butler Place in Philadelphia, but *England*, where I would be again among those who neither feared work nor abhorred those who must perform it and found no grace in indolence.

Fortunately, in the mood that was rapidly descending upon me, I was presented with an excuse to leave that uncivil company. One of the house slaves rushed in with a message that had just been brought across by a man from Butler Island. Mr. Butler requested I return quickly as possible. I was assured nothing was amiss with Mr. Butler or my babies or any other living soul on the island, but that I must come immediately. I assured my hostess of my deep regret to be called away from such a *pleasant* gathering. Yet another magnificent performance by the great actress!

I was not left to wonder long as to the nature of this urgent matter. Mr. Butler had sent a note to be conveyed to me as soon as I had departed from the other ladies.

My dear Fanny,

I regret to call you away so suddenly from a pleasant afternoon, but must tell you old Shadrach has died. I did not wish you to learn of this sad event while you were amongst the other ladies for fear you might be overcome, so high was your regard for him. It would also have appeared unseemly if the other ladies supposed you left their company to attend the funeral of a slave. Come quickly as you are able, for in the present heat there can be no delay in committing the body to the ground. Cooper London shall begin the service as soon as you arrive.

Your loving husband,
Pierce Butler

I was so affected by Shadrach's death I could not speak, but was not surprised, as the good old man had been declining. And I was warmed by Mr. Butler's action in sparing a man from the field to fetch me, and acknowledging his own responsibility to honor this life passed solely in service to his family. My heart was touched even by his affectionate signature. It had been some time since he had so tenderly addressed me.

I set to devising a winding sheet for Shadrach. This convention was not always observed on the plantation, but he was so revered for his long years of service to the estate, his diligence, and his knowledge of herbal medicines and healing that by Mr. Butler's express order, every aspect of the poor rites we extended should be conveyed. I helped the women prepare the sheet while the most expert of the carpenters finished planing perfectly smooth a yellow-pine coffin.

At dusk I went with Mr. Butler to the cabin of Cooper London. The coffin was laid on trestles in the bare yard in front of the cabin, where a large assemblage of the people had gathered, many of the men carrying pinewood torches, which sent up a glaring light in the darkening woods.

After Mr. Butler, even under these circumstances the supreme authority, signified by a nod that the proceedings might begin, the entire congregation uplifted their voices in a hymn, the first high wailing notes of which, sung all in unison, sent a thrill through me. When the chant ceased, Cooper London began to pray, and all the people knelt down in the sand, and I knelt beside them. Only my husband remained standing in the presence of the dead man and of the living God to whom his slaves were appealing for their comrade's soul. Although I reached for his hand, hoping this might encourage him to kneel with me, Mr. Butler turned away. I was profoundly moved by the power of the ceremony and the simple majesty of prayers imbued with awe by the dark, somber setting. The benediction began very typically, much like one to be heard in a conventional church, but I was overcome by tears when Cooper London concluded by calling for God's blessing upon their master, their mistress, and their children. I began to cry quite bitterly, mortified that Mr. Butler would not even kneel beside these poor people who honored him and his family with their prayers. The state of their lives so confounded me that tears seemed as legitimate a response to their miserable condition on earth as any prayer.

When Cooper London said, "Amen," we all rose, and the coffin was raised onto the shoulders of four of the strongest men, who surrendered their torches to others who walked beside them as we made our way to the people's burial ground. Then Cooper London recited aloud portions of the funeral service, holding out his much-worn prayer book. I stood surrounded by *my* slaves—I could no longer deny the implication—and pondered the grave dignity of these people standing on *slave* ground, not even free to be buried beside the few whites who had died on the plantation and who were buried in consecrated ground. I knelt again while the words were recited to proclaim to the living and the dead the everlasting covenant of freedom. I wondered what possible hope and sense the people beside me felt at hearing, "I am the resurrection and the life" as the vast river swept by, not far from where we stood in the near darkness, and the torchbearers drew closer to the grave.

If it had been within my power, I should have willed Mr. Butler to kneel down with us. I understood that in church in Philadelphia he would by custom have stood during the minister's prayers, but it seemed dreadfully cold of him not to kneel with *his* people, as a small token that in the sight of that *Master* to whom we all answer, all men are equal in prayer. But he remained perfectly erect among the weeping, prostrate assembly of his slaves.

When the coffin was lowered, the grave was found to be partially filled with water, hardly surprising, since the entire island was nearly a swamp from which the Altamaha was only suppressed by the high dykes built all around it. This discovery mightily distressed the slaves, whose crying and exclamations of grief rose all around us. Some of the men wanted to go in search of buckets with which they might bail out the water, but Mr. Butler silenced them.

"It would do no good. It will only fill again," he said, still looking down over all of us. "This water will not bother Shadrach now. It is only his body that is still *here*. He is at rest. He has gone home," my husband told them, alluding I suppose to Shadrach's final home, that *slave* heaven that awaited him. I wondered if the billowing clouds of heaven, which artists have drawn and which we have all envisioned replete with angels, were truly fields of white cotton for poor Shadrach to hoe.

When it came time to take leave of the people, as our path turned towards the house and theirs diverged to the Quarter, the slaves were most concerned by the degree of my crying. Mr. Butler took my arm, and one of the slaves surrendered a pine torch to him so that our way might be lit amid the complete darkness that had settled around us.

"Farewell, massa and missus. Lor, missus, don't you cry so!" they called out to me.

I could not speak to Mr. Butler as we walked on, but continued to cry, clinging to his arm, hardly able to see my way through the darkness and my tears. For a while he kept his own counsel and did not berate me, as was usually his wont, about how overly emotional I was concerning the realities of plantation life. Until he could contain himself no longer and complained, "*Surely* you have cried enough. Can you not control yourself? He was but a slave, a good man I grant you, but his time had come."

I wanted to tell him that I cried not for Shadrach alone, but that a man such as Cooper London, the spiritual leader of a community, was still subject to the driver's lash and his master's will. Without a right or a hope in the dreary world in which he lived, *still* he clung to the salvation of another world, another life. I could not tell Mr. Butler how deeply it shamed me that we should keep such an exemplary man in his abject state.

But I could not form words to express these feelings to my husband, and I cannot claim this was because I was still so overcome by tears. My sobbing had subsided sufficiently that I might have spoken sensibly, but I knew no words Mr. Butler should feel agreement with, and that I would only anger him further by my declarations against slavery. I decided it would be far wiser to continue as I had all along, by committing my feelings about this sad occasion to my journal. I could not determine if I should ever be able to bring forth the record I had maintained, yet I was determined to keep it, faithfully and accurately, and in a place where my husband should not discover it.

"You are very quiet, my dear," he said, opening the door for me and lighting the candles on our table. "I thought perhaps there was something you wished to say," he said with uncharacteristic gentleness.

I could only shake my head, so concerned as I was about trusting myself to speak about what I had just witnessed.

"Then perhaps we might have something to eat. A bit of refreshment to throw off this gloom," he said cheerfully. "Please call Mary and let us see what she can bring us," he said in anticipation, I am certain, of some wine.

"*Please*, Pierce," I beseeched him. "It is late. Surely she should not have to come out and wait upon us after what has transpired this evening."

"It is her duty to wait upon us *whenever* she is needed," he answered in annoyance. "As it is, very little is asked of her since you are always running to assist her."

"What is it you desire? I can easily procure it for you. Mary is probably still down in the Quarter with the other people. I know I could not eat a bite."

"Then do not trouble yourself," he said brusquely. "I was only thinking of you. Anything to lift this pall that envelops you."

"I know no refreshment which could achieve that until the suffering of these people comes to an end," I answered honestly, unable to keep my resolve to remain silent.

"Damnation, Fanny. I regret the day I foolishly agreed to allow you to come here. Your presence has afforded me nothing but trouble, and, so far as I can see, has brought you only anguish." He slammed his fist upon the table, shaking the crockery and glasses that were assembled there for the next day's breakfast. "Fact is, I regret the day I ever asked—" Then he hesitated, his face flushed with anger and his eyes, which once had looked at me so lovingly, focused coldly on me as if I were odious to him.

"Go ahead and say whatever you wish!" I cried. "Please, sir, do not be concerned with sparing *my* feelings."

"Gladly, then, since you insist. I rue the day I asked you to be my wife."

"Not half so much as I that I accepted," I cried, running from the room.

But there was nowhere I might escape save into the total darkness. I lingered in the adjoining room, composing myself to profess my longing to him for all we had once so deeply shared. I readied myself to beseech him not to permit the sadness of that day to further our estrangement. I longed to embrace the loving husband I had known, to comfort him and be comforted. But when I heard the sound of the cork being pulled from a bottle, I knew the time for speaking to my husband had passed away. I retired to a lonely bed.

24

The Written Word

Satisfied Mr. Ogden was handling the affairs of the plantations according to his own and his brother's best interests, my husband dared remain no longer on Butler Island. His rheumatism, originally benefiting from the mild winter, afflicted him terribly as humid weather and frequent rains settled over the region. As it turned warmer, the mosquitoes gathered round us with their incessant humming, making me fearful for all of our health. I bid Margery to begin packing up the children's things and started my own preparations, though my progress was slow once news of our departure became known.

"Missus, it is really so you are leaving us?" House Mary asked, a look of great sadness and worry in her mournful, dark eyes.

"Yes, Mary. You have seen how Mr. Butler suffers day and night. We must get him home to his doctors and a dryer climate. And I fear for the children with these clouds of mosquitoes." Immediately after I had spoken I felt ashamed of my words, since she and the others had among them so many children, whom I was abandoning to that humming pestilence.

"I will warm stones to wrap in flannel for his legs and set the carpenters to making wooden fans. Then all night long the people stand by your windows and fan so hard the mosquitoes blow away before they reach you or your babies. But don't you go, missus. *Please* don't you go."

"Mary, we must go. Thank you for all you have done to make us comfortable, but it would be dangerous for us to stay. And think how much easier your tasks shall be with only Mr. Odgen to cook for instead of so many extra mouths to feed," I said, trying to cheer her.

"Then it will be like it be before," she said, sighing deeply. "Not enough to eat. Harder work. No time to clean the infirmary or the cabins. No one to cut out dresses for the women or show them how to sew. No one to say the women must rest from the fields when they be heavy with child. No one to care—"

I knew she feared she had overstepped the bounds of allowable discourse by insinuating I was the only one who *cared* for them amid those who demanded their labor and chastised them with scourges. I wished to console her, to assure her that the small improvements I had wrought would remain and she need not fear on this account, but I knew how false such assurances would be. I had no authority over the regulation of the plantation and should not be present to know whether even the small, humane changes I had introduced would prevail. Mr. Odgen should soon have final word on all matters relating to the plantation, and so long as the profits continued to build year by year, and there occurred no significant loss of life or limb, his rules would go unchallenged.

"I am glad the women have enjoyed our sewing class," I said, watching her smile when I suggested she take on its leadership. "You have become an excellent seamstress and will manage quite well without me."

"Oh no, missus. I could not do it without missus. Tired as they be each night, the women would not come without missus there to teach them. Now there will be nobody to cut out the dresses," she said sadly.

"The time is so short, Mary," I said with regret. "But I *promise* with your help to cut out dresses before I leave for as many as I possibly can. I shall teach you so you may manage this on your own. But we must work quickly. Mr. Butler plans for us to leave the day after tomorrow."

"Thank you, missus," she said gratefully. "I will tell the women to bring what cloth they have. They will be glad. But without missus, this plantation will be like a funeral day when no one sings and the sun has no face to shine."

I had no ready response to Mary's words, comprehending all too well the harshness of their position without even one foolish Englishwoman to protest for them, and at the same time feeling such relief that my children and I were *escaping* that sad place. I longed to live once again in a world where workmen were paid for their labor, and dressed themselves and their families in decent clothing, and ate sufficient food, and tucked their children safely away to sleep at night in warm beds, secure in the knowledge that no one might "sell them off" on the morrow.

I determined to beseech my husband to give instruction to Mr. Odgen about the treatment of the women and to maintain the improved cleanliness in the cabins and the infirmary. I knew I must approach my requests cautiously, so angrily did Mr. Butler receive what he deemed my "interference" and recognizing as well that his affliction had made my husband's temper easily enraged.

I found him sitting in an armchair before the fire, which was built up very high despite the moderate temperature of the day, with both of his feet soaking in a large basin from which the steam was rising. Pierce was wrapped in blankets over his dressing gown and was sipping a toddy. His face was flushed with heat, and peering at me over his reading glasses, his countenance appeared so stern I wondered if I dare approach him.

Then his jocular mood surprised me. "It would seem, Fanny," he said with mock severity, "you might at least have the common decency not to come into this room abounding with such splendid health and good spirits. It is fairly *sickening* to a man in my condition."

Psyche's appearance with a kettle of hot water to replenish the basin for his feet spared me the necessity of a response. I was still debating what to say when quite uncharacteristically he laughed, gesticulating at my perplexed expression.

"Just look at you, Fanny! For once in your life, *speechless.*" He pointed to the chair beside him. "Please sit down. I meant for you to laugh," and then with a gallantry seldom showed towards me any longer, he said, "I did not intend to puzzle you, my dear. I meant only to praise how very well you look. In sad contrast to myself, I am afraid."

"I am sorry you are so ill, Pierce. Is there anything I might bring you?"

"Not unless you can cure this infernal rheumatism. I scarcely think I have sufficient joints to accommodate its new fury. But I am well cared for." He sipped his steaming toddy.

"May I assist with your packing? In your condition, you surely should not superintend it yourself."

"I have given House Mary careful instructions. There should be no difficulty. But you might check on their progress. You know how desultorily they perform any task if no one stands over them," he said disdainfully. "And you might ask Ogden to come see me. I have a few instructions for him."

"Might you spare a few moments before I call him?" I asked, sweetly as I could.

"*Of course.* I shall always have time for you," he said graciously, taking off his reading glasses and placing them on the small table beside him. "These ridiculous things do not help at all. I fear I am squinting quite as badly as Ogden. Now, what is it, my dear?" he asked attentively.

"It is a very small matter, Pierce. I would not even bring it to your attention, knowing how bad you feel, if we were not so soon departi—"

"Truly, Fanny, please just speak up," he said, showing his first impatience. "I cannot imagine why you, of all people, hesitate to speak your mind."

"It is only this. I have been thinking of how it will be after we have gone," I said cautiously, trying to make my way round to what I wished to ask.

"Funny you should mention it." His face brightened as if I'd said something that actually pleased him. "I have been sitting here all morning with nothing to occupy my mind except this misery," he said, looking down at his poor feet. "I am delighted that your thoughts, like my own, turn towards the happier times to come after we leave this place and return to our familiar occupations."

I said nothing. I could not bring myself to tell him how badly he had misread my meaning. My husband took my hand in both his own and caressed it gently.

"I cannot tell you how very happy I am, my dear," he said, "that you, also, are disturbed by this crossness between us. But it *will* be better, Fanny, when we are in Philadelphia once more and no longer marooned on this dreary island." Still holding my hand, he leaned back and looked attentively into my eyes. "Now please, my dear, tell me what concerns you."

I knew I must express my feelings immediately or there would not be time to beg his intercession. He would have issued orders to Mr. Ogden and never liked to contradict his directions, perceiving that as weakness. I realized I must act straight away, ill and uncomfortable as he was.

"Pierce, it is only this. I wondered if I might ask your help in one small matt—"

"You may ask anything you wish," he interrupted, "if you will just be quick about it," he said, his good humor contending with the terrible pain, which made him grimace as he gingerly moved his feet in their warm bath.

"I have been thinking of the small improvements in the people's lives here," I continued cautiously, not wanting to attribute any advancement to my own doing, as if I were again "finding fault," as he so often accused me.

"This matter of clean hands and faces and swept-out rooms?" he asked, his tone turning colder and I feared dismissive.

"Yes, all of that. But of greater concern, since we will be gone, is what directions shall be given Mr. Odgen regarding the maintenance of the infirmary. It has been quite improved," I said gratefully, "now that you have given Rose an assistant and the carpenters have made the first repairs. But additional work will be needed before we return again. And, of course, the rest period in the middle of the day for the pregnant women in their last months, which you so kindly authorized," I said appreciatively, inwardly seething I should be required to praise a slight reduction in the slave labor exacted from pregnant women as a *kindness.* "And the evening sewing classes so that the women may learn to make comfortable clothing for the people and keep themselves more presentable. This shall require another's attendance in my absence as well as a mere pittance for thread and cloth from time to time."

"And who did you think should carry on as seamstress, Fanny? Mr. Ogden, by any chance?" he asked laughing. "I doubt he has ever held a needle in his hand. Do you recommend that I send him to a dressmaking course?"

"You needn't ridicule me, Pierce," I answered sharply, feeling dangerously close to losing my temper. "I have asked House Mary to carry on with the sewing class. She is quite capable, and you cannot be insensible to the fact that most of your people go about in rags or are miserably ill clad in winter garments during the heat of summer. They have no time, understanding, or materials with which to construct new garments from summer-weight cloth. Surely you cannot object to Mary's teaching them what she has learned so they shall be more comfortable and in some small way better themselves?"

"I have no objection to anything that betters them so long as it also *benefits* the plantation. Otherwise, I am against it, Fanny. You cannot imagine I should favor any enterprise that takes time away from work. I have always been consistent in every instance in which you have *demanded* your improvements by telling you we are here to superintend *hard* work, not dressmaking and your other refinements."

"Then why did you allow me to make improvements or *refinements,* as you prefer to call my attempts to establish even a semblance of cleanliness or respect for human decency in this place?" I could no longer control my tone nor trust what I might say. I stood up and turned away, emboldened by the fact that his indisposition prevented my husband from following me.

But his supremacy quickly assailed me, even from the confines of his chair. "I did not consider it expedient, my dear," he said calmly, obviously determined to keep his temper in hand, "to endeavor to deter you from your role as Lady Bountiful once you had selected it, being already acquainted with the disastrous effects of impeding your headstrong will." He smiled, in what appeared a condescending manner to me, but which may have seemed gentlemanly and generous to him. "I saw no harm in providing you wherewithal to conduct your spring cleaning and the renovations to the infirmary or even your beloved sewing class, if such efforts pleased *you.*"

"You did not find these changes important?" I asked, requiring his answer, but fearing I already had received it. "You saw no need to relieve in even the *smallest* way the suffering of these poor people? Or to encourage even the tiniest shred of respectability in their appearance?"

"They have no time or need for respectability, Fanny. Work is what they know, and all they shall ever know. There was no harm in your improvements. They brought me respite from your constant complaining so that I was glad to approve them. But surely you cannot believe you were changing the nature of slavery," he said scornfully, "by teaching our people to sweep out their cabins and dressing them in new dresses? Do tell me, *please*, if I have missed some aspect of your grand intentions, as I do not always comprehend fully the ways of women of genius." By now the full sarcasm of his words could not possibly be mistaken.

"That was all it was to you, a temporary occupation to cure my dissatisfaction?" I asked, crestfallen not solely for my image in his eyes, but for my diminution in my own, if all my work had been a mockery of change, a pitiful pretense enacted only to appease me. "You *never* intended any of these benefits to endure beyond our stay here?"

"I said nothing of the sort, Fanny." He shook his head sadly. "I fear in your anger you hear opposition where there is none. By all means, let your improvements stand, and if House Mary can continue your sewing circle, I am happy to provide a bit of cloth. Why should I oppose it?"

"And you will give Mr. Ogden definite instructions that all improvements now in place shall be maintained for the future?" I asked this question, seeking nothing short of full assurance, and fearing the answer I was to receive.

"I shall, as always, expect Mr. Ogden to exercise his best judgment in managing my family's affairs in our absence. I *will* not saddle him with a list of petty requirements and obligations which may impede his progress and which bear no relation to producing greater harvests of rice or more numerous bales of cotton!"

"Then there is no more to say. I shall take leave of you now and return to my preparations for the journey." I had maintained civility towards him, I felt, but could not trust my tongue if I remained longer in that room.

"You have no more to say to your husband who languishes before you in this miserable state? No concern for *my* comfort. Your only worry is for the comfort of *slaves*?"

I hesitated to answer, such anger as I felt towards this man, my *husband,* who, despite being confined by his ailment to his chair, exerted over me and all in his dominion absolute sovereignty. All he had promised of a material nature was a pittance of cloth, but if I riled him further, even the improvements in rest and treatment of the women might be taken away. I was also addled by the extreme heat of that chamber with a mighty fire blazing and the steam rising from the foot basin. It did not escape me that while Mr. Butler suffered, as it was obvious he did, he had at least the luxury of enduring his affliction in comfort, well fed, and comfortably attired, beside a fire burning brighter than what a slave might be allowed to fuel a hundred days of fires. As he lifted his toddy to his lips, leaning back amid his cushions, I thought of the sad residents of his infirmary, who suffered much severer maladies and wondered if soon again they would be reduced to recovering upon a cold, dirt floor.

"I am sorry for your suffering, Pierce. *Indeed* I am. But I believe your affliction is attended as very best we can here. All around me there are those more in need of my concern than you, who may order anything you wish."

"You deem yourself more important in their lives than any service you have rendered them could *possibly* warrant," he said dismissively. Then shaking his head, professing his disbelief as if disclaiming to a chamber filled with people, "She concerns herself more for the welfare of slaves than for that of her own husband!"

"Pierce, in your heart, you know this is not so. It is absolutely unworthy of the man I know you to be to make such accusations."

"I know that you do, indeed, *need* my slaves more than I shall ever need them, even though you do not require their labor for yourself." He laughed aloud cruelly, perhaps strongly influenced by his powerful toddies. "You require their adulation, much as formerly you needed the adulation of your devoted audiences. Ah, I do believe I finally comprehend the rest of it," he said with an expression of revelation one might make upon a remarkable discovery. "You *love* my slaves. How disgraced I should be," he gasped, his deepest thoughts spilling out rapidly as water from an overturned glass, "for anyone to learn my wife values my slaves far more than she cares for my feelings. Please assure me that my fear is unfounded."

"How sad I am, sir, since once I felt so much love for you that I parted from my entire family to marry you, that if asked on Judgment Day, that time when every word must be spoken true, I should have to admit that your fear is correct."

When Psyche entered with a fresh toddy and word that Mary needed my instructions straight away on some matter related to our packing, I gladly left that room. I knew I had greatly angered my husband, and by his reckoning inflicted cruel insult, yet I felt the gravest injury was to my own hopes that love, or even some friendly understanding, might ever again exist between us. There was much blame I could rightly place upon my husband, yet I bitterly recognized my willfulness, sharp temper, and my inflammatory speeches. Butler Island had clearly provoked the worst aspects of my character.

While Mary and I finished packing our large trunks and the smaller portmanteaus to make accessible what was needed most for our journey, Psyche came to fetch me. It seemed Mr. Butler had called for me. My concern must have shown in my expression, since Psyche, always mild-mannered and reserved, assured me there was no need for worry since "Massa is much improved and no longer cursing like the drivers."

I hated to leave Mary alone to finish our packing, as I had noticed her wiping away tears when she did not think I could observe her. I assured her that I would return shortly, and I bid her take a much-needed rest in my absence. Just as I turned to leave the room, she seemed about to speak, but then turned away and busied herself folding garments and fitting them into the crowded space afforded by even our largest trunks. With regret and some trepidation, I went to answer my husband's summons.

As soon as I entered the sitting room, I discerned Mr. Butler's mood was much improved. He still sat by the fire, but it burned with far less intensity, and his feet, free from the steamy basin, were stretched out in his slippers on a footstool I had embroidered for him during a happier time. A small table beside him was arranged for tea, as if he had ordered it, in preparation for my arrival. His expression was so welcoming that I relaxed, determining that I had wrongly assumed he wished to resume our quarrel. He seemed much more intent on mending it.

"You will forgive me for not rising, my dear," he said, taking my hand. "But please do sit down. May I offer you a cup of tea?"

"It was good of you to think of it, Pierce. Please let me pour. You should not trouble yourself," I said, helping to arrange his cushions more comfortably behind his back.

"As you wish. I appreciate your solicitude. But I am feeling far better than when we met earlier today. In fact," he said, his eyes slightly downcast so that I could feel his remorse and actually perceived a few tears clinging to his dark, long lashes, "I am sorry my infernal rheumatism makes me so ill tempered. I fear I was very short with you earlier and beg your pardon."

I was quite surprised at this admission, since generally my husband took no responsibility for our disagreements and instead attributed them to my "theatrical personality" and his claim that I had been terribly indulged by my parents as a young child. But I heard nothing in his voice nor could I perceive anything in his demeanor that was not penitent and solicitous.

"I was equally at fault," I was moved to respond, his generosity becoming most contagious. I felt at least a *measure* of his accusation was not without merit. So overwrought as I had become by the condition of the slaves, perhaps I had not given his comfort the full consideration he was due. And my wifely attendance had been the only reason his family had ended their opposition to my accompanying him to Butler Island.

"We should not spend this quiet time together parsing fault. Let us just agree to be kinder towards each other," he said gallantly, smiling more warmly towards me than I could remember in several months.

"I am in full agreement," I answered happily, "and so relieved to see you feeling more yourself."

"Tomorrow, with only the assistance of my walking stick, I shall make it to the carriage without difficulty," he said with satisfaction. "Earlier this morning I feared I should have to delay the journey or make a spectacle of myself by being carried to my compartment like an ancient relic."

"I am relieved you need not suffer that indignity," I said gladly. "Are you sure there is nothing I might do to assist with your packing?" His easy, pleasant manner made me wish there were some service I could perform to ease his pain.

"Thank you, my dear. Everything has been well attended to by House Mary and the others except for one small thing," he answered, resting his head in his hand in the process of remembering it. "I have finished the books I brought down here, and naturally there is little here on the island, Ogden not being a man to read anything besides his accounts and a newspaper if it were thrust in his hand. So I thought I would take a look at the journal you have kept of your observations here. I am certain I should find it informative and *instructive*," he continued in a slightly mocking tone, which seemed to indicate the return of his displeasure.

Pleased as I had been at the return of my husband's thoughtfulness, his request to read my personal diary surprised me by its indelicacy. I stuttered making my refusal, recognizing much was expressed in my journal with which he would take issue. I had kept it faithfully, trying, as Elizabeth had advised, not to embellish but simply to document all I had witnessed about the slaves' daily life and treatment. I knew my husband would dissect and modify every statement I made about his *people*, just as he had removed from my earlier diary every reference to slavery. I could not abide his interference on this occasion, as I believed my account of the horrors I had observed on my husband's plantations would garner support for the abolitionist cause. I feared if my descriptions and opinions angered him, he might *improve* my journal by tossing it into the red-hot coals of his fire!

"It is a *personal* journal, dear Pierce," I said, trying not to bruise the civil tone of our conversation, though I felt betrayed, sensing his earlier pleasantries had been offered dishonestly in a ruse to obtain my journal. "I have not had time to review it again," I explained. "I should feel uncomfortable having you read it before I have fully studied it."

"You cannot show it to your own *husband*, Fanny? I should understand your hesitancy to share such an early version with editors, but to be so wary of criticism or comments from me is certainly most surprising. Where does this new fastidiousness spring from?" he asked coldly. "I have never known you to be so apprehensive of others' opinions, particularly my own. I thought Fanny Kemble simply tossed her impressions to the winds as soon as they occurred to her."

"But I am no longer Fanny Kemble. Perhaps you are acquainted with my husband, Mr. Butler?" I asked playfully, attempting to conceal my concern and yet determined he should not ever again censure my work. "In all seriousness, Pierce, did you not upbraid me for remarks I wrote casually about Philadelphians, expressed rashly before I knew that one day I should be living among them? I have learned the lesson of my thoughtlessness and am quite surprised that you do not support my private and careful examination of my impressions."

"I am reassured you have acquired American sensibility to such matters. Yet your past indiscretion establishes all the more why you should encourage my review. Please recall that everything you have observed here on St.

Simon's has been at the invitation of a gentleman to his *wife* to visit his plantations. I did not commission a book to be written about my plantations or the institution of slavery, nor did I invite a journalist to accompany me here."

"Nor have I embarked upon a new occupation." I smiled a smile I did not feel, hoping to calm him. "My journal reflects my deepest personal thoughts. I understand well that I am a guest here, privy to conversations and observations not made available to the public world, and I shall not abuse my privilege, but still I must retain the right to determine when my writing shall be shared and to whose eyes it shall be revealed."

"Bring it here at once, madam," he replied angrily. "I see it is useless to show you courtesy since you view all interest in your writing as censorious to your freedom. All I actually desired was to be amused during the many arduous hours of travel that lie ahead of us, but *now* I insist you bring me your infernal journal at once. I shall begin reading it immediately and will know before we leave this place if you have elected to weave false stories about plantation life to support your own sympathies."

I watched the remaining flames and red, glowing embers of the fire and dared not bring him my journal. In his wrath, I predicted it would soon be set ablaze and would be naught but ashes before an hour had passed.

"I command you as your husband to fetch me that journal," he cried, his composure lost and his face reddening in a most frightful way, close as I was to him. "I *will* know exactly what you have concocted. Every written word of yours belongs to me. I assure you I am in the right regarding my own property, which includes anything you possess. Your journal shall be read at my discretion. You shall not ever again humiliate me with your unfounded statements."

"You should not, sir, accuse me of writing fiction instead of fact," I said, quickly rising, not hoping to gain authority by my height, which was, of course, rather lacking, but wanting to move far as I could away from him, particularly since his indisposition should at least hinder his pursuit of me. "I shall not surrender it."

"Then I shall search for it!" he cried. "Call Mary here at once. And Psyche, too. I shall have them fetch others to search every inch of this house, every single crevice in the woodwork of this vast *mansion*, as I am certain you have inflated it in your descriptions," he said disdainfully, "until they find it. Then I shall read it, and you may apply to *me* to retrieve it."

I cannot say what it was that possessed me, but I felt suddenly a strength with which I had not been endowed but moments before. I looked directly into Mr. Butler's eyes, cold and sneering as they were, and said, "Then you shall be no more a gentleman, sir. And you shall regret it. For all you know, my journal may be secured upon my person," I told him. "What sort of gentleman would suffer his wife to be searched like a common thief, and by *slaves*," I implored him. "When all she holds in her possession is personal impressions in her own *private* journal. If you follow this course you shall be ridiculed for it, sir, and justly so. I cannot deny that you are my husband and the father of my children, but you shall not become my *jailer*."

"The very sight of you offends me," he said dismissively, I sensed more in defeat than anger. "Now leave me in peace. But first send me Ogden," he said in a more normal tone, recovering himself. "I think you shall find him in the kitchen with Mary having her darn his most prized shirt," he said sardonically. "Probably the only one he owns besides the one on his back. He was pleased you taught her to sew," he continued in a more conciliatory tone, by no means making apology, yet seeming by his tone to convey it. "I imagine he shall make good use of it."

The next morning rose unseasonably cold and rainy, so that amid the great commotion of our departure, we were forced to take time to bundle up ourselves and the children as best we could, lest we catch our death of cold going across the river to officially embark on the journey to Philadelphia. I had hoped to take leave from all whom I had come to know well during our short stay, but the rain came down so heavily it seemed a cruelty for them to huddle in their scant clothing to speak with us. "Farewell to you all," I called out standing under the shelter of the shallow entrance to that crude house that had been my home for almost five months. "I wish you all God's protection and thank you for your hard work and your kindness to me and our children," I said, purposely not including Mr. Butler, who would not appreciate my issuing statements on his behalf nor have felt any obligation to acknowledge kindness from those who were bound to serve him.

The grateful responses were too numerous to count. "Lord, thank you for missus that she come among the people." "Missus, safe jouney to massa, missus, and the little missuses." "Oh, missus, don't you go. We never see you more," someone cried out, and a crowd of children grabbed hold of the folds of my skirt and held on as if I were a raft offering safety to them on a dangerous sea. I longed to respond to each of them, but I feared Mr. Butler's impatience, standing there in the damp and rain on his poor, inflamed legs. Fan began to cry and could not be consoled, and Sal pulled at my hand, urging me to take her down to the waiting boat. Despite their sobbing faces, which told me how much the small comfort I had brought into their cruel lives, must signify to them, I turned away and walked straight ahead, determined I must not look back.

But then I felt a strong hand on my arm and turned to face Cooper London. Even as the rain came down on his broken hat, wetting his thick, greying hair, he thanked me. "Missus was good to pray with me," he said solemnly. "I shall not forget it. And the people will remember."

"I shall miss you, Cooper London. You are a fine preacher. As capable a minister as any I have ever heard in the great churches of England or in all of America," I said, taking his hand.

"Missus flatters London." He bowed his head humbly, and before stepping back so that the others, patiently waiting and deferring to him because of his status as their spiritual leader, might have their time, said, "There is not another planter's wife like missus in all of Georgia, Alabama, and there beyond." And then whispering so that no one else could hear, "And missus will not forget my prayer books and Bibles?"

"I will send them. I am not certain how yet I shall achieve it. But you shall have them."

Then more of the women crowded round for hugs and prayers and several showed me the partially sewn dresses we had just cut out that they had brought in the rain beneath their ragged clothes and shawls. They proudly revealed the progress they had already made by using minutes stolen from their precious sleep time to sew. Then Psyche stepped forward and pulled me to her side away from all the outstretched hands, so urgent was her need to speak.

"Missus, thank you for my children and my Joe." She looked at me through tear-filled eyes. "I did not know if I could live without them. And without you we should have been lost like those who wander in the swamp."

"I am so glad you are now safe," I told her, knowing that in slavery no one was really ever *safe* from misfortune or the capricious acts of a thoughtless master. I squeezed her hand. "Until next we meet."

"Oh, missus, something tells me that never will we see you again."

Would this were so, I thought, as this would mean slavery had been abolished and all the people before me made free. But deep inside me I feared that Psyche's intuition might be correct and that our separation would occur for a less satisfactory reason. "Do not worry, Psyche," I said reassuringly, determined not to reveal my dread. "Mr. Butler comes every year, and now seeing how comfortable I have made him, I believe he would be unwilling to come down here to live without my ministrations."

She smiled, gladdened by my words, and as I turned to go, I realized that in the throng I could not find Mary. Since early in the morning I had seen no trace of her. "Where is House Mary?" I asked, knowing that she and Psyche had been working early that morning and all the previous day together, and were so close that when they were not at work they and their families passed their time together. "I wanted so much to bid her farewell."

"She knows, missus," Psyche answered, looking somehow very troubled. "But she was too sad to see you off. She did not wish to make missus cry. She tells me to say she will miss you and her heart calls out for your safe journey."

I waved one last time and walked down to the boat. Soon I was lost in the rhythmic sound of the oars cutting the water and the unified singing of the oarsmen, whose faces also appeared forlorn. As I looked back, I was touched and saddened to see that no one had moved. Even though they could no more make out our faces than I could discern their own, as we drew further away with each cut of the oars, they stood there in the rain, bravely waving.

I had supposed I would be glad to go, to escape the endless suffering that was not in my power to alleviate or to destroy boldly as Joshua had once torn down the walls of Jericho. Yet as the island receded, I was not relieved, but deeply troubled for those poor souls left behind and for the vast, untold future of my own life, disturbed by this recent, painful sojourn and the difficult choices I would have to make when we returned to Philadelphia.

It was not until several days later that I had true occasion for intimate conversation with my husband since both Fan and Sal had taken cold and come down with fever and cough as soon as we set forth on our journey. Margery and I had struggled without sleep day and night attempting to comfort them. Even the first night when we lodged at a crude inn, hardly more than a barn, with food better suited to livestock than human beings, rooms were so scarce that Margery and I and the children were lodged in one room while Mr. Butler had to share his room with several gentlemen from another party.

It was a relief then to sit with my husband the next day on the train that carried us north, not withstanding cinders and suffocating heat, and to finally have a chance to talk with him. I was encouraged that his spirits seemed improved and hoped we might reach some accord before we returned to Butler Place and the bosom of his family. I gathered my impression of his mood was correct when at his own initiation he spoke to me agreeably about the passing scenery. He purchased a fruit drink for me from a man who passed through the cars selling them and struggled to open one of the stiff windows that I might be refreshed by the breeze.

So accommodating was his behavior that I felt moved to ask his opinion. "Pierce, do you not think it very odd House Mary did not come with the others to see us off? She *purposely* stayed away. I cannot understand it."

"Probably something occupied her that had nothing to do with us," he observed. "I hope you are not troubling yourself over it, Fanny." He patted my hand. "She was clearly devoted to you and the children."

"I cannot imagine what occupied her so completely that she could not say good-bye," I told him, unable to set my mind at ease about the matter. "Just the day before, she seemed moved to tell me something, but then changed her mind. She seemed distracted, and I was too absorbed with so many preparations and even our quarrel that I did not concern myself as I should have liked," I admitted sadly.

Mr. Butler spoke quietly, as if he were relaying a simple matter of no great importance, "Well, I should not worry too much about it now, my dear. It is of little concern since she will likely be gone in but a few days. And we shall never see her again."

"Why ever not? Where could she possibly go that we would not see her when we next visit the island?" I asked in horror, fully suspecting the dreaded answer I should receive.

"Actually she will be *sold* since you insist always on specific details."

"You have sold her!" I cried, unable to keep from raising my voice sharply, so shocked was I at his duplicity in selling off, as if she were indeed a horse or pig or a bale of cotton, a woman who had lived her entire life on his plantation, and whose education I had personally directed for her own good and for the benefit of the others.

"Keep your voice down, madam," he admonished me, seeing other passengers' eyes turning to watch us. "In fact, your anger is misplaced. She was not mine to sell, but is entirely the property of Mr. Ogden."

"Then why should *he* sell her? She works diligently as anyone on the plantation. And she has never given him or anyone else a moment's trouble."

"Oh, my dear, he has not decided to sell her as a punishment. This is completely a matter of business. I happened to tell him, as you had asked, about your sewing circle and how accomplished a seamstress Mary had become under your direction. We discussed the dresses you wished to be devised for the women to wear in warm weather and that Mary should superintend their making."

"What connection can the sewing of dresses have to sending her away?" I could not subdue my agitation, though my husband continued to direct me to lower my voice, as other passengers were beginning to whisper, observing us.

"If you will just allow me to proceed, I shall tell you as much as I know," he said quite moderately, keeping his own temper in hand. "Mr. Ogden, as you know, is a man of very few words, who keeps his own counsel. I had no idea what he intended by asking Mary to darn his shirt for him. I suppose it was his practical test of what I had reported to him of her sewing skills. It appears that Mr. Ogden, who follows the slave market very carefully, was paid a visit by a trader whose specialty is the sale of slaves with more refined skills. Ogden showed me the advertisement this man brought him from a notable South Carolina family particularly in need of a slave to assist their own seamstress in preparations for a large wedding. Ogden shall make a fair profit in just a few days when the sale can be concluded. Since the buyer is willing to take Mary's children as well, it shall work out for the best," he said, well satisfied at this transaction.

"She shall be sold away from all she has ever known. From every familiar association," I said, beginning to cry. "South Carolina might be as far as the moon for any hope of Mary's ever seeing her old mother and sisters and friends ever again. And were you never going to tell me? Was it your plan to wait until next year when we arrived and I wondered why she no longer waited upon us at table?"

"I did not inform you because you were already so disturbed by your separations from our people you might easily have become hysterical if you were told anything more," he said coldly. "You would have acted just as you did regarding Joe and Psyche, disturbing yourself and the entire plantation."

"It was appropriate to be upset by Joe and Psyche's circumstances, sir. Should such cruelty occur next year, I will again *beseech* you, with all my heart, to intervene on the side of decency."

"As for next year, since you persist in the insulting opinion that your own husband is not nearly so fit as yourself to determine the management of his—"

"That is not at all what I intend—"

"Madam, I have heard enough," he interrupted coldly. "You may be assured I have no intention of *ever* taking you back to Georgia. Besides the pain you have caused yourself, feeling every injury and difficulty of plantation life as if it were your own, you have created great dissatisfaction among the *people.* You encouraged their complaints and supported every lie they conjured up to excuse their own lazy, shiftless ways." Ever elegant, he deftly wiped away a cinder that had fallen on his cheek with his scented handkerchief. "I am sorry for your sadness about Mary, but this is what inevitably occurs when people become emotional about slaves, forgetting they are property to be worked or sold according to their master's best judgment. I know you are angry, Fanny, but I could not tell you yesterday for fear you would try to avert the sale. Mr. Ogden deserved the opportunity to freely dispose of his own property. He is quite grateful to you now, having made a nice profit, which without your aid would not have presented itself."

He spoke without emotion, as if his earlier anger had been banished from his voice along with any concern for justice for his people. But I seethed inside, knowing how intensely he wished to punish me by letting Mary be sold, when he could have easily appeased Ogden. He had denied his slaves the benefit of one who would have helped them achieve self-respect, even if fashioned only out of simple cloth. And poor Mary was to be deprived of the company of her old mother and father and the only friends she had ever known. Perhaps she even thought me duplicitous in the matter, grooming her for this fate, all the while pretending to be a kind woman, teaching her skills she might employ to help the others or to earn some small pittance for herself after her daily work was done.

Throughout that long train ride, I had much time to consider this wretched event and to reflect that if I, with the best of intentions, should have unwittingly committed a slave to her ruin, what miseries must occur when a mistress intentionally seeks to bring suffering to her slaves. Studying my husband's face, I could not determine if he had truly enjoyed wounding me with this dreadful occurrence of if he were so inured to slavery's everyday cruelties he failed to recognize the terrible thing that would soon take place. As I could not hold back my weeping, and it seemed little to disturb him, I concluded he must feel true enmity for me. Though I would not speak of this matter again, I could not consent to let my children's lives remain further contaminated by this foul institution even if I should have to beg their bread in the street. I would not tolerate being an unwitting instrument of these people's torment, nor could I ever convince Mr. Butler to emancipate his slaves, who represented far too great a fortune in human capital.

As the train rumbled on, I felt such despair that I prayed for an escape, *even* to the theatre, from whence I had been so pleased to retire. Feeling numb with sadness, I longed to return to the stage. There my words would be cleverly conceived and all my actions designed by playwrights with far greater eloquence than my own. I should be relieved from being cornered as I was on life's chessboard where every move seemed disastrous. I began to plot how I might flee with our children, while Mr. Butler ignored me, absorbed as he was by a humorous story in his magazine. The endless pine barrens of North Carolina passed by bleak and unwelcoming. The tall, spindly pine trees were shaken by the rough winds, as were my hopes.

25

"My Ain Countree"

We had not even time to wash the journey's dust from our faces when the letter arrived. I was naturally delighted to see the English stamps and chagrined that at first I did not recognize the handwriting. The letter was from my father, but the script was so changed from his graceful, steady hand that until I saw the salutation, I did not perceive he was its author. When I unfolded it, a short note fell out from Adelaide, who had evidently posted it, bidding me come at once, so serious was our father's condition.

His own letter told me he had taken to his bed possessed of some condition that wearied him to his bones and for which his physicians could find no remedy. He weakened daily, and much as he did not wish to sadden me by his own sad predicament, he longed to see me again and to meet his own dear granddaughters one time before his life should end. He had always imagined he should expire without illness at some great age, perhaps on the stage aptly playing a death scene, but now he feared his time had come. They gave him only months at best, and so he bid me come, both for himself and because I had missed my own mother's passing, which he knew had grieved me terribly. He sent me love and hoped that I might send him word immediately so that my anticipated visit should bring him hope.

I showed the letter to my husband, forgetting our estrangement in the sadness that came over me and longing that he might hold me as he once had with love and tenderness. I had not noticed until he showed me that my tears had fallen upon the pages, mixing with the blue ink. "My dear Fanny, please sit down," Pierce urged solicitously, "and let me pour you a glass of water. Then let us think what is best to do." He sent Margery off with the children, who were tired and famished and yet distraught to see me weeping openly before them.

"I must go to him, Pierce. As soon as passage can be arranged, I must go home. I should not forgive myself if I delayed and arrived too late to see him once more," I sobbed. "That comfort I admit is for myself, but he also implores me to come."

"My dear, I am so sorry, but please remember that you are exhausted and hungry and hardly yourself—"

"You cannot imagine I should feel differently about my father's dying request after I am rested?" I asked in amazement. "Nor can I eat or rest until the arrangements have been made to take me to him."

For once Pierce did not allow my outburst to incite his own short temper, but took me in his arms as I had wished and for one brief, pure moment, all I heard was the beating of our two hearts and the sound of the large clock ticking on the mantel.

"I shall make inquiries concerning your passage," he said reassuringly. "I shall handle your plan straight away. Now go refresh yourself, Fanny, and I shall send Catherine up later with warm milk and something light for you to eat. You will see, my dear, you shall feel better after a little nourishment."

"You will arrange passage for the children? And I must take Margery with me," I told him, thinking that I should require her care as much for *myself* as for the children, so anguished as I felt.

"I had not thought of Margery accompanying you," he said coolly, his solicitous tone somewhat abated.

"If I *must*, I can manage the children by myself. Although I see no reason why my journey should be made more arduous." I could not hide my displeasure, particularly as the discomfort of traveling with small children was only just behind me.

"I had not anticipated you should ask to take the children with you." He turned away from me to adjust the position of a porcelain ornament, a Chinese figurine on a small table, which did not seem to be positioned to his liking. "But let us discuss this later when you are rested and we have both had time to reflect."

"I shall not rest until we discuss my father's request!" I insisted, knowing full well I risked stirring his anger by raising my voice.

"He asks that you visit him immediately and so you shall," he answered calmly, as if that were all my father had requested.

"He asks to meet his granddaughters, Pierce. 'Before my life shall end,'" I quoted, determined not to relinquish that fact. "Surely you do not want to deny my father this pleasure. And Adelaide's note attests that his condition is quite serious."

My husband said nothing in response, his eyes still searching the letter, as if it were a forgery sent to us for some false purpose, a guise of my father's.

His expression grew so suspicious, I felt myself at once offended and accused.

"You said you are surprised I would *ask* to have our children accompany me. Why should you imagine I *need* your permission to honor my father's most reasonable wish? It would never occur to me that you would question a mother's wish to introduce her children to their own *grandfather*," I continued, willing myself to speak softly, but feeling I had been placed again upon a stage where I faced a tyrant. I am somewhat ashamed to recall that I moved and spoke as if the back rows of a crowded house watched my every word.

"I do not question why, as their mother, you desire to take them to London. But more importantly, my dear, I believe you forget that *I* am their father."

"How could I *ever* forget both they and I bear the name of Butler, your esteemed ancestor, Major Pierce Butler, who attended the Constitutional Convention and served in the United States Senate!" I answered hotly.

"At least he was not a common strolling minstrel practically *begging* for his supper like some of your illustrious forebears!" he shouted. And then, to his credit, ashamed of what he had said about my family, he apologized. "I *beg* your pardon. I should not have said that, nor had you any reason to bring my grandfather's name into this. All I had intended to explain," he said evenly, collecting himself, "is that as their father, it is my decision, and mine alone where my daughters shall spend their time. It is my right, at least in *this* country to determine when and where they may travel."

"Is it truly their welfare then for which you are so concerned?" I asked more solicitously. "I can understand you might have worried in the past when ocean travel was much more precarious. But I assure you, my father and I sailed here in utmost comfort and safety. The ocean air was wonderful, and the girls should have the benefit of the great enhancements they will enjoy in London and in the English countryside and during the journey itself."

"It is not the journey that I fear for them," he answered, this time avoiding my eyes.

"Surely you do not doubt they shall be greeted warmly and be well cared for by my family? Adelaide shall sing to them and teach them elocution while I visit with father. Our friends will welcome them, and they shall see all the sights of my girlhood."

"You force me to say what is very difficult for me, madam." In his discomfort with the pronouncement he was about to make, my husband retreated into excessive formality. "My concern has naught to do with the entertainments you should provide my children. Although I must say I doubt Fan should benefit much at her age from elocution or singing beyond the most elementary rhymes, even if she is part Kemble."

"Then what is it? Please tell me so we may dispense with guessing games."

"I fear that strained as relations are between us, you might seize this opportunity to run off with them. You are so high-strung and quite understandably overwrought by your father's health. I fear you would not return and should attempt to keep my children from me. I cannot permit that."

I beseeched him to reconsider, offering to sign any document he should devise, pledging to return. I urged him to secure our return passage on any date he might specify, which would again verify my intentions. But he would have no part of it, saying he did not trust me sufficiently regardless of what document I might sign, so hardened had my heart seemed towards him because of our great disagreement about slavery. He believed I might sign anything under duress and then once among my own people should distort his words until they would all be clamoring against him in a Kemble conclave. They would, he felt certain, encourage me never to return to his home.

I threatened to consult an attorney, hoping this might cause him to reconsider, so concerned as he always was for public opinion. He would not desire anyone of his acquaintance to see his carriage transporting me to an attorney's door for fear all of Philadelphia would soon speculate about the state of our relations.

"If you are determined to seek the advice of an attorney, then let no one say I stood in your way. But you shall find I know the law regarding my property, *including* my children," he continued angrily, "and you shall not take them anywhere, even around the park in a carriage, if I do not approve it."

"Am I to be a prisoner here as well?" I asked, looking around the delicately adorned walls of the drawing room in which we were arguing and where we had formerly spent convivial times. "Shall I be required to ask your leave to walk about the farm or the orchards or to go riding into town?"

"Do not make yourself ridiculous with these questions, Fanny. You are free to go wherever you wish. I have offered to secure your passage, but you shall not take my children. That is all there is to be said about the matter." He turned away from me and walked over to stand by the fire to light his cigar.

"I will not stand for such treatment, Pierce. I cannot live this way."

"What you will or will not stand be damned, madam," he said, disgustedly tossing his cigar into the fire. "You will not take my children to England without my permission. About that make no mistake," he insisted, moving so near I felt his breath upon my face. "Now you must excuse me," he said, leaving the room before I could contemplate a reply.

Through the closed door, I could still hear him speaking sharply to the servants, angrily shouting commands and knocking things about. I heard him calling for our carriage. Often when he was alone, I knew he preferred to ride his horse. In this instance, I was certain he believed if he left the carriage at my disposal, I might whisk our sleeping children from their beds, carry them into hiding, and then off to England!

I was tempted to prove that he could not so easily defeat me. I should not be too proud to take the farm cart. I would ask a stable hand to harness it for me and should not be ashamed to drive it myself before I would endure another night in his house whether or not he himself were there to torment me.

Then I considered the commotion I had just overheard and feared my husband had just issued instructions thwarting my escape. He might have made the servants fear him, or in the very sympathetic manner he adopted when it suited his purposes, he could have convinced them, so troubled was I at this sudden news of my father's failing health, that he feared I might do something rash. He would beseech them to support me in my despondency over my father, and tell them he hoped they understood it pained him that he must advise them of the sad state of my mind.

I went upstairs to take my bath, realizing that I was, indeed, not myself, even before this argument had enveloped us. I called for tea and some brandy, something I rarely took, but suffering such deep concern for my father and insulted that I had not the *right* to travel with my own children, I knew I should not sleep without it. When I was refreshed from my bath and had brushed my hair by the fire, I poured out tea and tried some of the brandy. But they did not quiet me, and though I finally settled down to bed, I could not rest. I waited, listening all night for the sound of my husband's carriage wheels turning over the gravel of the front walkway, but I had not heard them even by the time the rooster crowed.

I had breakfasted in my chamber and could not say what time my husband returned, nor did I wish to give him the pleasure of realizing how greatly his absence had disturbed me. Even an unhappy wife wonders where her husband has passed the night away from her, so that I felt no appetite for luncheon and was seated in the library trying to concentrate on the many letters which had been awaiting our arrival when I heard Mr. Butler's voice in the entry. The servants advised him that I alone in the library, but I made no effort to acknowledge him.

He knocked demurely, quite out of keeping with his usual authority, which propelled him into any closed room as if to do so were his undisputed right. When I answered, he entered quietly, offering me a small bouquet and *asking* if he might interrupt my work to speak with me. I was so taken aback by his kind tone that I did not respond in the cold manner in which I had planned to acknowledge him.

Pierce began by begging my pardon. He said he could not explain why he had behaved so abominably, and that, of course, I must take the children to see their grandfather. He explained he had passed the night at his cousin Amelia's home and was ashamed it had required her perseverance to make him see the injustice of his actions. I had assumed he had spent the night gambling or in low company. I was reassured he had been with his relatives, and that, for once, members of the Butler family had sided with me.

He said his cousin had severely chastised him for even thinking that an American lady—as I suppose I had then become—should undertake such a journey without a gentleman's protection. It would be unseemly, she had convinced him, if he did not accompany me, and how might he ever forgive himself if my fears were realized and my father succumbed without ever meeting his own grandchildren. She had cautioned him that everyone in Philadelphia should agree he was a heartless, cruel husband who deserved to experience the same ill treatment from his own daughters in his old age. He should not easily overcome this image of himself in society.

I almost responded bitterly that it grieved me his cousin's intervention was required to encourage him to comport himself humanely towards his own wife and her ailing father. My own temper should gladly have accommodated such an announcement. But I subdued my pride and answered that I should be delighted to have his protection and for my father to enjoy a visit from my entire family. I hoped Pierce might be entranced with London and the English countryside and agree to stay there for a while. I was sufficiently beguiled by my husband's apology and his shame at wronging me that I prayed new sights and associations and the absence of the issue of slavery would reconcile us.

When we arrived in London, it was apparent that my father's letter had in no way overstated his ill health. The recent Italian tour from which Adelaide had returned triumphantly would have been his proudest topic of conversation, but he did not mention it. Although the table beside his bedchamber was covered with news articles and notices, obviously arranged in hope of exciting even a small spark of interest in him, he was silent. I was uncertain if he realized who we were, so weary was the expression in his glazed eyes.

We stood for some time around his bed, waiting for even a small sign that he noticed our presence. I bathed his feverish face with a damp cloth and held his hand. Pierce rocked Fan, who fretted in his arms, and Sal stood at my side, her dark eyes solemnly assessing her grandfather. We waited in silence, my spirit bereft at the thought I might never again hear his voice. Even Pierce, usually first to offer his opinions or a wordy discourse on what should improve any situation, remained silent when it seemed death was clearly approaching to claim my father.

"Is my grandfather asleep with his eyes open?" Sal asked innocently, studying the situation. "Or is he pretending not to hear as you do sometimes when father is cross with you?"

For a moment we said nothing. I felt ashamed, wondering how much of the arguments between us, which I supposed had gone unnoticed by her young eyes, were vivid in her memory. I felt certain my father was in too weakened a state to hear her, but I was embarrassed she had observed so much of our discord.

"I should like to know, Mother," she went on. "Grandfather is breathing, don't you think?"

"Be quiet, Sal," Pierce admonished. "It is not polite to speculate in the presence of your elders about whether they are pretending not to listen or even if they are still breathing. Where did you learn such manners?" he asked, looking disdainfully at me.

Again, there was silence save for Fan's fretting. Then we were stirred by the sound of a dry, rasping voice, which arrested us, although it shared no resemblance to my father's deep voice when he had graced the stage.

"By all means let her speak. I like to hear her voice," my father whispered, the effort evidently requiring great energy on his part. "It is a *Kemble* voice," he said, smiling. "No doubt about that. And young lady," he said softly, "I have been very tired. Much too weary to talk. I was not *pretending* just now. But I am very skilled at it, I must say." He closed his eyes and took her small hand in his own. "I shall show you one day very soon." He gallantly kissed her hand before he settled back amid the bedclothes. "But now I must rest," he said peacefully closing his eyes. "Until this evening when I hope you shall dine with me."

The doctors said it was a miracle. They could not explain why my father's strength, so totally exhausted, was refreshed, or how a man who had refused all nourishment, even delicacies that had long been his favorites, should suddenly desire to eat again. I was so pleased I could hardly bear to leave his bedside. At first Pierce remained with me, but then sensing how bored he was, and wishing also to speak privately with my dear father, I urged him to go out. It was a godsend to have Margery to mind Fan and to watch Sal, who sat at the bottom of my father's bed with her dolls collected around her and a small diary in which she made a big show of writing her *secret* thoughts, I believe in imitation of my own efforts.

It was not long before my father was strong enough to sit in his chair or take a short walk down the hall to the upstairs parlor, where he might look out into Russell Square to watch the activities of couples strolling and children running round and round its graveled paths. As he ate again, one could see daily a difference as he regained his strength and his voice. After just a few days, the doctors were astounded to find him sitting in a chair laughing at the manuscript of a comic play sent for his review and walking more determinedly, hardly relying on my arm and beseeching us that he be allowed outside "this confounded house."

"You need not spend so much time attending me," he told me. "Seeing you is all the medicine I truly required. But now that I have daily doses, you should think more of yourself, Fanny. Our old friends all wish to see you, and surely you must pay calls with your husband. It is not the best idea to leave him so much on his own." He did not refer to anything more particular, yet sensitive as he was, I believe he recognized the estrangement between us.

"I will go out with him soon enough, Father. My proper place is here with you and the children. There will be time to go out when you are fully recovered."

I could tell something troubled him and urged him to share it. At first he struggled, as if it were too painful to put feelings to words, even for a man who had never been known for his reticence. He urged me to call Adelaide, whose strong voice we could hear completing her vocalizations in the drawing room below, to sit with him if I were so concerned about leaving him. Or if she could brook his intrusion and I should permit him to walk down a simple flight of stairs, he would sit quietly in a corner of the drawing room while her voice soared around him. Even she might occasionally take a brief pause and could then ascertain, to assuage her sister's qualms, that he was still breathing.

I finally insisted on knowing why he sought to escape my company when he avowed so strongly to enjoy it. Being very much my father's daughter, I would not desist until he finally confessed that Pierce had spoken with him. During one of those rare occasions when they were alone while I attended the children or took the rest my father insisted upon, Pierce had told my father how our marriage had suffered. He claimed I had been "bewitched" by abolitionist pamphlets before we journeyed to the South. This had made me incapable of assessing slavery fairly, and that rather than attending his needs, as had been the purpose for my accompanying him to his plantations, I had concerned myself with the welfare of the slaves in a most argumentative, demanding manner, which achieved little true benefit for the people and caused discord where only peaceful accord had formerly been known.

"He is greatly disturbed about a journal you kept while you were there, Fanny. He insists it must be terrible in its false statements or you would not refuse to let him read it. He asked my support for his position that as your husband and a gentleman he is responsible for your actions and should at the very least have access to your journal before it is made public. He maintains he still endures social injury from the insults to Philadelphia society made in your previous journal, and that you yourself regret remarks you hastily put to paper."

"What did you tell him, Father? What was your opinion?"

"I told him I had not much experience as a *gentleman*, never having been one, although I had played them often enough, but I was surprised a gentleman insisted on reading anyone's private thoughts against that person's will. I told him as a husband, I had never tried to censor anything your dear mother wished to write or say, and perhaps it was entirely my fault you had developed such appreciation for freely speaking your mind," he continued, smiling with pride and satisfaction. "As for slavery itself, I asked him how it could come as a surprise that an Englishwoman reviled it for the abominable institution that it is."

I could well imagine my husband's face, red with embarrassment and ugly with indignation, after such a conversation. He had surely imagined my father, particularly in his weakened state, would acquiesce to his own opinions and help rein in his headstrong daughter. In their short association in America, my father had been very grateful for Pierce's many accommodations to our family, offered without asking anything in return. My husband had appeared genuinely shocked that my father, from his sickbed, did not then reciprocate support in this one "small matter" of my journal.

"He is so incensed about this journal, Fanny, that I fear his wrath is disproportionate to any wrong you may ever have committed. If you will forgive me, I believe he exaggerates the effect your journal could have on public sentiment in support of slavery. I suggested while you are here you should both pursue activities you once enjoyed together. You must attend the theatre and museums, and go to call upon your old friends. I am certain you would still be received graciously at Court, and Pierce would enjoy that. Dear girl, you have been so isolated in Georgia or surrounded so completely by his Philadelphia relatives, whom you say distrust you, that you need fresh associations." He sipped appreciatively from the tea I brought him. "Have a dinner party, Fanny. I am *certain*, swayed as he is by public opinion, Pierce will be quite delighted to sit down to table with Dickens, Tennyson, and Liszt, a few of his American friends, and Kembles, naturally for good measure."

I assured him I would immediately issue invitations if such a party might restore tenderness to Pierce's eyes. Yet I feared even a private champagne reception with the Queen herself could not do that. I had not shared my fears even with Adelaide, but under the spell of my father's voice, I could not avoid tearfully confessing that my marriage seemed to be over.

If that were so, my father advised I should at once return to the stage while the London public still remembered me. I should divorce Pierce and allow the children to live with me in England. We would be welcome to reside with him as long as we wished, and the children should have every advantage. Their own Aunt Adelaide should give them singing lessons. He would teach them Shakespeare and assured they would acquire their mother's facility with languages when they traveled with me throughout Europe on tour. My father's old animation returned, as he pressed my hand and begged me to return home for good.

I acknowledged the temptation, since save the sorrow of finding him unwell, it had been pure pleasure to return to England. There was much excitement in a new country like America, and remarkable natural beauty, and certainly people of great brilliance, yet it was not my home. I did not attempt to sing it, particularly with Adelaide's rich soprano voice soaring up the staircase, but I reminded my father of a Scottish air which had been sung to us in the nursery. I recalled the chorus, which concluded:

"It's hame, and it's hame, hame fain would I be,
O hame, hame, hame to my ain countree!
When the flower is in the bud, and the leaf upon the tree,
The lark shall sing me hame to my ain countree!"

But happy as I felt to be in my adored home again among those who knew my every foible and still loved me, I told Father I could not consider such an arrangement. Pierce had convinced me American law would rule totally in his own favor, leaving me no rights to see our children without his permission. Even if the law were actually constituted in reverse, I told him I could not deprive my children of their father, nor rob Pierce of these lovely moments of their lives. We were a family. I had taken very seriously my vow "until death do us part," and should not break it lightly, nor could I ever return to the stage. I am not like you, I told him, a person who has longed for the stage as some men do for their bottle. I might come alive on it, yet I found no joy upon it.

"Then you must make him fall in love again, Fanny," my father urged. "This is possible even *without* potions. Though I fear, my dear, the true dilemma is that he fell in love with Juliet, a delightful, imaginary girl, with all a girl's innocence and passion for love, and then awakened to find he had married a *living*, breathing woman with real opinions about the world around her."

Thus began the rounds of visits. It was fortunate one of my father's servants had a young daughter who was available to mind the children, since Margery had taken leave to visit her family in Dublin. Devoted as she been to our family, even Pierce, sometimes so unyielding, could not deny her this visit. He actually assisted in making her preparations and insisted on paying for her passage. I was surprised by his generosity since Margery had shown more than once her absolute devotion to me, which seemed to annoy my husband. Nevertheless I was pleased by his consideration.

Then quickly my husband turned his attention to London society, and I was determined to please him. Once the servants were free to announce my father's health sufficiently improved to entertain visitors, Montague Place was lit not only by candlelight but by the delighted laughter of many visitors. These old friends and acquaintances constituted such a distinguished assemblage that even Pierce, who considered himself by birth and position so superior to all Kembles, felt himself to be in precisely the *right* company. We were visited one afternoon by Charles Dickens, whom Mr. Butler admired in spite of his openly expressed support for the abolishment of slavery, which had been repeated to my husband. Naturally in the presence of company, I made no mention of it, nor did anyone else, being well aware of my husband's holdings and his sentiments. We all conversed more about Mr. Dickens's growing celebrity and his hopes to soon travel to America to give readings from his most popular works. But it was no surprise to me that Mr. Dickens should so revile slavery, as his writing bespoke such understanding and compassion for the poor and oppressed. I wished my husband, who admired *Oliver Twist* when we read it together, could feel the same repulsion for slavery as he had felt for the cruel treatment of the poor children that Dickens depicted. Pierce permitted himself to be moved by fictional *stories*, but the reality of slavery, and the harsh conditions he himself imposed on hundreds of people, had no emotional effect on him. He brushed aside their stories as if they were grains of sand or bits of dust.

My father took up so wholeheartedly the mission to entertain my husband and make him feel important that the drawing room at Montague Place was filled every day with London's most celebrated artists and intellectuals. Pierce fairly glowed with good will, like the cat that drank up all the cream, when he was seated beside Lady Byron, who came by one day for tea. And to his delight, since he valued so highly aristocratic lineage, we were joined the same afternoon by Charles Greville, author of the Greville Papers, descendent of the Earls of Warwick.

Since Pierce thoroughly enjoyed music, he was greatly pleased that Adelaide's musician friends often stopped by in the late evening after their concerts. We were accustomed to coming home after dining out to find her entertaining Italian singers and even Franz Liszt, who accompanied her and praised her extravagantly when they performed at Stafford House in a benefit concert for the Poles. The Duchess of Sutherland had lent her magnificent house, and I watched with pleasure my husband's boyish awe of the great hall and its winding staircase carpeted in scarlet with marble balustrades and a ceiling of gold and white. The skylight was supported by magnificent gilt columns covered in carved roses. Sunlight poured down on the faces of the lovely ladies in the audience and on her fine collection of Paolo Caliari's Venetian paintings.

One evening when we came in, we found my father sitting over a glass of port with Felix Mendelssohn, who had greatly admired my mother and always called when he was in London. Pierce was charmed to learn that the inspiration for Mendelssohn's orchestral work "A Midsummer Night's Dream" had occurred while visiting the Grote's country house near Burnham Beeches, and that the overture had first been composed by him and performed in my own *mother's* drawing room. I witnessed my husband's wonder that Mendelssohn, when his presence was sought by all in high society, preferred the company of the *Kembles*, mere actors whom my husband felt he had granted distinction by marrying me. I observed that though Pierce prided himself in the flute playing that had originally moved me, he did not offer to demonstrate his skills in front of Mr. Mendelssohn.

Following my father's advice, I also accepted far more invitations than I should have desired to be certain my husband was entertained in keeping with all he felt should be accorded to someone of his standing in America. I accompanied him to Cranford Hall to visit the Berkeleys so that Pierce might resume his friendship with Henry Berkeley, whom he had met in America. Our dear family friend Lord Dacre expressly arranged a cricket match at his country home in Pierce's honor, as my husband had never seen it played. Afterwards there was a grand dinner on the lawn followed by an evening of music.

I wearied of so many visits and engagements, but was so pleased to again enjoy my husband's company and approbation that I was content, until

I began to observe signs of his old restlessness. One night after we had returned from a formal dinner at the Duke and Duchess of Allenby's newly redecorated London home, when I felt certain Pierce would accompany me upstairs, he chose instead to go out again by himself. I knew from past experience, it was the wiser course not to question my husband, yet I feared he sought not only late-night drinking and gaming companions, but was unfaithful to me. He received letters, which he was quick to snatch from the servants before I might see the name on the envelopes. I would not demean myself by spying or searching his chamber when he was out, but I noticed several times when he received his mail that the writing was feminine and written in the same hand. I thought on the rare occasions when he returned to me at night, caught up as I was in suspicion's inevitable web, that I detected about his person a perfume definitely not my own.

26

Opening Night

It was not Covent Garden, but through Matthew's growing theatrical acquaintances, and following the announcement that I would appear as Louisa Tarleton, mistress of the plantation, *The Poisoned Table* was finally booked at the Brighton Emporium. Matthew had despaired of finding an American theatre willing to stage his play after numerous rejections and even threats to run us out of town after a reading in a church. His dream of swaying public opinion towards the abolitionist cause had failed. Yet believing as I did in the power of *The Poisoned Table,* I encouraged Matthew to invest our small savings in travel to England to seek an audience.

We were at once uplifted by the fanciful sight of the Brighton Emporium, which contained a theatre and a music hall and possessed a lovely view of the water. London critics would review the premier if we were fortunate, and we would attract London theatregoers seeking something outside of the standard repertory. If our notices were good, which the play and performances should guarantee, we could contemplate an engagement to follow at a London theatre. My own fantasy of returning home in glory would be realized. And we would discourage the British public from siding with the Southerners by helping them see the human face of every slave.

Matthew was so convinced of our imminent success that, uncharacteristically, he invested generously in costumes and props. "It is not enough for the audience to hear impassioned speeches," he told me. "They must *feel* they have been transported to the dining room of a genuine plantation."

He, who had previously been satisfied to make do with sticks of furniture which threatened to fall to pieces if they were moved too roughly across a stage, and costumes and curtains which likely served double duty the same evening in someone's bedchamber, bought silver candelabras and handsome damask gowns for the ladies. He insisted upon a Persian carpet for the dining room floor and candlelit sconces on the walls. The table almost appeared bridal in decoration with a white, lace cloth and arrangements of fragrant white blossoms in a crystal vase. When I questioned so much expense and detail, Matthew assured me it was a necessity.

"You must appreciate the ironic contrast of this festive dinner table with what follows?" he asked impatiently. "The opening view of the table should appear tasteful and welcoming, before its poisons, hidden amid the graceful accoutrement, are revealed."

"We cannot afford your irony, Matthew. I mean that *literally*. Your audience must make do with simple pottery instead of fine china, and artificial flowers instead of fresh ones changed three times each week," I told him, examining the bills covering his desk. "Perhaps the cook could steal an item of meat less costly than an entire roast," I suggested. "And how could you spend so much on programs and posters? One would think we had pockets full of gold instead of holes."

"Your claims are ridiculous, Isabel," he said in exasperation, though he still kissed me. "Our costumes are old, but they have no holes."

"Because *I* have sewn them up!"

"We've nothing to be ashamed of, Isabel. We have earned our right to success and to spend a bit of money on this play. We need not proceed as if we must turn out all our pockets to find the price of a tablecloth."

"But you insisted we must not allow *The Poisoned Table* to pull the company down," I reminded him. "'We must give no one cause to claim this play received special considerations because it is my own,'" I recited back to him in convincing imitation of his earnest tone. "'Distressing as it would be to fail,'" you reminded us, 'it would be far worse to add to that humiliation, debts, which bankrupt us.'"

But Matthew had changed his mind. He insisted we must spare no expenditure that might enable *The Poisoned Table* to be well received so that its message and acclaim would carry it all the way back to America. The play would not be respected if we appeared to be a band of poor actors performing a different play each night with the players clothed in the costumes of the night before. He was determined to silence any impression we were a fledgling company without the ability to pay in advance for the furnishings on the stage or the handbills distributed about the town.

He hired a seamstress, as wardrobe mistress was no longer one of my responsibilities, and he began furnishing the dining room of the plantation house with every detail one might expect in a chamber where lavish meals were served. He labored over directions to the carpenters, who designed at the rear of the stage several large windows lightly veiled with curtains to allow the master to look through them to talk to the overseer and slaves.

They would stand on a platform behind the windows and be visible to the audience. Matthew accepted it was impossible to show on stage the dreadful beatings levied upon the slaves, but by obscuring the audience's view through curtains, they might still bear witness to this cruel world. It permitted him to have the roles of slaves acted by Indians and others of dark complexion who might pass as slaves. He obtained the services of several freedmen, and was able to cast in the role of Hecuba, the cook who wielded the poison, an aged mulatto woman from Barbados who had recently been set free in the will of her master, an old gentleman who brought her to England where he unexpectedly died.

I begged Matthew not to expend so much for our costumes and the very glasses that the master smashes into the fireplace in one of his angry rages. But he seemed unable to make any sacrifice of the splendid appointments he had envisioned. I tried accompanying him on his missions to the shops, hoping I might provide a steadying influence, yet in reality I seemed to inflame him to new heights of spending.

"You cannot imagine my dilemma," he told me playfully, taking my arm as we left an antique store carrying several paintings, someone's abandoned family oil portraits with which he wished to adorn the dining room walls. "I should like to be frugal as you wish me to be. But I must see you splendidly turned out for this role, which may well be your finest. And if I select lovely garments only for you, then I shall be accused of favoring you above everyone else." He tenderly kissed my hand. "So it must be the very best for everyone, and we shall have a magnificent performance."

There was an excited hum throughout the theatre. Looking out from the wings, I observed the audience's impatience for the play to begin. It was a small theatre, but we had filled the orchestra and most of the balcony, which was quite commendable for a new play by a playwright hardly known outside his own country. I hoped this good showing indicated English abhorrence for slavery, even if slave labor produced the Sea Island cotton upon which English commerce depended. I hoped it also revealed admiration for me, as I had been prominently portrayed in the posters and programs. It made me smile to think that Isabel Graves had come home to a following when once she had been forced to steal away in the night.

As the curtain parted, the figures on the stage were hardly visible. Then as the cook, Hecuba, her head bound up in a colorful kerchief, and two serving girls lit the candelabras in the center of the table, on buffets at both ends of the room, and another on a table by the rear windows, the room became illuminated. For a moment there was no conversation on the stage, only the deliberate and careful motions of the three women carefully arranging the place settings and exiting time to time to return with additional plates, an immense tureen, and serving pieces to place upon the table. Then they began to speak among themselves in the easy way that servants, no matter if they are free or enslaved, will do when they are among themselves and in no danger of being overheard.

Molly: (tauntingly as she arranges the silver) I know you say you going to do it, Hecuba. But I do not believe you. No matter what you say, you will not have nerve to do it. What do you think, Lula?

Lula: (soberly) I want no part of your fussin', Molly. You always cast trouble about you. (warning her) You keep away from me. I mind my own business and pay no mind to what anybody else do, master or slave. You do well to do the same. It not for you to wonder what Hecuba do or put some foolishness in her mind.

Hecuba: (laughing, straining as she moves the large tureen to the head of the table): You best just keep to your work so Missus have no cause to box your ears. I 'spect yours still be ringing from last night, Molly, the way she knock you on the ear with her book. You see soon enough what Hecuba will do or what she won't. (She stirs the tureen with a large silver ladle and then places the ladle beside the bowls next to the tureen.)

Molly: (pointedly) When you going to taste that gumbo, Hecuba? You know you always do when missus not looking or before she come to table. Why is tonight different, Hecuba? You always take your bowl or did you already spit in the sou—

Hecuba: (stepping towards her threateningly) You best not mess with me. Don't you start your trouble now or I give you some of my own and tell Missus where Massa lay these last three nights. Never in all my days I spit in a pot of soup or stew. Those dirty ways be more your way than mine. (mysteriously) I got my own plans. Just you wait and they be revealed in God's good time.

Molly: (moving close to Lula as if she fears Hecuba though she continues to jeer at her) Lula, she talk big but that is all she do. She will be afraid to do it when the time come.

Lula: (cautioning her) You be quiet now. You riling her. You know she still mad after what Missus say to her about the fish stew at luncheon.

Hecuba: (overhearing and responding angrily despite her resolve to be calm) Missus have no right to say I steal the stew. *(defiantly)* She say she measure out the cups of broth to the pot when I start to cook, but then when she measure it late morning, there be two cups missing. Even a child know some of the water boil away in the cooking. Many time I could steal plenty meal and milk and side meat from Massa's table and never I have. She got no cause to 'cuse me.

Lula: (soothingly) Missus know that. This whole ruckus all 'cause Samson stole the roast of beef she was savin' special for the preacher. *(laughing)* Missus want to be the one to serve him roast beef when all the other families give him pork and chicken. She trust Samson and then he do her this way.

Molly: (sadly but matter-of-factly) That why Massa flog Samson himself 'stead of leavin' it to the overseer. He say what Samson did be a crime against this house, along with the sin of thievery. *(warming to her subject)* That why he give him the full 150 lashes. Samson hold his tongue for the first fifty, though the blood be running down his back. But then he cry out so loud it make the people fall to their knees begging Massa to stop the beating. But he keep on 'til he give Samson the full number he had announced. When Samson fell to the ground, it seem there be no life left in him, Massa stood over him and tell him that Samson will work no more in the house. The very next day Massa sent him to the rice fields. No more easy life for him waiting table.

Hecuba: (defiantly) Massa should be struck down for beating Samson so. There no more loyal slave among all the people on this plantation. And if he stole one roast in all these years serving at Massa's table when he so hungry I hear his belly groaning from across the chamber, then Massa should have forgive him. He have roasts and chickens and pigs enough. He could have warned Samson and taken away his little meat that he give him and made him double his work. But beating him that way 'til the blood run down his sides—

(Hecuba has stopped setting the table. Overwrought as she feels, there is a power and force to her seething anger which makes the other two women back away, watching her apprehensively.)

Hecuba: (fiercely) Ever since Massa find cause to blame Samson, his back be always a mess of sores. He scared every day Massa may sell him away. The sores never have time to heal before the next beating. (angrily) I make him special salve from hog fat, spider webs, river mud, and ashes. Nothing Massa ever care to use. But when Massa see me prepare it, he throw it away instead of letting Samson be comforted. He let that useless Noah serve at table and wait on his guests, though Noah clumsier than if he tried to break everything he touch on purpose. Massa do anything just to spite Samson.

Lula: (cautioning) Missus already in bad temper, Hecuba. She 'bout snapped my head off 'cause little missus shoes not clean enough to suit her. You best watch that gumbo not burn, Hecuba. Or there be price to pay for us all.

Hecuba: (calmly reassuring her) Don't you worry, Lula. I watch that soup and I watch out for the people. (They busy themselves making the table ready, pouring glasses of milk and water into tumblers and making several trips from the larder to the table, carrying condiments).

I carefully watched the stage to be certain I came in on cue. I listened for sounds and signs the audience was happily engaged, and satisfied myself that they were fascinated, so still and quiet they had become. I prepared for my entrance, pleased that I looked particularly well with my golden hair arranged in a French twist, and with diamonds, paste of course, at my throat, accenting the daring neckline of my blue gown. I felt as handsome and haughty as Matthew had desired in his concept of Louisa Tarleton, and heard audible gasps and exclamations when I took the stage, much as audiences had once greeted Fanny Kemble herself. I pulled myself quickly out of the happy reverie into which this admiration had sent me, and following stage directions, walked imperiously up to Hecuba.

Mrs. Tarleton: (obviously annoyed) Hecuba, let me taste that soup immediately. (disdainfully sniffing the air) From the smell of it, I cannot imagine that we shall be able to eat it. (clapping her hands) Molly, open the windows before we all faint away from the odor of Hecuba's shrimp. (sniffing indignantly) It must be spoiled.

Hecuba: (with dangerous disrespect) I do not know what Missus be smelling, but it nothing belong to Hecuba. That gumbo made the way Missus tell me every time before.

Lula: (quickly interceding) Please, Missus, pay Hecuba no mind. She been cooking all morning over that hot stove 'til it make her temper hot. Please forgive Hecuba, Missus. (looking encouragingly to Hecuba) I sure she beg Missus pardon herself right now.

Mrs. Tarleton: (angrily) Hecuba best keep a civil tongue in her head without any reminder from you if she knows what is good for her. (clapping her hands) Molly, I already told you once. Open those windows. (turning to Hecuba) And you, get me a taste of that gumbo before everyone comes to the table.

Molly: (hesitant in her nervousness to disobey a command) Missus, I dare not. (looking out the rear window) Massa flogging someone. If I open the windows, Missus sure to hear the cries.

Mrs. Tarleton: (dismissively) It is only Samson. Bringing it upon himself again. (disdainfully) We have heard his whimpering enough by now to know it is of no consequence. Now open the window.

(When Molly opens the windows, the audience's view is still partially obscured by the curtains. Yet through them, it is still possible to see and hear the sound of the lash, wielded by Mr. Tarleton, descending upon a man's back, as well as his ensuing cries. Several slaves and the overseer observe the scene.)

Mrs. Tarleton: (impatiently) Hurry up now, Hecuba. I am waiting. And if this is like your usual cooking, it shall require all my talents to remedy the mess you have made of the seasoning before the others come to table. (with growing irritation) Be quick about it!

(Through the open window, the voices of Mr. Tarleton, Samson, and Mr. O'Toole, the overseer, become audible.)

Mr. Tarleton: (sighing) All right, Samson. That's enough for now. Get along with you and finish your work this time. The others are resting and eating. As soon as you finish, you may join them. You best hurry or the rest time shall be over. *(firmly)* Do you hear me, Samson? I am tired of your foolishness. I shall not tolerate your sassing Mr. O'Toole here. Next time, I've a good mind just to send you down river.

Samson: *(begging, on his knees)* Please, Massa, not that. Please Massa, not sell Samson away from all his family. Please, Massa, give Samson anoth—"

Mrs. Tarleton: *(annoyed at the disturbance)* Molly close that window. We've no cause to listen to that pitiful coward on his knees begging for mercy. After he has betrayed those who trusted him and treated him kindly. I've a good mind to ask your master to sell Samson away from here. He is more bother than he is worth. *(She takes the small bowl of gumbo from Hecuba's trembling hands and tastes it. Hecuba's face appears stricken at the sound of Mrs. Tarleton's words.)*

Lula: *(ingratiatingly)* Missus want a glass of lemonade while she waiting for the others?

Mrs. Tarleton: *(perturbed)* What I want, is an explanation from Hecuba of why this gumbo is so bitter? *(grimacing)* Whatever did you put in it to make it this way?

Hecuba: It is the same recipe Missus tell me. I add nothing but the shrimps the men bring me, same as always.

Mrs. Tarleton: *(summarily)* Something must be done about it. No one can eat it this way. Bring me the canisters of sugar and salt and be quick about it.

(Hecuba exits quickly stage right and returns holding the canisters before her and places them beside the tureen.)

Mrs. Tarleton: *(pouring a generous measure of sugar into the tureen and stirring it before she also adds a small amount of salt.)* Now, let us see if that improves it. *(She ladles a small amount into her bowl and daintily tastes it.)* Ah, that is much better. Your master shall be able to eat that and the children as well. Let that be a lesson to you, Hecuba. Do not serve us such bitter messes in the future.

Hecuba: *(meekly, but looking knowingly at Molly and Lula)* Yes, Missus. I will remember.

Mrs. Tarleton: Go ahead and serve it out. They will all be coming to the table. (critically) You have made it so hot, we shall all be glad to let it sit out in the air a bit. (jokingly to Hecuba) You would think that you intended to burn us all with this fiery gumbo of yours.

(The family assembles at the table. Mrs. Tarleton is seated at one end, and Mr. Tarleton, after kissing his wife, sits opposite her at the other end. Several young men and women, obviously older children, and two small girls fill the other seats. There is general laughter and greeting as might be expected at the beginning of a meal. Hecuba has left the room to attend the rest of the meal. Molly and Lula pass round biscuits and butter and refill glasses from the pitchers of water and milk. Then they stand motionless against the walls of the room, as if they are attached to them.)

Mr. Tarleton: (eating heartily) I enjoy a hearty gumbo after a hard day's work. (making smacking noises as he tastes it) I believe this is a sweeter recipe than you sometimes serve, my dear. Or is that just the good flavor of our fine shrimp?

Mrs. Tarleton: (with satisfaction) I am pleased you are enjoying it. I fear you nor anyone else would have willingly eaten it but moments ago. (staring at Hecuba) It was so bitter I could hardly stand it. You owe that it is palatable to a healthy portion of sugar. (taking a few spoonfuls herself) It is now very pleasing I think. (addressing the children) Now eat heartily. Food will not keep in this heat and we shall not waste it.

(For a few moments there is no further sound other than the spoons against the china bowls and glasses being lifted and bread plates adjusted. Suddenly, there is a loud cry as the youngest daughter, Anne Louise, reaching for her water, turns it over and leaps forward, crying out in obvious pain.)

Anne Louise: (imploringly) Mama, Mama, it hurts inside. Help me, Mama. I am on fire.

Mrs. Tarleton: (running to her daughter's side) What is it, precious baby? Are you ill? (feeling her forehead) She is perfectly cool to the touch. There is so sign of fever.

Anne Louise: (gasping, pointing to her mouth) It is inside. Something I ate.

Frederick: (crying out) Mother, my mouth is burning. (pointing to his half-eaten bowl of gumbo) I was fine until I ate that gumbo. It tastes sweet and then burns your insides.

(Another young man runs suddenly from the table and can be heard audibly retching in the bushes.)

Mrs. Tarleton: No one take another bite of this evil soup. (angrily calling out) Hecuba, Hecuba. Come here at once and answer for what you have served us.

(All the children are crying. Moments before, the dinner table was inviting and elegant. It is suddenly a setting of great disarray and hysteria. Mrs. Tarleton cradles one of the young girls in her arms. Lula and Molly do their best to comfort the others.)

Mr. Tarleton: (authoritatively) Hecuba! Hecuba! You have heard your mistress. Come here at once. You do not want to make me search for you. I promise you then it shall be worse for you.

Mrs. Tarleton: (placing the youngest child in Molly's arms) I will go see why she does not answer. (She exits stage right to the larder.)

Molly: (gently rocking the child) There, there, now baby. Don't you cry. Your mama will be back in just a moment. Soon I make you bread and milk and you be all better.

(Everyone seated around the table is very still. Except for the whimpering of the youngest child, the stage is eerily quiet for a table seating so many people.)

Mrs. Tarleton: (returning and appealing to her husband) She has vanished. Everything is left in readiness for dinner, but she is nowhere to be found.

Mr. Tarleton: (menacingly) I will find her. If I must ride straight through the night, I will find her. (going over to the window he leans out and shouts) You there, boy. Get your pappy and tell him to gather the others. Hecuba has run off. I want her back within the next hour. She must be found, and until she is, not a slave on this plantation shall have another mouthful to eat. Now run and tell the others.

Mrs. Tarleton: Molly and Lula, take the children up to bed. Everyone has been sickened by this meal. There is no point sitting here. No one shall eat another bite. (Both young women seem stunned, as if waiting for further orders, fearing to move without Mrs. Tarleton's order to do so.) Go ahead! (angrily) Did you not hear me? Has every slave on this plantation gone mad tonight? Do as you are told or you shall answer for it!

(Molly and Lula exit quickly gathering up the children of all ages and leaving only Mr. and Mrs. Tarleton on the stage.)

Mr. Tarleton: (taking his gold watch from his pocket and studying it) They have already wasted a quarter of an hour. (pacing back and forth) You can hear them shouting in the yard as if it were a party. I hope they took me seriously. There will be punishment for the whole plantation if she is not found straight away.

Mrs. Tarleton: They will find her soon enough. (agitated) But what will you do with her? I believe she has tried to poison us.

Mr. Tarleton: (resolutely) If that is the case, there is nothing I shall not do to her. And she shall deserve it all. (sighing wearily) This circumstance is most unjust to me. Normally I should sell off a recalcitrant slave, but how could I expect anyone to buy a cook who has nearly poisoned her own master and mistress and their children. After all that we have done for her. If I told the truth, which as a gentleman I am bound to do, no master in his right mind should want to have her near him or his family.

Mrs. Tarleton: (smiling cruelly) It would be as you say if she were sold as a cook. But not if she were sold as a common field hand. That is what she must be as soon as she is found. I will not have her around me or my children another day. Let her see how she shall enjoy field work. I predict she shall take to it as well as Samson.

Mr. Tarleton: It is not that simple, my dear. Hecuba is old. She will not be of any use in the field. Mr. O'Toole would complain that I had saddled him with a worthless old woman. The work would likely kill her.

Mrs. Tarleton: Then let it kill her. Was that not what she had in mind for our entire family?

Mr. Tarleton: You do not know yet. We must see what it was she put in the soup. Perhaps it was an accident, nothing she intended at all. She shall be chastised—forcefully, of course—and the incident may be forgotten.

Mrs. Tarleton: (with certainty) It was no accident. When I came down to taste the gumbo, I observed it tasted very bitter and asked Hecuba about it. She professed to taste nothing out of the ordinary. I added sugar to it, thinking the tomatoes were simply too sour. But now I am certain it was because she put something into the pot and thought to conceal her evil in the rich flavor of the soup.

(They are interrupted by the sudden entrance of a group of slaves, clad in ragged clothing as if they have just come from the field. They are dragging the struggling Hecuba before them and fling her at Mr. Tarleton's feet. Then they stand back in obvious fear.)

Mr. Tarleton: You thought you could bring sickness on us all and escape, Hecuba. But your evil scheme has failed. (coldly) Now, you had best tell us where you procured the poison you put into our soup. Who helped you with this murderous plan? (standing over the cowering woman) Speak up now or I shall beat every slave on this plantation until I know for certain who was trying to harm us. Answer me, woman. This is your last chance!

Hecuba: (rising to her feet) I have no poison, Massa. And no money to purchase any, and Massa know I never leave the plantation. I have no way to come by any poison.

Mrs. Tarleton: (accusingly) But you could make it. On Sunday after worship, I always see you walking and gathering up herbs and leaves in your basket.

Hecuba: I use those herbs to flavor Massa's food. (nervously) Missus knows there be plenty plants and roots in the woods and the fields to make good medicine and make Massa's food taste good. (appears deeply shocked) But poison! The good Lord would never forgive a soul for such a terrible thing. (She gasps and wipes her eyes with her apron.)

Mr. Tarleton: If it was not you, then it must have been Lula or Molly. They are the only others who help you with our food. (to his wife) Summon them immediately. They shall answer for what they have done, and they shall pay for it this very day.

(Mrs. Tarleton leaves stage right and can be heard ascending the stairs.)

Mr. Tarleton: (mildly turning to Hecuba) I am not in my right mind to accuse you after years of faithful service, Hecuba. It was the shock of seeing everyone stricken at our own table. (firmly) We shall set this immediately to rights.

(Hecuba looks dolefully at her master, but says nothing in response. She is clearly very afraid of what is about to occur.)

Mrs. Tarleton: (enters stage right dragging Lula and Molly) I leave them to you, my dear. I shall not speak a word to them after the unthinkable acts they have committed. (imploring her husband) I have just left the beds where our children are crying, their poor throats burning and raw from some evil potion. (shoving Molly and Lula forward so that they fall at Mr. Tarleton's feet) All they have known in this house is good treatment, and they repay us by poisoning us. Each week they attend church service, yet still they are so savage they do not hesitate to poison little children. On innocent babes they have perpetrated this crime! And the only reason they have not been successful was that they calculated incorrectly the amount of poison so that it only burned our mouths. I hope you will show no mercy towards these wicked wenches. The good Lord expects no less. Is it not written, "An eye for an eye and a tooth for a tooth"?

Mr. Tarleton: I do not know what eye or tooth we could take from them that should punish them properly for what they have committed. Unless we should force them to eat sufficient portions of this poisoned gumbo until they shall writhe in pain before they perish. But then I and this plantation should lose the value of two slaves and receive nothing in compensation save the temporary satisfaction of making them suffer for the evil they have wrought in a Christian home. (furiously approaching the window and calling out to men in the yard) Bring me my cat-o'-nine-tails. I shall know, if I must beat every slave on this plantation, who conspired in this attempted murder. And I shall begin with you two. (he speaks to the young women cowering at his feet) You deserve no mercy, but it shall go better for you if you quickly confess your crime and name anyone who assisted you. Though it shall dearly affect my pocketbook if I should beat you to your deaths, I will know tonight who the evil ones are on this plantation. And they will be sold down river and sent to the harshest labor I can find for them.

(A large leather whip is handed through the window to Mr. Tarleton. First he feels the separate lashes in his hands, separating them so that everyone can see them, and then very purposefully he strikes the floor several times so that the quiet stage is alive with the cracking sound of the leather.)

Mrs. Tarleton: Who shall go first or shall you punish them together? And shall I summon the people so that they may witness what happens to those who sin against this house?

Mr. Tarleton: (pulling them both up by their hair) Say now whatever you have to say that might explain your evil behavior and encourage me to go easy upon you. (When they do not answer he is clearly enraged.) Then I shall take you to the yard and beat you before every slave on this plantation. Whether you live or die is of little consequence to me, tricking old Hecuba as you have. When she brought you up to learn her craft so one day you might cook for the entire plantation and make something of yourselves. And this is how you repay us all. (He drags them towards stage left towards the doorway).

Mrs. Tarleton: Hecuba, stop your trembling and moaning. You should be relieved that the true criminals have been apprehended. Come to make up bowls of bread and milk for the children. This will soothe them until tomorrow when the doctor can attend them. Then put on the kettle for tea. I shall certainly want a cup. (annoyed that Hecuba stands immobile, frozen by the plight of Lula and Molly instead of minding her mistress's directions) Get along with you! Must I drive you like a mule!

Hecuba: (stands frozen in her tracks and cries out desperately) Please, Massa, stop. Do not harm those girls. They good girls and did not do this. I—I—with my own hands, I poisoned the soup. And I so sorry I did not know the measure of the powder from the roots so that it could have worked. Massa have no cause to treat Samson as he do. And the people starving on the rations Massa give. Yet I never steal the broth like Missus say I do.

Mr. Tarleton: (shoving Lula and Molly to the side) It would appear you are as accomplished a liar as you are a cook, Hecuba. But neither skill shall save you from the lash. (grabbing her roughly and pushing her through the door stage left)

Mrs. Tarleton: (calling after them) Show her no mercy. Tie her up so she may not avoid a single sting of the lash. Think of your children suffering upstairs. Kindly as you are, forgiving to all, this once let her have what she deserves. Think of your children.

Mr. Tarleton: (looking over his shoulder) Rest assured, my dear. Whether she lives or dies, this shall be the last night she spends on this plantation.

The curtain closes for a brief Intermission.

When I reached the dressing room, I was drenched in perspiration from the emotion of uttering such hateful lines. I had played villains often enough, and agreed with Matthew that evil characters presented the best opportunity to display an actor's skills. Yet while it was one thing to be Lady Macbeth or a murderous queen of the ancient Greeks, to portray slave-holders, who by all appearances looked like any other ladies or gentlemen one might pass in the street, was deeply disturbing. I took a drink of water and composed myself for the next scene when Louisa Tarleton learns of her husband's infidelities with his slaves during the punishment of Hecuba, which she watches through the window. As I stood in the wings, I was surprised not to hear a sound from the audience. While actors move about the stage, we become so engaged in the action that the audience is almost forgotten, but after every scene we search for any sign of their disposition.

Just before my entrance, I observed that though some members of the audience had taken their seats, rows that had previously been full remained vacant. I observed Matthew talking with someone in the rear of the theatre. They kept looking and gesturing towards the stage. Matthew seemed most distressed, his face very pale as he paced back and forth.

When I entered stage right I turned purposefully to the window, where from a decorous distance Mrs. Tarleton could watch the beating of Hecuba. After my husband had finished meting out her punishment, I was supposed to greet him, offer him refreshment, lemonade or wine, as if he were returning in the evening from his usual occupations about the plantation. Yet instead of the resumption of the interrupted dinner, Mrs. Tarleton is confronted with his treachery, for as this scene begins, under the duress of her beating, Hecuba cries out, "How can Massa blame Hecuba for betraying the family when he take Lula and Molly to bed whenever he please, even while Missus in the big house?"

Just as Mr. Tarleton joined me on stage, preparing to accept a glass of wine, a shocking disturbance occurred. The remaining audience members rose from their seats and began shouting. Some threw fruit and vegetables and pelted us with all manner of debris, including bottles and great wads of soiled newspapers. For the brief moment I remained on stage, frozen in amazement, I understood many theatre seats remained vacant since all the ladies had departed at intermission, as if by decree. Raucous insults continued as we hurried off stage, and there was a great outcry as Matthew made his way forward, hoping to regain order so we might resume the performance.

Yet the angry gentlemen would not return to their seats. They finally wearied of shouting insults at Matthew, having exhausted their supply of objects to hurl at us, and then arm in arm, clearly invigorated by their own performance, they left the theatre. I had by this time changed to street clothes and covered my head with a shawl so no one save my closest friends should recognize me as the haughty Louisa Tarleton. As I walked through the lobby of the theatre, hoping to encourage Matthew to leave with me, I was greeted by the shouts emanating from members of the company and friends, who had surrounded Matthew's prostrate body and were urging everyone to step back so the air might reach him.

I ran to him and tried to revive him with my moistened handkerchief and a sip of spirits, which one kind gentleman provided from his flask, but nothing seemed to lift him from his terrible faint. Several of the actors joined arms and carried him across the street where he might rest in our lodgings until a doctor could be found. Every few moments, he revived sufficiently to cough a dreadful cough that ripped through his poor chest, until he fell back into a troubled sleep. I asked the others to wait in the sitting room, fearing Matthew had fainted from the shame of seeing his play so grievously attacked, and when the doctor revived him, Matthew would be mortified to find himself surrounded by those who had witnessed his humiliation. I thought he could recover if only I could take him away to a quiet place in the English countryside to regain his strength. I prayed I would have the chance.

But when the doctor arrived, he listened briefly as I explained Matthew's sudden collapse, and then bid me sit across the room so he might examine his patient. I hated to leave Matthew's side for even a moment, yet stepped away and watched while the old man used his instruments to look into Matthew's nose and eyes and down his throat and rested his greasy head upon Matthew's chest to hear the sound of his heart and lungs.

"I am very sorry," he said, bringing me two bottles of medicine, one a thick red syrup and the other a sickly yellow. "There is little to be done for Mr. Harrison, I am afraid, at this stage of his disease. But these medicines will make him more comfortable for the little time that remains to him."

"I...I do not understand," I stammered, shocked by his words. "What do you mean, doctor? Matthew has not been treated for any disease."

"That I can easily believe by the sound of his lungs and the weakness of his heart. Nevertheless, he has long suffered with consumption, which has greatly diminished his strength. And now he has also contracted a serious infection of the throat."

"Then please prescribe some medicine to cure it. Truly, money is of no concern," I said desperately, thinking I would draw on all my savings and ask help from all the others, no matter how much it might take, to obtain the needed medicine.

"I am very sorry. But we have no medicine to cure his throat. What I have given you will help him sleep and may ease his breathing. If he were a stronger man, then perhaps he could survive this infection. But you see," he said, taking my hands, "he is very weak. You were not aware that he had consumption?" he asked curiously. "You never noticed that he was subject to spells of coughing?"

In truth, I had noticed the coughing and had asked Matthew about it. He always dismissed my concern saying that he had suffered since childhood from a weak chest. It ran in his family, but was no more than a minor inconvenience, certainly not a serious condition.

"Well, it is no matter now, my dear. I have known of other situations in which the decea—that is, the invalid," he quickly corrected himself, "goes to great lengths to conceal the effects of the disease, not wishing to draw attention to himself or to impose a burden on loved ones." He placed the bottles and his instructions on the table beside me. "Give him the medicine following my instructions, and he will be more comfortable. I shall come by tomorrow. I am very sorry, my dear. His time is short. No one can say how long he has, but I must warn you, Mr. Harrison has not long to live."

Looking at Matthew's pale face and thin body, racked alternately by chills and blazing fevers, I could not doubt the doctor's words. When Matthew woke after a coughing spell, I managed to spoon the medicine into his trembling lips. He grimaced and swallowed, far too weak to speak a single word to me. When I wiped his lips with my handkerchief, it came away stained with blood.

The next morning Matthew seemed slightly improved. He ate a few spoonfuls of soft-boiled egg, and after taking his medicine, which he complained tasted both sour and bitter, he enjoyed a cup of tea. I felt heartened that perhaps the doctor had erred and Matthew was strong enough to fight off his infection.

"I cannot remember fully all the events of last night," he told me. "Yet I recall enough to wonder if we even received a review since our performance was so rudely interrupted. Do you have the papers?"

I had hoped in his weakness Matthew might forget to inquire about reviews until so much time had passed it would be impossible to produce the newspapers. But when he asked me directly, I had to read him the notice we had received in the *Brighton Theatre Report,* which I had myself avoided reading until that moment.

It mentioned the audience's evident pleasure when "celebrated actress Isabel Graves took the stage. Conveying indeed the beauty and the arrogance of the mistress of a plantation, there were audible gasps from gentlemen in the audience when she appeared, recalling the reception once awarded to Fanny Kemble."

My heart soared at that reference, happy I had not imagined this warm reception. I hoped Fanny Kemble herself might read about it, wherever she might be. *I* was now the one gentlemen longed to see. Matthew proudly congratulated me, before he succumbed to another coughing spell, pleased how well he had predicted this role would suit me.

Then I was forced to read him the reviewer's scornful comments. "Whatever was Matthew Andrew Harrison, the noted American comedic playwright, thinking by bringing such a grisly drama to the Brighton stage?

Slavery may be a worthy matter for discussion among those concerned with commerce and the humane production of needed commodities such as cotton, which is most important to English interests. But to make this the subject of a play? Mr. Harrison, usually so skillful in the construction of his drawing room comedies, was certainly very imprudent in his writing of *The Poisoned Table*.

"Even the fine acting and lovely appearance of Miss Graves,"—it hurt me to read aloud positive notice of myself, so scathing as was this review of his own work—"could not mask the misguided sentiments and true vileness of this play, in which the cook on a plantation attempts to murder all the members of her master's family using poisonous roots she has gathered. Her plan is foiled as the tainted soup she serves the family is discovered by its bitter taste and burning aspect. Whether Mr. Harrison's 'poisoned table' is or is not a true metaphor for American slavery, we shall not know, since the play so disturbed the audience that at the first intermission, the gentlemen in the audience ushered away their ladies and then remained for the next scene only long enough to very vocally display their disdain for the play they had witnessed, many having no doubt secured tickets anticipating one of Mr. Harrison's delightful comedies.

"Theatre may indeed reveal insights into major issues of our times. But in this drama, the master and mistress of the plantation are so diabolically portrayed that even the sublime Miss Graves could not ameliorate the unconvincing depiction of her character, the mistress of Golden Isle. Plantation life is so odiously portrayed as to make one wonder how the American South could continue to exist if Mr. Harrison's rendering were accurate. This reviewer has not had opportunity to travel to America himself, but was fortunate to encounter, leaving the theatre with the other ladies, someone who had herself witnessed American slavery. This was no one less notable than the former queen of the British stage, our own Fanny Kemble, now retired from the theatre and wife to Pierce Butler, Esq., of Philadelphia, who owns two large Georgia plantations which she has visited. Mrs. Butler, who was not accompanied by her husband, expressed her dismay at Mr. Harrison's portrayal of the slaves themselves.

"'I have never concealed from my husband nor anyone of my acquaintance my loathing for slavery. Yet Mr. Harrison has not advanced the cause of abolition. In the first act, he has instead portrayed a trusted house servant as a demonic creature who tries to poison her master's entire family. In the time I spent on two Georgia plantations, I experienced only kindness and generous attentions from the slaves. I wish the gentlemen present opening night had not been so determined to protect their ladies so we might have been permitted to see the second and third acts and learn if Mr. Harrison's play possibly redeemed itself.'

"From what this reviewer witnessed, there will not likely be another opportunity to see this play upon the British or the American stage. If Mr. Harrison's reputation survives this dismal failure, let us hope he shall resume writing comedies to which his wit and style are so admirably suited."

After I finished reading that review, Matthew asked that I dim the lights and close all the curtains. I helped adjust the pillows comfortably behind him so that he did not rest flat on his back in case a fit of coughing should come over him. Then he asked if I might sit across the room in the easy chair to keep him company until he should drop off to sleep.

I was glad to oblige him and settled myself comfortably in a chair for the first time that day. After I was certain he was asleep, I decided I might well go to my own bed to rest. I was quite exhausted.

I must have drifted off when I heard his hoarse voice call out, "Isabel, was it truly that bad?"

"Of course not, my love. That was only one review. Besides, he did not see the entire play."

"How could Fanny Kemble not understand? Of all people, she should know I was showing that the atrocities waged by the slaveholders could drive a slave, even a loyal house servant, to commit desperate acts."

"She saw only one act, Matthew, like all the other ladies. She would have thought better of it if she had seen the entire play," I said consolingly, while I seethed that of all possible critics, *she* had condemned Matthew's work.

"There was one part that the reviewer stated correctly," he said, coughing sharply when he tried to speak. "He called you 'the sublime Isabel Graves.' You were completely convincing as Mrs. Tarleton. I have never seen you more regal."

"Thank you," I said, kissing his brow and plumping up the pillows. "Now you must rest, Matthew. And no more talking. It only makes the coughing worse."

"Just three words more." He smiled at me so sweetly so I shall never forget it and whispered, "I love you." Then he closed his eyes.

I sat with him to be certain he was breathing peacefully. I intended to observe him longer, but in the darkening room I closed my eyes in weariness and fell asleep.

I awoke startled to find that night had fallen, leaving the room in absolute darkness. It took me a moment to light the lamp so that I might see. And then I wished I could not. For as I crossed the room and came close to Matthew, I saw his chest was covered with blood and he lay very still. When I touched his face it felt cold and his eyes were locked in the fixed stare of the dead. I kissed his forehead and closed his eyes, and in that sad room I vowed I should continue to act and to perform for both of us. I should never forget him or the memory of the only true love I had ever known.

27

Urgent Reply Requested

We had been in England nearly six months, and my father was so nearly his former self, I had no excuse to offer my husband of why we should not go home. Pierce seemed anxious to return to his business affairs so I did not fear, despite his mysterious evenings out, that he had had forged a lasting alliance. I was upset by his lack of caring for me and our marriage, but I had no absolute evidence of his betrayals, just as I had not known whom he had gone to see the night we quarreled at Col. McIntyre's home.

Then a very odd incident occurred. I had been out riding on a splendid little mare Lord Dacre had kindly made available to me throughout our visit. It was a true pleasure to me to ride each morning through the older neighborhoods of London. On my more ambitious rides, I ventured to the outskirts of the city to the very countryside where my mother had insisted we pass holidays as children so we might run freely. I would come home tired yet so thoroughly refreshed by this exercise that even if Pierce were beset by one of his foul tempers when nothing pleased him and he perceived slights everywhere, I managed not to become provoked.

This particular morning I knew something was wrong as soon as I entered my father's front door. When letters were received, if we were out or slow in coming to breakfast, the servants placed our correspondence on a silver tray on a table in the foyer. When I examined the tray, I saw a letter addressed to me had already been opened. The seal was broken and the envelope torn, and no attempt had been made to conceal that it had been opened.

Still wearing my boots, my riding crop tucked beneath my arm, I read Margery's letter informing me that she should not be returning to America with us. She was sorry for any inconvenience to me and to our family, but knew that I would understand when she explained that she had seen again her old sweetheart and now had the opportunity to marry and remain near her aging parents. She did not know when we meant to sail, but wished to return to pack up some clothing she had not taken on her holiday, bid farewell to Fan and Sal, to whom she felt much attached, and assist with any preparations for the journey which I might require. As I was finishing this unexpected letter, my husband joined me.

"I have learned Margery is leaving us," I told him.

"Yes, I know," he said, clearly unashamed. "When I saw the letter was marked *urgent reply requested*, I felt I should not stand on ceremony, but should open the letter at once. I am glad I did so. With such an important request, she deserved an immediate response. This is good news for her," he said generously.

"As soon as I have changed, I shall write to her to offer our congratulations." I had considered admonishing him for opening my correspondence, but considered perhaps he had acted appropriately, considering the notation on the envelope.

"There is actually no need for you to do so." He smiled amiably. "I have already replied to her letter so I might send the boy out quickly to catch the last mail. She shall have it right away," he said with satisfaction.

"You answered without even consulting me?"

"What was there to consult about? Surely I might safely assume you should not oppose the woman's opportunity to marry." He shook his head, as if truly amazed by my response. "I assured her of our thanks and good wishes and enclosed payment for her last wages. I told her she need not trouble herself with the long coach ride here to gather a few belongings which we should be delighted to send on to her. I explained there would not be time for her visit in any case, since we shall sail in but a few days."

"Surely, we can find time to say good-bye to Margery? The children will never see her again, and think how devoted she has been to them!" I felt my anger rising, hard as I tried to contain it. "You had no right to respond to *my* letter or to determine when we shall sail as if I have no say at all."

"In truth, you do not, madam," he answered coldly, showing plainly my feelings did not concern him. "I informed you days ago that I could no longer remain here. I have been quite generous in abandoning my business concerns to bring you here. I was glad to accompany you, of course, but you need not act as if I have behaved unfairly towards you. It is time for us to go," he said peremptorily. "If you absolutely insist on staying longer, then I shall permit it, but you shall remain alone. I admire your fealty to your dear father, but you must admit he is much improved, and your place is therefore with your husband and children."

"But if Margery is gone, we shall need a nursemaid, Pierce. Might we not do better to advertise at once? Probably we shall find another Irish girl who wants to go to America. Why must we hurry off without a replacement?"

"Now I understand your concern, my dear," he said sympathetically, though I suspected trickery behind his smile. "You thought I expected you to make this voyage without any assistance." He patted my arm soothingly. "It was never my intention to treat you so thoughtlessly. Because I am very concerned for your welfare and that of our daughters, I have already placed an advertisement for a governess."

"But they are mere babies, Pierce. I can teach them everything they require at this point. I need help only with their daily care. Someone precisely like Margery. Certainly not a governess to issue orders like a countess."

"My dear, a governess is precisely what they need. And what they shall have," he said with determination. "It is time for them to have regular lessons and to stop running wild without a thought to proper comportment."

"I hardly think that they are wild. They are complimented on their lovely manners wherever we go, Pierce. You have yourself heard guests comment that Fan and Sal are the most accomplished little girls they have ever encountered."

"I have made my decision, Fanny," he said firmly, and then softened his tone, feigning hurt. "I had supposed you would be pleased for our daughters and for dear Margery as well, but I should have known better than to attempt to predict *your* feelings."

"If you cared about my feelings, you would consult me before placing an advertisement! I know a great deal more than *you* about the education of young girls. I attended the most celebrated girls' schools and was instructed by the finest teachers in England and France!"

"Please lower your voice. The children shall hear you or even *worse*, the servants. I have placed the advertisement. That it all there is to be said about it. I am certain I shall receive many suitable applicants and will set appointments with them right away. I have no objection to your being present if you can keep hold of your temper. Otherwise I will ask you to absent yourself, since if you are in one of your moods, I shall find it very difficult to interest anyone in the position."

I longed to pick up the large china vase filled with roses that sat on that table beside me and empty its contents over his head. But I said nothing, not trusting my temper, and sensing my mood, he immediately left the room. When the children came running in with my father to ask me to listen to the poems he had taught them to recite, I was so incensed I could not even pretend to listen. I began to cry, and the children stood watching me wide-eyed, uncertain of what they should say.

My husband informed me that three applicants should be interviewed that afternoon. He had set appointments and should receive them in the drawing room, one by one. I was invited to be present, and, in fact, he should welcome my impressions of their French accents, as he wished his daughters to have the best possible instruction in this language and acknowledged I spoke French as a native. But he cautioned me that I must limit my questions lest these interviews become inquisitions. Such accomplished candidates would not, he warned me, be amenable to my customarily severe scrutiny and criticism. If his behavior had not so distressed me, I should have laughed at his assessment of *my* comportment. In actuality, it was he who had found fault and expressed displeasure with my *low* origins and some of my acquaintances whom I had asked him to receive in Philadelphia.

The first applicant possessed lengthy credentials, remarkable for nothing save the abundance of commonplace knowledge she exhibited in her answers to our questions. I feared Sal already knew more of English composition than this elderly woman, a rather crusty personage dressed all in black. She answered so slowly any question directed to her that I wondered if her intellect was challenged by the effort of producing simple constructions in her own language.

The second applicant, a much younger woman whose demeanor was less forbidding and who had much experience instructing young children, as well as testimonials to confirm it, could not respond to me with a single word in French when I addressed her. She seemed surprised that this proficiency was expected, since the advertisement had not specified its necessity. I considered reassuring her that it need not prevent our engaging her, as this was an area in which I should be pleased to instruct my children, but one cold look from my husband, who must have sensed my support for this dedicated governess, silenced me.

"I am very sorry, Miss Higgs," he said, "We then must conclude our interview. I had not thought it necessary to stipulate that the governess must speak French. I thought it a basic accomplishment for anyone who sought to instruct children of the best families," he said disdainfully, "along with

English, penmanship, drawing, and piano. Forgive me if I have needlessly taken up your time."

As he ushered her out, I questioned why he had omitted a requirement he considered essential for young ladies. I worried what might prove to be his ulterior motivation, but was comforted by my hope that if the final candidate proved unsuitable, perhaps my husband would allow me to hire a nursemaid more like dear Margery. But the third candidate, Miss Gerard, was precisely to my husband's liking. Not only could she speak French fluently, she *was* French, reared in Paris in her early years. She had not been employed in several years as a governess, having had opportunity to travel as a lady's companion in order to see the world, and she showed us her quite creditable sketchbook featuring the most prominent sights of Europe and America.

"I believe travel is very beneficial to anyone's development," my husband remarked approvingly. "I am certain it is essential to both understand and convey to children the accomplishments of ancient and modern civilizations."

"And so enjoyable as well," Miss Gerard said, turning her lovely violet eyes upon him. "I was very fortunate that Lady Davenport afforded me such an opportunity," she continued, smiling with her perfectly white teeth, watching my husband's face as if I were not even present for the interview.

I observed his admiration for her figure, clothed by my tastes too flamboyantly for a governess. I did not fail to notice her very clear complexion, her dainty blonde curls, and her tiny feet. We were both female, yet there was very little else to claim as similarities, and silently I reprimanded myself for thinking in such terms. She was not a threat to *me*, and would be spending her time with our children, not as my companion. I doubted I should find good-natured camaraderie with her as I had with Margery, but I could see no serious impediment, save perhaps her youth, to prevent our engaging her. It was also apparent that my husband felt her testimonials from the family where she had instructed four children, and from Lady Davenport, quite sufficient, and she expressed her readiness to accept immediately, as soon as we should require her.

We sailed several days later on a very grey morning. I had beseeched my husband to allow us to delay for a few days until conditions were more favorable, as he knew how badly the children and I suffered from sea-sickness. But he would not permit this, maintaining that if we waited for better weather to depart, we might surely still encounter storms at sea. Therefore, the children and I suffered dreadfully amid the rolling waves that constantly rocked our ship for several days. Many of the other passengers were also stricken, although my husband and Miss Gerard endured the weather admirably.

"She is an absolute Titan," my husband told me, one afternoon when he came to look in upon me for a few moments as I tried to take a little broth. "You would be pleased at how hearty she is and how generously she has served the others, who are able now to come out and take the air from their deck chairs. She adjusts their blankets and brings them tea and broth and magazines. She will be a very kindly influence on our children. And a great help to you, my dear, as soon as you are well enough to sit for a bit in the sun."

The next morning, I felt stronger and saw through my porthole that the weather had cleared. I stood up and felt no more of the dreadful rocking beneath my feet. I washed my face and called for my bath and dressed myself completely for the first time in several days. I felt my appetite returning and decided I should enjoy some porridge and toast and good strong tea as soon as I had taken the air and walked once around the deck, just to be certain I was indeed fully mended.

When I emerged on deck, I found my daughters dressed in their matching blue flowered dresses and laughing as they stood on either side of their father, who was reclining in a deck chair. Miss Gerard, who sat in a chair beside them, saw my approach and sent the girls to welcome me. How I can remember my delight, after two such unpleasant days and nights, which had seemed endless, to hear their joyful laughter and to feel their dear hands, warmed from the sun, embracing me.

"Come see what Miss Gerard has shown us," Sal cried happily, her little sister running beside her. "There are porpoises following our ship. You can see them out there, Mother, if you only have patience and wait for them. Perhaps they are relations, Mother, of the ones we knew on Butler Island."

At that moment, Miss Gerard herself came up to acknowledge me, and I believe, as was fitting, to take charge of the girls, who were becoming quite boisterous in their enthusiasm over these wonderful mammals. I was glad for her assistance, finding myself a little less certain on my feet than I had anticipated, not having fully recovered from the weakening effects of my illness. When she approached us, bending near me to scoop up little Fan in her arms, I nearly swooned at the fragrance of her perfume. There was nothing offensive about it for those, who unlike myself, enjoy unsubtle scents owing more to the gardenia than the rose. But aside from a fragrance that I found so singularly unappealing, I was struck with its odd familiarity and tried to recall where I had recently encountered it. Then suddenly I remembered. It was the particular fragrance I had noticed once before upon my husband.

28

Philadelphia Prisoners

I kept silent regarding my suspicions, olfactory or otherwise, when we were safely reestablished at Butler Place. There was no one to whom I might confide them, and I certainly could not discuss my fears with Mr. Butler. He would have accused me of harboring unbecoming jealousy towards a simple governess and humiliating distrust for my own husband. I knew that his family, except his cousin Amelia, who had encouraged him to accompany me to London, agreed with every criticism my husband made of me and would deny any impropriety existed. My own family, having witnessed my husband's volatile temper and rapidly changing moods, knew I had not misrepresented his coldness and his late-night disappearances. But they were across the world, and I was all alone in Philadelphia.

Fortunately for me, another matter happily distracted me from the impertinent flirtations of Miss Gerard with my husband that I witnessed, and the more serious relationship between them, which I feared was conducted entirely in private. This was the sudden arrival, totally unanticipated by me and, I believe, also by my husband, of Jack, the young slave, who had been assigned to teach me to row and to accompany me on some of my long walks and rides on Butler Island. After my husband's outburst in which he blamed me for fomenting dissatisfaction among the *people*, I had not expected to see any of them ever again, particularly Jack, who was perceived to be my special favorite.

But it appeared that while we were in London, my husband's brother had approved Jack's transport to Philadelphia in an effort to save the young man's life. Since his early boyhood, Jack had always been of delicate health. He was very slight of build, light of complexion, probably due to Mr. King's partiality towards Jack's mother, and his constitution was not nearly strong enough to withstand the arduous work of the field. This had been tried when he was of the normal age to begin field work, but had been abandoned by both overseers and masters when it was established that Jack had a weak constitution and was not sufficiently adept with his hands to become an effective cooper, sawyer, or carpenter. In a setting such as Col. McIntyre's, where company was regularly entertained and a stable of horses maintained, he might have adapted well to life as an assistant butler, footman, or groom. But primitive as life was on Butler Island without an actual master's residence, and even on St. Simon's, where we dwelt in a spacious farmhouse, there was no appropriate occupation for Jack.

His assignment to me had allowed him to be spared the strenuous duties to which he was so ill suited. While Jack accompanied me on my jaunts or assisted me in the small horticultural improvements I endeavored to make on the island, others were relieved to no longer struggle with how to employ him. He proved a very willing and engaging companion for me, although he naturally could not read or write. Still he keenly questioned me about any information I shared with him and committed it quickly to memory, often exhibiting a lively mind and an imaginative nature. It occurred to me that had he been born a free man, he should have been a perfect candidate for university and might well have become a doctor or lawyer or some other worthy profession. But naturally, as a slave, such aspirations were ridiculous, and when we parted in Georgia, bravely as he tried to take leave of me, the only person with whom he could converse about the world beyond Butler Island, I read despair in his eyes. He must have worried what work would befall him after my departure, better suited as he was for dancing than for labor. I feared he would likely be sold away since Mr. Ogden or my own husband would surely recognize Jack's pleasing manners and appearance would make him valuable to a plantation where he might serve at table. He would be separated from his family and all that was familiar to him, and even if the planter who purchased him resided only as far distant as Savannah or Charleston, considering a slave's inability to travel, the Altamaha River would impose a barrier wide as a great ocean.

"As you have felt so concerned about the well-being of our people, Fanny," my husband said when Jack arrived, addressing me with more kindness than had been his wont in months, "I hope you may consent to see what you can do to raise his spirits. John says the boy is in a seriously weakened condition. They have starved him and fed him and bled him, and nothing brings about the slightest improvement."

"I will gladly see what I can do, but what malady afflicts him and why has he been brought here?" I was quite surprised, since it had never been the practice of those administering the plantations to take Butler slaves out of the South.

"While we were in London, my brother felt he had no other choice," my husband answered, stirring a generous amount of sugar into his tea. "Ogden sent him a report that Jack was failing daily. He was always thin, but his weight kept falling off no matter what they might try." He smiled approvingly. "Ogden is a good overseer and wants no valuable property to perish on his watch. He suggested it might be best to see if Jack would benefit from a change of scene and climate. Ogden rightly surmised that if he can find a purchaser who desires a pleasant-looking lad for assistant butler, weak and listless as Jack is, he would not fetch a good price."

"But what if even here he does not improve?" I asked anxiously, unable to continue with my own breakfast, thinking of poor Jack being starved, stuffed, and even bled, albeit with good intentions. "Has he been given plenty of rest and fresh air? Perhaps he should be brought here where he may accompany me on my morning rides, if he is strong enough."

"Rest he has had in good measure," my husband assured me, "odd as it is for Philadelphia servants to attend a slave. But with so much abolitionist interference he cannot be taken outside," he explained patiently. "There is far too great a risk he might be encouraged to escape since we cannot know with certainty who may be trusted. Jack may not leave John's house and shall be watched carefully."

I felt uncertain if my husband's words contained a veiled admonition to me, lest I harbored a plan to rescue Jack and spirit him with Elizabeth Hardwick's assistance to freedom in the protection of the abolitionists. Yet I was pleased when he asked if I would go later that day to visit Jack to see if this might raise his spirits. Since I had known the young man so well in better health, my husband and his brother thought he might confide in me what troubled him and that my attentions might succeed where medical interventions had failed.

"But I am to meet with Miss Gerard this afternoon," I reminded him. "We were to discuss the program for the girls' studies. That would have to be postponed." I did not care myself, but as he so often found fault with me, I did not wish to proceed until I was certain he approved this change in plans.

"Oh, certainly that may be postponed until tomorrow," he assured me. "I shall even speak with her, if it should be necessary, in your absence. This matter is far too serious to delay, and John sent round a message this morning that he shall greatly welcome your company at supper. You may see Jack this afternoon, and knowing that you shall wish to see him more than once," he added in a tone of great consideration, "I shall order the carriage to return for you after luncheon tomorrow."

I visited Jack in one of the attic chambers reserved for servants, where I found him gaunt and so grey in complexion he was hardly identifiable as the laughing young man I had seen but a few months before. A young servant girl sat with him, perhaps due to the perceived impropriety of having me remain in a bedchamber in isolated proximity to a male slave, even one in a gravely weakened condition. I quickly sent her away to fetch some water and wine and chicken broth, not because I felt they could truly benefit him, but to gain at least a few moments to speak privately. She gladly packed up her sewing and accepted my orders, pleased to leave that stifling chamber.

The chamber need not have been so miserably hot, even close to the roof as it was situated, as it was not overly warm on that spring day. But there was no circulation of air in the tiny room whose only window was tightly shut. The unpleasant fragrance of unwashed bedclothes and perspiration enveloped us. I immediately worked with all my strength to open the small window so fresh air might reach us. It was all I could do not to thrust my face into the small opening so I might inhale unpolluted air, yet I hesitated, knowing Jack's eyes were upon me. I did not want to convey to him that I found the odor of his chamber so noxious that I was frantic to dilute it.

"Oh, it is good you do that, missus," his hoarse voice said softly, and I could see he breathed appreciatively. "I *begged* them to open this window, but they would not permit it. They are afraid I will escape through it."

I felt indignant at such absurdity. Even painfully thin as he was, Jack could never pass through that tiny window. Anyone observing him should also have quickly determined he did not possess the energy to even raise himself from his poor bed.

"But are you taken out into the sun?" I asked, recalling that the hope in bringing him to Philadelphia was that he might improve from a change in climate.

"I stay only here, missus," he said, no emotion in his voice, still well versed in the slave's expected acquiescence to his master's directions.

"And there is no time for you to sit out in the fresh air?" I inquired, wondering how I or anyone should withstand such imprisonment. For that was precisely what it resembled, no matter what good intentions or concern for preserving a valuable asset of the estate had prompted this arrangement.

He did not answer, yet I did not require one, comprehending that they would not likely permit him to be carried outside if they even feared he could escape through a tiny, attic window. When the girl returned with the items I had requested, she stood by watching my every movement, I believe to be able to report to her master if I actually offered spirits to a *slave* and waited upon him. I quickly sent her away to obtain a particular food for me that I imagined should take her a long time to acquire. I moved the one hard chair nearer to the bed and proceeded to bathe Jack's face and arms with warm water. I could feel the heat of his fever, from whatever source it might emanate, through the thin cloth. I arranged the cushion from the chair behind him so that he might be more comfortable to drink and gingerly gave him first a few sips of water and then a few more of wine.

We continued in silence for several moments, I alternately offering him tiny sips of water and wine, and he swallowing laboriously and saying nothing, as if his strength were far too taxed by these feeble attempts at nourishment to utter a word. He managed finally to take a few mouthfuls of the chicken broth, although I could see that it brought him no pleasure and that he only did it to please me, so urgent was my coaxing. Then he lay back against his poor cushions and closed his eyes. I knew it might be only my imagination, yet I believed I detected a slight improvement in his color, and as I bathed his face, I saw that though his lips remained cracked and dry with fever, his forehead seemed cooler than before my ministering.

"Thank you, missus," he said gratefully, still not opening his eyes. "It is good that I see you before I die."

"You must not speak of dying," I told him, mustering all the encouragement I could summon. "You are a young man with many years ahead of you. I do not know what manner of fever this is, but you can survive it. With rest and food you will recover. Surely you know that?"

He opened his eyes, which were a surprising light brown, almost golden color I had not previously noticed, and gazed at me with far greater calm and ease. In fact, I was quite encouraged by how improved was his expression. My words had been expressed to console him, and, in truth, more as if I were reciting lines expected of a character in a play than from my own conviction. But his discernable improvement urged me to console him more.

"Think, Jack," I said, urging him to have hope. "For the first time in your life, there is absolutely *nothing* that you must do. You can lie here and rest while you gain your strength. You have no work. Just think of it."

"It was not work when I take missus around the island or to row on the river. Or to help missus plant her garden. When missus returns, I would do that work for missus again fast and sure." He sighed wearily and seemed to shiver, caught in another paroxysm of his fever.

"I am sorry," I said, sympathizing with him, "that those pleasant times are past. I do not believe I shall soon return to Butler Island, and at least for now such occupations would require more strength than you possess, Jack. We must think of something you can manage which will help to pass the time until you are well."

I did not say it, but I thought, until you are well enough to return to your life of drudgery, the ignorant *slavery* in which you shall die. Or even worse, until your health shall improve and you may be sold away.

"Perhaps you should like to draw, Jack?" I inquired. "I will leave with you this sketchbook that I use myself, along with pencils and charcoal, so that you might try your hand at rendering some of your favorite scenes from home or what you may have observed on your journey," I said cheerfully, hoping that my enthusiasm might be contagious. "I should not show them to anyone here if I were you, Jack," I whispered, "as some may object that a book of any sort is in your possession. But you might share these on Butler Island when you return home."

Even as I said this I wondered if the reverence we often feel for *home* had any meaning for someone who was *enslaved* to a place. I regretted at first that I had not brought my colors with me that he might be enlivened by the pleasure of applying bright hues to such images as he cared to make. It would have been my pleasure to give him the finest materials I possessed, yet I had not provided him with expensive colors, since should anyone observe them in his possession, they would think such a gift far too grand for a slave and might relieve him of them solely for that reason.

"Thank you, missus. But I have no hand to draw," he said wearily. "I have most forgotten all the scenes of home and it was so dark when we traveled. I was shut up in a compartment, and so I did not see many things I could put on paper."

I recalled once that I had seen Jack studying the worn remnants of an old prayer book, torn and broken along its spine, that Cooper London was showing him. Though I was not, I believe, considered someone to fear in this regard, reading, and particularly *teaching* a slave to read, was such an unforgivable crime I had observed them hastily put the book away when they became aware of my presence. I had never questioned Jack about this, not wanting to make him fearful, and secretly pleased he longed to read and tried with the limited means about him to learn a few words. I had made it a point to leave books unattended, even simple picture books of Sal's, when Jack might be about, knowing he possessed intelligence well beyond that needed to read their simple phrases on his own.

Recalling this, another fear took hold in me. I knew for any man convicted of teaching a slave to read, the penalty might well include death, if not merely a high fine and imprisonment. Such penalties could not be visited on a woman, so any actions of my own might result in severe consequences for Mr. Butler. Yet still I could not contain myself, looking at this miserable young man confined to his attic cell to waste away.

"It would have to be our deepest secret, Jack," I whispered to him, afraid to utter the words aloud. "But if you should wish to pass the time in trying to learn to read, I would help you." I fed him the last spoonful of broth and set the empty bowl on the floor at my feet, there being no table in the room.

He was silent, although his eyes opened wider at this news than at anything else I had told him. Even as I looked down in my nervousness, I felt certain his eyes were on my face.

"I would risk it if you would tell no one. *Absolutely no one.* I would find a book of simple composition and by the time you return home," I assured him, imagining that with his quick mind in only a few months he should have learned sufficiently to be able to continue on his own, "you should know how to read. I could not come often or others would be suspicious. And you would have to hide it beneath your mattress and never show it to anyone. But it would pass the time and the knowledge you should gain, no man could ever take from you."

At first he did not answer. At least not with words. His eyes were filled with gratitude, which they reflected tenderly, secure in the knowledge that no one save myself could hear his response. Then as we both heard the sound made by the feet of the servant girl climbing the steep stairs, he blurted out quickly, desperate as any man sentenced to a slow death day by day in slavery, "What purpose is there for me to learn to read, missus, when I have no prospect?"

I could not argue with his sad reasoning. It was not in my heart to try to convince him that his prospects were other than they appeared honestly to him, a life and death in servitude. But still I pressed the sketchbook and pencils into his hands and helped quickly conceal them beneath his poor covers.

At that moment, the girl burst in upon us, smiling knowingly, I thought, as if anticipating she should catch us in some secret alliance. Indeed, I had earlier perceived she found something very odd in my nursing a slave with wine and broth, valuable though he might have been, and clearly conversing familiarly with him. There was so much I wanted to say, yet I was silent. I could do little but take leave of him with a simple handshake.

"I will see you tomorrow, Jack," I said, "before I leave. And I shall give careful instructions for your care. Now you must rest."

The girl went over to shut the window. I heard her murmuring beneath her breath that she had no idea how it possibly came unfastened, but by the master's orders it must remain closed.

"Leave it be," I commanded, more harshly than I intended. "Let it remain open. I take full responsibility for it. There is no way to escape through it even if he had the strength to climb up there, and he shall not be left in a stifling room."

Though she clearly felt grave misgivings at my direction, she left the window open. Jack sighed and breathed deeply of the air, stirred by the breeze. I do not know if it actually comforted him or if he feigned contentment for my benefit, knowing that opening the window to his cell was all I could do to assist him.

"When shall I meet with Miss Gerard?" I asked my husband upon my return to Butler Place. I was eager to engage in the discussion of our daughters' education. Despite the restrictions Mr. Butler placed on my time with them, I was determined to influence Miss Gerard's plans for our daughters' lessons.

"Surely, you did not think life here was suspended in your absence?" my husband asked sarcastically. "I have already provided Miss Gerard the direction she required."

I could not understand why my simple inquiry about our Fan's and Sal's lessons should draw such a rancorous response from him. Yet observing his angry temper, I tried to harness my own, though I felt unfairly berated for my absence when it had occurred at his own request. So flushed was his face, even in the early afternoon, I concluded, once he breathed upon me, he had been drinking steadily since morning. No matter how he derided me, I resolved not to lose control and answer him in kind. From past experience I knew when this happened, my husband skillfully arranged to make it appear the fault of our disagreement was mine alone and that he had been provoked by my rude behavior.

"I went to your brother's house at your request, sir," I said, deliberately and politely as I could manage. "I was glad to go and offer assistance, particularly since this seemed to please *you*. Though this caused me to be away when I had planned to meet with Miss Gerard, it does not mean my interest in our daughters' well-being has lessened. Surely I did not forfeit my rights to help design the program for their study. I shall speak to Miss Gerard at once." I prepared to leave him to nurse his own bad temper.

"Indeed you shall not, madam." My husband stepped in front of me, barring my exit from the room. "I informed you before we returned to Butler Place that you should no longer superintend our children's education. And now that I have engaged the services of an accomplished governess, it is completely unnecessary and also unseemly that you impose yourself in this manner."

"*Impose* myself. You speak as if I were an interloper at a party. You may not wish to acknowledge it any longer, for whatever reason of your own prompts this cruelty," I said, meeting his eyes unflinchingly, "but I *am* their mother. And I shall always be. You can do nothing to change that!"

"Madam, you *shall* not coerce me to say words to a lady that ill befit a gentleman." My husband spoke firmly with his fists clenched and a malevolent expression, yet he stepped aside. "You are free to come and go. You are no prisoner, and I certainly am not your jailer. But if you intend to remain at Butler Place, you shall not hinder the course of study that Miss Gerard and I have established for our daughters. You are their mother. No one could witness Fan's unruly behavior and doubt that," he continued, laughing derisively. "But of far greater importance is that *I* am their father, and I shall not brook your interference."

Thus began my complete isolation from the daily life of my daughters. Inseparable as we had always been, it was very painful to me, but much worse than my own grief, was to witness their suffering. I had never allowed them to become pampered, spoiled creatures like so many American children, stuffed as they were with cakes and sweets and totally unaccomplished in all but the most rudimentary of studies. I had insisted they develop discipline, Sal more than Fan due to the difference in their ages, yet still I had encouraged them to run to me with their questions and discoveries, convinced such intellectual freedom was precisely what childhood should offer every child.

Under Miss Gerard's direction, such intellectual curiosity was forbidden. The children's lessons were rigidly controlled, and they could visit with me only at specially prescribed times of the day. I appealed to my husband, falsely assuming that despite his desire to prevent my involvement in our children's education, he could not be so base as to limit their time with me. But I learned this was entirely his intention. He acceded in all ways to Miss Gerard's opinions and informed me she had found our daughters more lacking in discipline than any children of their respective ages whom she had tutored. The reason for this, she felt certain, was the excessive freedom in which they had been indulged by me.

Soon I was reduced to daily appointments with my daughters, one hour before breakfast and another before their bedtime. Otherwise, we passed silently through the hallways of Butler Place, waving to each other surreptitiously when Miss Gerard was distracted and speaking formally to each other at meals where her stern regard for propriety, and my husband's stiff acquiescence, turned family meals into superficial exchanges among strangers devoid of the playfulness to which my children and I had been accustomed.

I soon understood I was being punished, not for genuine wrongdoing, other than being outspoken and not so ladylike by American standards as my husband had desired, but due to his own transgressions. I could no longer conceal from myself that Miss Gerard, my children's governess, was also Mr. Butler's mistress. They were very cautious in their intrigues. I never stumbled upon them in compromising situations, but it was apparent from my husband's flirtatious remarks and her cooing approbation for his stories that their relationship had deepened. My separation from my children was one of their precautions, lest I learn of an indiscretion my daughters had observed.

One evening, as I savored a precious, prescribed hour with dear little Fan in my lap, wrapped in her nightgown, Sal sat reading a book of stories in the lamplight by the fire.

"Mama, do you think Miss Gerard is pretty?" Fan asked, as I stroked her silky curls.

"Certainly she has a pleasant appearance," I said diplomatically as any woman might be expected to manage when describing the delicate, younger woman who seemed to have usurped her husband's affections.

"Papa thinks so as well," Fan said happily, clapping her hands. "Today when he came to the nursery to hear our lessons, he told Miss Gerard she is a delicate French rose blooming in an American garden."

I could not speak for a moment even though I knew both girls waited for my response. *He* could direct their lessons, but not *I*, who knew more of French and music and literature than he. *I* could not observe their lessons, could subject our daughters to his flirtation with their governess in their schoolroom.

"It is true, Mother," Sal joined in, closing her book and turning her solemn, dark eyes upon me. "Father says such pretty things to Miss Gerard. She *never* makes him cross. Maybe," she mused, "it's because she has no lessons like Fan and me to muddle when we are forgetful. But that does not explain why he is cross with you, Mother. You remember everything you read and know much more than Miss Gerard, even if she is a governess."

"Tomorrow Papa is going to play the flute for us!" Fan happily cried. "Like the shepherd in the story book."

"Perhaps not just like him," her older sister explained. "Since Papa will be accompanied. He gave Miss Gerard the music, Mother, that you and he used to play together when you first met. I asked if you could come to the schoolroom to play it for us. But Father said it was best not to bother you about it since you had so much on your mind."

I was furious I had been replaced by a *governess*. I wanted to interrupt my husband as he stood in the yard giving directions to the farm manager, but I knew if I showed my anger I should come away the worse for it. He would speak calmly and regretfully of my accusations and shake his head in feigned sorrow that my suspicious nature disturbed the entire household. He would smile ruefully and express his chagrin that I should base my suspicions on an *imagined* scent, common to Miss Gerard and to himself, indeed, a ridiculous thought, and the misunderstandings of our own children, who had simply misconstrued his cordiality to their governess. I knew I should come out completely in the wrong, and so I wrote to Elizabeth Sedgwick for advice. She was the only person, other than my own dear family so far away, to whom I might entrust my misery with absolute trust. I hoped that she, among her many friends, would find someone who could advise me of my rights.

It relieved my helplessness to know Elizabeth should soon respond to me. I longed to hear her soothing voice and look directly into her kind eyes.

But I dared not visit her to pose my questions for fear of what new rules concerning the children might be enacted in my absence. There was nothing to do but rise early to post the letter and then wait anxiously, perhaps for many days, before a reply should arrive from Lenox, Massachusetts.

A month passed, and still I had no word from Elizabeth. I continued the restricted visits with our daughters that my husband permitted, surely the most unnatural circumstance to which a mother has been subjected while residing in the same home as her own children. I tried to occupy myself with my writing, but found I had no heart to bring pen to paper, so desolate as I felt. At meals I could hardly induce myself to eat and noticed that my clothes began to hang unattractively upon me. I was further disturbed by Miss Gerard's continued ascendance in all matters governing our daughters. First, it had been only the content of their daily study, but then my husband informed me Miss Gerard disagreed with the indulgences I allowed the girls at meals, and since she had brought the matter to his attention, he concurred that adjustments should be made.

This was apparent when we next sat down to table. It had always been my custom, contrary to what I observed among American families, to restrict the amount of cakes and confections that my children were offered. In this regard, Miss Gerard had no disagreement with me, and I was pleased that she did not seek to garner my daughters' love by catering to their childish love for sweets. Yet I was horrified to witness the manner in which she asserted her authority over two girls who had always behaved most obligingly at table and never suffered for lack of appetite or good health.

She announced, obviously with Mr. Butler's approval, that henceforth the girls should be required to eat everything that was placed upon their plates. I saw the look of fear—there was no other word for it—pass across Sal's face when she saw that Miss Gerard clearly intended to determine which foods to put on their plates and the size of portions to be served them. There was to be neither choice nor possibility of declining peas or artichokes or potted meat or those dreadful, pasty lima beans, which seemed prevalent in Pennsylvania. Miss Gerard informed them that she knew best what would nourish their bodies and incline them to achieve the best results in their studies.

Poor little Fan ventured to state, very politely, "Miss Gerard, if you please, I do not like tomatoes. I have tried, but I cannot like them at all. I will eat more spinach if you like and potatoes. But please none of that yellow sauce for me," she said, with almost a curtsey in her tiny voice.

Miss Gerard made no answer, but ladled a large serving of stewed tomatoes on to a plate beside a slice of lamb and several potatoes, nicely browned with parsley. I am, admittedly, not the most reliable chronicler of Miss Gerard's motivations, yet I am certain I am accurate in remembering that she smiled before she liberally applied the hated sauce to Fan's plate.

After it had been placed before her, Fan surveyed her food with much dismay and then said very respectfully, "I think perhaps you did not understand, Miss Gerard. I cannot bear to eat that sauce. It makes me feel very ill indeed."

"It is not for you to determine, *Frances*," Miss Gerard answered firmly, using the name by which no one in our family addressed Fan, "what you *can* and *cannot* bear to eat. I am a far better judge than you of what is required to help your little bones grow and make you wise and strong." She smiled encouragingly, and then said sharply, "I shall not tell you again. That is your supper. Now eat it. Every morsel. If you will not eat it then you shall be sent at once to your room and you shall not join us at table tomorrow. We have neither time nor patience for spoiled little girls who cannot do as they are told."

Fan said nothing more and lowered her head over the food that was abhorrent to her. I watched as she picked up her fork and secured a tiny bite of spinach that had been untainted by the sauce. As she sipped her milk, I saw her dear little eyes were brimming with tears. I imagined my husband would intervene, so tenderly did he love Fan, despite his annoyance at her impetuous behavior. Enamored as he was of Miss Gerard, I thought as a gentleman he could not sit by and watch his daughter be tormented. And Fan's healthy, sturdy little body should certainly have allayed any fears he had that her health suffered from malnourishment.

But Mr. Butler said nothing. He seemed absorbed in thought or perhaps in his glass of wine, which he turned in his slender fingers while ignoring the battle mounting at his table. Fan sank down in her chair and began to eat mechanically, bite by bite, as if each morsel were an unpleasant task to be consumed without any hope of pleasure. I observed that she held her breath as she swallowed the lima beans whole, one by one. I could contain myself no longer.

"Here, Fan," I said, reaching for her plate. "I shall take yours since I am very partial to tomatoes and Mrs. Martin's good sauce. I am certain there are modifications we might discuss later," I said politely as I could. "But for now, Miss Gerard, will you please serve Fan a plate without tomatoes or sauce and with some extra spinach. We should both be very much obliged."

Miss Gerard could not oppose me before the children. I was, after all, still the lady of house and other servants were present. Yet she could not completely suppress her anger. It was evidenced by the knocking of the serving spoons against the platters and the cold manner with which she regarded Fan and me. I knew I should pay heavily for my actions when I was next alone with my husband, whose face was flushed, on this occasion more with anger than with wine. It was still worth it to me, upbraided as I would certainly be to see an end to Fan's tears and a fleeting look of joyful thanks from Sal, who picked up her fork as if it were no longer a hated implement.

"How dare you interfere in this way?" Mr. Butler asked as soon as we were alone in the drawing room. "Did I not make it sufficiently plain that Miss Gerard shall have oversight over the children's studies and health?"

"I cannot now, nor will I ever, abide the tormenting of children, sir. There was no reason to force Fan to eat that sauce, which honestly is a *dreadful* mess of flour and fat. There is no health in it. Nor must she eat tomatoes to remain healthy. It is just a foolish cruelty, sir, and far beneath your stature as a gentleman to allow it."

"Ah, so now *you*, who are very far below me in birth, intend to lecture me on what becomes a gentleman?" Without even asking if I objected to his smoking, a courtesy he had always shown me in the past, he lit a cigar. "I believe Miss Gerard's directions to the children are completely reasonable, and I shall not permit you to hinder her wise attempts to teach my daughters to properly comport themselves."

"They are my daughters as well, sir, I do remind you. And I will not sit by silently while a governess brings them regularly to tears. They have always been such happy girls with dispositions as temperate as a summer breeze. Just look what she has done to them!"

"If you cannot tolerate being present when they learn manners, which a proper mother should have previously taught them, I suggest you absent yourself at meals." He smiled briefly considering his own suggestion. "In fact, I shall inform the servants at once that henceforth you shall take your meals privately in the small sitting room. This way you shall not be disturbed nor shall you become an impediment to Miss Gerard's instruction of the girls. She tells me Fan is very headstrong. I have not the slightest doubt from whom this tendency emanates."

"You shall not keep me from our daughters, Pierce," I said, desperately catching hold of his sleeve since he was clearly preparing to leave me. "I am their mother. I have as much right as you to see to them. You cannot shut me out of their lives!"

"I think you shall find, Fanny," he said calmly, not succumbing to rage as I had hoped he would so I might catch him in the wrong, "that this is not the case. I do not dispute, of course, that the girls feel an understandable attachment to their mother, but nevertheless the girls are *my* daughters, and as their father I shall by right and law determine what is best for them. To this reality you would do well to accustom yourself."

"Just as I must also accept all that Miss Gerard really is to you and why you condone her cruelty to our daughters?"

For a moment when Mr. Butler did not answer and the room stood terribly silent, I feared when he stepped forward he might strike me. He had never done so, yet I felt his conduct with Miss Gerard had unleashed the true vulgarity of his nature and his penchant for cruelty. Then he seemed to perceive my unspoken thoughts and caught hold of himself. He smiled and stepped back, observing me gently, as if we were not enemies but once again a husband and wife whose relations, though strained, were not to be abandoned.

He said ruefully, "You hurt and shame me terribly with your base suspicions, madam. It is unseemly to make such accusations against a gentleman without an ounce of justification. I care not for the injury you seek to do me, but for the sake of *poor* Miss Gerard, I pray you have not voiced these ridiculous imaginings elsewhere. This would be unspeakable."

Then, as he turned to leave the room, no doubt to rejoin her, he reached into his waistcoat pocket to retrieve a letter. The seal was opened, and I could discern the handwriting on the envelope was Elizabeth's. He had invaded my privacy to read it. As I reached for the letter, he held it slightly above my grasp.

"I do beg your pardon," he said. "A servant had placed it with my other mail, no doubt misreading the inscription, and I began to read it. Naturally I stopped immediately when I saw it had been misdirected, but curiously enough, your great friend Elizabeth, certainly not one of my strongest admirers, appears to understand your situation with far greater clarity than you do yourself."

I could not subject myself to the further indignity of reading Elizabeth's letter in his presence. If it truly confirmed there was no favorable resolution to the insufferable position in which Mr. Butler had placed me, I determined not to grant him the satisfaction of observing my reaction. Accomplished actress that I had been, I did not believe I could conceal my disappointment if Elizabeth's research established that my children and I must remain his prisoners. I walked calmly, with as much dignity as I could muster, to the privacy of my own chamber. As I unfolded the pages covered by Elizabeth's distinctive hand, I considered how filled with anticipation I should have been at their appearance, had my husband not already obliterated my hope.

February 23, 1843
My dearest Fanny,

You cannot imagine my sorrow to receive your letter and to learn all you endure from your husband. It grieves me you should suffer this alone. I would gladly come to you, but as you know, I should not be welcome in his house. Just as gladly should I welcome you and your darling girls to spend as long as you wish here with us at Lenox, either in our house or in a dear little cottage it should give me so much pleasure to equip for you.

I could not tell, dear Fanny, from your letter how irreparable is the rift in your relations, but I suspect that the doubts I had always hoped were false on my part have now been shown to be correct. I could not believe that you and Mr. Butler were suited in temperament, nor did I think his intellect was worthy of your own, and now that your stand against slavery, that abominable institution, has turned him against you, I fear there can be no remedy to reunite you. Even if your fears that he has lost all affection for you are warranted, I must still remind you that at least in all public ways, he maintains the highest regard for you.

And sadly, my dear friend, I must advise you against accepting my own invitation unless you have Mr. Butler's specific consent. It is my painful duty to advise you that what he has expressed to you as his rights, truly his absolute authority over all decisions governing his daughters, as he calls them, is correct. It is evil and unconscionable that a devoted wife and mother is not recognized under American law. I have consulted Father and learned lawyers of our Society and am assured it is so. Until they are twenty-one years of age, they shall be governed absolutely by his will.

I understand you are anxious to receive my advice so I shall refrain from writing in the detail that I would usually employ. I am certain the advice I must offer shall certainly be unwelcome to you. I fear it is accurate that you have no legal standing with which to dispute Mr. Butler's authority over your daughters. Should you cause him to experience serious provocation, he could, according to the law in America, not God's Law, prevent you from seeing them at all until they are twenty-one. I do believe that upon his honor as a gentleman he would not deny the mother of his children, nor his young daughters, the sight of each other, and I believe that his own relations should advise him that such a stance should place him in the wrong in the sight of all polite society.

Knowing this, I advise you my dear Fanny to restrain your temper and your justifiable rage at injustice done to one who so deeply loves her children. Remain in his household as long as it is bearable so you may be an influence to mitigate his abuse.

Perhaps if you convince Mr. Butler that you accept his authority, and upon your honor pledge to uphold it, he will consent for you and the girls to spend part of the summer here to escape the dreadful heat of Philadelphia. It is far cooler here and there is opportunity to bathe.

In closing, my dear Fanny, I urge you to keep writing. The journal that you have maintained so carefully thus far must be shared. Your eyes have borne witness to the daily crimes committed wittingly or unwittingly by owners of slaves. Such matters must become public to people throughout our nation if this evil is ever to be ended. I hope you realize fully the power that your knowledge and celebrity give you if this journal were to be published.

Forgive me, I should not blame you if you should wonder how a true friend could have heart to speak of slavery at such a sad time when you are sorely beset with your own problems. As I revere you and your sensitivity to the pain of others, dear Fanny, I hope that you shall believe that I comprehend the immensity of your suffering. Only it cannot escape my thoughts to imagine how much worse are the conditions of slaves. Imagine if you were not Mr. Butler's wife but instead one of his slaves. He might determine not only to deny you free access to your children, but he might sell either you or them, separating you forever, on just a moment's whim.

I am grieved for you and for little Fan and Sal. Yet I am most ashamed and grieved for our entire nation when I conceive of the horror that is perpetrated daily upon our poor black brothers, solely due to the color of their skin. I should understand if you ran in disgust back to England. I am certain America and Americans looked far different to you when you observed us from the stage, long before you knew how your husband's fortunes were made.

Please let me know when you decide what you wish to do, and in any way you may wish, you know I shall help you. Father also asks me to convey his great affection for you and your children and urges me to encourage you to think of our home as your own. You are always welcome. I fear, Fanny, that perhaps no man should have been a suitable husband for you, such as the covenants of marriage are now constructed. But I embrace you in your stand for a mother's rights and responsibility to assure her children's welfare. And I know that you are good and kind.

With all my love,
Elizabeth

The verdict Elizabeth sent me regarding my circumstances made me weep with rage, so that soon the letter I held was wet and rumpled in my hands. It humiliated me beyond comprehension that while I suffered this news, my husband was undoubtedly reveling in his victory, having read this letter intended only for my eyes.

My maid conveyed to me the message that Mr. Butler wished to see me in the drawing room as soon as was convenient. I considered bidding her to tell him I was indisposed and should gladly see him on the morrow, but was afraid this should encourage him to feel even more confident of his own authority and more certain of my hopeless defeat. I bathed my face and combed my hair, trying with whatever means I could to make myself more composed as I prepared to meet him. Observing my mottled complexion in the glass, and recalling his unkind remarks even when I was still secure in his love, I feared he might remark what a shame it was the conventions of society would not permit me to apply stage makeup.

Mr. Butler stood politely when I entered the drawing room, extending his hand and leading me to sit beside him on the sofa, as if this were the most companionable of meetings. If he noticed my distress, he made no mention of it and seemed inclined to be gracious, offering me tea and cordials. It made me shudder to recognize this was but his version of the victor's dance.

For just a moment, in my weakness, I began to wonder if I had perhaps misjudged his intentions, so solicitous was he of my comfort. Having observed my trembling, my husband placed more wood on the fire and pressed tea upon me, imagining that I was cold. He spoke for a moment of matters relating to the dairy. A new manner of pressing the sweet butter had been devised which he believer would be to my liking. He thought I might like to see the three new calves that had just been born, and as he politely shared this simple news, I enjoyed the pleasant rhythm of his voice and longed not to be required to say anything that should return us to our established, argumentative roles. But I knew our intended conversation must take place. The fate of my precious children depended upon it, and so I looked to him expectantly and sipped my tea, determined to say nothing that should invoke his anger, and waited for him to speak.

"You were much distressed when we parted earlier," he said softly. "I am sorry for my part in that and for accidentally reading a small portion of your letter. But now let us move past this to make our arrangements so that there shall be no more scenes before the children or the servants."

Ah, it is all about appearances, I thought. *Now we are truly at the heart of it. He is not concerned for the children's benefit, just that there shall be no gossip among the servants.*

But I said nothing and waited for him to proceed. Only he did not. He was clearly waiting for me to respond. The amiable sight of husband and wife seated companionably before the fire seemed a false scene in a play. I struggled to consider what I might reasonably say that should not inflame him, nor cause me to express sentiments I did not feel or knew to be untrue. I could not restrain myself.

"Sir, you *could* not have read but a small portion of Elizabeth's letter as you earlier claimed, to conclude her opinion confirmed your own regarding your legal *property*, our children. I am certain you read her entire letter. But putting that aside, let us consider how we shall proceed. I want nothing more than to spend time with them every day, as much as possible." I could no longer keep my voice from rising, nor could I contain my anguish. "I wish them to run freely to me for comfort and to share with me the small joys and adventures of their days. I do not desire to be in your way, sir, nor to have further angry disputes with you. I wish only to be their mother. I cannot stand by and allow my children to become strangers," I affirmed strongly as I dared. "Certainly, you cannot wish your children to grow up not knowing their own mother?"

"I understand your distress if you have come to believe such a thing, Fanny. I do not wish to separate you from my daughters. I believe you will find what I propose now a most reasonable arrangement."

"The only arrangement that I should find reasonable, sir," I replied, struggling to regain my composure, "would be for me to once again assume my proper role in supervising our daughters' care, including the food they eat, the clothes they wear, and their deportment, and conferring with you, sir, to determine the course of study that shall be set forth for them."

"It *cannot* be as you desire. I have engaged a governess to perform many of the tasks you describe. Yet *no one* shall oppose your spending time each day with my daughters. Surely you cannot imagine I should wish to separate my children from so accomplished a mother."

My daughters, my daughters. It made me want to scream with all my might.

"Then, pray, what do you propose, sir? If it is so reasonable then please advise me so we may begin this new arrangement and put our differences to rest."

He smiled then with a sly expression, fleeting in its duration, but which sorely frightened me, so aware of his treachery had I become. I sensed also that he delayed his answer purposefully, enjoying holding me at his mercy.

"It is truly not dissimilar from what I originally proposed. I believe you will simply see it more clearly now, much as Elizabeth does. You shall have private time with the girls each morning for one hour after they are dressed *before* they have their breakfast. And I shall not mind whether you spend this time with them in the nursery or outside walking, since I know it is often your custom to rise early and go out to walk or ride." He smiled contentedly, obviously impressed with the great beneficence he was bestowing upon me.

"Then afterwards may I breakfast with them?" I asked hopefully. "Even in the nursery, if you prefer, so we shall not disturb you. It would be a great pleasure to us and so natural after just exercising together."

"Madam, you demand far too much, no matter what you are offered," he said in annoyance. "They shall breakfast with me. Surely you can concede that you are not the only parent who wishes to enjoy their society. And naturally you understand that my affairs often keep me away during the day. Are you proposing that *I*, their father, should not then see them at all?"

"Of course not. I meant nothing of the sort," I hurriedly assured him. "I see you are fair in the arrangements you propose. Only you might reconsider and let me join you for breakfast," I proposed. "Is it not the American custom for fathers *and* mothers to share this meal with their children?"

"Perhaps," he conceded, "under more normal circumstances in which the mothers in question do not constantly oppose the efforts of governesses seeking merely to control the conduct of their undisciplined charges," he answered sanctimoniously. "I believe your performance yesterday evening provides sufficient evidence of why this is not possible. You *cannot*, madam, prevent yourself from trying to change every arrangement Miss Gerard makes, no matter how sound."

I wished with all my heart to protest the injustice of such claims, yet knew that if I said more I would likely set him further against me. So sternly did he then look at me, I imagined he should welcome my open defiance as cause to further punish me by keeping me from our children.

"You shall also have another hour with the girls immediately following supper, Fanny. I shall in most instances already be out for the evening and you may therefore have no reason to fear that I shall interrupt your time with them. Then they shall prepare for bed, and if they have comported themselves reasonably and done all that Miss Gerard has required of them— and naturally she, not *I*, must determine that—you may then spend a half hour with them supervising their prayers before bed."

"And so I am to be excluded from all meals served in this household forever more?" I could not control the anger I felt at the very idea that my conduct should pose such a threat to our daughters or to the propriety of our meal times, that I must be banished.

Yet he did not meet my anger with his own, but told me calmly that as matters stood between us, there could be no possibility of our continuing to dine together, since it was not in my power or my nature to assure him there would be no further scenes. He was convinced of his fair conduct towards me in all arrangements he had made for my comfort, as well as in the generous funds he advanced for my maintenance. He was certain no gentleman of his acquaintance provided greater resources for his wife's amusement and comfort.

"But what if I should not consent to this unnatural arrangement?" I asked, boldly as I could.

"Then, madam, you shall not see my daughters at all," he said hotly. "I shall not brook your interference or your demands! Do not doubt that I shall exercise my rights in this regard under the law. And though her presumptions are amusing, I have my own legal counsel and need not depend on Elizabeth Sedgwick's opinions, or those of her friends, to define my rights."

"Then I shall leave this house. I will find my own lodgings, perhaps a nearby cottage, or I shall go to live with Elizabeth and her father. And the girls shall come to live with me!"

"This shall not take place," he replied so sharply his voice might well have cut stone. "There is no court in the land that would ever allow you to take two daughters from the care of their loving father, who provides generously for their every want. If you wish to live apart from me, although please keep in mind that I have *not* asked you to do so, nor should it ever occur to me to ask my wife to vacate our home and my protection, I should, of course, allow any reasonable accommodation. And if you find a setting that I deem appropriate, I should probably be inclined to allow my daughters to visit with you for short holidays or perhaps during a portion of the summer."

"So you mean even to determine *where* I may live, sir? You seek to establish conditions that shall rob me of our children and force me from our home, and yet that is not sufficient? You also expect to be permitted to inspect the premises I should select for my own residence."

"Oh, come, Fanny, please spare us both these emotional displays," he said, dismissively. "Surely nothing I would require in the way of a suitable accommodation could prove so confining to you. I am certain if you consider my proposal overnight, you will conclude it *is* the most reasonable plan if you value the children's needs over your own. Oh, and there is but one small, additional promise I should require of you if you are to remain at Butler Place," he then quickly added, as if it were but a small detail that had for a moment eluded his memory.

I waited. I knew it could not be a minor requirement or he should not make such a point of it. I feared some greater humiliation awaited me. Might he actually debase me further by informing me Miss Gerard should accompany him in my place when he went out in the evenings?

"I do not consider the promise I must exact from you anything but reasonable in view of Elizabeth's recent comments," he continued slowly.

I tried to keep my face immobile so that he might not gloat over his success in injuring me. I felt something ominous was about to descend upon me.

"If you determine that you wish to stay in this household and remain a part of my daughters' daily lives, then you shall agree, and I shall require it in writing, that you will not communicate by letter nor shall you receive at Butler Place, even in my absence, any member of the Sedgwick family."

"By this, I then assume I am to become your prisoner. You intend that I shall have no contact with my closest friends in America. Will that be enough, sir? Or are you going to demand that I shall not communicate with my own father, our daughters' grandfather, as well? Am I to have no rights at all?"

"Naturally, I should never suggest anything so unfair. But certainly you cannot imagine I should permit you to remain in contact with those who are enemies of this house. And not, I might add, due to any unfriendly action I have taken to provoke their disdain. *You* have inflamed them with lies about me because you share their desire to abolish slavery, an institution you revile, but one which has placed those lovely pearls around your neck." He pointed to the lustrous double strand of pearls I wore, which he had presented me shortly after we were engaged.

I was mortified by his words, though reflecting on them now from the vantage of years, why one item of adornment should suddenly have seemed so loathsome when all we owned was produced by slavery's sad harvest, I cannot say. Perhaps it was the combination of his arrogant, condemning stare and his scornful laughter. I did not take time even to release the clasp from this symbol of our former love, which he used to accuse me of hypocrisy, living as I did on the profits of his plantations. I tore the necklace from my neck, so hateful did its presence and its source feel to me, and threw it at his feet. I heard the sound of pearls coming loose and rolling towards him across the highly polished wooden floor.

"No matter, Mrs. Butler," he said, very unruffled, as if I had accidentally dropped a comb or broken some inconsequential ornament. "If you no longer like pearls, then so be it." He stooped to retrieve several that that had come to rest at the edge of the Persian rug. "I know others who shall be glad to receive them," he said cruelly.

When I turned to look at him, shocked, despite what I had long suspected, that he should speak so blatantly of his infidelities, he quickly discerned his error.

"I meant only, of course, that my daughters should be delighted to receive such pearls."

"I care not what you do with them, Pierce. If it is your plan to insult me, then I wish you would give them to the first beggar you pass in the street."

"Please spare me your theatrics. You are no longer on the stage, and there is no audience." His voice grew cold as if he were speaking to a subordinate whom he held in absolute contempt. "And if it should please you to continue throwing about and destroying my gifts to you, well, then, I suppose I shall have to endure it. I am, *after all*, only a simple American man of business, not at all versed in the ways and customs of someone as worldly as yourself. Forgive me, as I have not had the advantages of your upbringing," he said disdainfully.

"It is unspeakable, sir, you should treat me in this way. If not for the sake of our daughters, two lovely little girls who shall be heartbroken by your decrees, then show compassion because you once swore you *loved* me better than anyone in the world. You said I held your heart in my hand."

"I was an infatuated fool, madam. Now there, I have admitted it. Does it make you feel better to know I see now how foolish was my fantasy? Indeed, I believe I fell in love with Juliet, not *you*, at all. And we both know that in the bright light of this room or in any other, she is gone forever. So there is no love left to me," he said softly, as if he truly felt himself to be a sadly injured party. "I was the fool that all Philadelphia told me I was to make such a choice."

"It ill becomes any man who calls himself a gentleman to express such feelings, Pierce. I never claimed to be Juliet, and certainly I am no longer a girl, nor was I one when I met you." I answered matter-of-factly as if his words bore no sting for me, but I knew my cheeks were burning. "Do not imagine for a moment that I imagined *you* to be Romeo when we first met and fell in love. I thought you were a *man*, flesh and blood, accomplished and humorous and gallant in your pursuit of me, but certainly not a romantic lover in a play. And as you know, Romeo and Juliet died tragically after a marriage of one day. This certainly was not the marriage I hoped for, and if you did, I regret that our hopes were not more harmonious."

"I will not deny you know Shakespeare better than I. There can be no doubt of that." He moved angrily towards me with a look suggesting that only by the strongest exertion of will could he restrain himself from shaking me. "But I shall no longer abide your temper and your foul moods. You must decide by morning whether to remain here under the conditions I have outlined. I shall have your answer, and if it is in the affirmative, I shall expect your acquiescence when you are alone with our daughters as well as when you are in my presence. Now I am going out," he said, passing by me quickly so that I should understand unequivocally that our interview had concluded and no further discussion should pass between us. "I do not know what hour I shall return. I have urgent business that requires my immediate attention."

He turned back, smiling slyly, after considering his reflection in the glass. We both knew the nature of his *business* and that I would make no inquiries concerning it.

29

An Empty House

The porter entered my dressing room at the New Hope Theatre, a select venue twenty miles outside of Philadelphia, after the closing performance of *Much Ado About Nothing*. He struggled with an elaborate arrangement of roses and lilies and a heavy basket piled high with festive tins of delicacies and several gold foil-wrapped bottles of champagne.

"My goodness, Eddie," I exclaimed, looking up from my dressing table, where I was removing the last of my stage makeup before leaving the theatre. "Who sent all of this?"

"I cannot say, Miss Isabel," Eddie said, setting it all down on my table. "The gentleman who brought it is waiting outside. I asked if I might take you his card, but he said he preferred not to send one in," he explained apologetically, nervously pushing back his shaggy blond hair, as if he, and not this unknown gentleman, were behaving oddly. "He asked me to inform you that an old friend wishes to speak with you."

"This is very odd, Eddie. Why would someone present such lavish gifts and then refuse to send in his name? Did you notice anything peculiar about him?" I asked curiously, considering that no old friend I could recall should have the resources to purchase all of the bounty assembled on my table. Unless...

"Was he a rather portly gentleman past middle age with muttonchops and heavy chin whiskers going grey?" I asked apprehensively, wondering if Mr. James could actually be so despicable as to call himself my *friend* and dare to appear at my door after what he had done to me. I speculated that he had learned of my success and come to claim credit for training the actress whom a reviewer had generously described as "the most beautiful Beatrice to grace the American stage."

The review further attested that "just as Benedick justly calls Beatrice 'Lady Disdain,' Graves's lines are spoken with withering hauteur. She brings to this role, as she does to all others, her artistic signature. Philadelphians who treasure the theatre must make a special effort to see her as Portia next month in a new production of *The Merchant of Venice*, and we must strongly advocate for increased engagements to assure her sustained presence in our city. Her interpretations are so inspired, this reviewer recommends one should either see Isabel Graves, wherever she may be appearing this theatre season, or remain at home with a good book."

When I had so happily read those admiring words, I thought longingly of Matthew, to whom they would have meant so much. I did not doubt that I merited praise for my talents and even the beauty that had been evident since I was a girl. But I knew without Matthew's invitation to join his company and his encouragement and designation of me as his preferred leading lady, such praise would never have come to me. It was unbearable to lose his love so soon and to know that *The Poisoned Table*, his most important play, had dealt him a fatal blow.

"Miss Isabel, I don't believe you heard me," Eddie said, standing very close to me and touching my arm to gain my attention.

"I'm sorry. What did you say?" I asked hurriedly, embarrassed he had watched while I was caught in reverie, smiling like a girl receiving her first compliment from a young man.

"Only that the gentleman waiting to see you is not the least bit portly. He is clean-shaven, and I should never describe him as being 'past middle age.' He is still a young man."

"What color is his hair?" I asked, no longer fearing the unknown caller could be Mr. James and finding myself very curious to discover his identity.

"I cannot say, miss. He is wearing a black silk hat so I cannot tell you more than I have done. He insists if I do not allow him to pay his respects, you will be quite angry when you learn I have turned away a dear friend whom you have not seen in some time."

I could see from his worried expression that Eddie, on whom I regularly relied, was concerned I might find him responsible for preventing me from seeing someone truly important to me. As a well-known actress, I had attracted admirers in many cities, although since my abandonment by Pierce Butler, I had never again allowed myself to become dependent on any man save Matthew. I occasionally allowed gentlemen to take me dancing or to dinners in fine restaurants when it seemed necessary for the good of the company, but I rarely permitted one to escort me home, not wanting to create the impression that any man might possess me, nor that I would suffer fools who wished to display an actress on their arm to impress their companions. The hurt that often still woke me in the night from troubled dreams of Pierce Butler, made me wary of gentlemen who were intrigued by my celebrity, yet made disparaging comments revealing their feelings of superiority towards anyone who worked for a living. Actresses to them, no matter how celebrated, were only slightly above women who walked the streets.

"Show him in, Eddie. I suppose you must," I wearily agreed. "But please stay close by."

"Of course, miss. I will be near. And I shall be listening out if he tries anything bothersome and needs encouragement to be on his way."

The man whom Eddie admitted to my dressing room was not immediately recognizable to me since the tall silk hat pulled down tightly on his head shadowed his brow, and a long dark cape enveloped him. Yet when he turned to face me saying, "Good evening, Isabel, it is so kind of you to receive an old friend," I recognized his voice as if I had heard it regularly rather than after an absence of several years. When he took off his hat and gloves and smiled at me, there could no longer be any doubt of his identity. Pierce Butler stood confidently before me, holding out his hand, seemingly oblivious to the possibility that I might not welcome him.

"I do not believe you dared come here," I said coldly. "Surely you cannot imagine I should actually *desire* the company of someone who left me homeless and friendless. Whe—when—," I found my voice breaking with anger at the shock of facing him, "when you had promised to marry me."

He who always savored the last word in every conversation, was for a change speechless. I had not invited him to sit down, and so ever proper, he stood in front of me, stone silent, looking admiringly at me.

"Please leave at once," I managed to say, not meeting his eyes, but speaking to the wall above his head. "Or you shall be shown out."

"I shall go then," he said quietly, "since my presence disturbs you. But not before complimenting your performance tonight. I have never seen Beatrice better portrayed, not even by Fanny Kemble!" he exclaimed. "And reading how the reviewers sing your praises, I am clearly not alone in that opinion."

"I did not know she played Beatrice," I admitted, shamefully abandoning my resolve not to speak to him, and longing like a schoolgirl for any words that would show me to be the superior player.

"Of course she did. Along with everything *else*," he said disdainfully, as if he had tired of speaking of her or thinking of her at all. "I am certain you have played most of the same roles. And though she had that wonderful voice, I must say you were a finer Ophelia."

At this point I had regained my composure and was prepared to insist that he leave. Yet as he approached me, I was not afraid when I smelled alcohol on his breath and saw he was unsteady on his feet. I considered with pleasure that circumstances had changed so much between us that perhaps he had consumed a quantity of spirits to muster the courage to speak to *me*. Just as I turned towards to door to summon Eddie, Mr. Butler seemed to sense my intent.

"You know, Fanny agreed with me," he said quickly. "When we saw you in New York, she admitted you were far more graceful than she and that you conveyed Ophelia's madness with much greater conviction. She said she had never portrayed Ophelia as well as you did that night."

Fanny Kemble had seen me perform Shakespeare! She had actually been in the audience of a theatre in which I was appearing and not managed to steal the audience's attention from me, though she merely sat among them. I had been aware of her presence only when she had seen me in *The Poisoned Table* and had helped to bring about its doom.

"She *said* that?" I asked, despite my efforts to appear disinterested, unable to conceal my surprise and delight that one who had always upstaged me should have praised me. "She came to see *me*?"

"My *dear* wife always attends the theatre, even though she no longer adorns its stage in all her glory," he said disdainfully. "We went to see you since those we were visiting in New York City had procured the tickets. But for me it was certainly not the first time," he confessed. "I have attended your performances on as many occasions as I could possibly manage," he admitted, taking my hand tenderly. "I was proud to see how well you were received and that your prowess increased every time I saw you."

"You almost destroyed me," I said angrily, recovering myself and snatching away the hand that he clutched. "I have suffered many injuries in my life," I told him, tears filling my eyes as I recalled my horrors, "but nothing was so dreadful as being abandoned by you. And knowing that you had gone off to marry *her* with no thought for what would become of me. Or even if I were—"

"If you were what?" he asked tenderly, his eyes fixed upon my face. For once he seemed enthralled by my voice instead of contemplating his next response.

I did not answer, regaining my ability to breathe, and realizing how close I had come to telling him about the baby I had lost and of Mr. Meacham, parts of my past I had told no one and had no desire to reveal to him.

"If I were even alive," I finally uttered, my survival seeming a safer topic than trusting him with the story of the baby he had not known had even been conceived. "Before my success there was much misery and struggle," I said, my voice trembling as I remembered my life after I parted from Mr. Meacham, when his gift of money was all that stood between me and ruin. "While you and Fanny Kemble traveled to London or were celebrated in Philadelphia, New York, Boston, and St. Louis, enjoying the best of everything, I lived in rooming houses. Some days, meals of cold porridge and gristly beef and greasy vegetables were all I ate. You slept in featherbeds with silk comforters while I often traveled all night, sleeping best I could in stagecoaches and freezing carriages or in lumpy beds in cold attic chambers, the least costly the theatre company could engage for our tours.

"You never gave a thought to me in those days, Mr. Butler. Whether I lived or died. It is only now that I have some degree of celebrity that you think of me at all."

"That is not so, Isabel. I have thought of you most every day since we parted," he claimed passionately. "I am so sorry for how you suffered. I was a cad, I admit it. But those days are past. Surely now that you are secure and people stand in long lines to purchase tickets to your every performance, you can find it in your heart to forgive a man who once wronged you because he was foolishly smitten by another. Dear Isabel," he said, again grasping my hand and dropping to his knees at my feet, "surely you know that it was not just I, but an entire nation that hung on her every word?"

Boldly he kissed my hand, and completely against my own will, I felt myself trembling to feel his touch again. I summoned all of an actress's resolve to keep my face immobile as I recovered and pulled my hand free, almost knocking him over.

"I forgive you *nothing*, sir," I said, seething with rage for every wrong I had suffered from his cruelty. "If you were truly a gentleman, you would not have come here. Just the sight of you brings back the most appalling memories. Now leave me, *please*. Or I shall be forced to have you thrown out."

"Well, isn't the little filly feeling her oats," he exclaimed crudely, even admiringly. "I've no aversion to a bit of spirit in a woman," he said, rising and approaching me. "Come now, Isabel, admit it. You know you have missed me. Why put on this show of coldness when I could feel just now how your breath quickened when I touched you. Married though I am, it is in name only. I was bewitched by Fanny Kemble, but she is *nothing* to me now," he insisted. "If once again I could take you in my arms, it should be just the way it was when we met. And I *promise* you," he said, leering and approaching closer, "I would not be the only one who should rejoi—"

"Get out this minute," I said, pushing him back with all my might. "You sicken me, drunken lout that you—"

"*Lout!*" he angrily exclaimed. "How dare *you*, a common shopgirl when I met you, call *me* a lout? You put on the airs of a grand lady when you have no right to them. No one, male or female, shall call Pierce Butler a lout!" he shouted in rage, his face mere inches from my own.

I had waited to cry out for Eddie, hoping to avoid a scene, but since Mr. Butler had created one, there was no need to remain silent any longer. But just as I prepared to shout for assistance, Eddie burst into the chamber, and seeing Mr. Butler looming over me, grabbed him by the back of his coat, scooping up his cape and silk hat in his other hand, and dragged him from the room.

"Now settle down, sir, and go peaceably," he instructed him, not unkindly, from his superior height and strength not fearing Mr. Butler at all. "Leave now without further disturbance or I shall have to call for an officer."

Mr. Butler, enraged as he was, put up little protest, though he continued to mutter under his breath about "someone of low birth thinking herself above a gentleman from one of the finest families in America!"

When we observed him walking angrily away, Eddie asked if he should go down to arrange a carriage for me and if I should wish to take the basket of delicacies and wines home with me.

"If you have no use for it, Eddie, please give it to anyone you like or toss everything in the rubbish bin. Just so long as none of it is here tomorrow to remind me of him." Then I shuddered, my eyes again filled with tears as I thought of Pierce Butler's audacity in supposing he should begin again with me and that I should be glad to see him.

"There, there, Miss Isabel," Eddie said soothingly, wiping my eyes with his own handkerchief. "There is nothing to worry about now. He is gone," he said, looking out the window. "I do not believe he will be back for more." He shook his shaggy head in disbelief. "I suppose there is no telling, miss, how an admirer may carry on when he is so taken with a great actress. But how could he imagine that a lady like yourself would have anything to do with the likes of him?"

30

In Retreat

I agreed to stay. Humiliated as I was by Mr. Butler's conditions, I had no choice but to accept them. I could not leave my children under the complete domination of Miss Gerard, who fairly gloated with importance whenever I encountered her. I no longer saw her at meals, outcast as I was, yet it was from her hand that the children were released to me and to her once again I surrendered them. Brave as I tried to be, it was extremely difficult not to burst into tears when Fan's tiny fingers had to be pried from their hold on my sleeve at the conclusion of our brief morning visit, and I had to listen helplessly to her pitiful crying as she was pulled away.

With such daily sadness, I forgot my husband's other cruel requirement until he called me into his study one evening, insisting that I take down the letter to Elizabeth Sedgwick he was prepared to dictate. I refused to participate in the demeaning exercise of allowing him to put words into my mouth, but I did consent for him to review the letter I agreed to send straight away. Much as it sickened me to be controlled in this way, I knew without this concession he might further restrict my visits with our daughters, claiming that I had not abided by my own promise in this matter. It was the shortest and most constrained letter Elizabeth would ever receive from me, and I could not imagine what she would make of it. I vowed at some point I must manage to post a letter to her outside of the servants' sight so that Mr. Butler would not know about it. I must let her know how I longed to continue our normal correspondence, an exchange that brought great solace to me. The letter I signed and showed him read:

My dear Elizabeth,

I hope you are well and pray you know that you are always in my thoughts. Since it is Mr. Butler's express wish that for the benefit of our daughters I now limit my correspondence, I am unable to write to you at this time. He asks also that you refrain from communicating with me, as I shall not be able to respond. At the present it seems impossible for me to visit you in Lenox this summer with Fan and Sal. I shall hope for a change in this situation in the future. But for now, I know

you will accept these circumstances and shall support me by honoring Mr. Butler's
wishes.

Please express my love and deep regard to your father and Maria and all of
the family.

With deepest love,
Fanny

After signing such a letter, which Mr. Butler immediately sent a servant to post, I felt the nails had been hammered into my own coffin. Isolated as my life had become, living largely apart from my own children and separated by a wide ocean from my family, it was grim to additionally be prevented from sharing my thoughts with my dearest friend. For several years we had been accustomed to writing at least weekly to each other, and my Georgia journal had evolved as a series of letters to her. Conversing with her, even by letter, and visiting her and her family each summer had become so much a part of my life that I felt this censure heavily, as I am certain Mr. Butler fully intended.

Still, as I had learned by my parents' example, and from my own experience as an actress, many adversities feel so monumental they might consume us, but nonetheless we persevere and endure to act another day. I pressed into every moment that I spent with my daughters new stories to amuse them, prepared pictures and drawings and favorite songs, and did anything I could think of which might bring them joy and let them feel my love for them. Listening to their prayers, sharing a good-night song, and holding them close before we parted each night was especially dear to me. Yet I also felt quite bereft I could not see them freely every day, nor hug them whenever their mood or mine suggested it, as would any normal mother.

I rode even more than before, since exercise had always been my greatest distraction from sorrow, and Mr. Butler, to his credit, gave me free access to his stables. If anyone of his acquaintance saw me out on my morning or afternoon rides, he should not have held the slightest suspicion of my personal anguish, as the riding enhanced my figure and brought color to my cheeks. I read and wrote as much as I could, but it was hard to concentrate when at any moment the children's voices might waft to me across the lawn or from the drawing room or the library as I passed through the house. Loving mother as I had always been, I could at any moment suffer the pain of seeing one of my children catch sight of me and commence running happily to join me, only to be apprehended like a fleeing thief by Miss Gerard. It was a position I should have found unimaginable even a few months before. Despite the dreadful suffering I had witnessed there, I began to long for my days on Butler Island, where at least I had been free to spend as much time as I wanted with my own children. I reflected on precious memories of being interrupted at my sewing or writing or as I sat by the fire conversing with their father, by the sound of their little feet padding happily toward me and the joy of their unbridled laughter.

Since I had so much time to myself, I asked Mr. Butler if I might go once again to visit Jack. I had in every way exceeded to his wishes, so I did not see why he should not willingly grant this small request, particularly since he and his brother had expressly requested that my initial visit be made. I hoped they would permit me to take Jack outside for fresh air, which I knew would do him good. I had resolved to persuade them by insisting it was essential to do something quickly to save this valuable property. I believed an appeal to their pocketbooks might be successful, but had been waiting several days for an answer while Mr. Butler conferred with his brother.

"It was generous of you, Fanny, to make that offer," Mr. Butler said one afternoon when he returned to Butler Place from a business meeting with his brother. He spoke in a friendly voice quite different from the tone that had colored all our recent conversation. "I did appreciate it, and John asked me to personally express his thanks," he continued courteously. "However, today I learned very sad news. Jack suddenly passed away in his sleep. They found him yesterday when they took him his breakfast."

I was quite overcome, thinking of poor Jack lying in his attic room, dying lonely and desolate. My tears came forth freely so that even Mr. Butler, who was no longer inclined to feel kindly towards me in any way, began to comfort me and offered me his handkerchief.

"It is quite remarkable, Fanny," he said. "When they were cleaning the room, they found this sketchbook beneath the bed." He held it out to me. "The sketches are in charcoal and pencil, and though naturally very primitive some are actually quite pleasing," he said with obvious surprise. "I do not know who taught him, since clearly he could not have learned on his own. Poor fellow." He shook his head. "I thought it might amuse you to look at them. They are mostly of you and the children. Otherwise I should have disposed of them as they are of no use to me, and, of course, have no value. But I *am* sorry, Fanny," he said, patting my hand. "I know it is hard to lose a slave whom one has come to feel particular affection for, as you did for our Jack."

After he had left me, I opened the sketchbook and was amazed to see, after Mr. Butler's scant praise, sensitive drawings of genuine strength. There were several scenes of Butler Island, the landing on the river, the rice mill and the fruit trees near the infirmary. There were a few others he had started and abandoned as if they displeased him. I could well understand his discouragement, as charcoal can be a most exacting drawing material, and he had never had instruction or chance to experiment with it until I placed some in his hand in that dismal attic room. It impressed and touched me how well he had drawn completely from memory. The only portrait was of me with Fan and Sal. I was rocking Fan while Sal labored at my feet over lessons on her slate. The final drawing showed Jack and me, as we used to walk together on the narrow dykes of the island. I was carrying a basket of the type I often filled with shells, flowers, leaves, and other specimens, which I would bring back with me to amuse the girls. Jack was carrying the large staff that he had insisted upon from our very first walk, his only weapon with which to defend me from the snakes that often crossed our path. I was surprised and saddened by even his careful rendering of the very pattern of my frock, which he had not seen in many months. It was the most finished drawing, the one to which he had obviously given his closest attention. All that it lacked was the signature, which, of course, he could not render.

I considered his talent, raw and untutored as it had been, and discovered only by chance through my desire to give him a retreat from boredom in the sad cell where he had died. The final drawing, his gift to me, comforted me, since he had chosen to draw, his only means of recording any memory, our walks together. I hoped, although he had been a slave, that in moments of our time together, he had found some small degree of pleasure. I closed the sketchbook for fear my tears should mar his drawings. I recalled his last words to me, and wondered if I, too, lacked any prospect.

* * *

I was startled by a burst of screaming and commotion. I had arisen un-characteristically early and gone out to ride, finding it the only antidote to the bad dreams that overtook me. After an energetic and bracing canter down to the wharves, I came back refreshed. I thought I should have time to hurriedly bathe and then wait to have my own breakfast after my morning hour with the children. I could not stand to squander even a moment of this time with them.

But as soon as I entered the main door, I was confronted by a frantic, screaming Fan, who came racing towards me with Miss Gerard running angrily after her and Sal following close behind. Several of the servants stood watching nervously as Fan eluded her pursuers and ran into my arms, where she tried to hide among my skirts, beseeching me all the while to save her from Miss Gerard.

I could not, for good reason, feel liking for Miss Gerard, but I was shocked to find my small daughter so terrified of her. Fan's face was red from crying, her hair was in wild disarray, and I could feel her trembling as she pressed herself against me.

"Frances, you will come back here this instant," Miss Gerard commanded, grabbing Fan's arm and trying hard to break her hold on my gown. "You cannot hide in your mother's skirts like a *baby*. If your father becomes aware of this outrageous behavior, he may well determine you have not earned the privilege of spending time with your mother today or *any* other day," she threatened.

I felt Fan collapse beneath my skirts while her hands desperately clasped my ankles. It was dreadful to have her clinging piteously to me as Miss Gerard tried to grab hold of her little legs to wrench her away. The servants had never witnessed such a display in all the time my children had been among them. Sal's terrified eyes followed me, waiting to see what I should do to end this terrible display. My past instructions to "treat others kindly as you would wish to be treated" had still to be sounding in her head. I had admonished, "Let me never find *you* chastising your little sister. When she aggravates you and your temper is enraged, you must find me and I *will* intervene."

"Unhand my daughter *at once*," I shouted, truly from a mother's instinct, hardly realizing that my riding crop was still in my hand and that I was brandishing it at Miss Gerard. I gathered Fan up in my arms and sat down with her in one of the large chairs in the entry. Sal ran over to stand beside us, putting her arm around my neck and bending over her little sister.

"Mrs. Butler, surely, you do not intend to reward Frances's deplorable behavior in this manner," Miss Gerard said, approaching us with the absolute expectation that I would surrender Fan into her care. "And Sarah, you come with me immediately," she said firmly to Sal. "We shall return to the nursery and get on with our lessons."

"They shall not move from where they are," I told her, "and you shall not come a step closer until I discern what has so terribly disturbed them. Please, Miss Gerard, I must have a few moments to speak privately with my daughters."

"And if I will not comply? Do you intend to hit me with that riding crop?" she asked haughtily.

"I *am* sorry if I upset you, Miss Gerard," I said regretfully. "I had been riding and hardly realized it was still in my hand. But I assure you I have never *struck* anyone with a riding crop or anything else." Even, I reflected, during my sojourn in Georgia among slaves when no one would have spoken ill of me for doing so at the slightest provocation.

"That is indeed reassuring," Miss Gerard said insolently, dabbing at her face with her handkerchief. "Appearances being as they are, I nearly fainted when I saw you clutching it. I detest violence of any kind."

"But Miss Gerard struck Fan with her hairbrush because she did not dress herself quickly enough," Sal exclaimed, her words bursting forth indignantly. "Fan always struggles with her buttons. I *told* Miss Gerard, Mother, and asked if I might help Fan since you always wished me to assist her. But Miss Gerard said we must stop babying Fan. Then she struck her two more times. Once with the side with bristles and once with the other."

Miss Gerard laughed, calling such accusations "ridiculous" and exclaiming over the vivid nature of Sarah's *imagination*. She maintained she had only used the hairbrush as a means to encourage Fan, who always refused to rise when she was instructed to do so and never even tried to fasten her buttons, as any child of her age should have been able. "Indeed, I only *touched* her with the hairbrush," Miss Gerard declared. "Her tears were a result of her own dreadful temper, certainly not from any pain inflicted by me."

I sensed Sal was preparing to speak in her sister's defense and so quickly whispered in her ear to discourage her. I knew any further outburst, honest and accurate as I was sure it should be, would only infuriate Miss Gerard, and Mr. Butler as well, as soon as it was reported to him.

"Nothing further shall be gained by accusations," I said, catching my breath and managing to regain my normal speaking voice. "I shall bring the children back to the nursery when they have composed themselves, Miss Gerard. For the moment, they shall remain with me."

"But Mr. Butler has given express directions not to allow them to remain with—"

"I assure you, Miss Gerard, I will speak to Mr. Butler. I am certain he gives you very careful directions. But there is a grave misunderstanding if you imagine his instructions allow you to chastise our children with their hairbrushes."

She left defiantly, muttering beneath her breath in a way that was certainly disrespectful to me. Yet I felt victorious observing the happiness on my children's faces as she retreated from the room. I was certain that even set against me as by then Mr. Butler certainly was, he would not condone the beating of his own children and would respond favorably to the letter I hurriedly wrote and had delivered to him.

My husband had been out very late the previous evening and I had overheard the servants whispering among themselves that he was quite out of temper about a newspaper article. I imagined it to be some trifling matter in which he had not received the attention to which he felt entitled by his position in Philadelphia society. I did not give it further consideration, tired as I was of his insatiable vanity and preoccupation with society. Yet I was concerned that if he were in bad temper he might be unreceptive to my entreaties that he end at once our children's ill treatment by Miss Gerard.

As the maids were tidying the drawing room and Mr. Butler's study, I heard further mention of this same article, as well as derisive laughter towards Miss Gerard, who had just passed by on her way to the nursery, carefully avoiding me. But again, since the servants' remarks were not made to me and stopped as soon as my presence was observed, I thought it far better to ignore them. I could not ascertain the content of their remarks or the reason behind their laughter, and it seemed beneath my *own* dignity to inquire into servants' gossip. I was pleased that when I looked sharply in their direction, their conversation ceased.

A little later, as I ate my solitary luncheon in my chamber, I was brought a note from Mr. Butler. He had returned and would see me that evening, and for the moment, also gave me this reply:

Dear Fanny,

You are correct that I have, indeed, given no instruction to Miss Gerard to physically chastise my daughters with a hairbrush or any other object. Truly nothing disgusts me more than cruelty towards children. I have sent word to Miss Gerard that such correction, if indeed it did occur, must desist at once and cannot be repeated. You know how headstrong Fan can be, but nonetheless, I will have her disciplined suitably. I cannot abide any further scenes before the servants. You were wise to intervene as you did on the children's behalf. We shall speak further this evening.

Respectfully yours,
Pierce Butler

I was pleased to receive such an agreeable note from my husband regarding our children's care. It seemed for once we concurred in a matter regarding them. I replied that I should be happy to see him when he returned that evening and was pleased the girls had put the incident behind them and were happily engaged in their music lessons when I had last seen them. Though I did not dare mention my thoughts to Mr. Butler, I was intrigued by the contradictions residing within a man who was greatly disturbed by his daughter's punishment with a hairbrush and yet remained completely unmoved by the sight of slave children torn from their mothers' arms to be sold away, or to the condition of his slaves who labored in all weather, starving for want of sufficient food, wearing only flea-infested rags and subjected to the driver's scourge for even the slightest infraction.

When my children's unhappy outbursts became more frequent. I tried for their sake to absent myself as much as possible from wherever in the house and grounds they were being instructed by Miss Gerard. Yet when our paths crossed, which inevitably they did, since Butler Place was hardly so capacious as to make us strangers, they cried out for me in their misery. I began to feel rather than alleviating their suffering by my proximity, our separation proved a constant reminder to them of theirs and my unhappiness. Tears came to my own eyes when I overheard Fan entreating, "Please, Miss Gerard. You may hit me all you wish with my brush or even Sal's, which is much larger, if you will only let me have my supper with my mother!"

Mr. Butler and I became quite strangers to each other. For rare gatherings of the family at our home or John Butler's or for social calls Mr. Butler deemed essential in polite society, we appeared together. There were times I can recall when for the sake of the children, we conversed quite civilly as we watched them in their pursuits with dogs or ponies or in games about the grounds. But it was still quite contrived, and I found it hard to accept that we had once been such tender companions.

I knew my husband's sentiments about slavery would never change, ingrained and inseparable as they were to his self-interest, but I hoped we might find again some common ground. We were not so long married that I could not recall the pleasure of our courtship and romance. I was not so naïve as to believe nothing had transpired between him and Miss Gerard, yet wondered if perhaps their flirtation had come to an end since Mr. Butler seemed not so eager to take her part and had even thanked me for my intervention. I hoped if he were genuinely remorseful, a true reconciliation might still be forged between us. I felt with certainty Mr. Butler had been the one mainly in the wrong, but determined for the sake of our children I should be willing to apologize for a great number of sins I had not committed, in addition to those matters in which I had transgressed, if we could but put the past behind us and return to a shared life.

Then all such charitable feelings and loving hopes faded for me with great finality. One morning, as I casually read the newspapers which had been brought in with my tea, I saw two articles about Mr. Butler that truly outraged and hurt me. I had until that time considered him cold and unfair in the separation he forced on the children and me, yet his cruelties had not been public. I had felt humiliated by his treatment of me and his despicable conduct with Miss Gerard, but at least these had been private humiliations.

I read that James Schott, as fine and generous a man as I had met in America, had arrived unexpectedly at his New York home to find Mr. Butler in a drunken state making improper overtures to his wife, Ellen. I accepted that one should not believe everything one reads in the newspapers, yet the account presented, with the exception of the extent of my husband's arrogance, was very similar in both the New York and the Philadelphia newspapers. My husband had insisted James Schott fight a duel with him, even though the poor man could hardly put sufficient weight upon his right foot so that he might stand normally. It was a horrifying spectacle, and the fact that no one was injured caused me to wonder if Mr. Butler had, indeed, still been intoxicated when they met on the alleged field of honor.

Mr. Butler had known when we were in Georgia how disturbed I was by poor Mr. Wylie's death as a result of his quarrel with Dr. Hazzard. I was disgusted by this American preoccupation with honor and of upholding it in the most dishonorable way, as in Mr. Butler's insistence that his ill, avowed friend stand up with him. I was humiliated by his actions, which were certainly the talk now of Philadelphia and New York, and surely Baltimore, since the duel had taken place met in Maryland. I felt ashamed that I should be brought to ridicule by my husband and that we were no doubt the first subject of gossip in several American cities. The sensational articles were likely passed around like bonbons. I wondered if Ellen Schott had been, like me, my husband's victim, or whether she might be implicated in this adultery. I anticipated my husband's angry denials, and since I already held my own suspicions about Miss Gerard, was disconsolate, surrounded as I was by Mr. Butler's family and associates and barred from communication with Elizabeth, the only American friend to whom I might confide.

I recalled the unkind remarks Mr. Butler had made about my origins, suggesting that he had lowered himself by marrying *me*, a mere actress humbly descended from other actors, and how he had refused to entertain my actor friends at our home. He, who cared so much for propriety, had no concern for the many times he had dishonored me and our marriage. I thought of occasions when he had become infuriated when I asked where he planned to spend the evening. He had repeatedly left our home in anger and returned late at night, if he returned at all, without any explanation. I recalled the perfume about his person that I had assumed was Miss Gerard's. Perhaps it had been Ellen Schott's all along. Or perhaps both wore the same scent, which I had come to despise. Maybe Mr. Butler had made them presents of a perfume he selected for all his paramours. In my dismay, I envisioned countless betrayals.

Had I not been so afraid of frightening my children, I would have angrily hurled my teapot through Mr. Butler's ancestral mirror over the fireplace. If he had been home, I should not have been able to prevent myself from attacking him for his cowardice in not warning me such sensational articles would be appearing, even if he denied their voracity. I could not think what to tell the girls if they overheard gossip that must already be reverberating around Philadelphia. I saw that our own servants were aware of the scandal and could better understand both the embarrassed laughter and the whispers, as well as sympathetic glances I had noticed that morning from the maids who brought in my breakfast and cleared away my tray.

Thinking of my dear daughters only made it worse. I could not protect them, nor could I take them away with me. I imagined a lawyer advising me that even if this most regrettable matter had received attention in the press, I possessed no proof Mr. Butler had actually committed an offense. The scurrilous articles might be libelous depictions of a misunderstanding between friends.

I overheard Miss Gerard's quarrelsome voice directing Fan and Sal as they prepared to go out for their walk. A disagreement ensued when the girls wished to go down to the dairy without their governess, and Fan cried out for me in protest. Miss Gerard angrily reprimanded her and told her to release her hold on the banisters or she would strike her with a ruler. Sal threatened in a bossy voice to complain to her father, whom she said had told her they should not be physically punished any longer. The angry and fearful voices of my girls and Miss Gerard's indignation rose so that I prepared to intercede. But before I descended the stairs so my daughters could see me, they had somehow reached a compromise and had left the house with her.

I waited a few moments until I was certain I should not encounter them and risk further dissension when the girls would wish to accompany me. Then I hurried downstairs to embark on a brisk walk in a direction I knew they would not likely choose. Fresh air and exercise would help me decide what I should say when I faced my husband. I must convince him Miss Gerard's cruelty continued despite his orders, and that this caused not only my own suffering, for which I was certain he had little care, but made our dear children live in fear of her. I did not know what to say about the newspaper articles, but felt if I ignored them he should only use me more unfairly and assume he was not required to make any answer for his disrespectful actions. I put on my hat and cloak, not so much as protection from the weather, which threatened rain, but in hopes no one should recognize me and stop to converse with me.

Just as I prepared to leave, one of the servants came running forth to hand me a letter. She indicated that Mr. Butler had just returned and directed this letter be brought to me as soon as he learned it had arrived. He was engaged in the library with several gentlemen at that moment and could not be disturbed, but he had instructed her to entrust it to no hand but mine. She reiterated again his insistence that I should have it at once.

Even in my distressed state, my mood was transformed when I recognized the handwriting as Elizabeth's. My husband had obviously relented in his anger towards me and had sent this letter as a peace offering. As much as I cherished the letter in its own right, as the words of my dearest friend, the knowledge that it represented my husband's recanting of his harsh demand that I break with her gave me hope that he, too, wished us to be reconciled. As I left the house walking rapidly in the morning air, I felt I should soon be reunited with my children's father. Since he had extended this olive branch to me, I should be willing to meet him graciously in the spirit of forgiveness despite those dreadful articles displaying my humiliation. I would not ask him to confess his infidelities if he would but promise that they had come to an end.

I paused beneath my favorite maple tree to read Elizabeth's letter. I was surprised she had written it after the admonitions in my own letter, yet on consideration, it seemed so like her to always remain vigilant and to never retreat in her devotion to a friend. I no longer possess that original letter, but I recall vividly her assurances to me:

I am so troubled by the tone of your letter, my dear Fanny. It is your own hand, yet the voice does not resemble yours, as if some force required you to express words under duress. I shall not speculate further save to acknowledge that I perceive you are unhappy. Since you say that you may not visit in Lenox, allow me to say only that if you need me I should gladly meet you in New York or Boston or even Philadelphia, if there should be a way. It this is not possible, then, dear Fanny, you should go home to London to your father. You must have the loving counsel of someone who reveres you as I do.

My circumstances were unchanged but seemed much more bearable since my dearest friend had been returned to me. I rushed back to the house, hoping Pierce's business would soon be concluded so that I might thank him and express my fondest hope that we might soon again live as husband and wife with genuine accord between us. I reflected on his generosity in making this overture despite how vehemently Elizabeth condemned slavery and encouraged me to express my opposition. I resolved, still hurt as I was, to meet him with forgiveness and to pledge to repair our marriage.

I was told Mr. Butler's guests had departed and that he awaited me in his study. He requested that I join him there as soon as possible since he was eager to speak with me. I thought of going upstairs to freshen myself so that I might appear at my very best for our reunion, but considered it more prudent not to keep my husband waiting. I wished him to know at once how pleased I was to find him eager to restore happier relations between us.

My smile faded the moment I entered his study and saw the stern expression with which my husband regarded me. There was nothing in his face or manner to indicate the good feelings I had assumed had prompted his release of Elizabeth's letter or his support of my intervention with Miss Gerard over the hairbrush incident. He offered me a chair beside his desk.

Cold as our relations had been, I was not surprised he did not kiss me in greeting, yet was taken aback when he did not smile or even offer me his hand.

"I shall trouble you now for the letter from Elizabeth Sedgwick," he said coldly, extending his hand to receive it, in much the tone he would have addressed a servant suspected of secreting household valuables about her person.

"Whatever do you mean by that request, sir?" I asked playfully, smiling at first, supposing he was attempting a joke about this letter which had come between us. "Thank you very much for changing your position about my correspondence with Elizabeth."

"Why would you assume I had a change of heart about your communicating with that *person*," he said contemptuously, "who along with her family is an enemy to this household?"

"Sir, I cannot imagine that someone as thoughtful and civil as Elizabeth Sedgwick could be considered an enemy to *any* household. I believed you had changed your mind about my corresponding with her since earlier this morning her letter was brought to me at your direction." I kept my voice calm although I trembled at this unexpected turn in our conversation.

Mr. Butler did not answer at first, but sat up stiffly in his chair, examining me critically, his expression cold and hard, recalling the stare which the slave women had called his "flogging face." Try as I did to remain unperturbed, I found myself unsettled by it.

"Do you find me so capricious in my actions that you imagined I should wish you to renew your communication with her when I had recently forbidden it?"

"I have never called you capricious, Pierce, nor have I done so now. What should I possibly have construed, save that you wished me to read her letter when it was presented to me at your own request?" I thought I had outwitted him there. I did not think he would deny the orders he had given.

"It was not your business to *construe* anything about my intentions, Fanny, but to merely follow my wishes as you had promised. Surely you did not fail to understand the letter you wrote to Elizabeth, which I had approved. If you imagined I had changed my instructions to you, you should have asked me to clarify them *before* you disobeyed me."

I then understood Elizabeth's letter had simply provided my husband the means to trick me so I should appear in violation of our agreement. He had no desire to reconcile with me. I saw that my foolish hopes in that regard had been dashed like a small boat upon the rocks.

"Please surrender her letter, Fanny. You have admitted yourself that you received it."

"But not that I committed any wrong in doing so." I pulled the folded letter from the pocket of my cloak and flung it on his desk. "There, you may have it. I have nothing to conceal, and though you wrongly take this piece of paper, which is so precious because it comes from one so dear to me, nothing you can do shall alter the fact that Elizabeth is my friend and shall *always* be."

"You do not behave honorably in breaking your promise, madam, but at least one can say you are steadfast in your opinions," he said condescendingly, taking the letter and placing it, like damning evidence, in one of the locked compartments of his desk.

"You may go now. There is nothing more we need discuss at present," he said, not looking up as he dismissed me from his company.

I cannot describe the fury that took hold of me. He, who had publicly humiliated me and repeatedly dishonored our marriage, had the audacity to impugn *my* honor. I admit it has never been my forte to conceal my strongest emotions, particularly when I am angry, and standing there before him, I felt I should explode with indignation. I wanted to strike him, so maddening was his own complacency as he sat there ignoring me, absorbed in composing a letter in his careful, regular hand while I was consumed by despair.

"Did you not hear me?" he asked crossly, looking up from his writing, surprised and displeased that I had not left the room. "I told you that our conversation was concluded."

I know he felt my agitation, though he certainly did not acknowledge it, continuing to write with concentration, pausing only to take a sip from his glass of neat whiskey, humming to himself as if he were quite alone. I was seized with great longing to reach over and grasp his crystal inkwell and fling its contents across his desk, destroying his work and his calm in a pool of ink. I was close to indulging in this childish act when I noticed something quite arresting near his elbow. He was so engrossed in his writing and in his pretense of granting me no further notice that he did not perceive my awareness of his papers.

Without even straining to have a better look, I could determine that one open letter and an envelope addressed in the same hand appeared to be from a lady. The delicacy of the handwriting could certainly not be attributed to any gentleman, and the stationery was distinctly feminine. I could discern the salutation and the first few lines which read:

My darling Pierce,

How can I bear to be parted from you who give my life meaning? Your kisses are still on my lips and in my heart, and if I could, I should never..."

In my carelessness as I leaned over his secretary, deeply immersed in this infamous letter, my shadow fell over him and startled his concentration. One look at my stricken face, which bore the expression of one betrayed, told my husband that I had been able to discern the nature of the letter. He snatched it away quickly, saying angrily, "Have you no shame, Fanny? I should never have believed you would stoop to reading another's personal correspondence."

"It is what you have driven me to, sir," I answered, unable to conceal my tears of rage and grief that his former love for me had come to this when I had hoped that very day we might reconcile. "I do not dispute I read what I should not, but the letter about which you are so infuriated today is from my dearest friend, not a *paramour*, as is so clearly the case with your own!" My voice rang out in my rage. "How can you treat me so dishonorably? Are these letters from Ellen Schott or Miss Gerard or someone else entirely?"

My husband rapidly secreted his letters inside his desk and approached me with open hatred that was frightening to see. He pressed me roughly against the wall and spoke so directly into my face that I could smell the whiskey on his breath as he sharply pinioned my arms behind me. "You have seen nothing! Do you hear me? You have no complaint against me, not one that should be recognized in any court in the land. Not because of a reporter's fancy or your jealous rage over letters I receive from my friends. Now leave me at once before you cause me to do something I shall regret!"

I could no longer conceal from myself that my husband's infidelities continued and that he shunned me and might even harm me, so impassioned as he was against me. I feared he had become so perfidious that in order to pain me further, he might direct Miss Gerard to exact harsher demands of our dear daughters. His furious anger towards me so confused his reason that he might allow injury to his own children, whom he dearly loved.

Miserable though it made me to leave our dear girls, who hugged me and beseeched me not to leave them, I knew it would be far worse for them if I stayed and provoked their father. I understood my husband's vindictive nature well enough to feel assured he would exercise his power to hold me prisoner in his home, as I had no money with which to escape him. He would never allow me to go to Elizabeth, nor even if she had provided me the money would he have allowed our daughters to visit me at her home in Lenox, so I resolved my only course was to return to England. I should be helped by the company of my father and family and many old friends and would be able to think more clearly about the future. I knew that Mr. Butler, who cared dearly for the good opinion of society, would not wish it publicly discussed that he had denied his wife a visit to see her elderly father.

"It is a splendid idea, Fanny," he told me, actually coming to the drawing room to see me rather than responding to my note, since by that time almost all our communication occurred through letters. "You should by all means visit your father. I shall personally see to it you have everything you require for your journey," he assured me. "I know you shall worry about the girls, but I will instruct them to write to you every week. And, of course, Miss Gerard shall watch over them carefully. Feel under no obligation to return quickly and suit yourself entirely on that matter, Fanny, since we shall manage very well."

"But I shall not manage so well without our children. Will you not consent to let them come with me? My father should be so happy to see them again."

"How can you imagine I should even *consider* such a thing," he asked coldly, "after you defied our agreement regarding Elizabeth Sedgwick? I cannot trust you and have no assurance you might not attempt to keep our children in England against my will."

I was tempted to bring up his own treachery, yet knowing I could not win such an argument, I submitted to his will. Still, I beseeched him, "But I shall miss them so much, Pierce. I could never bear for them to think that I am abandoning them."

"There, there, my dear," he said almost kindly, patting my shoulder, disarming me by apparently relenting in his harsh demeanor. "You are allowing yourself to become overwrought by these quarrels which have come between us. It should never *occur* to my children to think their mother could abandon them. No one, not even *I*, Fanny, angry as you sometimes make me with your ceaseless questioning and your defiance, could imagine you should desert my daughters. Devoted as you are to them, such a thought is preposterous."

31

In Exile

I sailed from New York in October of 1845 and asked Elizabeth to meet me there. Mr. Butler, delighted, I suspect, that I was departing without further argument regarding the children, easily agreed to my spending several days visiting friends before I departed for England. So few inquiries did he make about my New York plans that I was not placed in the false position of either deceiving or defying him. He seemed to wish only to be spared my society and to be assured that for all appearances, he had performed every service a husband ought towards a wife embarking on a journey. And he wanted all of Philadelphia to see that our children remained with him at Butler Place.

I ordered tea as soon as the train was underway to New York, hoping to steady myself, as my heart was beating much faster than its regular rhythm. I was certain everyone traveling in my compartment must be able to hear it. I left my bread unbuttered and enjoyed but a few sips of my tea, finding I was too nervous to consume it. For the first time since I had been a schoolgirl, I had no precise plan for my future.

I already missed my dear girls. We had exchanged miniatures and other keepsakes so we should never lose sight of each other during this separation, which I had not represented to them as being as lengthy as I feared it might turn out to be. It had been very difficult not to confess to them the sadness that oppressed me. In the first moments of my journey, I took out their likenesses that I might study their dear faces, yet saw instead their tearful eyes and trembling lips as they had struggled not to cry at our parting. I vowed to find some manner of work to support myself well so I would have a home where I could comfortably receive them. I also resolved to give Mr. Butler absolutely no cause to find fault with me, try as he might to do so.

I set great store in what Elizabeth should advise me and was so anxious to speak with her that though the train moved towards New York City with considerable speed, it seemed to crawl slower than the rudest conveyance. I was certain that with Elizabeth's and my father's assistance, I should study the law and find a way Mr. Butler's treachery might be turned against him, at least so far as the guardianship of the girls was concerned. I recognized that unless forced to do so by law, my husband would never permit our daughters to reside with me permanently. I could at least dream of long visits when our precious time together should not be marred by quarrels and cruel restrictions. I imagined a happy reunion with my daughters in England instead of America, which had become for me a sad symbol of my failed marriage and my broken hopes. I was certain I could not resume my solitary confinement at Butler Place.

I began to cry with joy as soon as I saw Elizabeth's kind face at Pennsylvania Station. As she reached forward to enfold me in a welcoming embrace, I felt my body relax so completely that I feared I might collapse. For so long, I had been holding in all my feelings not even daring to write to her, that it was quite overwhelming to find myself all at once in her presence and able to speak freely to her of any matter of my choosing.

"Fanny, you are much changed since last we met," she said sadly. "You do not look *frail* or unwell," she hurried to assure me, observing, I am sure, my reaction to her words. "I do not imagine you should ever look weak, even if you were dying. But you seem weary to a degree much greater than the toll this journey should exact. You are so very pale, yet what worries me most is your expression." She held my chin gently but firmly in her hand and tucked a lap robe around me for the carriage ride to the hotel she had engaged for us. "You look *frightened*, my dear Fanny. I thought, save when called for on the stage, this was never an emotion which appeared on your face."

Elizabeth put me to bed as if I were a tired child. Knowing I was completely under her protection, I savored my first good rest in months, and when I awoke, partook gratefully of the food she had arranged for us. I felt embarrassed she had been sitting all afternoon in our chamber watching me sleep, but in her gracious way, she assured me that this had been no bother to her. She had been reading and editing articles for the next publication of the Society of Abolitionists and had been completely occupied in her work.

While I ate hungrily of the sandwiches and soup and cold chicken she had set out for me, she told me of a plan that had just occurred to her. Now that I was separated from Mr. Butler, and should soon have an entire ocean between us, it was the perfect occasion to publish the journal I had kept while residing on his plantations. She implored me to let the mission of liberating the slaves, literally thousands of souls, and the power of my words to do so, bring fresh purpose to my life in this time of sadness. There was little I could do to thwart Mr. Butler's will under current law, but while separated from my daughters, I might at least advance the cause of freedom.

Much as I shared her revulsion towards slavery, I could not give my permission for publication. "I am still his *wife*, Elizabeth," I insisted, "and though I find both his livelihood and his betrayals reprehensible, so should I be if I publish an account of what I saw only in a private context as his invited guest."

"Your scruples do you credit, my dear Fanny, but to what purpose do you preserve them," she argued, as she served our tea and added more coal to the fire against the chilly afternoon. "Surely, after all the ways in which he has injured you and continues to wrong you, you cannot still feel you must protect Mr. Butler?" she insisted. "Your silence injures the cause of freedom. If your journal were brought forth and read widely in the North, we should gain support for abolition daily, as no one could doubt your sincerity and the terrible authenticity of your accounts. I hope you do not suppose," she said cautiously, looking thoughtfully for any change in my expression, "that Mr. Butler shall come to love you again if only you remain silent on this issue?"

I acknowledged it unlikely Mr. Butler and I should ever live again as husband and wife. Yet for the sake of our daughters, whom we both held dear, I hoped to prevail upon his former love for me to find a way he might allow them to regularly visit me. I knew if I enraged my husband, as the publication of my journal would surely do, I should never hope to see my daughters until each had reached the age of twenty-one. I also feared such a long separation would embitter them towards me, living as they would be, totally in his presence, or at the very least, might turn us into strangers. I would be wiser to secure a steady occupation in England and to wait for Mr. Butler to discern on his own that I posed no threat to his way of life and no harm to our daughters. Perhaps, I reflected, if I should again gain public notice by my craft, it would raise my worth in his eyes.

"You cling to the desperate hopes of a *slave*, Fanny," Elizabeth said sadly, "who believes if she obeys her master and never complains, her lot will be better, though all the evidence in the world indicates he will do whatever most profits his pocketbook and cares no more for her devotion than if she were a pig or a cow."

"What would you have me do, Elizabeth?" I implored her. "You do not disdain those slaves who are afraid to run away from bondage for fear of snakes and dogs, endless swamps and starvation. I admit freely I am not nearly so brave as characters I have portrayed upon the stage. But I could not live if my girls were taken forever from me. I cannot afford the risk this might occur. You say it shall not happen, but only one who has lived among the masters can fully comprehend their cruelty."

My friend had no answer but to hug me and promised not to press me further about my journal. She asked if I had come to regret my marriage to Mr. Butler, which had placed my freedom in such jeopardy. I might instead have remained on the stage where I had been so admired and recognized, and by this time should have amassed a fortune. If I had not abandoned the theatre, she insisted, I should never have suffered in isolation, dependent on the largesse of this small-minded man.

"But you forget, Elizabeth, I never aspired to the theatre. Such fame as I attracted was nothing I coveted for myself. It was all to save my family from ruin, a loyal daughter's romantic role. Yet if not for that life, I should never have known love as Mr. Butler once loved me." Speaking to her of that lost time, it returned to me, and I could recall the rare joy of seeing his face tender with love across a room and the feel of his hand when he first came to call for me and I had not wished to surrender it after we had exchanged greetings. And special moments of new affection that I could not possibly describe, even to a dear friend, but which were undeniably inscribed in my memories of my marriage. Despite the charges that are often made about actors' mores, called as they are to portray scenes of love upon a stage before many eyes, no man had ever genuinely touched me as Mr. Butler had.

"But was it really you, your *true* self, Mr. Butler loved or merely Juliet?" Elizabeth inquired gently.

I could not, of course, answer her question, for who can fathom absolutely the feelings of her own heart, much less that of another's, especially one whose love has turned against her. I told her there was no possible benefit in looking back. The most valuable lesson I had learned upon the stage was that a true actor must always look forward since no scene may be played again. No matter how poorly acted, with dropped lines and missed cues, a good play moves relentlessly onward following life. The actor must always be preparing for her next scene, never looking behind her. This was all I knew to do.

My father was delighted to introduce me once again to the London theatrical world. He maintained I had improved, both in appearance and voice, and was no longer just a talented girl, but was a handsome woman with a full, rich voice. He said it possessed warm colors that were not present when I was young, and so new roles should be open to me. I feared at first this was but his chivalrous way of conveying that I was too old to portray Juliet and Portia any longer, but he said that was not his meaning. He had known actresses far my senior who had credibly acted Juliet, and felt it was not vanity for him to claim that as a young man, and even when he was old enough to be that young man's father, he had always effectively played his part as Mercutio *or* Romeo.

And so once again I began to earn my own bread. I was relieved to no longer be dependent on my husband, but I found no greater joy in portraying Lady Macbeth or Calpurnia than I had years past as Juliet. Like any actress who has come out of retirement, I felt great relief when a critic declared, "Fanny Kemble's voice is fine, if not finer than it was before. She has lost no luster in her absence from the stage." And from another writer, "Although we know that she has been living in America and raising a family, not generally thought to be an actress's finest preparation, we find her brilliance, like fine wine, has but matured with age."

I saved money, every penny that I possibly could, since my hope remained to earn a sum sufficient to allow me to purchase a small farm in Lenox near Elizabeth, where the girls might visit me during vacations. I hoped if I lived very modestly and my reputation flourished, Mr. Butler could not deny me the chance to see our daughters in America, even if he would not permit them to come to me and their grandfather in London. After so much time spent in isolation while my husband went out alone in the evenings, I enjoyed London parties, plays, and concerts and making rounds of visits to friends. Yet I was ever cautious to do nothing that might draw Mr. Butler's wrath.

Letters from the girls were my greatest pleasure on any day when they arrived. Their words could not make up for our separation, but reading their poems and stories and responding to them, almost the moment their letters reached my hands, I felt still closely attached to them. Their sweet drawings I displayed about my chamber and my drawing room as if they had been sketches by famous artists, and I sent them my own renderings of London scenes.

My bank account grew from my own earnings and from the allowance Mr. Butler sent regularly. I was far happier than in my last years, subjugated to Mr. Butler's will, yet a great weariness came over me after my long hours and my lonely life separated from my children. I wondered how many years I could continue touring and playing the same roles over and over until I should have earned a sufficient amount to purchase my farm. I feared that even living frugally, it should require so long a time to amass a worthy sum that my girls might well be grown ladies by the time I would be able to welcome them for a pleasant summer visit.

Then my father offered me a legacy. He could not repay, nor would I have accepted the return of, the large sum I made over to him when I married Mr. Butler. It was long gone and had served its purpose in settling family debts. Yet he offered something far better than money when he passed on to me his mantle. Even well beyond the age most actors left the stage, my father had not departed entirely from the theatre. He had sought financial security, and, beyond that, for a man who had begun acting as a mere boy, he knew no other life. He had never found time for amusements, always touring, and even when in town, he kept an actor's late hours, and the theatre and the company of other players were his only recreation. Since the death of my mother, his soul's companion, he had been desperately lonely. He began offering readings of Shakespearean comedies and tragedies, playing all the roles himself, and whenever he gave these recitations, my father attracted large audiences.

I had never imagined that I might also possess the voice and presence to enrapture audiences by reading to them for several hours. This was precisely what he suggested one evening when I came in late from the theatre. He was waiting for me beside a table covered with scripts and pages of notes in his own precise hand. I was much discouraged to find he wanted to converse about plays. I was so weary I wanted nothing more to do with the theatre that night and longed for my bed. But he would not hear of it.

"My dear, I have been concerned about you lately," he said kindly, pouring me a small snifter of brandy and placing a footstool beneath my tired feet.

"I am grateful for your concern, Father. But it is nothing that sleep cannot mend. I will be much better in the morning." I put down my snifter, hardly touched, and prepared to kiss him good-night. I knew he should be content to sit up late perusing his manuscripts.

"No, wait," he insisted. "I require but a few moments of your time."

I sat down, puzzled by his insistence, and honestly a little annoyed by it. I thought he above all others, should recognize the exhaustion in an actor's face that no makeup could conceal at the conclusion of a strenuous performance and might allow me to go unimpeded to my bed. I am ashamed

I did not recognize at that moment the gift he was prepared to give by allowing me to take his place, since he had always maintained he should never leave the stage and planned to die upon it.

"You must earn a better living, Fanny, if you are to get your farm and have a place for Fan and Sal to visit," he said. "And you shall not earn even a portion of the sum that I once accepted from you from your current pursuits." He sipped his own brandy. "As actors age, we cannot, as you know, continue to play Romeo or Juliet, Hamlet or Ophelia. And I have even passed beyond playing Lear and Macbeth, since even my readings now exhaust me. Some evenings when I begin, I wonder how I shall ever make it all the way to the play's conclusion. Even as I have abridged the plays to make it possible for one voice to read for several hours, still I long to further shorten them, and so it is time for me to cease this enterprise. I shall continue with my pupils. There are still many things I can teach these would-be princes and kings. But you may now take my place giving readings and may choose from any of the plays I have arranged. They are laid out for you here, every one of Shakespeare's plays that I have read to audiences, along with my notations. Not that *you* should even require them," he added graciously.

I recognized his delicacy in saying *should* and *may*, rather than insisting that I follow his lead, yet I protested, believing with all my heart, that no one would come to hear me. He was England's hero, not I. Audiences had adored him for fifty years without interruption, unlike my brief and furious fame, and though he had aged, he was still a fine figure of a man. It seemed to me a grave injustice of nature that women aged less favorably than men, and I told him then that I held no illusion that I should present nearly so admirable an appearance in a lecture hall as did he.

"I will not listen to such foolishness," he told me. "Surely you do not really believe it in your own heart. It is only the effect of this dreadful marriage of yours, beating you down, ruining your confidence."

"But I would not know how to begin, Father," I answered nervously, truly feeling the shyness and inadequacy he had perceived. "I know nothing about renting a hall or managing the publicity. Who would put out the handbills and what play would best suit me?" I glanced nervously at the laden table. "I should not know where to start or how—"

"You must start where you began, Fanny, with *Romeo and Juliet*. And if you consent, I shall handle all the arrangements. You shall not worry about a detail. You have always said you treasured Shakespeare's plays *themselves*, not acting a part in them. Now you have opportunity to interpret every character for your public. Audiences are still devoted to you, and their enthusiasm shall provide the means to reclaim your children. So, my pet," he said tenderly, stroking my cheek as he had done since I was a tiny child. "What do you say?"

I could not refuse.

(April, 23, 1847: London *Herald*)
"Juliet Reigns Again"
by Ames Fielding

For a fortunate audience of 250 at Worthingham Hall tonight, there could be no more delightful and appropriate way to celebrate the great bard's birthday than by witnessing Mrs. Pierce Butler's (nee Fanny Kemble) stirring reading of *Romeo and Juliet*, the very play in which she made her Covent Garden debut nearly twenty years ago. In the tradition of her father, the esteemed Charles Kemble, whose Romeo and Mercutio are still unsurpassed and who adapted the Shakespeare plays that his daughter reads, Mrs. Butler's inflections and her rich voice were superb. She hardly seems to glance at the play script before her as she makes the entire play come alive with her captivating personality.

For some time, London audiences have had opportunity to enjoy staged readings by literary lions as diverse as Dickens and Thackeray. There is understandably great excitement and fascination in hearing authors and poets read from their *own* works, but what makes the readings of Mrs. Butler, and her father before her, so exceptional, are the actors' gifts with which they bring fully alive the language of each play.

Mrs. Butler is in her own right an accomplished writer, having published when still a mere girl the play *Francis I*, which was well received at Covent Garden. Her journals, dating from her girlhood to her first impressions of America when she toured with her father before marrying Philadelphian Pierce Mease Butler, have also been widely read. Her short pieces, in current magazines and reviews, are written with the same intelligence and vitality that characterize her longer works. It is our opinion her exceptional capacity to interpret plays results from the unusual union within her between actor and writer.

Over the next four months, Mrs. Butler is engaged to give readings of twelve of Shakespeare's plays for audiences in England, Scotland, and Ireland. She also anticipates a tour of France and Italy since she is fluent in the languages of those countries. We are delighted to have this daughter of

England's most famous theatrical family once again in our midst, although we recognize that the call of her husband and children will likely send her across the ocean to America before very long. Therefore, we exhort all who enjoy theatre and who admire Shakespeare's tragedies, comedies, and histories to attend Mrs. Butler's readings.

Welcome home, fair Juliet!

(May 14, 1847: *The London Courier*)
"The Play's the Thing"
by Ethan Potts

Indeed, no one need argue with Shakespeare. The play is definitely the thing, particularly when one has the opportunity to hear Shakespeare's works brought to life in readings by Fanny Kemble. She is, in actuality, Mrs. Pierce Butler of Philadelphia, but to London theatre audiences she is, and shall always be, the lovely daughter of Charles Kemble, who created great sensation with her splendid portrayals of Julia and Portia when but a girl. Now her powers of expression and her magnificent voice have matured so that whether one hears her read *Macbeth*, as I did several nights ago, or *The Tempest*, several weeks previously, the effect is magnificent.

Even the lesser characters, which one has come to perceive as mere plot devices, take on new meaning and consequence in Mrs. Butler's portrayals. Through nuance of voice and delivery, an entire cast stands before her audience without even benefit of costumes or scenery. It is, indeed, extraordinary that so notable an actress, whose stage presence is unmistakable as her beautifully modulated voice, manages to disappear before our very eyes so that nothing eclipses the power of Shakespeare's words. There is no other actor in memory, save her father, Charles Kemble, to match her in this regard. And her effectiveness is not governed by whether the characters she portrays are male or female, old or young. Mrs. Butler imbues every line of a play with transcendent understanding so that her audiences wish her readings, like sublime poetry, should never end.

I knew Ames Fielding's assumption that I would be called home by a loving husband was sadly erroneous. Yet I missed Fan and Sal so terribly that I could not be parted from them any longer. I reasoned that with my excellent reviews and drawing on my past reputation, I should be able to support myself by giving readings in America as well. I hoped that time had softened Pierce's hostility, and I should return now on a different footing. I had just been offered an engagement that would bring me over five hundred pounds. Added to my savings, I felt this sum would be sufficient to purchase the small farm and cottage that could become my home in America.

Considering the insufferable heat of Philadelphia in summer, I hoped Pierce might permit the girls to join me at the cottage for part of each summer and that he himself might be persuaded to pay us a visit. If all of England found me so engaging for months on end, I prayed it would be possible for my own husband to enjoy my company for a few weeks. And though I feared from past knowledge of his habits what associations he might have made during my absence, I still hoped our separation had helped him recall happier memories of our years together when not a rancorous word passed between us.

I planned first to treat my father and myself to a short holiday. Adelaide would come to us in London, and then we should all take a cottage together near Surrey, where mother had loved to go. The cottage was situated near enough to London for me to perform there, and friends might come and go as they pleased. I was apprehensive of how I might appear to Pierce after two years' separation, and hoped that country living, with its abundant exercise and fresh air, should help me replenish myself after my very arduous schedule.

When Adelaide arrived, I observed right away something was very wrong. She seemed distracted despite all of our father's playful attentions and a festive meal prepared in her honor. When he had finally retired, in his gentlemanly way leaving us to chat alone, I begged her to tell me what was troubling her. I feared she was seriously ill or that some terrible financial worry consumed her.

"I worry for *you*, Fanny," she said, taking my hand and moving closer to me on the settee. "I assumed you had not yet told Father, and so mentioned nothing in front of him at supper. But surely before you leave you plan to tell him what awaits you on your return. You mustn't allow him to hear from others."

"What would you have me tell him, Adelaide?" I asked in bewilderment. "I cannot imagine what secret you think I have concealed from Father. He knows I hope to reconcile with my husband, although who knows how he will receive me. Or if he has continued associations which dishonor me," I admitted sadly.

"You really are not aware of what Mr. Butler has done?" she asked incredulously. "I am so disturbed by his actions, Fanny, I can hardly call him by his Christian name."

I feared another of his embarrassing liaisons. When I had been longing for peace and, if not love, then at least companionship, it seemed I was to return home to humiliation. I wondered if I should be confronted by his infidelities within our own circle in Philadelphia, or if he had sought liaisons in other cities, making it likely this disgrace would again be reported in newspapers, shaming our daughters and following me to every locality my readings might take me.

"What has he done, Adelaide?" I cried out. "Whoever she is, please tell me that there is not a *child* involved!"

"I am so sorry, dear Fanny," she said, her resonant voice still breaking with the difficulty of conveying the hurtful news. "Mr. Butler is suing you for divorce on the grounds of *desertion*. I learned from Amanda Stephenson. She came to call on us in Rome. It is evidently the talk of Philadelphia. She assumed I knew and wondered if you will be defending yourself against the charge."

"Defending myself!" I could not stifle my indignation. "How can I be accused of desertion when he has always known my whereabouts in my *father's* own home? I should never have left Mr. Butler's home at all if he had not persecuted me by his deliberate insults and deprivations. I feared his animosity towards me might even lead him to antagonize our own dear children simply to torment me! *He* is the one who had dishonored our marriage." I felt so cruelly used that despite my best attempts, I found myself weeping in Adelaide's arms.

We canceled our holiday plans and my engagements so that I might set off immediately from Liverpool for America. Adelaide offered to accompany me, as did my father, but I could not let her break so many commitments to her own public in the height of her popularity, and I feared for my father to be present during arguments that would surely ensue. He would not suffer Mr. Butler to insult me in person or in the press. I was concerned that my father's love for me and his sterling sense of honor could compel him to demand my husband acknowledge his perfidy. I knew Mr. Butler should dearly love to give my father satisfaction in a duel, and in my father's death, a likely result for an old man who had only dueled upon the stage, exact his own revenge.

I sailed for New York on a stormy day, which seemed appropriate to my miserable state of mind. As the dark water swirled around the ship, which was rocked steadily by the wind and waves, I suffered seasickness and also anguished in my fear my children should be lost to me. If I were found *guilty* of desertion, then a judge might refuse me right to communicate with my own daughters even by letter, much less allow them to visit me.

Taking the air on the deck, feeling the light rain falling on my wrist in the space my cloak did not cover, I glanced down at the delicate gold watch Mr. Butler had given me after we were engaged. The face was growing damp so that I could not even read the numbers or see its tiny hands. I took it gently in my hands, remembering the pleasure I had felt when he had presented it with the loving wish that it should always adorn my arm. I examined it for a moment longer, preparing to fasten it once again about my wrist, but then I changed my mind. I leaned over the rail and tossed this golden trinket into the churning ocean. I cared no longer for time or possessions. Only for my children.

32

Exile's Return

I registered at a small hotel, clean and comfortable, but certainly not fashionable, so that I might stay as far as possible from anyone who might know Mr. Butler or our circumstances. I spoke to no one, save Elizabeth, to whom my father had written on my behalf when I set sail so unexpectedly. He had inquired if she or her father could recommend an attorney, since even in matters of publishing, Mr. Butler had always insisted on reviewing my papers and contracts, and if any detail warranted legal review, he enlisted the services of his family's attorney. My father had cautioned me to make no statements to friends or members of the press and to refrain from attempts to see my children until I had advice of counsel.

I met with Thaddeus Winship, Esq., at his offices, which occupied one floor of his townhome overlooking a lovely park. I was ushered from his waiting room immediately into a private meeting room with so much secrecy I feared his assistants thought I was indeed a disreputable woman. I knew that divorce was considered improper in Philadelphia society and wore my most somber garment, a grey tweed suit, instead of the bright colors I preferred, hoping to appear the model of sober motherhood. I recognized that Mr. Butler accused me of being an unnatural mother, more wrongful than wronged against, so that it might prove difficult to find an attorney to defend me against charges brought by the scion of one of America's leading families.

Mr. Winship was, to use one of my father's expressions, "a very solid citizen" who amply filled out the front of his dark grey suit. His graying hair was parted precisely, as if with a ruler, and the muted design of his blue tie, his crisp white cuffs, and his earnest manner seemed so carefully regulated as to make impossible imagining his adopting any other demeanor. It was very difficult to envision him casually dressed, even as a boy. Since Carlyle & Winship had been in operation since 1778, I assumed he had been destined from birth to be an attorney, no doubt reading law at his father's side.

"Very honored to meet you, Mrs. Butler," he said politely and most discreetly, barely touching my hand when he took it in his own. "I saw you years ago on the stage. I am not a great one for the theatre, I must admit, but seeing you *with* your father, now that was an entirely different matter. I still vividly recall it."

I nodded appreciatively and waited. I was accustomed to such pleasantries, particularly with Americans, who studied me very closely, even if my business were simply to acquire a packet of pins and several bolts of cloth, fascinated as they were by my former celebrity. They seemed surprised to find a member of the acting profession had a personality that differed widely from the roles she played upon the stage. They could not believe I performed ordinary, daily tasks such as reading the newspaper and making sandwiches for tea, or that when I spoke in a shop, I did so in ordinary voice and not as if I were declaiming lines upon a stage.

"Yet...ah...nevertheless," he continued, stammering slightly at having to make reference to such a delicate matter as my occupation, "I would hold off a bit from engaging in that...ah... sort of endeavor now that you are home. I mean absolutely no disrespect, dear lady. But in matters of this sort, there are those of my profession who try to portray the accused party as a person of tainted character. Therefore, we must not give them any cause to comment about your profession. We must portray you as a devoted wife and mother, *not* an actress." Then, hurriedly, lest I had taken offense, he assured me, "Though I have had accounts from friends who heard you in London, that your readings are magnificent. But I hope you shall not be engaging in them now." Lines of concern accented his smooth, pink face. "At least until this matter has been settled."

So it seemed in addition to the five hundred pounds I had lost by canceling an incomparable engagement to be present to defend myself, I should also be required to forfeit all income from readings. When I should have reasonably anticipated strong American interest in my readings, all doors were closed to me.

"May I see my children, Mr. Winship?" I asked anxiously. "I have been separated from them by great distance, and now it pains me most of all to stand a few miles from their door and yet be unable to approach them. I assure you, sir, they would run gladly into my arms."

"I am certain you are correct, Mrs. Butler," he said gallantly. "Who would not wish to greet you?" He patted my hand sympathetically. "Perhaps the saddest aspect of a divorce is the condition of the children, which is why I rarely consent to become involved in such proceedings. But from the Sedgwicks' description of your situation, and the considerable gossip surrounding Mr. Butler's associations, it would appear you are the wronged party, and *he* has behaved abominably."

No words could have brought me greater solace. To hear a learned man of the law acknowledge that I was the injured party, rather than the one who had dishonored my marriage commitment, brought tears to my eyes.

"Then you are hopeful, Mr. Winship? I am very pleased to hear it. It has been dreadful to find myself accused of deserting my husband and children when that was never the case. I am so gratified you perceive we shall be victorious," I said happily.

Mr. Winship made it immediately clear I had misunderstood his meaning. Though he had no doubt as to my honor and my devotion to my family, not even the Sedgwicks' testimonials and the evidence of Mr. Butler's erratic behavior would make it likely I should prevail. He assured me his defense of me would be vigorous, yet he feared the law was on Mr. Butler's side. Then he passed me a substantial folder of documents to sign in order to retain him to answer Mr. Butler's complaint. There was also a detailed summary of the financial obligations that should result from such representation. I could not imagine how to manage them without depleting completely the money I had been saving to purchase a home where my children could reside with me.

As I responded to his questions, Mr. Winship carefully noted my answers in the file before him, and as I came better to understand his expressions, I sadly discerned that my answers did not please him. I could not state that Mr. Butler had *ever* asked me to leave his home. He simply made the conditions of my living there so degrading that no mother with any regard for her children or herself could have consented to remain there under his persecution. He had not declined to appear with me in society, though there were many evenings he went out, refusing to advise me of where he was going, and he had barred me from eating meals at his table as if I were a miscreant and not his wife and the mother of his children. He *had* provided all necessary funds to support my daily needs, but he had also interfered in my contracts with my *own* publisher, entered into before I had become his wife.

Even in the matter of my husband's infidelities, humiliating incidents that I had never imagined having to recount to any man, Mr. Winship was not encouraging. He blushed himself at my disquietude in relating them and at Mr. Butler's shameful behavior. Then he advised me that though the duel with Mr. Schott would be admissible, the love letters I had seen had most certainly been destroyed, and mention of both the former and the latter, he feared would be reported in the newspapers, bringing shameful attention to my daughters, and would likely offer little benefit to my defense. He listened patiently, but concluded I had no actual verification Mr. Butler had conducted himself inappropriately with Miss Gerard, and that a judge should find ridiculous any allusion to the fragrance of her perfume upon him as evidence. Raising such matters would open a line of inquiry in which Mr. Butler's attorneys might well assert that my obsession with my pursuits as an actress and writer had driven this loving husband, who had shown his devotion to me so publicly, to seek other *company* because I was not a true wife to him.

The cruelest blow was to learn that Mr. Butler might successfully establish evidence that I had deserted him. He had not denied me money, nor had he ever beaten me. Only on that one occasion in his study had he even touched me roughly. He had not disparaged me in the presence of others, and if he chose not to take his meals with me nor have me share them with our children, there was nothing in the *legal* interpretation of the marriage vows that established that he must do so. I could establish no pattern of actions by my husband which forced me to leave Butler Place, yet there could be no denying I had left my husband's home of my own accord and had been away for more than two years.

"But he knew where I was at all times, sir, and never once asked me to return," I protested. "And when originally I proposed to leave Butler Place to visit my ill father in England, Mr. Butler agreed heartily I should go."

"And you have written proof of this?" he asked hopefully.

"No. Save for the monthly allowance he sent to my father's house, which he had offered to provide. I had not even asked him to commit anything towards my expenses," I was careful to explain.

"The record of that monthly allowance will benefit him far more than it shall assist you in court, Mrs. Butler," he said sorrowfully. "It demonstrates that he maintained his devotion to you, behaving responsibly as your protector, even though you had deserted him and his children."

"I did not desert my children. We corresponded weekly the entire time I was away, and on my part, sometimes far more often than that."

"Well, now, that is *something*. We should be able to make a point with that for your right to visitation."

I ran to greet Fan and Sal in Mr. Winship's office, not caring who witnessed our eager hugs, so determined was I not to squander a moment of our visit. I had hoped they might spend the night with me at the hotel, but this would not be permitted. I could take them out to luncheon and for a walk in the park, yet had been instructed by Mr. Winship to be certain to return no later than three o'clock. Otherwise, he could not promise that future visits would be allowed.

I was so delighted to see my dear girls I would have bought them four luncheons each and sweets and any amusement they could imagine, but like me, they wished only to be together. They had grown so tall that I could no longer think of them as my babies, even Fan, who still had her curls. At thirteen, Sal, who quickly told me I was the only person who still called her by that baby name, was quite a young lady, and Fan, still impetuous and spontaneous, was determined to do everything for herself. When I tried to help her cut her meat and later tidy up after the ice I had purchased for her in the park began to drip, she politely objected.

"Thank you all the same. But I have been doing everything for myself for ages, Mother. I am quite grown up, you know."

Fan's independence and Sal's impatience with my hugs were only natural effects of our long separation. I understood and yet still felt saddened to see how much they had changed in my absence. My sorrow grew as they began to pose the questions I had known they would inevitably ask.

"Why did you want to be away from us, Mother?" Fan asked, who had called me Mama all her life. "Father said you preferred to read to people in England than to stay at home with us."

"Did you leave because of your disagreements with Father about slavery, Mother?" Sal asked. "Miss Gerard says Father is a very wise and kind man and would never treat *anyone* unkindly. She says that everyone in the South who can afford to do so has slaves, so, of course, Father does as well. But she says you do not agree with slavery, which has to do with your being foreign born." She studied my face carefully. "I do not believe that people should own other people," she said very seriously. "I should not like to be forced to work in someone's fields or sold at market. I told Miss Gerard so, and I am not foreign born."

They spoke about their studies, and I was reassured to find them very bright and reading well beyond their years. Of the fine quality of their writing I knew much more since we had been fast correspondents. Sal showed me a picture she had recently drawn of a new colt down at the farm.

It was far better formed than I should have accomplished at her age. Fan was soon walking hand in hand with me as if we had never been parted, so that I was very happy and then quite amazed when our time was so quickly over. When Mr. Winship returned after escorting the girls to the carriage waiting to take them home, I asked if Mr. Butler had driven to meet them. I hoped he had so he should see for himself I had returned them well fed and healthy and in good spirits.

"Yes, he was there, Mrs. Butler, to see that they were returned on time," Mr. Winship explained. "After such a satisfactory visit, we shall be able to make a very good case for arranging another one quite soon."

"Did he say anything? Was there any indication of his mood?" I asked, anxious to be reassured Mr. Butler should not oppose my seeing them soon again.

Mr. Winship said Mr. Butler had taken out his watch and noted the time carefully, mumbling under his breath words of which he was uncertain. I asked if he were being truly honest or if he simply did not *wish* to tell me what Mr. Butler had said. Mr. Winship smiled and said that he could not catch Mr. Butler's precise words, but he thought he seemed very disappointed.

That told me all that I required. I was as positive as if I had been present myself that he had said critically, "I see that they are back on time. Their mother, the *great actress* has always kept me and everyone else waiting for her. The very first time I hoped she would be delayed, she is punctual!"

The Complaint of Mr. Pierce Mease Butler, Esq., in the matter of Pierce Mease Butler, Esq., vs. Frances Anne Kemble Butler, City of Philadelphia, Philadelphia County, Pennsylvania

July 14, 1848

Statement of the Complaint:

It was only with deepest regret, recognizing that my wife had no intention of reconciling with me, that I filed suit to divorce my wife, Frances Anne Kemble Butler, on grounds of her desertion of her duties to me and my children, Frances, age ten, and Sarah, age thirteen. I had endeavored by every means within my power, including that of providing ample financial support to my wife throughout her almost three-year absence from my home, to entreat her to return to her family.

Several times previously, she had abandoned our home for days at a time, and in each instance, for the sake of our children and due to my abiding love for her, I welcomed her back. Yet her recent, prolonged absence and cruel abandonment of our children and her responsibilities as my wife, as well as her continued appearances in plays in which she portrays characters whose morals and very sanity are in question, necessitated my action. I had repeatedly beseeched her to amend her ways by adhering to the pledge she made me upon our betrothal, to leave the stage and devote herself to the duties of married life. However, she has persisted, against my specific instructions, in such improper performances and in publishing journals and other materials that are unsuitable to a wife and mother. No man, even one dedicated to Christian principles and the belief that the marriage bond is a sacred covenant, can continue to remain silent in the face of such shameful treatment.

In suing for the dissolution of our marriage, I seek to protect my young daughters, as it saddens me deeply to separate myself from a lady for whom I have held the most tender affection. Yet for the sake of these impressionable young ladies, I must sever connections with their mother from genuine fear that if she should return to my home, they will witness and emulate her example and lead themselves, and the husbands with whom they shall one day be joined, on a journey perilous to their immortal souls.

Save for my daughters, whose youth until recently sheltered them from awareness of their mother's actions, I should be willing to forgive her trespasses and endeavor out of love and a fervent hope to save her soul to forgive her past transgressions and begin anew. However, as their father, I cannot in good conscience welcome their unrepentant mother's return to our home. She deems her desertion justifiable since I would not submit to the management she wished to impose upon our children, which I, as their father, found unsuitable and improper. Even when I employed a highly qualified English governess, thinking that my wife would be pleased our children should be instructed by her own countrywoman, she insulted the governess regularly, interfering with all attempts to provide reasonable discipline to our children, further diminishing this lady's authority over our daughters.

If I were to now allow Mrs. Butler to return to my home as wife and mother, I am certain she would once again create havoc by vacating my home whenever it suits her whim or if she should experience displeasure over the simplest detail of daily life. My daughters, who have been subjected to her previous desertions, have already too often cried themselves to sleep longing for her.

The actions of Frances Anne Kemble Butler have harmed not just my honor and the sanctity of our Christian home, but have severely injured my livelihood and my reputation. When we became engaged, as previously stated, my wife promised to leave the stage and desist from the publication of diaries and observations, which although perhaps acceptable for an actress, were unsuitable for the wife of a gentleman. Yet she has, on numerous occasions, violated this promise, most particularly during the last two years, in vulgar halls throughout Europe (I have attached theatrical performances and readings). In addition, when I first made it known to my wife how strongly I objected to the sensational nature of her writings, whose publication would occasion true hurt and serious insult to those who had generously entertained her in their homes, she insisted nevertheless in doing so, refusing to recognize my right as her husband to regulate these materials that should affect our future. When I intervened, as was my responsibility and my duty, she became violently oppositional, resorting to offensive language and once, in a fit of temper, destroyed priceless porcelain that had been in my family for generations.

Prior to our marriage, Mrs. Butler had not concerned herself with the nature of my property, which, as is commonly known, consists of several Georgia plantations in rice and cotton. Once she learned that I supported her and our family with an estate run through the effective and humane management of over eight hundred slaves, she became overwrought on the matter of abolition. She was never silent about the subject, even enlisting the intercession of her abolitionist friends, the Sedgwicks of Lowell, Massachusetts, in her attempts to condemn slavery. Without my permission, she participated in the meetings of their Society when she visited them, and expressly against my consent, she maintained correspondence with Elizabeth Sedgwick after I had advised her that the entire Sedgwick family was an enemy to our family and its fortunes.

Furthermore, in 1838, while accompanying me to Georgia for my annual assessment of the estate consisting of Butler Island and Hampton Point on St. Simon's Island, she became so critical of the overseer's direction of my interests that she interrupted for days the regular operation of these plantations, causing a loss of income as well as serious damage to discipline among the slaves. Her interference was so persistent that the overseer, a man patient beyond measure, threatened to leave my employ, a truly disastrous prospect. Despite my entreaties that she desist in activities unbecoming to a planter's wife and my expenditure of countless dollars on unnecessary enterprises of her own conception to improve the plantations, nothing would satisfy her short of my freeing all my slaves and experiencing financial ruin. Her behavior was so disruptive that to prevent my family's financial ruin, I was forced to stipulate that she should never again accompany me when I visited my Georgia plantations.

In summation, Frances Anne Kemble Butler has disgracefully conducted herself as my wife and as mother to my children, defying my reasonable requests to *restrain her outbursts and bringing shame and humiliation down upon me and these precious daughters. Before long, these young ladies shall naturally assume their rightful places in Philadelphia society. I cannot permit their reputations to be sullied by their mother's ungovernable behavior and her disregard for the conventions of society that wisely regulate our attitudes towards those around us. I appeal to the Court as a man of business and a planter, certainly no match in rhetoric or presentation with a noted actress, to recognize that devoted as I have been to my wife throughout our marriage, I am concerned her improper actions shall continue, leading to irreparable damage to my financial position and to my personal reputation. I regretfully admit my own failure to guide my wife more persuasively in the performance of her duties and responsibilities to her family. I bear Mrs. Butler no ill will, but after much prayer and reflection, have concluded the dissolution of our marriage is in the best interests of my beloved daughters, upon whom her disturbing influence shall then be mitigated.*

Respectfully submitted,
Pierce Mease Butler, Esq.

"We can do very little to answer such charges, Mrs. Butler," Mr. Winship advised me, "overstated and sanctimonious as they are. Mr. Butler seems a man content to alter memory and fact whenever this suits his purpose."

"But surely we must challenge his lies! He impugns *my* integrity when the dishonor was all his own. I should never have returned to the theatre if I had not needed to provide for myself, and he speaks of my absence as if I had indulged in mysterious escapades throughout the capitals of Europe rather than seeking refuge in my own father's home." I found myself pacing around Mr. Winship's office in my agitation. "And what of *his* numerous infidelities? Surely, we must testify that from the early days of my marriage I *suspected* he was unfaithful and then discovered he had betrayed me! Again and again."

"My dear Mrs. Butler, please be reassured. We shall of course introduce the infidelities, but only *very* carefully, so as not to injure your dear daughters. We must prove that Mr. Butler's terrible financial speculations threatened your daughters' future and made it necessary for you to pursue your own living." He spoke with the determination of a seasoned director convincing a veteran actress to undertake a role she feels is unsuited to her talents and her temperament. "That, I am afraid, is the best I can do for you, my dear lady. We shall not win this suit, but we shall ameliorate the settlement for you and your daughters. We cannot permit him to gamble away their fortune or keep them from your sight."

"But it is beastly I should be shown so completely in the wrong when *he* drove me from his home. I understand full well American justice recognizes a father's rights as if he were a king, but Mr. Butler has deprived a devoted mother of every right towards her own children. And in forcing me to write that terrible letter to Elizabeth Sedgwick, he has denied even my right to free speech!"

"Though you were coerced to write it," Mr. Winship said carefully, "no one witnessed that coercion. The letter is in your hand, is it not?"

"Are you saying even *you* disbelieve me and take him at his word?"

"*Of course* not, dear lady. I am only telling you how it will appear in court."

"And though he spreads these atrocious lies, you say I should not defend myself. How can that be possible?"

"I shall proceed however you direct, but we will do best to argue that he must settle property on each of your daughters so that his rash speculations, of which I am finding considerable evidence," he said, thumbing through his file of papers, "shall not leave them without a proper provision. We shall insist you must have substantial visits with them every year until they reach majority and are free to visit whomever they please. If he shall agree to those terms, I advise you to surrender your defense."

"And not fight for custody of my children so that they shall not remain with a dishonorable father? And see them but once or twice a year?" I asked, my anger at such unfair treatment bringing me to tears.

"Or risk not being permitted to see them at all, dear lady. And discovering that he has gambled away their patrimony. I understand your grave displeasure with my counsel," he said sympathetically, patting my hand, "yet it is the best the law can do for you."

"Then do whatever it is you must do," I exclaimed angrily. "But this law is an abomination towards every wife and mother. This law be *damned!*"

"Your sentiments are easily understood, Mrs. Butler, and you are not the first to express them in this chamber," he said kindly, offering me his handkerchief.

Though it took weeks in the courts to conclude such miserable proceedings, I accepted that the matter of Butler vs. Butler should proceed much as Mr. Winship had set forth. At first, Mr. Butler insisted he was being sorely persecuted and that his sound investments for his daughters' future should be much restricted by this unwarranted intrusion. But Mr. Winship successfully introduced testimony revealing Mr. Butler's gambling debts and speculations, which despite the magnitude of his holdings, were quite considerable and which threatened the foundation of his estate.

Contrary to what was generally expected, perhaps even out of sympathy for me and belief in the greater veracity of my accounts than in Mr. Butler's harsh accusations, the judge ordered Mr. Butler to make provisions for each of our daughters, over which a bank, and not he, should retain full authority until they reached majority. I was awarded the right, once I obtained "a suitable permanent lodging," to a visit of at least one month's duration with my daughters each summer until they should come of age. And during the year, I might see them for short visits in Philadelphia when sufficient notice was provided and a setting was selected that met with Mr. Butler's approval. I determined after this development I should select John Butler's house for my Philadelphia visits, and defy them not to admit me, or Mr. Butler to declare such a setting unsuitable.

In early 1849, I purchased a lovely little cottage in Lenox near Elizabeth called "The Perch," because it sat upon a hill overlooking a lake and grassy meadows. It had not the extensive farmland I had anticipated, but the interruption in my income from readings, and Mr. Winship's charges had taken their toll on my savings, and I thought it best to be prudent and expedient in finding a permanent home where my girls might visit. They came for a wonderful month that summer, where we were truly riotous in our happiness, bathing and fishing in the lake, taking long walks, and gathering wild flowers.

Fan was still so young she could spend this time without a worry, thinking no further ahead than determining at breakfast how she might spend her day. But Sal, who seemed much more than just three years older than her sister, thought ahead to the fall and boarding school, new friends, and dances where she should attract admirers.

"It is very sad about you and Father," she confided. "I do not see that this divorce has made either of you happier. And now that Fan and I shall both be off at school, there is no further need, I should think, for Miss Gerard to remain at all. I hardly know what there is for her to do besides serve Father at tea. They are always whispering together. He says they are only discussing Fan and me, but I believe there is too much laughter in it for that. And Miss Gerard laughs very little when she is alone with us."

I did not inquire further about their governess and whether her father's behavior actually suggested something improper about Miss Gerard's role in the household. I understood the severe limits of my authority over decisions regarding my daughters, and sad as I was to think of little Fan being sent away to school sooner than I preferred, I was relieved my dear girls should not constantly be around Mr. Butler and Miss Gerard. I vowed to myself I should quickly find out the dates of their holidays and make plans, no matter where my readings might take me, to be with them anytime they were free to be with me.

When Fan asked how they should now address their letters to me, it surprised me, I suppose, because I had not even considered it. I wrote down the address for "The Perch" and praised her for remembering to obtain this piece of information.

"But that is not what I meant, Mother," she said impatiently, handing back the piece of stationery. "I mean now that you are no longer married to Father."

"Oh, I see. I am Fanny Kemble, Fan," I told her happily, taking pleasure in the sound of it. "It has been a while. But that is who I am once again. And I believe that is who I shall always remain."

I knew I should be delighted to read the accounts of Butler vs. Butler and learn Pierce Butler had divorced his wife for *desertion*. I should have rejoiced at any hurt or disappointment that caused Fanny Kemble to suffer, since her fame and fortune had been assured and lovingly managed by Charles Kemble, while my father had virtually sold me to Mr. James to improve his own. She had destroyed poor Matthew's play as blithely as if she were swatting a gnat. She had not accomplished this all on her own, as the audience had been filled with detractors, but when she was interviewed, the wife of a planter who had witnessed slavery with her own eyes, who might have saved *The Poisoned Table* with but a few words from her famous mouth, she instead called it false.

I remember by heart her remarks to critics more easily than the most difficult passage I have memorized in a lengthy role. Her most damning comments are burned into *my* memory. Even in his final weakness, when my dear Matthew asked me to read him the notices, I could not entirely protect him from the condemnation she had spoken in her high-flown way to the reporters. But at least her most vicious comments I only became aware of after Matthew's death. I read the review quickly and was so infuriated by her injustice to Matthew that I tore the Brighton Theatre Report to bits and threw them in the fire. Yet try as I did, her words lingered in my head and in my heart. I recall them still, and even more wrenching was the interview I read later in the Pennsylvania Theatre Gazette:

"I cannot question Mr. Harrison's good intention," said former actress Fanny Kemble, now Mrs. Pierce Butler of Philadelphia. But the plot he weaves is injurious to the very slaves themselves. In all the weeks I spent on two different plantations, I never once heard of slaves trying to harm their masters, let alone poison them. Rather than advancing the cause of abolition or urging through his play more humane treatment, Mr. Harrison has written a play that will only instill fear of these poor people. I never saw evidence of such evil actions by slaves as Mr. Harrison has put forth. I was quite surprised to learn he is an American playwright. I surely thought from the lack of humanity with which he has drawn the characters of slaves that he had never even seen a slave."

I hated her cold dismissal, she who should have known far better than any other theatre patron how a playwright's symbols may not precisely match real life. Even I, who had witnessed more humane slavery, if such a phrase can be used to describe the condition of well-fed slaves, who were decently clothed and worked often beside their masters and mistresses, could conceive the desire *and* the resolve to poison those who held one and one's children in bondage.

I wanted to relish her suffering and to gloat that her costly attorney and her eloquent testimony had not abated her downfall. She had *lost*. She, who had plagued me since I was a girl, was suffering the fate of other wronged wives. No exception would be made for her. I should have reveled in her misery.

But I could not do it. I could not hate Fanny Kemble. Perhaps Pierce Butler's visit to my dressing room, drunken, leering wastrel that he had become when he was still her husband, and yet deceiving her much as he had deceived me, made it impossible for me to savor her misfortune. I considered that if she had not stolen his affection, he might have married me, and the humiliation in court she had recently endured might well have been my own.

I knew I would never have summoned the courage to leave Pierce Butler. I would have remained in that lovely white cottage believing whatever tales he chose to tell me and waiting for him to marry me, accepting whatever excuses he offered. I would not have met Matthew and had my chance to regain the stage and should never have known the true love of a good man. Our time together had been cut tragically short, yet I had known unselfish love from a man sweetly devoted to my happiness. Understanding precisely what Fanny Kemble had known of love with Pierce Butler, who had been my teacher as well in the devil's own deceits, I realized she had suffered terrible sadness without the antidote of joy.

I wanted to hate her. I wanted to take pleasure in her public defeat. But I could not. It surprised me that I did not savor her unhappiness like the sauce to the most savory roast. But I could not.

33

The Hand of Fate

Whenever anyone speaks of the hand of fate, I always imagine a giant hand holding a long wooden spoon such as the slaves employed to stir the huge caldron of corn grits on Butler Island. During my sojourn at that sad place, I was surprised to overhear, on a few occasions, older slaves cautioning their children not to "tempt the hand of Fate or something worse be stirred into the meal." Watching as they suffered daily hardships and cruelties, I marveled they could believe that a hand, even a partly beneficent one, protected them.

I mentioned my puzzlement on this subject once to Jack as we walked about the island, and he had asked my permission to speak freely before he gave his answer. Friendly as was the tone of our daily discourse, I saw he still feared offending me. When I convinced him I truly wished him to speak his mind, he stopped beside a place in the path where we were shaded from sight by a heavy growth of palmettos with their sharp, spiky leaves.

He told me the old *people* were wise to warn the young folks, and even though he was young himself, he had heard talk of dreadful times on plantations where all the food was cooked centrally at a great outdoor fire in a caldron tended by several of the women deemed too old for field work. Daily or once each week, depending on the custom of the particular place, all the women would come forward with great wooden buckets into which their family's share of this porridge, the mainstay of their diet, would be poured. If an overseer should be angered by runaways or dissent among the *people,* he could stir into the porridge in this common caldron an evil concoction. It was not a fatal poison, but it was sufficiently powerful to bring a plague of stomach ailments to every family on the plantation. Until the behavior that had angered the overseer was corrected, all the slaves were forced to eat that tainted food or risk starvation if they abstained. Jack could not remember an instance when this punishment had occurred on the Butler plantations, but some of the older men and women had experienced this suffering in their youth on other plantations and could not easily forget it.

Bright as Jack was, I believed he might not comprehend metaphor and explained such admonitions to the young might not always be literally intended. Perhaps the elders had wished to impress on the younger *people* that even a bad situation might be made worse. Could it not be, I asked, that in the case of a reasonable overseer, the older *people* hoped to prevent the young folks from provoking him and bringing about worse treatment or assuring his replacement by a crueler taskmaster?

Jack acknowledged that this *could* be, though he could not speculate since he had been raised on another saying that derived from that same caldron. If there was a person on the plantation who appeared to be untrustworthy, stealing from others or trying to court favor with the overseer by informing on matters among the *people*, it was said, "If you sup with him, you best use a long-handled spoon."

"Now missus," Jack reasoned that day, "if old Fate not stirring up his trouble with a spoon, then how come there be so much talk about it?"

I had no ready answer for Jack, and to this very day have no clear impression of the form in which Fate may move. If it does not move in the amorphous realm occupied by souls and angels, I have no true answer. Nor do I know what provokes Fate when, time-to-time, I have tried without success to appease him. Though I must say that the hand of Fate stirred very different courses for Mr. Butler and me after our divorce.

At first, Mr. Butler felt victorious and vindicated for every wrong he alleged he had suffered at my hand. He was relieved for all of Philadelphia to see he had committed no offense save that of selecting an inappropriate wife who had bewitched him with her actress's wiles. Yet in his exuberance over his victory in court, Mr. Butler began to speculate even more unwisely. I no longer communicated directly with him but heard from old friends that he had taken to drinking even more heavily and traveled with a crowd known for its extravagance. He hosted large parties with lavish refreshments described to me by Sal, who was much preoccupied with such details. He frequented gambling establishments and card games at the several clubs to which he belonged, and when he traveled, at parties held late at night among the gentlemen after the ladies had retired, gambling for stakes that proved outrageous in the sober, light of day.

During school holidays when I saw my daughters, I inquired about their father for politeness sake. I did not wish them to feel I despised him, and though Mr. Winship had at least secured a provision for their future, I hoped Mr. Butler had not suffered further damage to his holdings, which might irreversibly destroy their inheritance. I had seen my daughters described in an article as the wealthiest young ladies in America, but had reason to suspect from Sal's reference to the sale of horses and a property in Philadelphia and even some rare jewelry that had belonged to his Aunt Frances, that Mr. Butler's financial situation was none too secure.

"I think it strange, Mother," Fan said, looking quite the young lady and hardly recognizable as the child she had been so recently, "that you inquire about Father and he should wish to know so little of you. Would you not agree this is odd?"

"I really cannot say, Fan. Perhaps I am just naturally more curious," I told her, not wanting to make much of it, and reassured at least he did not try to prejudice our daughters against me.

"It has little to do with curiosity," Sal said quickly, repeating words I could tell had been said often in her presence. "Father says Fanny Kemble does not laugh or breathe or stop to admire a painting without someone writing an article about it."

Mr. Butler overstated my popularity, as my every statement and whim were not so frequently discussed as when I had been a young actress, scarcely more than a girl. It was my readings that received frequent notice in the papers. They were in such demand and so widely attended, I could schedule them every evening of the week *and* on Sunday afternoons, if I so desired. Between my travels I rested in Lenox, but scarcely had time to replenish myself before I set off again for another destination. My short pieces and articles were also quickly published, so for the first time since leaving Mr. Butler's home, I felt no worry about my future. I purchased a new horse without concerning myself too terribly about the price and, without feeling frivolous, spent more on clothes than I had spent in five years. Despite what some may claim about the English, I ate well and supplied my company with very good food, much of it raised on my own farm and in my garden.

As the 1850s progressed, my bank account grew so that I could easily send money to my father, treat the girls to excursions, and provide them with horses of their very own at "The Perch." During the same years, Mr. Butler's fortunes declined precipitously. At first, he carefully kept up appearances, announcing he should let Butler Place "for a time," since he preferred to stay in town concentrating on his investments. When he surrendered his memberships in several elite clubs, he informed the girls this was because his business concerns required all of his attention. But then he gradually stopped making any excuses, always paying their school fees late, so that even *I* was asked about it. He suggested the girls spend longer summer vacations with me rather than the month specified in our divorce decree. He indicated his leniency simply reflected his opinion that I had reformed. In fact, I had so admirably comported myself, he was pleased to see I was quite accepted in society.

Yet the truth was sadly apparent to me. He actually welcomed my shouldering the responsibility for our daughters during the summer months because he struggled to meet his daily expenses. Acquaintances told me Mr. Butler's gambling had become even more desperate, and he had acquired a reputation for being one to whom credit should be extended only if there was little expectation of being repaid for a long time. At restaurants where he had always stepped forward to take the check, no matter how elaborate the fare or how numerous his companions, he became suddenly reticent when the bill arrived. His pocketbook remained in his pocket and his eyes were turned elsewhere while another gentleman settled the bill. His wardrobe was not nearly as distinguished as it once had been, nor did he maintain his own carriage in town. He seemed often under the influence of alcohol, but as one of his old *friends* informed me at a reception after one of my readings when this gentleman seemed willing to disparage Mr. Butler amid the gay flutter of my resurrected celebrity, "poor Butler will not be standing anyone champagne much longer. Unless it is the dregs at the bottom of the bottle."

Then the crash of 1857 shook the financial foundation of even America's wealthiest families. I learned from Fan and Sal that their father's fortunes were severely damaged. They appealed to me for spending money and for clothing, which I gladly provided. Yet I was confounded that despite Fan's requests for funds to purchase a new riding habit, dresses, and evening clothes, she always came out with me in old garments. My curiosity did not permit me to refrain from inquiring why she had bothered to ask me for the money if she did not intend to spend it.

"It is only that I have been so busy, Mother," she said haltingly, turning away from me, as if even her own ears registered the false sound of her words. "I intended to make those purchases. I have simply been engaged with other matters."

I was greatly surprised by Fan's delay in selecting new her wardrobe, as she had always longed for finery more than any child I knew. It seemed particularly odd that a young lady who enjoyed, to a degree which displeased me, the opportunity to ride her father's finest horse wearing stylish riding apparel, should ride with me in the very habit she had complained was dreadfully worn. I said nothing, but Fan could see that I was dismayed. An awkward silence came over us like a cloud.

"I *am* sorry, Mother," Fan said apologetically, "for not using your gift as I said I should. But I still have *some* of it," she said hurriedly to reassure me. "I simply had other obligations which needed to be settled."

"You have not fallen into debt, Fan?" I asked in horror. "If that is what has happened, you must tell me at once, and I shall help you settle it." Still recalling my dear father's improvident business decisions to save Covent Garden and the terrible debts that followed, as well as Mr. Butler's financial excesses, I prayed this financial curse had not fallen upon my own daughter.

"It is nothing like that," she reassured me. "I have been careful. And Father has always been very generous to Sal and me."

"Well, then, what is it?" I asked sharply, and then fearing I had responded harshly, I adjusted my tone. "You are an accomplished young lady, soon to be of age, like your sister. You know your own mind and should not be made to feel you must account for every penny of my gift. I must apologize to *you*. I was much too insistent."

"No, Mother, I owe you an explanation. I deceived you when I made my request. I *did* need to replace the clothing we discussed, but it was never my intention to do so. If I had told you the actual reason I required money, I feared you would withhold it, and I could not blame you if you had."

She confessed to me while we rode in my carriage on a fine Sunday afternoon for what should have been a happy time, concluding with an elegant tea. Her words were wrought with so many tears I thought the movement of the carriage disturbed her further and directed the coachman to take us off the boulevard into a stand of trees, that she might compose herself. With my arm around her, we sat silently for a moment while she regained her voice.

Just as a summer thunderstorm suddenly comes down in torrents, Fan opened her heart. Her father's situation was far worse than she and Sal had ever expressed or had come to my attention through gossip. In the past, he possessed such great wealth in reserve he had always the means to cover his debts if the risks he took with his investments or on horse races proved too extreme.

But suddenly that had changed. Her father had never asked her to appeal to me for money. Yet she had observed his dismay when he tried to quickly conceal the bills and creditors' complaints delivered daily to their door, and she knew his circumstances were dire. Lawyers and agents for his creditors waited for him at his brother's home and at any establishment he was known to frequent, since he never responded to their letters and calls. When she saw he had begun to dispose of family silver, paintings, and antiques, pretending he had merely tired of them and intended to acquire more fashionable replacements, she requested money from me for rather frivolous items, which she knew I would grant her, so she might give the money to her father for the essentials of daily life. She had also sold jewelry, and when members of my family made a substantial gift to her in celebration of her eighteenth birthday, she had made this sum over to him "for safekeeping."

I recalled in a new light my conversation with Sal from several weeks before. She had told me her father stayed home more in the evenings. "I think it would please you, Mother, to see that Father is far less extravagant in his habits. I know you worry about Fan's and my fortunes. I am not so much at home myself now, but almost any time I return, he is there himself, sitting with gentlemen in his library and only very rarely going out to parties."

Once she had turned twenty-one and Mr. Butler could no longer prevent her coming to me, I enjoyed more visits with Sal. It had also pleased me that, though he might still lawfully deny Fan's free access to me, he had not recently chosen to do so. We enjoyed longer visits in which we could talk leisurely. I learned the thoughts and fancies that occurred to her, not saddled, as we had previously been, by our awareness that the time allotted for our visits was ticking rapidly away.

Faced with Fan's stricken face as she cried beside me, I understood that Mr. Butler was willing to suffer having Fan see more of me so she might entreat me for money. This was the only reason he allowed me the luxury of more time with her before she reached marjority. He witnessed my increasing success, as it was again reported everywhere, including news of my upcoming tour of England, and he was so consumed by his own disastrous affairs that he could not perceive the shame he brought to his own daughters.

"Fan, you must *never* think I begrudge your being a loving daughter to your father," I assured her. "You were kind to give him all your own pocket money. But I shall not have you want for anything while I have a penny to my name." I pressed into her hand all the money in my pocketbook, save what I required to pay for our tea. "I shall begin paying regular allowances to you and Sal. Please do not trouble yourself to give me an account of how you spend the money," I reassured her, attempting to stroke the worry from her face. "I should prefer that you do not," I added quickly, thinking it would distress me greatly to learn with certainty I was supporting Pierce Butler. "I will not have my girl worrying over money and feeling so terribly sad," I told her, kissing her and wiping her eyes. "I am sure your father will make a financial recovery, as he has done so several times before. He still possesses one of the largest estates in all of America."

In honesty, I must confess I shed bitter tears by my daughter's side as I reflected grimly on Mr. Butler's *possessions*, who resided in Georgia ceaselessly toiling to tend his cotton and his rice. It also surprised me, as much acrimony as had passed between us, that I could still shed a few tears for that man who caused so much suffering to our daughters and to those poor souls he enslaved, maintained in rags.

My engagements required me to return to London. It seemed the cruelest of circumstances that when I finally encountered no more interference from Mr. Butler and could freely spend as much time as I desired with our daughters, I was required to leave them. Even had not the commitments of Fan's schooling interceded, her devotion to her father would have prevented her from leaving him alone in his struggles, nor would Sal have departed America without her sister. So I returned alone to resume the readings that had previously afforded me much solace from my loneliness. I began with *Julius Caesar* in a cycle that included *Romeo and Juliet*, *Richard III*, *The Tempest*, and *King Lear*. I followed my father's arrangements of each play. My tour took me to small theatres and concert halls, churches and town halls, and always, the houses were full. I could not quite believe it, but nevertheless it was so.

One evening, I had just completed *Romeo and Juliet* and was preparing to have a cup of hot tea before taking a carriage back to our house on Russell Square when a woman stepped out of the throng of audience members waiting to speak with me. I was quite accustomed to these attentions by this time, though still made very uncomfortable by them, and wished it were possible after a reading for the audience to vanish quickly as if it had been all a dream. Yet I knew it was my duty to be gracious and grateful to those who came to see me, and so I turned my face encouragingly to her. I expected a passing greeting, but this lady, whom I judged to be slightly younger than I, and though my vanity made me loathe to admit it, fresher looking and possessed of far greater beauty, beseeched me to have a private word.

As there was a small dressing room nearby and nothing frightening or unusual in her appearance, I agreed to speak privately with her. She was far too finely dressed for it to seem she was coming to me, as so many did, to appeal for money. I was frankly curious what she might want and wondered if she might herself be an actress, so dignified and graceful was her bearing. When we were seated in the dressing room, I before the mirror, and she in a small slipper chair to my side, I asked her what she wished to discuss.

For a moment, she said nothing, but stared at me, both at my person and at my reflection, watching with such wonder I did begin to feel alarmed that I had shut myself away with someone who was not right in her own mind. But then she broke her silence, speaking softly in an English voice tempered with tones I recognized in American speech.

"My name is Isabel Graves," she said finally. "I do not expect you to recall my name, if ever you knew it. But I have thought of you every day since I was a girl."

This was such a strange avowal I did not know how I should respond. Could she really have admired me since we were girls? I searched her face, but could not recall any association with her name. Until suddenly it came to me.

"Why, you are quite famous in your own right, Miss Graves," I exclaimed. "And very modest to think I should not recall *your* name. Please forgive my poor memory for faces. I am honored you came to my reading. It must have been boring for an accomplished actress to watch me *read* all the parts."

"No, it was quite wonderful to see one actress assume so many roles," she graciously assured me. "And I am flattered," she said gratefully, as if she truly took pleasure in it, "that you know of my work."

"It was my pleasure to see you as Portia, a role I have always particularly admired, and also as Ophelia," I told her "at a small New York theatre. I cannot recall which one after all these years." I tried to remember details, sensing they were important to her, so fixedly did she watch my face. "Our going to see you was Mr. Butler's suggestion. He said that he had known of you in Philadelphia."

Immediately the words left my mouth, I saw I had disturbed her. I had intended to please her by praising her work, which I have found, when warranted, all performers appreciate, but in doing so, I had instead troubled her. I handed her a lace handkerchief that had been lying on the dressing table, and, taking her hand to stop her trembling, I begged her to explain. "Please tell me what I have done to upset you. I meant only to express my admiration for your accomplishments."

Still, she said nothing but did not allow her eyes to leave my own, even as they began to fill with tears.

"Just now I recalled another time I thought your acting brilliant." She seemed so very sad I wanted to lift her spirits. "I do not recall the name of the play. Like so many, it did not last. It opened *and* closed the same day in Brighton. But still I remember how beautiful you were—and so very believable—even in that awful play." When her crying intensified, I feared somehow I had further injured her. "I am so sorry. I seem once again to have said something that has upset you."

"Truly, you've no cause to apologize," she said wiping away her tears. "You could not know it would be so painful to hear you speak of Brighton and *The Poisoned Table* after so many years. Or that your husband should spea—"

"My *former* husband," I hurried to correct her. I did not wish her to suppose I was still married to Mr. Butler.

"Yes, of course. Excuse me." She again wiped her eyes and took a small sip of the tea I offered her. "You said before he knew *of* me in Philadelphia. Yet actually I was once well acquainted with Pierce Butler," she told me, as if it were a confession. "Before you were married, of course," she assured me.

I understood her meaning at once, as well as how painful it was for her to speak to me. "I am so very sorry," I said, pitying her for a hurt that seemed still fresh.

"I have hated you for so long, I came here this evening hoping that your reading should be wretched and not the splendid performance that it was."

I said nothing, watching her tormented face, baffled at how to receive such a strange compliment.

"It was not just his betrayal, though Mr. Butler was very cruel to me," she went on. "I cannot bear to say how sorely he harmed me."

"Nor can I say that you were the only person he injured," I said, recalling the deceptions and the duels and my pain at the loss of him.

"I am sorry for your unhappiness as well," she said sympathetically. "I do not believe the terrible things he said in the newspapers."

"Thank you. It has been very painful to become a public spectacle, but Mr. Butler no longer has the power to hurt me," I said, relieved this was the case and that no one else held such disdain for me. Until I considered she had admitted harboring hatred for me. I had to ask her, "Is it not possible that your resentment was misplaced? By your own account, it was *he*, not I, who harmed you."

"His injury was only part of it. The worst wrong was when *you* were chosen over me to be Juliet," she said accusingly, and the hatred that had only been mentioned was uncovered in her eyes.

"I do not remember even *meeting* you before," I replied, unable to hide my perplexity and wondering if her mind were addled. "Like you, I have played Juliet many times. Though I do not recall competing with you or appearing in any company with which you were associated."

"You would not remember," she said sadly, the anger retreating from her voice. "It was before your debut at Covent Garden. I had been taken to read for your father. I was the perfect choice to be Juliet. My hair was a mass of pure golden ringlets at that time. I knew the part well and possessed the fresh figure and face. I *was* Juliet. But you were chosen. I was asked to be your understudy because your father was the manager and had selected you when I was far better suited to the role," she said bitterly.

"Life is such a strange master," I said calmly, hoping to soothe her. "I know you shan't believe me, but if I had been given any say in the matter, you surely should have been cast as Juliet. I can see, even now after these many years, you were always far more beautiful than I, and certainly I am more suited to these armchair readings I give."

"No, that is not so," she insisted straight away. "You give them majestically. I had thought to hear a reading of an entire play should be frightfully dull, yet I have never understood Shakespeare's meanings more clearly nor heard his words come so completely alive."

"That is by far the nicest compliment I have received," I told her. "Perhaps it is made even more special knowing that the giver has overcome so much past unhappiness to express it," Then, impulsively, I kissed her cheek, moved by the abiding sorrow in her face.

"I feel no hatred any longer," she said gently, breathing deeply and then seeming visibly to release her enmity with her breath. "All these years I thought you knew and took pleasure in your defeat of me. I see now you knew nothing about it."

"And I pray you do not believe I had complicity in Mr. Butler's cruelties?" I found my own eyes filling with tears as I thought not only of her sorrow, but of my own suffering at his hands.

"None of it matters any longer," she reassured me, reaching into her handbag to find a handkerchief for me. "My anger fades now that I have finally seen you perform. I could never allow myself to do so before."

"Why *did* you come after so many years?" I asked, intense curiosity helping to restore my composure. "To this of all plays, considering our history?"

"I am home for a few weeks, after many years apart from my family. A friend who knew nothing of my past sorrow had procured the ticket for me so that there was no way graciously I might refuse. Now I am glad that I did not. Your reading was a rare performance, and it has helped to speak of the past."

"Is it truly helpful to revive the past?" I asked, since it was often quite painful to me, the bits and pieces of it that came to me in waking moments, and the tangled memories with which it distorted my dreams.

"I believe you misunderstand me," she said with a firm dignity, which had not at first been evident in her manner. "There is absolutely no cure for past wrongs except perhaps in plays where villains receive their due. Yet it has helped me to witness the genius of your reading this evening. I shall no longer feel I was passed over for an inferior rival. Nor will I consider my slight an act of fate. It was as it should have been, on merit."

Then she left me. Though I called after her, eager to ask her to dine with me, she departed quickly, having offered more comfort, I feared, than she had received.

She had not revealed the complete nature of her association with Mr. Butler, yet from my painful familiarity with his many exploits, I was certain he had made her suffer. I felt a stony anger take hold of me and wished I might shout at him for the pain he had brought to me and my children, and to this sorrowful lady who had just left my dressing room, and to all the poor souls whom he had bought and sold.

Mr. Butler did not possess his *people* much longer, but not by way of the emancipation I had hoped for as a young woman, enraged by their suffering and not fully cognizant of the vast wealth they represented. So excessive were Mr. Butler's accumulating debts, literally hundreds of thousands of dollars, he was finally left with only one way to satisfy them. On March 2nd and 3rd of 1859, he sold at the Savannah, Georgia, racetrack all the slaves he owned apart from his brother, four hundred and thirty-six souls, men, women and children. This auction of slaves, the largest to have ever taken place in the South at that time, occasioned much attention in New York and Philadelphia, where Mr. Butler was widely known and his fortune under great scrutiny. In London, where I was about to present a new season of readings, I learned of this tragic sale through correspondence with Elizabeth, who sent me a copy of the New York *Tribune* describing it.

Others might have read the long article with general interest, in the manner in which we all seek out accounts of historic or tragic events. Yet even after the space of many years, my interest was not casual. I read urgently, seeking any detail that might acquaint me with the particular fates of actual beings whom I had known, whose hands had reached out to me for help, and whose hopes now seemed dismal as the day we had parted in a cold rain.

I cannot say how others conceived the vision of over four hundred people being sold away from the plantations where they had likely lived all their lives, never to see again their mothers, fathers, brothers and sisters, and children. Perhaps lacking any memory of their faces, other readers thought it humane and generous that husbands and wives and children of very young age were to be sold as lots that could not to be separated. I could not fathom, if places were reversed, being parted from my dear sister, Adelaide, or my father, or to have my children wrenched away from me, since they would be long past the age of inclusion for sale with their mother.

What the reporter presented as a kindness seemed to me only a convenience perpetrated by those who cared little for the destiny of these people, only for the best return on an investment. Young children, considered of little present financial consequence, could be raised to great worth but might never attain full value grieving for their mothers and lacking their care. Husbands might "kick up a fuss," just as Mr. King had feared would be the case with Joe, who *fussed* about leaving his wife and children, and thus become intractable workers, the worst of all slaves. These, I was certain, were the true reasons behind the decisions to sell some families together.

I sensed the reporter's horror to observe potential masters and overseers rudely examining the women's bodies to determine if they would be likely *breeders* or if their endless labor and return to field work soon after childbirth had left them ruptured too severely to bring forth new slaves. I pictured this writer as someone accustomed to attending sporting events at a racetrack or seeing horses sold in such a place, but never imagining this dreadful auction of actual beings, who begged those who examined them to purchase their loved ones as well.

I had once visited the Savannah racetrack with my husband when he considered acquiring racehorses, at that time enjoying this pursuit so favored by many wealthy gentlemen. I recalled it as a pretty place at the edge of woods several miles out of town on a spring day when the air was fragrant with blooming pink and purple azaleas. It was warm, but not unduly hot, so it was pleasant walking about, the ladies with their pastel-colored parasols and the gentlemen in light suits.

The place was evidently quite changed by the time of the auction of Mr. Butler's slaves. There was, for good reason, none of the celebration and good spirits that normally attend race days, but instead a mood of perseverance to business on the part of the purchasers and unrestrained mourning on the part of those to be sold. The reporter indicated that it had rained for four days without pause so that the track itself and the roads leading to it were deep in mud and navigable only by carriages. For this reason, there were no casual passersby, only those miserably awaiting sale and those who had come to acquire them. Had it not been raining, perhaps some provision might have been made to exercise the slaves outside, under armed guard lest they tried to escape. But as it was, the slaves had been huddled together in pitiful family groups in a room behind the grandstand, scarcely twenty feet wide and a hundred feet long, a place formerly used for the storage of goods and livestock awaiting sale.

Blessed though I am with the gift of imagining, I cannot conceive the horror of over four hundred *people*, eating, sleeping, and attending to all bodily wants in this space, never stepping outside for even a breath of air. I picture them clinging to each other as grandparents and their children and grandchildren, aunts, uncles, and cousins all accept that they shall shortly be sold off in all directions and shall probably never see each other again. They grasp tightly their few goods, bits of clothing and finery, items they have struggled to obtain by completing all manner of extra work.

I read that unlike some sales, where the slaves are stripped of their own property, since as chattel they have no right to the claim of any, these slaves were allowed to keep possession of their own rightful goods. Had such collections been made, I learned, easily more than one thousand dollars more might have been raised for Mr. Butler's creditors.

While huddled in their family groups with these few possessions, the slaves were subject to continuing inspections by prospective purchasers. They could be observed walking along, pushing away the overtures of slaves who did not interest them, and pausing whenever they wished to make their examinations. Mouths were thrust open, just as with horses, so that masters might judge better the age of slaves and determine if any abscess might be evident to the touch or easily discerned by an unpleasing breath.

The reporter noted that the most fortunate slaves in this large assembly might be those adjudged to be lame. Although poorly healed limbs and deformities were not normally construed as anything but an affliction, under these circumstances, if no one sought to purchase a slave unfit for toil, the slave might be allowed to purchase his own freedom. Had he been whole, he would have been unlikely to amass, through even years of labor on his own time, the fifteen hundred or two thousand dollars that would be required. But at such a sale, where there was no desire to transport *useless* slaves back to the plantation, a crippled man or woman might purchase freedom for only four or five hundred dollars. This seemed at least a small benefit of affliction, I thought, until I realized that once free, there would be no place these poor slaves might go to seek their living. Poor as it was, they were accustomed to having their food supplied as well as their rude shelter, and it seemed improbable anyone would hire them. They would have the temporary joy of obtaining their freedom, yet without friends or shelter, they might well have acquired it at the price of their lives.

As I looked down the list of chattel, numbered in family lots for sale, I read rapidly, searching for the names of slaves I had known. I loathed accepting their fate, but neither could I escape it by refusing to read their names. Many were not there, having either perished before this sad date or, belonging to John Butler's holdings, been left to work the plantation. Many of the names were so common, *Mary*s, *Sue*s, *George*s, and *Tom*s, that I could not tell with any certainty if they were the slaves I had known. But there were two names about which I could not delude myself.

I noticed Number 349 first, arrested as I was by his name, *Lowden*. He was described as aged 54, a cotton hand, and was sold in a lot along with Tom, 12, a cotton hand, Judge Will, 55, a rice hand, Hagar, 50, a cotton hand, Silas, 13, a prime cotton boy, Lettia, 11, a prime cotton girl, and a boy by the same name, Lowden, age 13, who also worked in cotton. There was no one, of course, that I might ask, but I feared by his age and a supposed misspelling of his name that this man might indeed be Cooper London. So skilled as he had been in both the making of barrels and the guarding of souls, I wondered how he should have fallen to the life of a field hand in cotton. I wished I knew if he had received the few Bibles I had managed to send to him and brought them with him in his own small bundle as he awaited sale, so that he might minister again when he reached his new plantation, or if in this miserable circumstance he had abandoned his faith. In my grief, I agonized that perhaps these Bibles, *my* gift, had been the instrument of his ruin. Perhaps a spiteful overseer had accused him of teaching others to read and spoiling them for their brutish labor. I prayed it was not he, but another poor soul without his gifts, sent away to labor in some unknown master's cotton fields.

But hope as I might for the salvation of Cooper London, there could be little hope for Number 114, woman Sikey, age 43, sold in a lot with Allen Jeffrey, 46, rice hand and sawyer at the steam mill, along with a boy Watty, age 5, of infirm legs. So poor Psyche, saved twenty years before, had not escaped a second time. I could not know if Joe, valued highly as he had always been, had been left behind on Butler Island or if he had perished from a snake bite or at someone else's whim, been given away as a *gift*, as Mr. Butler had intended once before. Might Allen Jeffrey be her new husband? I wondered if it was a marriage of their own choosing or arranged for the sake of a more appealing sale along with a poor infirm boy, who might or might not be their son.

It was a beastly spectacle of our modern times on the edge of that pretty city, so revered for its lovely architecture and genteel customs. The reporter noted that after the sale was completed, Mr. Butler, who had been present, gave every adult slave a parting gift of one dollar. When he bade them farewell as they left behind every familiar association, he handed them four twenty-five cent pieces. Caring always about appearances, it did not surprise me to learn he had obtained all new coins, fresh from the mint. Passing out those shiny coins, as if their newness increased their value, struck me as the final insult to those who had labored their entire lives for him.

I was certain after studying the article for several hours that Mr. Butler, who had realized over three hundred thousand dollars from the auction, had relaxed entirely the reins of his conscience to split up those slave families, selling them off in all directions. I then resolved to sever every prohibition I had held against publishing the journal of my sojourn on Mr. Butler's plantations. Its time had come.

34

Emancipation

In 1860, Fan traveled alone to see me in London since Sal had recently married Owen Wister, but she presented to me their shared entreaty not to publish my journal. They knew Elizabeth strongly supported my recent decision to publish and had implored me for years to make my diary public. I had shared with them the letter in which she beeched me "for the sake of all who are still in bondage" to proceed without delay.

"You must not do this, Mother," Fan insisted, speaking with great urgency, equal to Elizabeth's own. "I understand you feel you must speak out according to your beliefs and you have always abhorred slavery. But from across the ocean you cannot feel the present mood in America."

"You speak as if I have been away for ten years instead of just a few," I insisted. "Elizabeth has begged me for years to bring out my journal," I reminded her. "I do not know in good conscience that I can still refuse her."

"The plantations are all Father has left. If you publish now you will *destroy* him. What do you and Elizabeth propose for the slaves working the land who belong to Uncle John?" Fan asked angrily. "Slavery is all they have ever known, and the *abolitionists* never propose anything reasonable for the future of those they wish to set free!" Her dark eyes grew very bright as she struggled to control her anger. Then her hands clutched at my sleeve while she implored me with words. "I beg you, Mother, think more of your own daughters and of a man you once loved than of the speeches you wish to make and the readings you might give," she said passionately. I felt accusation as well as entreaty in her words, revealing her father's beliefs when I had once thought she would share my own.

"Sal feels just as you do?" I asked, wondering how two daughters of mine should mature so beautifully in their abilities and their gifts, yet be so unfeeling towards the plight of others. It affected me deeply that Fan should so closely resemble me in temperament but should oppose so vehemently the abolishment of the institution that seemed the greatest evil I could perceive.

"Not entirely," she answered frankly, exhibiting the honesty she had possessed since she learned to speak. "Sal and Owen believe as you do, and, of course, Owen's family is from the North, but Sal *is* afraid for Father, who has been lately so despondent. But you are correct that my views are more similar to Father's own. Slavery shall not be abolished so soon as Elizabeth believes, and the slaves are not yet prepared to live as free men."

"Then what shall prepare them, may I ask? Continued slavery and suffering!" I felt my face grow hot with agitation.

"I beg your pardon, Mother," she said, taking my hand. "I did not wish for us to argue. I *am* twenty-two, you know, and had hoped you would care as much for my opinion in this matter as you do for Sal's. Yet I see you are determined to publish. Fanny Kemble may be wherever she pleases when this journal appears, while *we* shall be in America when it is talked about over tea and supper and in the all the newspapers. Sal and I shall hear animated conversation turn to whispers when we walk into drawing rooms. No one shall care for our opinions since, of course, we are not *Fanny Kemble*," she said mockingly, "merely her daughters by that *evil* slave owner." Then her face turned very white, much as it had when she was a small girl and became so angered by some perceived wrong that she could no longer speak. She coughed and stuttered with rage.

I tried to calm her, offering her water and leading her to the sofa where we might sit down to talk more comfortably, but she would not be quieted, reminding me of an actress determined to passionately declaim her favorite speech, even at a seated rehearsal without makeup or costumes.

"You know Father never intended to be a slaveholder! He only inherited them, Mother," she insisted. "Yet when you speak against slavery, you make it seem men like father created it and that ending it shall be simple as closing a door. But we shall be caught up in whatever occurs. Father talks of managing the plantations without an overseer to save money, though his health will *never* stand the Georgia heat. We shall try to prevent him, though I am sure you believe personal matters and fortunes should not now be of any concern, only the 'cessation of the scourge of slavery' you are always decrying," she said angrily, breaking into tears. "Honestly, Mother, I should not know what to do if you publish that journal!"

And so I put aside Elizabeth's entreaties and promised Fan I would wait. Elizabeth was my dearest friend, and I shared so strongly her convictions, but Fan was my daughter.

Early the next year I returned to America and to "The Perch," where I lived joyfully on my small farm, replenishing myself with the more peaceful art of writing after my exhausting tour schedule. I have felt since childhood a great happiness when surrounded by growing things, whether they be animal or vegetable. Since my farm was worked by free men who were paid fairly for their labor and who lived in neat cottages, I felt easy in their company, unlike the dreadful guilt and shame I had felt around slaves. I told Elizabeth one evening, as we sat upon my porch savoring good English tea, that the best way to increase public support to abolish slavery would be for Southerners to visit the farms of New England, where they would see the efficiency of our operations and the high quality of our produce, achieved *without* slavery by the diligence of workers humanely treated and fairly paid. Those Southerners, if they were truly Christian, should rejoice at the opportunity to escape the horrible system in which they were embroiled, by paying wages, which would reduce only modestly the profits they enjoyed.

Fan ridiculed my position when I wrote to her in Philadelphia describing this discussion with Elizabeth. I had not literally expected such an experiment to be enacted, naturally not imagining Southerners should willingly admit the cruelties of slavery and offer to remunerate their slaves, nor believing that my small farm should reasonably be compared to the operation of a vast plantation. But then she responded immediately with a letter so vehement in her disagreement that I could imagine her standing angrily before me. She insisted I deliberately sought to overlook the planter's dilemma by equating the raising of my small acres of wheat and a kitchen garden with the management of a plantation producing thousands of pounds of rice and cotton. No planter could afford to maintain hundreds of slaves in the conditions of a free farm, and I was disingenuous to even suggest it.

I wished she might visit me so we could sit and talk over our positions with Elizabeth and other members of her Society. I felt certain their eloquence would convince Fan, where my mere mother's arguments had failed, of the rightness of any sacrifices necessary to end slavery's evil dominion. Fan sent answer by return post that she would instead soon be traveling to Georgia with her father. His interests on the plantations urgently required his care, and she would accompany him to look after his welfare, so troubled was he now by his rheumatism and a lung ailment that she hoped the warmer weather might improve. She wrote that I ascribed the very worst motives to her father's actions, but hoped in this instance even I should admit that he was behaving admirably. Despite his poor health and the great unrest throughout the country, he was hazarding this grueling and dangerous journey in order to see to the needs of the *people*. As his fellow planters studied their future, he wished to join in their discussion. He could have pled ill health and rested in comfort in Philadelphia, but he would not shirk his responsibilities to his *people* or to his Georgia and South Carolina friends and neighbors.

I begged her to reconsider the mounting dangers and not to accompany him. If he chose to make such a journey it was unquestionably his choice to make, but a young lady should not be traveling into a region where there was daily news of increasing turmoil. I beseeched her to stay home and even implored Sal to exert an older sister's influence so Fan might change her mind.

But Fan traveled to Georgia and later returned safely to Philadelphia with her father. I believe there was considerable mockery at my expense since I, who never in my youth agreed to follow anyone's caution, had admonished my own daughter for adhering to the actions prompted by her own conscience.

I arrived in Baltimore more than thirty-five years after I set out for that city following my abandonment by Pierce Butler. I had been helpless, completely dependent on Thomas Meacham's kindness on that earlier journey. This time I traveled by carriage, a well-appointed private carriage I could easily afford, bound for the Harbor Theatre, where I had a six-month engagement appearing in a changing repertory of contemporary comedies and Shakespeare's plays. Mine was the most prominent name in our billing save for a young tragedian I had never met but whose handsome likeness had appeared on the advertisements that were sent to me with the materials to engage me. He was by far my junior, truly a mere boy, and it made me feel quite aged that often I should be cast in several of the productions as his mother. No woman, even one totally lacking in vanity, would wish to appear beside a young man in the first bloom of his attractiveness while a younger actress is cast as the object of his romantic interest.

I was handsomely paid and provided with my own maid at the theatre and a spacious, sunny apartment in a row house just a short, pleasant walk away. I had been consulted in the selection of the season's offerings, a consideration I had only previously been afforded by Matthew, and felt I had attained a new height in my popularity. The only aspect of the arrangements that disturbed me was that I shared equal billing with this dashing young man. I had retained my youthful figure and my golden hair and so seemed easily ten years younger than my age, particularly upon the stage, yet still to appear night after night with a young man over whom women regularly made fools of themselves made me uneasy. I feared I should soon be spoken of as an "older actress" by detracting critics and as a "great lady of the stage" by their kinder counterparts. It seemed dreadfully unfair I had not been paired with a romantic lead but was instead forced to play roles suited to an older actress while having to observe this remarkably handsome young man cast opposite someone who would not have compared to me in my prime. I nervously awaited our introduction at our first rehearsal and carefully planned how I should attire myself and wear my hair to appear my most youthful. I determined I should not be caught ill-prepared and forced to meet him when I looked weary and worn.

But one evening before we had been officially introduced, the maid brought a gentleman's card to me in the parlor where I was reading. Taking it from the silver tray, I nearly dropped it, surprised as I was to find *John Wilkes Booth* calling upon me. Every time he performed, ladies sent flowers to his dressing room containing hidden notes begging for a meeting, and young girls offered to sacrifice their virtue to him. I was surprised he should seek out my company before our first rehearsal, popular favorite that he was. He came from an established acting family like the Kembles, and though considerable gossip about a common-law marriage in England had attended his father Junius's arrival in America, the Booths had achieved the stature of theatrical royalty in America. John's older brother, Edwin, was a celebrated tragedian, yet the family's greatest hopes seemed to be placed in this younger brother. Many had declared him the handsomest man they had ever seen, with a voice and stage presence never observed before in one so young.

I would have taken more time with my hair and dress if I had been forewarned the young actor who had bewitched America would be standing at my door. As it was, there was nothing for it but to invite him in. If I sent him away, I should seem unfriendly and self-important and would have to meet him anyway the following week upon the stage.

Despite his reputation, nothing prepared me for the full effect of seeing John Wilkes Booth in person. In the theatre, one expected to be charmed by the appearance of actors upon the stage in all their makeup and finery. It was sometimes disappointing to find, meeting them on the street, that a nose that had seemed noble was overly large or someone's wavy chestnut hair was a wig and another's complexion mottled in the light of day. But Booth appeared anything other than ordinary as he strode self-assuredly into my parlor. I am certain the maid had asked to take his cloak. When he unfurled this black silk garment so that its red lining flashed, I realized he had not surrendered it in order to display himself to greatest advantage before me. He was elegantly attired in a black suit that smartly accented his absolutely black eyes, more luminous than any I have seen before or since in a man or a woman, and his thick, wavy black hair curled over the velvet collar of his coat. His thick mustache made a startling contrast against his face, as his complexion was the palest ivory. I have known men of much taller stature, yet have never encountered anyone with a more finely developed physique. Although he was an actor, one might have looked at his broad shoulders and his powerful arms and supposed him to be a laborer. At the same time, there was about him an animal grace usually found only in dancers. I had no desire to buoy his vanity with my admiration, yet it was very difficult not to stare at him.

"Good evening, Miss Graves," he said, bending gallantly to take my hand and kiss it, while holding in his other his kid gloves. "It is good of you to see me without a formal appointment," he continued cordially, his cultured Southern heritage apparent in his accent as well as his manners. "I am honored to meet you."

"As it turns out, I was not engaged this evening. Except with my reading, which can certainly be postponed. So I am delighted to see you. We will soon be spending so much time together that it is well we should become acquainted. May I offer you some refreshment, Mr. Booth? Some coffee or a cordial?"

"You must call me, John," he said smiling widely, revealing his perfect white teeth. "We are colleagues after all. And thank you, but I desire nothing save your company."

"Very well, but then you must call me Isabel."

"But I could not possibly do so," he said solemnly. "It would not be proper. It should seem disrespectful in view of—" He stopped awkwardly, suddenly perceiving the indelicacy of his words.

"In view of the difference in our ages," I responded, finishing his thought. "You need not be embarrassed, John. I assure you, I do not try to conceal my age. It shall be no surprise to anyone that I am old enough to be your mother. But we are actors who shall share the same stage for many performances, so do not let this disturb you."

"It is preposterous to think of you as anyone's mother," he protested, falling to his knees in front of me, his face paler still as he conveyed the foolishness of such an idea.

"Please, get up," I scolded him. "We are in my parlor, *not* on a stage. Surely, this is no place for such theatrics."

He rose, looking quite hurt, as if I had seriously chastised him, and took his place on the settee beside me, a little closer than I should have preferred.

"I meant no insult, dear lady. I am merely overcome to play regularly beside you, who have been Juliet, Portia, and Ophelia, beloved by audiences on two continents. And Louisa Tarleton, mistress of an entire plantation."

"You saw *The Poisoned Table*?" I asked in shock, before considering the impossibility for him to have seen this play, performed only once, likely before he was born. At that moment, he was still a glorious boy.

"I did *not* see it. As a Southerner, I should never have attended such a misguided play, distorting as it did our way of life, a fine system beneficial to both master and slave. But I learned of it from a collector's perspective. Just recently I was in London and had opportunity to purchase a collection of programs and playbills. One of the offerings, I am certain due to your reputation and your great beauty, was the playbill and the advertisement for *The Poisoned Table*. Though it was impetuous to come hurrying over here this evening without invitation, I was hoping," he said sweetly, turning the full force of his coal black eyes and long lashes upon me, "you might consent to sign them, increasing their value to the world, but most particularly to *me*, ten thousand fold."

I intended at first to refuse him, so terrible as it was to think again about this play, which had destroyed Matthew. Lovely as the drawings were, exhibiting me in the exquisite gown Matthew had insisted should be designed for me, I shuddered remembering the play's reception and wished to decline his request. Until I considered how odd it should seem to Booth that I refuse such an innocent request by the man I should appear with daily for months to come. I took up my writing pen and dipped it in the peacock blue ink that I favored at that time.

"Come them closer to the light," I told him. "I shall be glad to oblige you. I fear you shall not find my signature very distinguished, but you are welcome to it."

Then something very odd occurred. I believed he was looking over my shoulder so as to more closely examine my signature. And without any warning, he leaned over and I felt the tickle of his mustache as he kissed my neck. Before I could think what to say or do, he had kissed me again, and despite my disapproval of his actions, I felt an excitement that I had not felt in many years.

Quickly recovering myself, I pulled away from his embrace. "Sir, you forget yourself," I insisted, expressing more outrage than I genuinely felt.

"No, dear lady, I do not forget myself at all," he whispered, moving closer to me. "It is true I have no right to kiss even the hem of your dress, but whether or not I have the right, I must tell you I adore you." He tightened his grasp on my hand and then tenderly kissed it again. "You may reject me, as a lady clearly has right to do, but I believe just now, before your reason ruled your emotions, you were *glad* I kissed you. I do not believe you truly wish me to leave you."

"Then you are mistaken. And now you must go," I insisted, though it was with the greatest difficulty I forced myself to stand up and move away from him.

"I cannot refuse a lady's bidding," he answered gallantly, never taking his eyes from my own. "If you are certain that you wish me to go."

I insisted that he leave, although I longed to feel his kisses and be able to return them. Yet I knew, in truth, he could be my son, and I would feel ashamed even to play a love scene with him upon the stage, much less in my parlor.

"You must go, John," I insisted. "It is late. It shames me to ask this question, one which no lady should ever ask a gentleman, but why should a young man like yourself, desired by young ladies across America, be so enamored of someone my age?"

"My dear lady, you do yourself a dreadful injustice in posing such a question," he answered without apprehension or nervousness. "You are far lovelier than you imagine. And please consider that while many ladies make their admiration known to me, it does not mean I return it. I cannot predict who shall win my heart. Yet I always know when it has occurred," he said, carressing me with his magnificent eyes.

"It is best for both of us if you go now," I told him, fearing if I did not insist immediately I might succumb to his charm. I could not deceive myself sufficiently to believe he found me so captivating. I did not know if he simply sought another conquest, and in my life had learned through painful experience that supposed *gentlemen* practiced such deceit.

"If you permit me to stay I should make you very happy. But since it is your wish, I shall leave," he said, surrendering my hand. "Though I promise you, dear lady, it shall not be best for me."

"Thank you for calling," I said, rising and walking him to the door, attempting to bid him farewell as if it had been the most ordinary social call. "I shall see you Monday at rehearsal." I prepared to close the door.

"One day I shall achieve true greatness," he declared proudly, still intent on convincing me he should remain. "When this occurs, everyone shall have heard of John Wilkes Booth. Will you not be sorry then that you turned me away?"

At first I was tempted to slap his face, so insulting was his caution that I should rue the day I passed up the *honor* of giving myself to him as so many others had done. But having suffered painfully far more insulting and harmful advances, I was not truly angry with this impetuous boy. I had no fear of him or anything he might do to me. If he had tried to overpower me, I should have called to the servants, and only felt sorry for him, rebuffed peacock that he was.

"I believe you have *already* achieved greatness," I complimented him. "Any week of the year, can you not be engaged to play a different one of Shakespeare's heroes each night? For any performance when you appear, every ticket in the house is sold. You have achieved fame, which many older actors shall never know. Though you come from a famous family of actors, you are more renowned now than your father or even Edwin."

"But I seek something much more important than theatrical greatness. I cannot say now what I shall accomplish. But when I am called to action, I shall change the course of history."

"Is it then politics?" I asked. "Do you intend to hold public office? Might you run for president?" I inquired, thinking he should be the most magnetic of candidates, although severely hampered since women could not vote. And men might detest him if they observed how their ladies looked at him.

"I do not know yet what I shall do, but it will not be elective office. I shall still appear on the stage so long as audiences come to see me. But, I must also fight for the South and our way of life, which no one shall take away." With these last words, his remarkable eyes grew distant, as all their warmth seemed to depart, subdued by his determination.

"Then I shall watch with interest to see what course you take," I said, ascending my front steps. "Good-night, John. Until next week at the theatre."

"Good-night, Isabel. I shall treasure your signature. Lest you think I am a boastful fool whenever it may turn out that I truly achieve my greatness, you shall not need to search to discern it. When the time comes," he said proudly, "my accomplishments shall be widely known throughout the country. I shall play a role far greater than any in which I might be cast upon the stage."

The tensions in the South I had warned Fan about grew worse, and the muffled voices calling for secession turned into loud cries that could not be silenced. On April 10, 1861, Brigadier General Beauregard, commanding a provisional Southern force at Charleston, South Carolina, surrounded the harbor and demanded the surrender of the Union garrison at Fort Sumter. On April 12th, Beauregard's Confederate batteries opened fire on the fort, and by April 13th, Major Anderson, the Union officer in command, surrendered the fort. The unrest I had feared would threaten Fan's safety had erupted into a war that threatened the future of the United States. I had always abhorred violence, whether it were directed against one person or waged by one army against another, but if the Union emerged victorious, I saw there could finally be an end to slavery.

Distressing duty that it was, I helped to hand out weapons and equipment to the new recruits in my own town square, many of whom were young men hardly past boyhood. My friends and neighbors donated food and provisions to accompany the new soldiers off to battle against the Confederacy. Standing on my authority as an older woman, whose authority they had become accustomed to recognize as workers on my farm, I sent a few disappointed boys home. They dreamed of glorious battle bedecked in new uniforms with brass buttons, and in the way of boys, could not fathom a conflict where the stricken would not rise up to fight again, and where the valleys would lie drenched in blood and covered with the bodies of the wounded and the dead. I told them to go home to care for their mothers and sisters and tend their fathers' farms so that there would be something to come back to, and to apply again when they had begun to shave and could fill out a man's jacket. I hoped even as I said these words, *gently* as I could and still be heard, that by the time they returned, the war should be over. The Union would be victorious, and the slaves would be free. The

Confederate Army could not survive long, I hoped, despite the fervor of the Southerners and their determination to prevail in what they deemed a war of honor, much in the way that as individuals they, just like Mr. Butler, favored duels.

(August 20, 1861: *Richmond Herald-Dispatch*)
"Leading Citizen Falsely Arrested"
by Samuel Davis Stephens

Yesterday morning in an unprecedented attack on decency, Pierce Butler, Esq., a prominent and wealthy Philadelphian, who has resided long and peacefully in that city, was arrested at his residence on Walnut Street by marshals acting on order of the President of the United States. Mr. Butler, who was unarmed, was immediately shackled and chained as if he were a common criminal rather than one of the most notable men of this country.

Mr. Butler's landlady, whose name shall not be mentioned here to prevent further harassment by authorities of the United States, indicated that though he was indeed crestfallen to be subjected to such an outrage, "he still comported himself as a gentleman, as always is his custom."

Although there was no reason to suspect him of any unlawful action, Mr. Butler was subjected to an intrusive search of his person and his chamber and personal furnishings, office, and all his trunks, which had been prepared for a railway journey. These were overhauled and extensively searched by the marshals. Nothing of an injurious or improper nature was found in Mr. Butler's personal effects. He was, however, by order of the president, forced to vacate his residence and was taken to New York Harbor, where he will be confined in durance vile at Fort Lafayette.

All men of good character must protest such treatment of an upstanding citizen, the grandson of a Revolutionary War hero, and a noted civic leader in his own right. To seize a man like Mr. Butler in such a violent manner bespeaks the treachery of the government and must be attributed to the fact that Mr. Butler owns cotton and rice plantations in the South. Though born in Philadelphia, Mr. Butler has always supported the right of the states to determine the matter of slavery and is no doubt being persecuted due to his unswerving loyalty to the region where his grandfather, Major Pierce Butler, settled after his marriage to the former Polly Middleton of South Carolina.

Such was Mr. Butler's calm and brave demeanor, that even after such an unwarranted search and affront to his dignity, he delivered himself up without protest to those who had been charged to arrest him. His landlady, terribly distressed by his harsh usage by the marshals, asked in concern, "Mr. Butler, when shall you return?"

He answered calmly, "Do not despair, madam. I shall return as soon as the war is over. And that cannot possibly be very long."

Due to the successes already achieved by the Confederate forces, it seems likely that Mr. Butler's prediction shall soon be realized by a commanding victory over an unjust and oppressive government. As he was taken away from his residence in chains, Mr. Butler's only concern was for the safety of his beloved daughters. He is a devoted father to Sarah, married to Dr. Owen Wister of Philadelphia, and to Frances, who assists him in the management of his estate. He has been sole guardian to both daughters since his divorce from the British actress Fanny Kemble, whom he sued for desertion when she abandoned him and his young daughters to pursue her theatrical engagements. Mr. Butler's family had opposed the marriage, but in his kind-hearted and trusting manner, he would not be dissuaded.

(August 20, 1861, New York *Star-Ledger*)
Pierce Butler Arrested in Philadelphia
By
Mortimer A. Kilpatrick

Yesterday morning a dispatch was received from Secretary of War Cameron authorizing the arrest of Mr. Pierce Butler, one of the country's leading citizens and until financial reverses in 1857, considered one of the wealthiest men in America. Butler was captured by United States marshals at a boarding house on Broad Street where he makes his residence. The arrest order was issued based on notification by sources, which remain anonymous at this time, of activities undertaken by Mr. Butler in which he has allegedly conspired to aid Confederate forces, and "during a period of public excitement has carried out actions unfavorable to the government of the United States of America."

After Mr. Butler was placed in the hands of deputies, the chief marshal thoroughly searched the premises, both Mr. Butler's personal chambers and his offices, as well as trunks that had been readied for a forthcoming journey. Incriminating findings included large sums of money, correspondence to the Confederate authorities, a supply of pistols and ammunition, and secession cockades. These rosettes, most often affixed to hats and coats, have been used by the rebel forces to demonstrate their defiance of the United States government. It has been widely published that those displaying these inflammatory rosettes shall be arrested under suspicion of traitorous acts towards the United States.

Mr. Butler's aforementioned illegal property has been confiscated, and he has been taken to Fort Lafayette in New York Harbor, where he will be held. An authority knowledgeable about the case reports that Mr. Butler, owner of a large estate consisting of two Georgia plantations in rice and cotton, was in the South just prior to the attack upon Fort Sumter. He had only recently returned to Philadelphia after time spent at Butler Island and St. Simon's Island, Georgia, and in Charleston, South Carolina.

Fan and Sal were horrified that their father had been arrested and imprisoned, both for his sake and their own, as with all the notoriety the case had received, they were likely to be perceived by some as the daughters of a traitor. Even Fan, who sympathized strongly with the Confederacy, worried that while she had been traveling with her father, so concerned for his health, he had placed her in grave danger. She might easily have been arrested as his accomplice.

We learned he was imprisoned in a section of Fort Lafayette reserved for political prisoners. He had been so inflamed with passion regarding slavery and states' rights, I could not know what extreme actions he might have undertaken to defend his interests and to injure the cause of the Union. I would not, even for the sake of past affection, have tried to assist him had it not been for the anguish of our daughters.

Accompanied by Sal and Owen, keeping Fan away from a matter in which her own sympathies might be suspect, I went to Washington to call on several friends with access to Mr. Lincoln's ear to learn what might be done for Mr. Butler. It was arranged through their kind intervention for Sal and Owen to speak to Mr. Benson, an assistant to Secretary of War Samuel Seward. So heartfelt were Sal's words on her father's behalf, even though she expressed her disapproval for his misplaced loyalties, that it was arranged for her to personally submit a petition to President Lincoln. Sal implored me to accompany her, thinking that my known sympathy for the Union cause would assist her. I had offered a series of readings to raise funds for medical supplies for the soldiers, which had attracted large audiences. I made as well appearances before the troops, who seemed to enjoy my readings and my remarks, even if I were no longer young.

But I declined, feeling that Sal and Owen had done well without me and that this was not a matter in which I wished to be associated. If their efforts failed and my involvement become known, and Mr. Butler were forced to remain in prison for the war's duration, he would surely blame me.

President Lincoln, with beneficence truly undeserved by Mr. Butler, offered to free him if he agreed to sign a document promising to immediately and permanently desist from any activity or associations to harm or lead to the overthrow of the United States of America, and despite his ownership of property, not to travel to the Southern states without a passport permitting his travel. Under special order of the President, Sal visited her father at Fort Lafayette to present the document that would free him if he but agreed to sign it.

She reported that she found him angry and irritated as a caged tiger, continually pacing the confines of his cell. She was allowed to provide him with food and necessities for his comfort, and when she felt his mood was somewhat improved, had presented the letter for his signature. "If it is signed and witnessed now, Father," Sal told him, "you may depart with me at once. Owen is waiting in the carriage to drive you to Philadelphia. You shall be home in time to have supper and sleep in your own bed."

But he would not consider signing the document. He knocked it to the floor and ground his heel upon it.

"Yet he did not destroy it, did he?" I asked, smiling at my insight into this man who had for so many years controlled my life and that of those I loved most. "He did not burn it with his cigar nor tear it to bits?"

"No, he did not destroy it," she admitted, sighing. "But he absolutely refused to sign it and carried on most outrageously about the friends who shall rise up to arrange his escape. I fear he will spend the entire war in that cell, since if he will not accept this opportunity, I do not believe there shall be another."

"Do not worry, Sal," I said, soothingly as I could. "That he has kept the letter tells me that he will sign it. In his own time."

I was correct. Five weeks of prison food and confinement in a damp cell changed Mr. Butler's mind. He called for an officer to witness his signature and pledged to abstain from providing any further assistance to the Confederacy. Proud as he was, I am certain it injured him mightily to be required to ask permission to visit his own plantations, but he accepted all the terms of the agreement and went home, where Fan lavished attention upon him, making him soothing broths and custards to help him regain his strength.

His actions, foiled before they could achieve any meaningful threat to the Union, still encouraged me to take my own stand. Mr. Butler had had *his* say to support the slaveholders, and I was determined to have my own for the cause of freedom.

Journal of a Residence on a Georgian Plantation 1838–1839 finally appeared in 1863, first in London in May, and then released by Harper & Bros. in July in the United States. By then, I had resided in England for over a year and had been prompted to action not solely by Mr. Butler's treachery, but also by the blindness of the English newspapers and my *own* esteemed friends, who seemed prepared to recognize the ascendancy of the Confederacy. I had been greatly alarmed to hear speeches by British government officials, as well as conversations in drawing rooms where friends and acquaintances expressed support for the Southerners and the new nation they had formed. It appeared so long as their cotton continued to arrive in England, there would be no opposition to the cause of the Confederacy. The Southerners were perceived as chivalrous gentlemen, and some Englishmen even believed that the workers in Northern factories lived much harsher lives than the slaves of the South, whom they believed had every need attended to by their benevolent masters.

A few months after its publication, I heard my journal credited with influencing English opinion to oppose the Confederacy to a degree that even my considerable vanity would make it difficult for me to believe. I have reflected much upon this matter, as in later life one has more and more time to mull over the past, and I believe the Confederacy's grave defeats at Gettysburg and Vicksburg had already shown that the dreadful war could not be won by the Southern states.

It is absolutely true that even after President Lincoln issued the Emancipation Proclamation in early 1863, the battle against slavery was not won. The Proclamation stated that "all persons held as slaves within any State or designated part of a State, the people whereof shall then be in rebellion against the United States, shall be then, thenceforward, and forever free; and the Executive Government of the United States, including the military and naval authority thereof, will recognize and maintain the freedom of such persons, and will do no act or acts to repress such persons, or any of them, in any efforts they may make for their actual freedom..." Despite the powerful language of its pronouncements, the Proclamation could only be enforced in areas under the control of the Union forces. The terrible war and the bloodshed continued, and many slaves were still living in conditions of slavery unchanged by words issued in Washington.

I came to see that my journal, as well as the writings of others, helped convince individuals in America and Europe, who believed in humane slavery, that it was an evil myth. In England, where slavery had been long abolished, the journal was read not only by people notable for their titles and positions, but also by everyday working people in meetings and town halls. These were the same people who cheered in the streets when copies of the Proclamation were circulated. As more people read my description of what had cruelly transpired on Georgia plantations before my very eyes, they knew that the Proclamation, finally decreed, must be enforced.

As a writer, I had anticipated my journal would be criticized and some readers might complain of my lack of delicacy in describing the horrors of plantation life, but I had not expected to be accused of manufacturing the entire record or altering it to advance my political beliefs and to injure Mr. Butler. Some also sought to vilify me for delaying publication for so many years out of deference first to my husband and later to my children, and yet others unfairly insisted I cared nothing for the cause of abolition but finally published my journal purely for financial gain. About that they were again sadly mistaken.

I was grateful to the friends who stood by me, particularly those of long personal attachment such as Elizabeth Sedgwick, to whom it was dedicated. She and members of her Society of Abolitionists refuted allegations that my journal was only a recent invention by circulating portions of the journal that had been shared with them many years before its publication and which were identical, save for a few corrections, to the published text. I was also touched when Lady Grey vouched for the authenticity of the work by writing to the London newspapers and telling all whom she met in daily society that she had heard the same accounts when I had read them aloud at the home of her grandmother, Lady Dacre, years before when she was but a girl.

As a young girl, I sometimes sat up with my dear father, sipping tea from his cup through long, harrowing nights as we waited for first light when newspapers reached the streets and we should know the verdicts of reviewers. So many years later, I will admit to feeling hurt by attacks made against my journal as well as my personal integrity by publications and writers I had always respected. Yet when the review in the August 1863 edition of the *Atlantic Monthly* appeared, I felt happily that every purpose I had ever envisioned for writing and publishing my journal had been justified. Though I should like to quote it in its entirety, I restrict myself to but a few passages in deference to those who accuse me of excess. The reviewer wrote:

Now, at last, we have no general statement, no single, sickening incident, but the diary of the mistress of plantations of seven hundred slaves, living under the most favorable circumstances, upon the islands at the mouth of the Altamaha River, in Georgia. It is a journal, kept from day to day, of the actual ordinary life of the plantation, where the slaves belonged to educated, intelligent, and what are called the most respectable people.... It is the record of ghastly undeceiving...of the details of a system so wantonly, brutally, and damnably unjust, inhuman, and degrading that it blights the country, paralyzes civilization, and vitiates human nature itself.... This is not a book that a woman such as Mrs. Kemble publishes without a solemn sense of responsibility. A sadder book the human hand never wrote, nor one more likely to arrest the thoughts of all those in the world who watch our war and are yet not steeled to persuasion and conviction.... It is a noble service, nobly done.

I shall confess I read this entire review, though not at least aloud, many times. It helped in small measure to ameliorate the pain I suffered at Fan's disapproval. We are now reconciled, and I have spent long and happy evenings in her company at Butler Place and at her home in England with her dear husband, Rev. James Leigh, but I fear my determination to make public what she felt was "inviolately private" caused a great rift between us for a long time.

And speaking of the passage of time, there is nothing else with such power to heal us. Now that I no longer read plays aloud to audiences, I still read Shakespeare to myself and sometimes travel further back to seek what inspired him in the writings of the ancients. As he wisely told us, "There is nothing new under the sun." And long before he wrote Troilus and Cressida, or considered the balm of time, Geoffrey Chaucer wrote in *Troilus and Criseyde* that "as tyme hem hurt, a tyme doth hem cure."

And so it has been with Fan and me. Once we had time enough to know each other in a setting unspoiled by slavery or even its arguments, our hurts did heal.

Even those who claim I wrote my journal to slander Pierce Butler cannot know how little enmity I bore him once I learned what a moral pauper he had become, chiefly by the curse of slavery, which he had wielded over others and which in the end destroyed him. I took no pleasure knowing that in the last years of his life, stripped of his fortune, with naught left but his deteriorating plantations, he became a pitiful man. Fan returned with him to Butler Island after the end of the war to try and reclaim his property. They were determined to gather together those of his former slaves who wanted to return, and by paying them small actual *wages*, to operate his rice plantation as it had been once before. He planned to live there year-round, superintending all his own affairs, and living in the overseer's house we had once shared and which had not been improved by another quarter century. Fan, always loyal to him, stayed with him until the summer heat and the pestilential mosquitoes were insufferable, and then, with regret, she left him there. Fan begged him to accompany her and to stay the summer with her and James in Philadelphia, but he refused to leave Butler Island.

He died of malarial fever in August of 1867 before his former slaves could obtain a doctor from Darien. I suspect he died alone in that small, dilapidated house, he who had possessed vast properties and had once commanded hundreds of thousands of dollars. I suppose his dying words were heard by none save those he had formerly enslaved. There was no longer a Cooper London to offer a prayer for Mr. Butler. I wondered if any of the freed men who had been part of Cooper London's congregation might still have been present, and if they had *knelt* in prayer for Mr. Butler, though he had refused to kneel for Shadrach in the days when Mr. Butler was truly the absolute master of that sad universe.

35

Last Acts

"Isabel, have you heard the news?" Dolly St. Claire asked excitedly, as I joined her on the terrace overlooking her charming garden on a quiet London morning. I was staying with her for two months since we had become good friends when she visited New York City. She had admired my acting and come to my dressing room to present her compliments. Then, after a few late suppers and a small reception where she introduced me to her New York friends, she had invited me to visit her in London, and the time had finally presented itself.

"About what, Dolly?" I studied her face carefully, wondering what exciting tale made her eyes so unusually bright.

"Fanny Kemble is giving up her readings. There is never a spare ticket to any of them—even the tired old histories I could not enjoy with a stage filled with actors—but nevertheless she is bringing them to an end."

"I wonder why?" I asked in surprise. "She gave a remarkable performance when I saw her on my last visit. She read for over two hours without a single pause, and hardly looked at the pages, as if she had memorized the entire play. I do not know how she manages to do it night after night."

"Well, then, perhaps that is why she is retiring. The poor old thing, Kemble stock or not, is worn out."

"You are calling *Fanny Kemble* a 'poor old thing'?" I asked playfully. "What must you say at my expense? I am, after all, only four years younger than she."

"Now, Isabel, I have nothing but praise for you *or* Fanny Kemble for that matter. I mean no disrespect to her in saying you seem more youthful. It is simply a matter of fact. Just as no one can dispute her readings are exceptional."

"I do not understand how one actress brought so many characters to life, even the famous male roles. No one else could carry it off."

"Evidently Fanny herself believes *you* could manage it. Which is why she has asked you to her retirement party."

"I've received no invitation," I told her, surprised by such a claim. "You must be mistaken."

"She did not send it through the post. I dined with her the other day, and when she heard you are staying with me, she asked me to invite you." She whispered confidentially as she leaned forward to pour me more tea. "I am telling you so you won't be caught unawares. She wants *you* to take over her readings. She is confident you could continue them better than any other actress."

"But I have no desire to take this over. I am *not* an imitation Fanny Kemble," I said sharply, unable to conceal my dismay, recalling that time more than fifty years before when I had been asked to be her understudy. I had declined at that time, and the intervening years had not made me feel any better about the prospect.

"Well, then you tell Fanny. These readings were her father's legacy that she has carried on, and now she wishes to entrust them to you."

So many prominent people attended "Fanny's Farewell," as it was called, that I prayed I might be lost in the throng and it would be impossible for her to make her request. I would be safely installed in America, secure in my own pursuits, before she recalled that we had not discussed this matter. I knew it would annoy Dolly, who had promised I would stay for the farewell dinner following the reception, yet I planned to steal away while everyone milled around the hors d'oeuvres and champagne before dinner. I sidled over to the lady's lounge, so that if I were detected, I might pretend I was not leaving, but merely powdering my nose. I waited in the shadows in a corner of the room, partially concealed by potted palms, and then when no one appeared to be looking, I walked cautiously down the hall. Suddenly, a rich, resonant voice, an unmistakable voice, called out to me.

"Oh, there you are, Isabel! I feared I had missed you all together," Fanny Kemble exclaimed, drawing near and taking my hand in a gesture that looked gentle but which felt quite commanding.

"I am sorry, Fanny," I said, feeling trapped in my attempted escape yet trying to appear simply rushed. "It is a lovely party, and thank you for asking Dolly to invite me." I glanced at my watch nervously in the most obvious of stage gestures. "But I must go now. I wish you happiness in whatever you do next."

"Please, just one moment," she said, fixing her large, dark eyes upon me, unchanged in their power, even though her face was worn and certainly no longer recognizable as Juliet's. "There is something I must ask you before you go." She motioned to a small sitting room just behind us. "I promise we will be but a few moments." She looked back at the guests going in to dinner. "I cannot keep them waiting."

There seemed no way to leave without offending her, so I sat down beside her on a small green-patterned sofa. As she turned to face me in the quiet light of that small room, I wished I could be anywhere but there. I composed my face to convey courtesy, but had no intention to offer her any encouragement. I wanted no part of Fanny Kemble's leavings.

"I had not intended to ask you to consider this with so little discussion. I had hoped we might talk later tonight after everyone else had gone, but now I find that you will be unable to stay," she rambled on. I sensed I was not the only one who was apprehensive. She seemed very unlike the confident Fanny Kemble known to the world.

"I cannot understand, Fanny. If you wanted so badly to speak with me, why did you wait until this evening? I have been in London for nearly two months." I felt my resolve growing.

"I only learned you were here when I dined with Dolly, and did not believe you would come to see me. But just as you *have* done, I thought you would accompany Dolly to my party if she asked you." She sighed deeply as if truly discomfited, so that unsympathetic as I had been towards her request, I reached out to her.

"What is it?" I asked. "What troubles you on a night like this when everyone is here to toast you?"

"They have come to bid me farewell, Isabel. I shall never hear an audience applaud ever again."

"I doubt that. You may always return if you should wish it. Audiences will gladly welcome you." I smiled at her. "You know that."

"I could return, but it is not what I *wish* to do. I want to spend more time in the country reading and writing for whatever time remains."

"You should not speak so gloomily. I am sure you have many years ahead of you. You are only in your—"

"Pardon me, Miss Fanny," a maid said insistently. "They have sent me looking for you. They are waiting for you to begin."

"Tell them I will be along in just a few moments. Tell then I am sorry but I must say good-bye to an old friend."

An old friend. An old friend. How strange to hear her refer to me this way after what I had felt for a lifetime.

"It is awkward to speak hurriedly of such an important matter," she continued tentatively, carefully choosing her words, "but there is not time to ask you properly in the way I had wished. You know the versions of Shakespeare's plays I read were arranged by my father and first read by him?"

Everyone knew that. I nodded, and waited for her to proceed.

"For that reason, they have always been very precious to me. I should hate to have his legacy end with my departure from this pursuit. I have thought very hard about which actress would have the capacity to take them on. Not many should have the voice to master so many roles."

"I am sure you shall find many willing to try," I assured her, still wondering why she had chosen me. "But none who shall manage half so well as you."

"That is kind of you to say, but there is one actress who could carry it off as well. Perhaps even better," she insisted. "I have seen you perform brilliantly, and others extol you. Please say you will do it, Isabel. Surely some time before long, even youthful in appearance as you are, you must leave the stage. If you continue my readings, they will provide for you, and my father's artistry shall live on as well."

"I mean no discourtesy, Fanny, particularly on this night when you are so specially honored, but why do you suddenly care one way or another about my future?"

"I never meant you harm. That night you came to my dressing room I thought you believed me." Her eyes began to tear so that for a moment she seemed overcome. "I told you, I did not want to be Juliet," she finally continued. "I did it to help my family and had no idea how much it hurt you. I did not even know you existed."

"I know that," I conceded, though it was difficult, after so many years detesting her.

"I admit freely this is for my father...and for myself, Isabel. Yet it is a way to give back something that was taken from you," she said simply, no longer pressuring me to accept her offer.

"I am grateful, but am not nearly ready to leave the stage I fought so hard to attain. And I do not believe one can be given back all things which have been lost."

"Very well said, I am sure. But certainly there is no reason not to look back and try to make amends."

"I prefer to look forward," I told her. "Thank you for thinking of me, Fanny. Now I must be going. And you must return to your guests," I urged her, noticing the servant had returned to her position outside the door.

"You will not take even a day to think it over?" she asked almost tenderly, as if genuinely concerned not just for her own and her father's legacy, but for me as well. "So you may be certain you have decided according to your best interests and shall not be left with regrets."

"I am not plagued by regrets," I answered honestly. "I am saddened by many turns of life that have hurt me, but I can accept the choices I have made. Are you so troubled by them?" I asked as I rose.

She smiled as she came to stand companionably beside me as if we *were* good friends. "I do not feel entitled to them with all I have enjoyed. How many can say they have called Tennyson *Alfred* or dined with Dickens or had Mendelssohn play selections from *A Midsummer Night's Dream* in their own drawing room? Or been escorted about London by so brilliant a young man as Henry James?"

"Even so," I asked, truly wanting to know her answer, since I had never known fully how to measure the hurts of my own life against its triumphs. "What of your sadness?" I felt ashamed by my need to understand if even Fanny Kemble, who had received the adulation of thousands, suffered day to day. "Does it still pain you now...that is...your marriage?"

"I suffered much more than the loss of a husband's love. A mother's loss of years of her children's lives is the most painful loss I can imagine. I do not know if you can understand. Do you have children?"

"I did not marry." Her eyes searched my face for a longer answer, yet that was the only one I offered. I would not confide the way in which I had almost became a mother or that Pierce Butler had been the father.

"That surprises me, Isabel, lovely as you were. I should have imagined you had many opportunities. Was there not any man you could love?"

"I did not say I had not *loved*." Try as I did, I could not keep the sharpness from my voice at her presumption. "But there was only one man whose love was true joy to me. That was Matthew Harrison."

"Why did you not marry him?" she asked, clearly interested, not desiring to hurt me.

"I should have, in time, I am sure. But he died." This was all I had resolved to say, yet standing so close to her and realizing how she had had condemned Matthew's play, the words burst forth from me. "You killed him. I do not believe *you* even remember his name. But when his play appeared in Brighton, you said terrible things about it though like you, he was trying to put an end to slavery. He was already ill, but your cruel words, broke his heart."

"I had no idea. You certainly cannot believe I intended to harm him." Her large eyes, luminous in their way as John Booth's, filled with tears. "If I had believed that wretched play should have advanced the cost of abolition, I would have praised it to the heavens. But I felt then it would have only harmed the cause of freedom. I hope you can believe me."

I had no reason to doubt her and prepared to go until she called me back and spoke to me as if bestowing a great gift. "It may not matter to you, Isabel. But despite your sorrows, you have known something I have never known."

I could not imagine what that might be. She possessed far more education than I, had achieved great fame as an actress *and* a writer, owned her own farm and remained close to a loving family. I watched her face, waiting for her to tell me.

"You have known true love, when I have known only admiration. Even Pierce Butler, during the brief time when we were happy, felt not love for me, but only infatuation." She smiled ruefully. "I have never known romantic love save on the stage."

I believe she offered this sad revelation as a parting gift, an acknowledgment that worldly and accomplished as she might be, I had bested her. She made this admission to ease my heart, yet in truth, I felt only sadness in place of the last remnants of my old anger.

"I really must go in, Isabel," she said, pressing my hand in hers. "Are you sure you will not change your mind? Not about the readings," she continued hurriedly, "but will you stay for dinner?"

"No, I must go. But I hope that we shall see each other again," I said, surprised that I actually meant this pleasantry.

"At our age, one may not take anything for granted. I intend to live more quietly now. It will be a genuine pleasure to have freedom to do precisely as I please. Yet even so, I cannot imagine I shall be calling on you in America."

"Still, I will not say good-bye, Fanny. Tonight, of all nights, I shall say, 'farewell.' I hope you will enjoy your new freedom."

She held me back as I tried to take leave of her, again taking my arm.

"Isabel, I doubt your Matthew in his play or I in my journal fully understood freedom *or* slavery. Even I, who witnessed slavery close at hand,

372

could not comprehend it, nor write about it powerfully as I wished, or of my own imprisonment controlled as I was by my husband."

By this time there were no longer only servants coming in pursuit of her. Gentlemen and ladies, elegant in dinner dress, were approaching us, though someone in the front seemed to restrain them, perceiving a serious conversation was taking place between us. Their impending arrival made her speak rapidly. Though we did not know each other well, we were at that moment bound so closely together that she chose to confide in me.

"Isabel, would you not relish the chance of living into the next century when so many changes shall be possible?"

"How do you know there shall be? People are always speaking of change, but most things seem to remain as they have always been."

"That may be so. But my dear friend Elizabeth always predicted that in the new century women shall come finally to be respected as men's equals, which clearly they have always been. I know I am too old, but I should love to see it. Even a glimpse. And to know how the grandchildren and great-grandchildren of slaves shall fare when slavery is only the memory of dreadful stories passed down in whispered voices late at night, but nothing known to anyone still living."

"I must go," I said awkwardly, feeling I must depart before the other guests descended upon us. "Good-night, Fanny. I wish you great happiness tonight and in this next season of your life."

"Perhaps it would be wiser, Isabel, in this *last* season of our lives, though I am, of course, older than you, to wish each other a happy death," she said.

I was uncertain if she intended a grim joke or if she spoke seriously. She seemed startled by my expression since I could not contain my feeling of discomfort that she should speak of death on her night of triumph. Hard as I had struggled, I wanted so much more of life before I should be forced to part from it, and had no wish to contemplate death. But she would not leave the subject, much as I have seen an actress slow the pace of a speech, so attached as she has become to her favorite lines.

"I do not know you well enough to guess what you should choose, Isabel," she said, whispering so those approaching should not hear. "But if I could choose my own death, I should like to gallop full speed on a handsome horse with the wind in my face, spirited forward faster and faster until perhaps my hair should catch in low branches and I should break my neck and die instantly. So long as the horse should survive unscathed to gallop on."

I hardly knew how to respond to such a strange avowal and wished to leave her. "Then I suppose I am glad I never learned to ride, Fanny," I said smiling, with what I hoped was an actress's best comic timing, "so I need not share your grisly vision."

"Well stated," she said, smiling at my response. "Thank you for coming, even if you will not take up my readings."

Then she held out her hand to me. As I took it, I thought better of such a formal gesture and embraced her.

"Good-night, Fanny," I said. "Still, I will not say good-bye. Who knows where life may take us and when we may meet again."

"I doubt we shall, Isabel. I think this likely is good-bye," she said gently.

"Then you do not believe in heaven?"

"If it does exist, I am not certain I should deserve to go there," she said smiling quite devilishly. "And other than ministers, who naturally must proclaim it, the people I have known most convinced that heaven awaited them were the slaves on Butler Island. Those poor souls, so totally deprived of freedom on earth, had as their sustaining hope, attaining freedom in the world to come."

"I have never given it much thought," I confessed. "It has always seemed so very far away. How sad if it is the only hope supporting those who are enslaved in this life."

"You are wise not to worry about it," she advised quickly, as several servants and a number of her guests led her away. "I should just live," she called out to me, as she placed her hand in the crook of one gentleman's arm. "And let death and heaven attend to themselves."

-THE END-